EYE OF THE BEHOLDER

EYE OF THE BEHOLDER

Robyn Anderson

ARROW

Arrow Books Limited
20 Vauxhall Bridge Road, London SW1V 2SA

An imprint of Random House UK Ltd

London Melbourne Sydney Auckland
Johannesburg and agencies throughout
the world

First published in 1991 by Random Century Group

Arrow edition 1992

1 3 5 7 9 10 8 6 4 2

Printed and bound in Great Britain by
Cox & Wyman Ltd, Reading, Berks.

ISBN 0 09 997080 5

For Mum, Iain, Katie, James and Heather

CHAPTER 1

❖❖❖❖❖❖❖❖❖❖❖❖❖

'MY MIND may be trapped within my body, my body may be imprisoned within these walls, but my spirit is forever free.'

The small quotation was roughly carved in the wall of the cell, slightly below eye level for an average man sitting on the floor. Tanner could imagine the author huddled in the corner chipping away at the wall. Perhaps he had been one of those Irish political prisoners or some poor devil awaiting the gallows, trying to leave some part of himself for posterity.

Tanner turned his attention to the far wall, where a lush growth of mildew clustered around a dark patch caused by seeping water or sewage. He inhaled cautiously; the smell still sickened him even after all these weeks. Yet it could have been worse—he could be on one of the prison hulks moored on the Thames or crammed into one of the convict ships bound for Australia. The thought of Australia prompted him to reach into his pocket and draw out a letter. Tanner didn't open it—he didn't need to—he knew every word by heart, for such insignificant items as letters became lifelines in these overcrowded prison cells.

He gazed for a moment at his brother's firm, familiar hand. Tanner returned the letter to his pocket. It was so full of optimism about the colonies that were growing so fast and had so many free settlers they would soon have to stop sending convicts. There was land for the taking, and gold, gold that would make any man with the heart to dig rich beyond belief.

Tanner smiled; he and his brother had always been out of place in the life to which they were born, never able to accept that there was no alternative to the poverty and drudgery of their class. Their neighbours had called them dreamers to their face and troublemakers behind their back. 'A right pair' was the common term for them, but they were not entirely alike, for his brother's attempts at betterment were based on the belief that those who

1

truly tried, succeeded, while his own ventures proceeded from the premise that there had to be a way to circumvent the prejudicial system and turn it to his advantage.

Tanner pursed his lips thoughtfully. His worldly cynicism had left him alone in gaol, while his brother with his childlike naivety had a wife, two children and a chance to strike it rich.

Tanner's eyes wandered to the mildew again, following the course of the damp patch as it meandered along the cracks in the stonework, finally making its way to the floor. He pondered the minor miracle that had brought his brother's letter to him. He so seldom went back to the old neighbourhood and there were so few people there who would keep the letter for him. His thoughts turned to Flo and the dingy, two-roomed house so like the one in which he'd grown up. Flo with the hard voice and the soft heart.

'Tanner!' He turned slowly to face the guard who had barked his name. Everyone moved slowly in the gaol, their expression one of insolence, except for those who had been broken and stripped by the system. The haunted desolation of their eyes made the others cling tighter to their wall of defiance. 'That's him, Sir.' The guard addressed a supercilious looking barrister who picked his way warily across the floor of the outer cell. 'Tanner.' Tanner rose slowly to his feet. 'Over here you, you got a visitor.' Tanner regarded the barrister with increasing interest.

'Alone.' The lawyer turned his imperious beak on the guard and waited for him to retreat to a polite distance before addressing Tanner. 'My name is Binns. I've been retained by some business associates of yours to represent you.'

'Represent me?' Binns had dropped his voice to a level that Tanner could hardly hear, and for a moment he wasn't sure he'd interpreted him correctly. He had all but accepted that he would be convicted, and the arrival of this expensive barrister had made him curious rather than hopeful.

'Your associates are, shall we say, concerned about you.' The beginnings of a smile flickered across Tanner's lips—he could well imagine those fine and proper gentlemen being concerned about what he might say, how he might involve them, how much damage he might do to their precious reputations but not about him personally. 'They feel,' the barrister continued, 'that it would be in all of our best interests if you were acquitted.'

2

'It would certainly be in mine,' Tanner grinned, but the humour was lost on Binns.

'Furthermore, they feel it would be in your best interests to leave London.'

'Leave London?'

'England, for preference. You're a sailor they tell me, go back to the sea.'

Tanner was too surprised to speak. He knew they'd be worried about him involving them in the smuggling, but not so worried that they'd want him out of the country. After all, it was not for the smuggling that he'd been arrested and he'd hardly be likely to admit to it just to get them into trouble. It didn't make any sense.

'Make up your mind quickly, I don't want to be in this place any longer than I have to.' Binns glanced disgustedly around the cell, his gaze finally resting on Tanner. Tanner took a deep breath—there was no choice. He may have resigned himself to a stint in prison but this was hope and in this prison any hope had to be seized without question or pause.

'I have a sudden yearning for distant places.' The barrister's face tightened into what might have been a smile.

'Good, I'll tell my clients I have your word on it.'

'For what it's worth.'

'It may be worth nothing,' Binns' eyes narrowed and his voice chilled, 'but breaking it could cost you a great deal. Do you understand?' Tanner nodded and the expression that passed for a smile crossed Binns' face again. 'Now about the charges . . .'

'I didn't assault her,' Tanner interrupted.

Binns' look forestalled further comment. 'My appearance in court virtually guarantees your acquittal. The girl is a mere strumpet who lives above the stables at the inn. Her auntie is a drunk and the local louts and the police didn't arrive until after the assault.'

'I didn't assault her.' Tanner tried again, but his words made no impression. Binns was an expert in his field—the verbal thrust and parry of the cross-examination and the skilful interpretation of the letter of the law were his concern, not guilt or innocence, justice or truth. 'It was an accident.' Tanner softened his tone. Many times he had taken liberties with the truth but not this time. This time he was telling it straight, and the fact that it was poetic justice that no one believed him didn't make it any easier for him to control the mounting annoyance he felt at Binns' indifference.

'You were caught standing over the girl with a piece of wood in your hand.' It was not an accusation but a statement of a fact, and although the man offended Tanner the statement did not.

'It was dark,' Tanner began slowly. 'I'd doubled back after I'd led the police away from the warehouse and your clients. They'd had time to get away and I thought it was safe to go back. I was running across the courtyard between the warehouse and the inn and—'

'No,' Binns interrupted him. 'Under no circumstances will you mention my clients or your association with them.'

'I'd no intention of mentioning Carstairs or his fine and proper friends.'

'And you mustn't say running.' Binns thought for a moment. 'You were stumbling about, lost.' He nodded, happy with the explanation.

'While I was stumbling about,' Tanner continued, 'I knocked over a pile of crates and they smashed on top of the girl. I was pulling them off her when the old lady came out. I—'

'Was it a piece of crate you were holding when she saw you?'

'Yes, of course.'

'Excellent, excellent.' One of Tanner's cell mates belched and groaned. Binns took a step backward.

'It was an accident.' Tanner raised his voice in an attempt to hold Binns' attention. 'I didn't even see the girl, I didn't know she was there.'

'Why were you pulling the crates off her if you didn't know she was there?'

'I heard her moaning.'

'Did anyone see you before you were found standing over the girl?'

'No.'

'Did anyone see you strike her?'

'I didn't strike her.'

'Was it dark?'

'Yes.' The barrister had been firing the questions in rapid succession. Now he paused to think.

4

'The old woman,' he said thoughtfully.

'She was drunk,' Tanner snapped, 'and if I'd had the money to buy her off she'd have dropped the whole thing then and there.' One of Tanner's cell mates began vomiting. Binns covered his mouth and nose with a handkerchief and backed away.

'I think I have enough. Your story fits in quite well with the established facts.'

'That's because it's the truth.' Tanner moved closer to the bars as if his presence would halt Binns' retreat, for surely the man didn't have enough information to mount a defence. Tanner felt an inkling of panic penetrate his self-control. 'Look, if you ask the girl . . .' His voice trailed away. Binns wasn't listening to him, he was looking at him, sizing him up.

'You speak rather well for what you are. I'll send you some clean clothes and make sure they allow you access to a razor and water for washing. You may well pass for a gentleman if you mind your manners.' Binns looked across at the guard and signalled his intention to leave. 'By-the-by, hearing's set for 10.30 tomorrow morning.'

Tanner turned his back to the bars and faced the interior of the cell and his cell mates. Thieves, murderers and bullies they may be, but they offended him less than the man who had offered him his freedom or the gentlemen who had hired him to do so.

CHAPTER 2

✦✦✦✦✦✦✦✦✦✦✦✦✦

'Blind she is, blind,' the old woman shrieked at the magistrate, 'and no good for nothin' no more.' She peered out from under the brim of a misshapen hat, her hair yellowed from dirt and age, her skin yellowed from too much alcohol. She wore every item of clothing she possessed: dresses layered one on top of the other, vests and bodices, and three coats all in the same state of disrepair. Her breath reeked of beer and her voice retained a raucous quality despite her attempts to turn it to a piteous whine. 'Healthy she was and strong too, a good worker, got a good wage she did. Now look at 'er, useless.' The magistrate made an attempt to interrupt but she didn't give him a chance. 'Lots of likely lads after 'er, too. None of them will want 'er now, you mark my words. Ruined she is, and me too old and sick to be caring for 'er and not a penny did 'e offer—'

'Will you answer the question, Madam, please?' The old woman looked at Tanner's barrister as if she hadn't noticed him before. 'Did you see what happened?'

'It was like I told 'im.' She indicated the Queen's Counsel. 'Out I come to see what happened and there 'e were stood over 'er with a great lump of wood in 'is hand.'

'What kind of wood?' The barrister snapped.

'What do you mean, what kind of wood?'

'A stick from a tree, perhaps?' Binns dropped his voice to a warm cajoling tone.

'No,' she came back at him, 'a lump of wood from one of them crates.'

'What crates?'

'Them ones what was lying broken all round.'

'The ones my client claims he accidentally knocked on top of the girl?' The woman didn't answer. 'Could my client have been lifting the broken crates away from the girl?'

'When I come out 'e was stood over 'er holding a lump of

6

wood.' It was the only thing she knew, the only thing that mattered.

'Why did you come out of the beer house—was it closing time, or had you run out of money?'

'No,' she said indignantly. 'I come out because of the crash.'

'What crash?'

'The crash them crates made when they fell down.'

'The crates my client claims to have knocked over inadvertently, while he was stumbling around in the dark.' He paused for effect. 'The crates he was trying to lift off the unfortunate girl when you came out to see what was going on.'

'When I come out 'e was stood over 'er with a lump of wood in 'is hand.'

'Your Worship,' Tanner's counsel addressed the bench, 'Constable Fipps has already testified that he made his arrest based on this woman's say so. My client will testify that he was lost in an unfamiliar part of the city and that he was going to the inn to ask directions. In the darkness of the courtyard, he didn't see the crates and walked into them, knocking them down. He had no idea the girl was hiding there and, in fact, he was trying to rescue the poor unfortunate child when this—' his inflection indicated his distaste, '—this woman appeared screaming all kinds of accusations. As you can see there is nothing in her testimony to refute my client's claims and I ask that the charges be dismissed.'

'Dismissed!' the old woman shrieked. 'Dismissed, and 'er blinded for life and not a penny from 'im for all 'er pain. You ask 'er what 'e done to 'er. Blinded 'er 'e did.'

'Enough!' The magistrate roared. 'Enough, Madam. One more word from you and I will charge you with contempt of court and *you* will go to gaol, do you understand?'

'Yes, Your Worship,' she murmured. She understood, probably better than he did. She'd seen his quick appraisal of Tanner's clothes, his deferential nod to Tanner's barrister. She understood all right.

The magistrate beckoned the Queen's Counsel to the bench. 'Are you willing to withdraw the charges?'

'Of course, Your Worship. I didn't realise until this morning that Mr Binns was representing this case.' He included Tanner's barrister in his halted explanation. 'I'm sure we could have settled this out of court if I'd known. I'm sorry.'

'So be it.' The magistrate cut him short. 'The charges have

been withdrawn,' he announced to the court.

'All rise—' the bailiff began.

For the first time since he'd come into the court, Tanner allowed himself to look at the girl. It was only a fleeting glance as the old woman dragged her from the building, but enough to remind him of the pale, delicate form he'd found lying bruised and bleeding amongst the splintered remains of the crates. Then Binns propelled him towards a side entrance and pushed him into a laneway. He began to speak in that same barely audible whisper that he'd employed in the prison.

'My clients would like to know when you are leaving London.'

'As soon as I can. It may take some time to raise the necessary funds, unless of course your clients would be willing to advance me a little travelling money.'

Tanner had an accent that didn't really come from anywhere. He'd been born in England but had travelled to the Americas and Africa and to more parts of the European coast than a man should be able to get to by boat. He could play the gentleman, but the impersonation always held a hint of satire and Binns found the strange quality of his voice and his attitude very irritating.

'Mr Tanner, let me warn you that if you should try to extort money from my clients you will face a charge much harsher than the one that has just been withdrawn, and all the pressures that were brought to bear to assure your acquittal here will be turned against you to ensure your conviction. Do I make myself clear?'

'Perfectly.' Tanner gave a bemused bow.

Binns turned towards the door, then stopped. 'Get out of England, Tanner, before my clients find it necessary to put you in your place.' He departed, leaving Tanner alone in the empty lane.

Tanner smiled—he was too relieved to be offended or intimidated by anything Binns might say. He had no doubt that Binns was serious and he'd certainly make himself scarce but, at that moment, all that mattered was that he was free.

He walked up the lane along the side of the court building towards the front entrance. He was a bit out of pocket; maybe he should go back to sea. He was breathing deeply, the air sweet compared to that within the gaol, and it made him feel light-headed and quickened his pulse.

He turned the corner, heading back past the court. He would

go to see Flo, he decided, collect his kit, maybe borrow some money, then go some place where there was laughter and decent food. His smile broadened.

'There you are, you slimy, miserly bastard.' The old woman materialised in front of him, weaving back and forward like a snake and backing him up against the wall. 'Blinded 'er, 'e did,' she yelled at the passers-by, who merely averted their eyes and quickened their pace. 'Blinded 'er and not a penny from 'im.' Tanner didn't look at the girl despite the old woman's attempts to push her in front of him. 'Assault, that's what it was,' she screamed.

'That's it, old woman.' Tanner grasped her by the shoulders and the feel of her sickened him. 'That's it, it's over.' He let her go, pushing her away slightly as he released her. 'There is no money—I don't have any money, so go peddle your misery elsewhere.' He turned to go but she grabbed his hand. 'It's over.' He forced the harsh sound between his teeth as he tried to pull himself free.

'Over is it? Over for 'er and I'm not going to be responsible for it. Finished she is, useless to 'erself and everyone else.' She dragged the girl forward so that Tanner could no longer ignore her. 'Well, there's no help for it and I've got meself to think about.' The woman was backing away but Tanner didn't notice—his attention was held by dark, unseeing eyes. 'Leave 'er on the streets to starve, put 'er to the workhouse.' With each phrase the old woman moved further away from Tanner and closer to the dim alley. 'Take 'er for yourself, she's young and not been 'ad.' The alley was one step away. 'Do what you like, it's on your 'ead now.' She turned and ran with more speed than Tanner would have credited to her age. He made to follow her.

'Auntie!' The anguished cry caught him mid-stride. The girl extended her hand and took a hesitant step forward. 'Auntie?' She stopped, tears welled in her eyes and desperation took hold of her trembling voice. 'Auntie.'

'She's gone,' Tanner said flatly. The girl faced him: she was beautiful despite the filthy, ragged clothes, the long black, unkept hair, with tear stains and terror on her face. She was small and so terribly thin.

'Who—who are you?' she stammered.

'I'm . . . My name is John Tanner.' She caught her breath and started to back away from him. 'Look, it was an accident, not like your auntie said. I ran into the crates—' She continued backing away until suddenly she tripped. Instinctively, Tanner reached out to catch her. She twisted and turned, trying to get free. To prevent her struggling any further, Tanner caught her to his chest. She sobbed hopelessly then became quite still. Tanner loosened his grip, and she raised her hands to touch his shoulders and then his face.

'You're so big,' she said.

'Please don't be afraid of me. I didn't mean to hurt you. What my barrister said in the court was the truth. I know how it must have looked to your auntie, but believe me it was an accident.' Tanner could hear the sound of his own voice; he was speaking too quickly, trying to say too much too soon. He steadied himself. 'I'm sorry, truly sorry.' He let her go and she stood before him, a thin, frightened child. Tanner's voice dried in his mouth. There was nothing he could say, no explanation that would take away the blindness or the fear and despair that he read in her face.

His silence seemed to last an eternity, the rattle of the carriages and the tramp of feet masking any indication of his presence from the girl. More terrifying than the man who blinded her was the possibility of being left alone. She inhaled sharply, lifting her head and trying to sense some presence. There were people walking past—she could hear them—and she tried to call out, but hardly any sound escaped her lips.

'Oh God, help me,' she whispered as she extended her hand.

'It's all right.' Tanner's voice sounded loud because of his close proximity to her. She jumped back, but he caught her hand. 'It's all right,' he insisted. 'I won't hurt you, I never meant to hurt you.' His grip was firm but not tight and his voice was warm and genuine, so different to the way she had thought it would be. He led her forward and she came—there was nothing else for her to do, no way she could run from him, no one who would help her. 'I'll take you home,' he said gently. 'It's the room above the stables isn't it?' She nodded. Tanner linked her arm through his. 'It's a fair step. Can you walk that far?'

'Yes,' she murmured, then shook her head vaguely. She was so confused, he was so different to what she had expected, the size of him and the sound of him and the way that he acted. He contradicted everything she thought to be fact. He said it had been an accident as if he expected her to believe him, he said he'd take her home as if he expected that Auntie would be there. Confusion turned to panic and she missed her step, stumbling and almost falling, but he caught her as before, allowing her a moment to regain herself before moving off again.

'I can't remember your name,' he apologised. 'They read it out in court but—'

'Amy.' She saved him making the rest of the explanation.

'And you've no parents?'

'No, they died of fever when I was twelve. It took my little brother, too.'

'And you've no other family?'

'No.'

'Just your auntie?'

'She's not my auntie.'

'But she's been looking after you?'

'She takes in orphans if she can get them work because the law lets her take their pay until they're sixteen, then she throws them out.'

'How old are you?'

'Near sixteen.'

Tanner felt a strange, sinking feeling in the pit of his stomach and the old woman's words, which he had tried so hard to ignore, forced themselves back into his consciousness. 'Leave her in the street to starve, put her to the workhouse, do what you like, it's on your head now.' Tanner slowed his pace—there was no longer any urgency. When they reached the stables it didn't surprise him to find the old woman gone.

'She owes us for the room.' The proprietor's wife was a broad, hard-faced woman.

'Is there anything left up there that belongs to the girl?' Tanner asked.

'Girl's got no belongings, nothing but what she's stood up in, and if she wants to keep that room you'll be paying for it aforehand.' There was no charity in the woman's face, and even though Tanner pleaded the girl's case, arguing that there would be work she could do to pay her way, he knew it was a waste of time.

'Perhaps there's a coat or wrap upstairs, something . . .'

'I told you, the old woman took it all.'

'The London nights can be awfully cold.' Tanner directed his

11

anger at the woman, but it was the situation that infuriated him. Despite all the hard things that he'd done in his life, Tanner couldn't just walk away and leave the girl. The proprietor's wife gave them one last cold look, turned on her heel and went inside.

Tanner took the girl's arm and guided her back into the street. He knew the direction he was taking, the only alternative left to him, and it turned his feet to lead and put a heaviness in his heart that made it hard for him to speak.

The girl was silent, too. It had been a long walk and she was tired and hungry. She was too afraid to think for every thought led to despair—she had no place to go, no way to live, she didn't know where she was or where she was going. Her only guide, her only hope, was the man who had blinded her and he was so anxious to be rid of her that any minute he might just walk away and leave her standing there. She gripped his arm so tightly that her nails dug into his wrist, but he didn't respond.

By the time they reached their destination Amy had lost all track of time. Her feet plodded one after the other, her body drawn on by the man's insistent pace. He began to mount some stairs without warning her, and she tripped and fell heavily. He helped her to her feet.

'I'm sorry.' His voice sounded so strained that it terrified her. 'There are about five steps.' There was a deep sadness in his tone and she would have given anything to be able to turn and run. She heard the clang of a bell and the sound of a door opening. Then his voice came, still heavy and sad. 'I've a girl here, she's blind and she's nowhere to go.' The woman who opened the door of the workhouse was a picture of efficiency without a trace of humanity.

'If she's got some kind of sickness she don't belong here.'

'She's not sick, she's blind.' Tanner's voice was tight as he enunciated each word clearly.

'She don't belong in a workhouse, she belongs in a hospital.' Tanner's aggression had made the woman's decision for her.

'No, no, no.' A small, round-eyed man appeared from an office off to the left. 'No, I'm sorry Mrs Perkins, but you're wrong. Blindness isn't a disease, she can't go to a hospital.'

'She don't belong here,' the woman insisted.

'I don't see why not,' the man said brightly. 'Some of our old people can barely see.'

'It's different for the old.'

'But she could sit with them.'

'We don't need no more useless people here.' She was adamant, almost threatening.

'She's no more useless than that poor wretch that lost his legs.'

'Well he don't belong here neither.' The woman was unrelenting. 'What about the asylum? I mean, it's an affliction isn't it, something in the head.'

'No.' Somewhere in the building a child was screaming, and a sickening stench that was either cooking or washing wafted through an open door at the rear. A sickly waif was in the corner on his knees scrubbing the floor. 'It's our Christian duty, Mrs Perkins.'

'We have our duty to our employers too, may I remind you, Sir.'

Tanner looked down at Amy's face: it was deathly white, her lips were taut and tears welled in her eyes. He said nothing, simply turned her round and marched out of the door and down the stairs. They'd gone a fair distance before Amy found her voice.

'Auntie said I could still be a whore.' Tanner was totally unprepared for the remark and, even though Amy waited for him to comment, he didn't. 'She said I looked all right and that some men weren't fussy and that some madam might take me on, not that she'd pay anything for me.' The strain of controlling her voice became too much for Amy and the last words came between sobs.

Tanner kept on walking, but his mind was reeling from the shock of her suggestion. He'd seen them along the docks, girls no older than she, their faces hardened by their experiences and their bodies hardened by use and abuse. He tried to speak but no words came. Instead, he quickened his pace as if to outrun the thought. The variation in his gait caused Amy to miss her step. He saved her from falling yet again and she clutched at his arm, holding it tightly until the trembling that had taken hold of her passed. He took her hand and linked it through his arm again.

'I used to live near here when I was a child.' Tanner had found his voice, which still sounded heavy and strained. 'I've a friend, a lady, she's minding my kit. We'll go there—she'll help.'

It wasn't far to Flo's house. Tanner had known her all his

life and he'd taken advantage of her more than once. She was a good woman, too good in fact, and even though Tanner knew it was unreasonable of him to expect her to take the girl he was desperate.

'You, you devil,' she greeted Tanner. 'Where the hell have you been? I told you I had a man on the *Sea Queen* and I wanted your stuff out of here before he came back. Hell to pay there was, me trying to think up every excuse under the sun.' She moved away from the door to let them enter. 'Who's this then?' She inclined her head towards the girl.

'Amy, this is Flo.' Tanner introduced them. Flo scarcely acknowledged the girl.

'Well, what's the excuse this time? Some business matter to be taken care of up north, or some private matter to be avoided down here?'

'I've been in gaol.'

'Well-deserved too, I should think.'

'I was innocent, Flo.'

'Oh yes.'

'I was accused of assaulting Amy and blinding her, and the charges were withdrawn.' Flo took a long look at Amy, examining her minutely.

'Don't look blind to me. Blind people's got funny eyes.'

'She is blind Flo, believe me, and she's got nowhere to go and no way of supporting herself.'

Flo continued examining her, then leant close to her ear and said in a loud voice: 'Would you like to sit down, dearie?'

'She's blind Flo, not deaf.' Tanner took Amy's arm and led her to a chair. Then he drew Flo to the far side of the room, which acted as a kitchen. 'Flo, I didn't mean to blind her, it wasn't my fault. I can't think what I'm going to do with her— I've tried everywhere, the workhouse, the hospital, the asylum, they won't take her. I don't know what to do, short of selling her to some madam or leaving her on the street.' The desperation in Tanner's voice was genuine, but Flo had seen it put there by design too many times to believe him now.

'Not this time.' She faced him squarely. 'I know your ways, bring her here, tell me her sad story, then off you go into the night and me left with her. It never changes, puppies and kittens it was when we was young and your poor, old parents when

14

you took to the sea, but not this me lad, not this.' Her voice had risen and she ignored Tanner's attempts to quiet her. 'I've a good man now and I'll not ruin that just so you can go on your way with a clear conscience.' Tanner was aware that Amy had heard every word, and he tried to find a way to change their meaning.

'You don't understand,' he said, 'I just came here to get my kit and I thought you might let the girl wash and lend her some clean clothes.'

'Ha! I'm hardly her size.'

'You used to be.' There was a teasing intimacy in Tanner's voice.

'Well, I suppose there might be a dress or two I used to wear,' she said grudgingly. 'Old they'd be now and a bit out of fashion, but they were my favourites and I've never had the heart to cut them up.' The dresses that Flo produced had been made for formal occasions—weddings, funerals and the day the new Archbishop rode through the streets in an open carriage. They were simple gowns but nicely trimmed. She paraded them in front of the girl. 'Well dearie, what do you think?'

'They're lovely,' Tanner answered. 'Is there some place where she could wash and try them on?'

'There's water in the other room. Does she need any help?'

'I don't know, Flo, why don't you ask her?' Something in Flo's attitude to the girl offended Tanner—it was as if she thought the child's feelings and intellect had somehow vanished with her sight.

'Can you manage by yourself?' Flo said loudly.

'If you can put my hand on the basin and let me feel where everything is, I think I'll be all right.'

'Well, it's this way.' Flo moved toward the other room. 'I'll just light the lamp for you.'

'I don't need one.'

'No, no, of course not.' Flo hesitantly took the girl's hand and led her from the room. She returned a moment later.

'I don't suppose you have any shoes?' Tanner asked.

'What do you take me for, the local emporium?'

Tanner looked tired and appealing. 'Please help me, Flo.'

Flo's eyes narrowed determinedly. 'Don't bother using that tone with me. You're not going to dump her here, and don't go pretending that isn't why you came.'

Tanner knew that he'd handled it badly, rushing in too quickly, not letting Flo get the feel of the girl first, then feeding her the story piece by piece. He sighed with frustration and rubbed at the stiffness in his neck.

'Flo, she's got nothing. I just thought you might have a few things to spare.'

'Oh yes, dresses, shoes, what else?'

'A coat or wrap, something to keep her warm, perhaps a case or bag to keep them in.' She laughed at the nerve of him.

'Anything else?'

'A meal and a place to stay for the night.'

'No chance, me old love.'

'But Flo, I haven't eaten since this morning and then it was prison food. I haven't had a decent meal in . . .' He shrugged. 'And I don't think the girl's ever had one.' Flo took a deep breath to harden her resolve.

'I might have a pair of shoes she can wear, bought them off some hawker, I did. I knew in me heart they were too small but he had your charming ways.' She looked at him accusingly. 'But that's it boyo, no coat, no bag, no meal and bed. Me man comes home tonight and I want you and her and all your stuff out of here.'

As Amy washed and dressed she tried to ignore their conversation, but the volume had slowly risen until she heard Tanner's voice unmistakable and clear.

'For heaven's sake Flo, you know how I live, always getting into trouble or getting out of it, living it up on my ill-gotten gains or paying for them in gaol. It's no life for a girl, any girl, let alone one like her.'

Amy felt a tightness in her throat. She hated him and feared him for what he'd done to her, but he was all she had.

'Put meself out for you, alter my plans, change my life, 'cause you can't accept responsibility for nothing!' Flo's voice was hard, bitter with the memory of all she'd done for this man who would never care for her as much as she cared for him. 'Just like it was with your poor old parents. Them dying of fever and your brother off to Australia and you God knows where and me left with it all. I got the fever too you know, and there was none to care for me. My life turned around so you could go your own sweet, merry way. Well, not this time.' She paused, but not long

16

enough for him to speak. 'I'll get them shoes, then you'll be off.'
She left the room without waiting for a reply.

Amy heard her coming and fumbled for the comb. She needed
to be doing something so that it didn't look as if she'd been
eavesdropping. Flo lit the lamp and stood looking at her.

'Well now, you do look a treat, just like I did at your age,
'course, I wasn't as pretty as you.' Flo searched for the shoes
as she spoke. 'I've got a pair of shoes here just might fit you.'
She handed them to the girl. 'Put them on dearie, then you best
be off.' They walked to the main room together. 'Well, what
do you think?' Flo demanded.

'She looks beautiful,' Tanner said honestly.

Flo smiled with satisfaction. 'There's your stuff over there.'
She inclined her head towards the corner, then moved to open
the door. Tanner collected his kit with one hand and Amy with
the other.

'You're a hard woman, Flo.' He bent to kiss her cheek as he
passed.

She watched him leave as she had so many times before, and
although in the past she had cursed herself for giving in, this
time she cursed herself for standing firm.

CHAPTER 3

++++++++++++++

TANNER LINGERED outside Flo's house, half expecting her to call him back. He had no idea of what to do next, and he looked about him hoping for some inspiration. None came. Reluctantly he moved off, now guiding the girl as if it was second nature to him.

He stopped after a while. It was not yet dark but a swirling, November fog was descending on them, blocking out the last vestiges of the sun's light and warmth. He pulled his heavy seaman's coat from his bag and put it around the girl's shoulders.

Amy thanked him, but her voice was so muted by an overwhelming sense of panic that he did not hear her. She knew he had tried every way possible to be rid of her and she wished with all her heart that she had some other place to go, some other person to care for her. She prayed to God with all her being that her sight would return so that she could run from him. Her body ached from all the unaccustomed exercise and she was hungry, too. Although meals had always been few and far between, today she seemed to feel the hunger more, as if it was there to remind her of what would happen if she was left alone.

Tanner stopped walking, closed his eyes and tried to think. 'Food and shelter,' he said.

'What?' Amy's voice was strained.

'Something to eat, a place to rest.' He looked at the row of monotonous little houses—every street looked the same, unless you'd been born there. 'There's a pub not far from here, serves up a terrible stew but in very large quantities. I reckon we could share a plate.'

The pub had virtually nothing to recommend it—it was small, smoky, dirty and crowded—however it was warm and cheap. Tanner settled Amy at a table then went to get the stew and a tankard of beer. He didn't have much money, just enough to buy a meal and little else. Tanner jiggled his coins as he watched the rough mob ahead of him. They were drunk and abusive, demanding service and spoiling for a fight. He ignored them, refusing to retaliate even when they pushed and jostled him. His freedom was too sweet to waste in a brawl over a plate of stew.

At first Amy simply sat at the table, welcoming the respite and the warmth of the room, but the smell of food made her hungry and the hunger made her impatient and slowly the impatience became concern. He'd been too long, she thought, and he'd tried every other way of getting rid of her. All he had to do was walk off and leave her. She stood up slowly, clutching the table. She wanted to scream out his name or run into the street after him, but she couldn't, she couldn't move. Her chest heaved in a sob but no sound escaped, then tears rolled down her cheeks and her body wavered back and forth as she hung on to the table for support.

Tanner almost dropped the stew when he saw her. She looked so pale that he thought she was ill. He grabbed her by the shoulders. 'Amy, what is it, what's happened?'

She threw her arms around him and cried uncontrollably—it didn't matter that he'd blinded her, it didn't matter at all, if only he'd stay with her, if only he wouldn't leave her alone.

At first Tanner thought someone must have hurt her, and he looked around the room but could glean no hint of who or how. He caressed her hair and patted her shoulder, waiting for the sobs to stop. She quietened finally and he turned her face towards him.

'Tell me what's wrong.'

'You were so long, I thought . . . I thought you weren't coming back.'

'No.' He extended the word as if to belittle the idea. 'I wouldn't just go off and leave you.' It was the truth, even though the idea had not occurred to him before and it shocked him to realise that somehow, over the last few hours, he'd become responsible for a fifteen-year-old girl. He gave her a reassuring hug. 'Now you sit down and have a sip of this beer.' He handed her the mug. 'And we better eat this stew before it gets cold.' She drank too much of the beer and she drank it too quickly. It made her feel warm and dizzy.

'What will you do with me?' she asked sadly.

'I don't know,' Tanner replied. Accepting responsibility for her was one thing, discharging it would be completely different. 'But I'll not just walk off and leave you.'

'Promise?' Amy reached out to touch him.

'A promise from me isn't worth much,' he smiled wearily, 'but there's one I've got to keep.' He took her hand in his as if the contact could maintain the fragile trust that his next words might easily shatter. 'I have to leave the country.' She didn't react, not at all. She sat motionless, holding her breath, waiting for his next words. 'I won't leave you anywhere you don't want to be and if it comes to that I could always take you with me, but I have to leave and soon.' Tanner had chosen his words carefully, but not until he'd finished speaking did he truly realise what he was offering her.

'Why?' she stammered. 'Why must you leave?' Tanner was loath to tell her the truth, but she had a right to know at least some of it.

'I did something not quite legal for some people who are afraid I'll put them in. They got the barrister for me on the understanding that I would leave the country.' Tanner shook his head irritably; it still didn't make sense and the more he thought about it the less sense it made.

'Where will you go?' Her question drew Tanner from his deliberation.

'I don't know—Africa, the Americas.' He thought as he spoke. 'I could probably work a passage for you, but that would leave us precious little in the way of funds once we got there.' She had expected him to say Scotland or Ireland, Europe at the furthest, and the thought of Africa or the Americas stunned her completely. He gave her hand a gentle squeeze then placed the fork in it and put the plate of stew in front of her. 'You eat what you can of this, and I'll have what's left.'

She ate slowly, feeling for the food with her fork, trying not to make a mess. In a world of darkness, where everything relied on touch, finding food on a plate was one of the most difficult problems of all. The stew was a cold, congealed mess by the time she handed it over to Tanner, but weeks of prison fare had taught him to expect nothing better. Yet he longed for a more pleasing taste.

'I'm going to get more beer.' He stood up. 'I'm not running away, I'm not going to leave you.' She smiled for the first time since he had met her, for the first time since the accident.

He turned to watch her as he waited to get the beer. She looked so vulnerable and alone, somehow, over the course of the meal, and the anger and the frustration of being left with her had vanished. Even the guilt was beginning to give way to genuine compassion. Two young men came close to her and Tanner found himself watching them. One of them was too handsome to be real—tall, lean, graceful, a veritable Adonis. The other man was shorter and clumsy and had not one redeeming feature, and Tanner wondered if the former had chosen the latter as companion in order to accentuate his own good looks. They pushed close to Amy as they made their way to their seats, and something in their demeanour made Tanner anxious to get back to her. As he drew near Tanner could see that they were far too involved in their own conversation to take any notice of Amy and, feeling slightly foolish, he sat down beside her.

'Mr Tanner,' she murmured.

'Certainly is,' he said brightly. 'How did you know?'

'I didn't,' Amy smiled 'I just wanted it to be you.' She reached out for his hand, but got the beer mug instead.

'You want some more?' He misconstrued the gesture but she didn't decline.

Although Amy had only a few sips of the beer, her exhaustion, combined with the fact that she'd never drunk beer before, made her very susceptible to its effects. She felt her head becoming heavy and her eyes begin to close. Tanner moved to put his arm around her and magically his shoulder was there for her to rest her head on just as it became too heavy to hold up.

Tanner felt her relax into sleep. He was uncomfortable—the position he'd put himself into in order to take her weight was not a natural one and the muscles he had to use to hold her there were already tired—a day of walking after weeks of just sitting in prison had made him stiff. He looked idly around the tavern; it was warm, and if they stayed there until closing time they would only have to spend half the night sleeping in the street.

A group of travellers came in, amongst them a portly man complaining loudly that their carriage wheel had lost its rim and that they had been forced to walk some distance to this, the only shelter. They hung their coats by the door and took over the area closest to the fire. Tanner smiled to himself—no one from this part of town ever left their belongings unattended. There were two women in the group, a couple of old maids unless Tanner missed his guess. The smaller of the two had been wearing a wool cape and carrying a green portmanteau, and Tanner wondered if he dared risk taking them for Amy.

'Australia!'

'Shush!'

Tanner turned in the direction of the voice. The command had come from the good-looking young man he'd noticed before, who was trying to quieten his startled companion. They were huddled together, their faces intent, looking for all the world as if they were planning to rob the Bank of England. Tanner strained to hear them, which wasn't hard as the insistence had made the good-looking one raise his voice also.

'I tell you Joey, we'll be rich. Rich like we could never be here, not for all our hard work, nor thieving, nor cheating neither. Think of it Joey, gold!' And his eyes shone to match the word. Joey began to shake his head. 'It's true, I tell you. They've found gold and there's a rush on to see who'll get there first. It's our chance Joey.' His voice was silk and Tanner knew he got his own way, right or wrong, every time.

'Australia.' Joey managed to speak at last.

'Yes Joey, Australia.'

'How would we get there?'

'By ship.' Joey was shaking his head. 'We'll sign on as crew and jump ship when we get to Melbourne. Then we'll just join the crowd. It'll work I tell you.'

'No, no, I've heard tell how some captains will come after you if you jump ship and bring you back and it goes hard on you when they do.' He looked appealingly at his friend. 'I don't like the sea, Davis. It's a hard life and I've not got the stomach for it.' There was a hint of agitation about Davis' mouth, but none showed in his voice.

'There's a ship,' he said softly, 'The *Lady Ann*, it sails for Australia within the week. The Master's name's Buchanan, a fair and easy going man but careful with the way he picks his crew. Most are men he's sailed with for years but there's a few openings this time out and, him being a decent, Christian gentleman, he'll be taken in by the right tale of woe, especially if he thinks a man's got family here to come home to.'

Joey was still unconvinced and so the conversation continued, Joey reiterating his fears and Davis countering every objection. Tanner lost interest in them. He glanced across at the travellers, who were deep in conversation, and he looked again at the coats. If he was to steal the cape for Amy he must do it now, before the crowd began to dwindle. He roused her gently.

'Where are we going?' she asked.

'Just do everything exactly as I say or we'll both end up in gaol.' It never occurred to him that she might have some moral objection to stealing and he didn't feel the need for any further explanation. He guided her towards the door, manoeuvring her so that she stood between the travellers and their coats. He bent down as if to retrieve something dropped and rose with the portmanteau in his hand. A quick look round told him that no one had noticed so he turned, collecting the cape in the same movement, then taking Amy by the arm, he walked unhurriedly from the inn.

Outside he moved with great speed, pushing and pulling her this way and that, ducking down this alley then that lane, in and out of the back streets that he'd known since he was a child. He stopped at the back of the old church, a popular place for tramps although none were there that night. The church was on high ground but was sheltered from the north wind. Tanner put the cape around Amy, then settled her in the doorway. He lay down beside her and put his coat over the two of them. Amy felt the light wool of the cape.

'Where did you get this?'

'Shall we say it's on loan for an indefinite period?'

'You stole it!' Her voice held such a ludicrous touch of righteous indignation that Tanner laughed at her.

'It's the middle of the night,' he began sarcastically, 'we've no money, no place to go, no one to help us.' His tone mellowed slightly. 'What was I supposed to do? You're cold now, and by morning you would be frozen.' He paused, but she didn't speak. 'How did anyone with an auntie like yours develop such high moral standards?'

'My father . . .' She stopped. 'She's not my auntie, and you could go to gaol.'

'Only if I'm caught.'

Amy didn't argue—her utter dependence on him made it seem

23

unwise—but it was wrong to steal, it was against the law. She untangled her arms from the cape and felt his chest and shoulders. He was so much bigger than she had imagined, and he sounded different too. She forced her mind back to the night of the accident, to the very last things she had seen.

She had been up in her room above the stables when she heard yelling from the warehouse on the other side of the courtyard. She'd looked out of the window but had been unable to see anything, so she'd gone downstairs. There had been enough light from her window and from the back door of the inn for her to be able to see him quite clearly. He was running across from the warehouse, a small, thin, angular man with grey hair she'd thought him to be, a gentleman all dressed up in a fine suit with a silk embroidered vest that shone as brightly as the silver handle on his walking cane. He'd yelled at her and she'd turned to run. Then had come the pain and the darkness.

She'd been so certain that she'd been hit with the cane, but Auntie had said it was a lump of wood. Amy frowned—that was not the only inconsistency. All had agreed that it had been dark, so the candle in her room must have gone out and someone must have closed the inn door. The crates had still been standing when she fell, at least she'd thought so, because she'd ducked behind them and the man had followed her. Amy moved restlessly. Perhaps it had been as Tanner had said, perhaps he'd stumbled and knocked the crates down.

The rest she'd had in the tavern had refreshed her a little, and the cold and her thoughts made it hard to sleep. Her arm still lay across his chest, he was so much bigger than she'd expected. The idea didn't occur suddenly nor did it manifest itself through logical thought, if anything it had to fight its way through a tide of rejection—that Tanner may not have been the one who had blinded her. He may have come later when her candle had burned down and the inn door had been shut, and in the darkness knocked the crates down on top of her as she lay where her assailant had left her.

It was only an idea, a possibility, and she didn't want to accept it, for she'd be just as blind whether he caused it or not, just as alone but without the tenuous hold of guilt, and he'd resent the way he'd been imprisoned because of her, the way he'd had to lie and steal because of her and he'd dump her there and then.

She felt the same panic she'd experienced outside the court house when Auntie had left, the same terror that had seized her in the workhouse and when they'd mentioned the asylum, and she tightened her grip on Tanner.

'What's wrong?' he asked. She didn't answer. 'Amy?' he insisted.

'What are the Americas like?' It was the only thing she could think to ask.

'Big,' he said, 'so big that in the north it can be as cold as you've ever been here and, at the same time, further south it can be hotter than you can imagine, then at the tip of South America it's cold again.'

'What part were you thinking of going to?' she asked. It seemed incredible to her that he was willing to take her with him. It frightened her, but at the same time the idea excited her.

'I don't know.' He spoke casually, voicing his thoughts as they came to him. 'Maybe not the Americas.'

'Africa?'

'No.' His answer came with such a cold anger that Amy dared ask no more. Africa, for Tanner, was a bitter memory. It was his first ship away from England and he'd been lured there by the promise of higher pay. It was legal they'd told him and he'd jumped at the chance, but by the end of the trip he'd sworn before God that he'd break any law or die of starvation before he'd work on a slave trader again. He came out of his reverie aware of her hand on his chest. He patted it gently. 'We might go to Australia.'

'Australia?'

'Mmmm.' The thought had been hovering at the back of Tanner's mind ever since he'd heard the young men talking in the pub. 'I've a brother there. He's got a wife and a couple of youngsters.'

'If I come with you would you leave me with them?' she asked. Tanner smiled—she was quick, there was no denying that.

'I won't leave you anywhere you don't want to be.' It surprised him how easily the words of commitment came and how sincerely he meant them. He'd spent his whole life avoiding such promises, despite the effort of many a likely spinster. 'My brother wants me to go prospecting with him, and if you come with me we'll all just pitch in together, be one big happy family.' The idea appealed to him more and more as he thought about it. Of course, if there were gold strikes ship's captains would be wary of a man

25

wanting to work a one-way passage for his ward; still, it wasn't an insurmountable problem, not if the captain the young man had mentioned was as soft as he said.

Amy knew nothing about Australia, she didn't even really know where it was, and although the thought of going there didn't evoke the same panic as the workhouse or the asylum, she still felt ill at ease.

'Have you ever been to Australia?' she asked.

'No.' She waited for him to say more, but he was too busy plotting a way to get her on the ship.

'Is it far away?'

'Yes.'

'Further than Africa?'

'Yes.'

'Further than the Americas?'

'Yes.' He was only half listening to her questions.

'Will it take long to get there?' The hint of concern in her voice caught his attention.

'Australia is about as far away as you can get from here and, yes, it will take a long time to get there, so if you don't want to come with me now's the time to say so.' He studied her as he spoke. 'I have to go, Amy, and if you come with me I'll do my best to care for you. I doubt you could be any worse off than you are here, unless of course there's someone you've not told me about.'

'I've no one, you know that,' she said, and he was sorry for reviving the bitter memory.

'Well, you'll have friends there—my brother has a very friendly family.' She seemed unconvinced. 'I've found that people are pretty much the same the world over, some good, some bad. It's true there's less people in Australia, but that tends to draw people together. Remember, you may well be more alone on the busiest street in the largest city than on the smallest boat in the emptiest sea.' He waited for his words to have effect.

'What's it like, the sea?' she asked. There was no apprehension in her voice.

'Most people get seasick first time out,' he said.

'Did you?'

'No.' He smiled. 'I get seasick every time.'

CHAPTER 4

++++++++++++++

T HE ICY chill came just before the dawn. Tanner woke to find the girl shivering beside him. He rubbed her shoulders and she tried to move, to push herself closer to him.

'My feet!' she exclaimed. 'I can't feel my feet.' He sat up and began to massage them for her. He looked about him: the dull, grey dawn was creeping slowly amongst the shadows and the fog, which had abated to a mist, was beginning to clear.

'They're better now,' she lied, for the absence of feeling had been replaced by a burning sensation that his ministration only made worse. She felt him move away from her, then heard him fidgeting with something.

'What are you doing?'

'When I acquired that cape you're wearing, I also purloined a small, green portmanteau, the contents of which might just fit you.' He paused and grunted with exasperation. 'Unfortunately, it's locked: There, got it.' He removed the contents one by one, placing them in Amy's hands and telling her what they were. 'They're ladies underthings,' he said, oddly embarrassed despite his many experiences with such items. 'Night-dress, brush, comb, wash cloth, wool stockings—we could put a pair of them on you now. There's a shawl, too, that you can wear.' He laughed suddenly, gleefully, like a man who'd won a prize.

'What is it?'

'A writing set.' He grinned at her puzzled face. 'I've a letter here from my brother, sent all the way from Australia, postage mark on the envelope says so. With this writing set I can write another letter, a reasonable forgery of my brother's hand, a heartbroken letter thanking me for all I'd done to try to find a doctor who could cure you, his beloved daughter, begging me to forsake my wife and business and find some way to bring you home to him as he has no money left, having spent it all in the hope of finding a cure. Then I put my letter in his envelope.'

27

He hesitated, testing the viability of his idea.

'I only saw one doctor,' she said wistfully. 'The one who got up in court to say that I was really blind.' It had never occurred to Tanner that there might be any doubt about her blindness, or a cure for it.

'Did he say it could be cured?'

'No, he said it couldn't.'

'I'm sorry,' Tanner said softly. Amy smiled with such sweet sadness that all the joy of his new plan left him. 'If I could change it, take back that night . . .' She reached out and touched his lips with her hand, silencing him before his words released the tears she was fighting to control.

'Now, what do we do once you've written the letter?'

'Find Captain Buchanan of the *Lady Ann*.' Tanner was grateful for the change of subject. 'We're going to have to play a little game of pretend from now until we reach Australia.' Recalling her stalward morality he decided to make it sound like a game, hoping to mitigate the deception.

'You want me to pose as your niece. Call you Uncle, talk about my poor parents waiting for me in Australia. We'll have to say I've been blind for a while, seeing as I can't describe the place, and you'd better tell me a lot more about what it's like to sail— I imagine that's how I came to be here.' She paused thoughtfully, unaware of his mounting astonishment. 'If you're supposed to have a wife and business here it couldn't have been you who brought me from Australia, so whoever did bring me from Australia isn't available to take me home.' Tanner stared at her in amazement—there was a brightness in her face and firmness in her voice that was so alien to everything he knew of her. Her brows were knitted and her mouth pursed. 'We could say,' she continued slowly, 'that a good friend of the family, whose husband had died, was returning to England and offered to take me with her.' She smiled triumphantly.

'I think you've managed to get the gist of my idea.' The surprise showed in his voice and she was pleased that she'd impressed him.

'I'm fifteen, not five, and I'm blind, not daft.'

'So I see,' he said mockingly.

She responded to the challenge. 'I know what you're asking me to do is wrong, but that doesn't mean that I won't be any good at it.'

'Really?' Tanner teased.

'It's against everything my father taught me, but after three years with Auntie I've learnt that if you live under a person's protection you do as they say and you do it well.'

Tanner grinned at the serious, young face. 'Well, if you can think of some other way to get on that ship, one of which your father might approve, by all means let me know.' Amy bowed her head—it was for her that he was being forced to lie. Tanner patted her hand reassuringly. 'It's not too late to change your mind.'

'And do what?' she asked miserably.

'Once we're on that ship, if we get on it, you can't change your mind, you have to go on with the pretence and you can't make any mistakes.' His voice had become serious, deep and slow, emphasising the importance of what he was saying. 'It's always the high-minded, pious types that bring you down. They believe the world is evil and look for evil in all they meet.' He started to repack the bag. 'Self-involved people are easiest to deceive. You're pretty, young, and female, so most men will consider you incapable of fooling them. Women won't be so kind—they'll resent your youth and beauty but your blindness will disconcert them.'

She was helping him pack, beaming up at him in a way that halted Tanner's discourse. Adolescent girls were given to infatuation, and he wasn't very good at living up to other peoples expectations.

'You were going to tell me about the sea,' she said.

'Amy,' he began, then stopped. Whatever his misgivings there was little he could do to change things now.

'Yes?'

'Why don't we walk and talk at the same time?' He helped her to her feet and guided her towards the dock, telling her all he knew of the trip out from Australia and all he'd heard of the country itself as they searched amongst the ships for the *Lady Ann*. At mid-morning they stopped to rest while Tanner wrote his brother's letter, and it was well past lunch time when they found the *Lady Ann*.

'Captain's not aboard.' The boatswain answered Tanner's inquiry in a voice that probably never dropped below a yell. 'Taking tea.' He indicated a small row of weathered shops that nestled incongruously amongst the warehouses. In front of one hung a

29

swinging, wooden sign with the words 'Tea Shop' neatly carved on it. Tanner paused at the entrance to count the few coins he had left.

'What's wrong?' Amy asked.

'If I ask you what you'd like, you can order tea and toast, but if I ask you if you want anything, you'll have to say 'No' even if I insist. Do you understand?'

'Of course,' she smiled, 'you've no money.' He took her arm and led her into the shop. Neat was the right word for it—polished tables, well-swept floors, a simple but wholesome bill of fare.

Tanner picked Captain Buchanan as soon as he entered the shop, but he asked the waitress just to be sure and she confirmed his guess. He chose a table near the captain and sat Amy down facing him. The waitress came to take their order.

'I believe there's a Captain Buchanan here?' Tanner asked loudly. She was surprised to be asked the question again but gave little sign of it.

'Him over there,' she said, cocking her head in the captain's direction. Tanner looked nervously at the captain, smiled and nodded in acknowledgement. The captain returned the gesture. Tanner asked Amy what she'd like and she ordered tea and toast. He moved restlessly in his seat, turning to face the captain then turning back again. Finally he stood up with a sudden, jerky movement. He was still dressed in the gentleman's clothes his barrister had provided, but he affected the way of a seaman.

'Begging your pardon, sir,' he said, then waited for the captain to signal him to continue. 'I hear you're Australia bound and I was wondering if you had a full crew.' Tanner glanced over his shoulder at Amy and the captain followed his gaze.

'Crew's not complete yet but I've no room for men who only want a one-way trip.'

'No, sir, no.' Tanner sounded sincere. 'It's 'cause the *Lady Ann*'s coming straight back that I was hoping to sail on her.' He glanced at Amy again, and the captain's curiosity got the better of him.

'Sit down,' he said. Tanner complied. 'Now, why so anxious for a round trip to Australia?' Buchanan had once been a good-looking man with aristocratic features, but he had a bluntness about him that made him seem uncomfortable in polite society. Tanner inclined his head towards the girl.

'My niece,' he said then, fumbling in his pocket, he produced the letter he had written in his brother's name. The captain studied him for a moment, took the letter, opened it and read.

My Dearest Brother,

How can I thank you for all you've done and how can I ask you to do more? Yet, ask I must, for although I still have faith that one day my child will see again I no longer have the funds to pay for further treatment. Still, I do not regret the money spent only that there is no more, not even enough to pay for her fare home.

I cannot tell you how much her mother and I long to see her and to care for her, but believe me only such a longing could prompt me to ask what I now ask. I know the time you have taken away from your new business must have cost you dearly, but I must ask you to make one more sacrifice.

Please, bring my daughter home to me.

I know I have no right to ask you to make the trip but you are the only one she knows, the only one she trusts. I have no right to ask you to pay for her fare but I have nothing left.

I beg your good wife's pardon and your own. Believe me, Brother, I would not ask if there was any other way.

I close with deepest regard for your loving kindness,

Robert Tanner

The captain refolded the letter, glanced at the postage mark and handed it back to Tanner.

'What business are you in?'

'I was hoping for a partnership with some gentlemen in the importing business.' Tanner couldn't resist the ironic twist of the truth. The captain regarded his clothes.

'This business of yours, it doesn't earn enough to pay your fare?'

'Not mine nor hers neither, sir,' Tanner said bitterly. 'Business is gone sir, house, everything gone, wasted on one useless cure after another, thieves or cranks most of them.' His anger seemed to give way to sorrow. 'I promised my wife I'd leave the sea, but it's all I know.' He looked earnestly at the captain's face. 'She's living with her family since we lost our house. Perhaps it's for the best, she won't be so lonely. You see—' He paused as if he was unsure of his decision. '—I want to work a passage

31

for the girl, then make some kind of living for myself.'

The captain nodded, apparently considering Tanner's words, but his eyes were on the girl and his mind was full of unselfish, brotherly love. He asked the usual questions about Tanner's previous ships. Tanner mentioned some he'd sailed on and some he hadn't but that he was certain the captain couldn't check.

'We sail within the week,' the captain said at last.

'Does that mean you'll take us on?' The captain smiled and nodded. 'When can I take the girl aboard, sir? It's hard for her to get to know a place.'

'Now, if you've a mind to do some work while we're in port.'

'Gladly, gladly, thank you, sir.' He backed away towards his table. 'I'll write my wife. She knew what I intended and she'll be glad it's settled. Thank you, sir.'

He sat at the table and took Amy's hand. 'Did you hear?' he murmured.

'Most of it.' She squeezed his hand. 'You'd better write your letter, Uncle John.'

CHAPTER 5

◆◆◆◆◆◆◆◆◆◆◆◆◆◆

T HE *LADY ANN* was primarily a cargo ship, small and fast, although she had provision for a few passengers. On this voyage the owners, all pillars of the church, had afforded free passage to a vicar, his wife, their infant son and their housekeeper. The vicar was an utterly devout man who had little time for anything but his religion. His wife, a small, fussy woman, had finally found purpose with the birth of her child and now devoted herself entirely to it. Amy shared a cabin with the housekeeper.

The vicar had described his housekeeper as a kindly woman who would be overjoyed at the prospect of caring for one less fortunate than herself. In fact she was neither kindly nor capable of feeling joy. When Tanner had warned Amy to be careful of the self-righteous he might well have had Miss Sharpe in mind.

Tanner was surprised to find the passengers all on board when he arrived and that all but a few of the crew had returned from leave. Most of the men had served together for years and they had a basic mistrust of newcomers.

Aside from Tanner and the two young men from the tavern, there were only two other newcomers: the nephew of one of the seamen and the son of an old friend of the captain. These two came to the crew by right of birth, so Tanner found himself faced with a choice between isolation or an association with Joey and Davis, neither of which he relished. Something about Davis irritated him, although he could not have said what it was.

The *Lady Ann* sailed exactly on time, in fine weather with a good wind. Tanner had taken a position far below his capabilities. He was a fine navigator, though he'd not the papers to say so and smuggling had taught him tricks the tried and true sailor never learned. The boatswain found him to be quick and reliable and the thinking of that rather limited man never took him beyond that. The old crew, if they were impressed by his ability, made no comment. Joey and Davis didn't have the experience to judge him, nor did the young midshipman. Tanner considered that the other officers were far too involved with more important matters to spend their time observing him. So it came as a considerable shock to him when, not two weeks out, he was called to the captain's cabin.

'Smuggling was it, or piracy?' Buchanan barely allowed enough time to be sure they were alone.

'Sir?' Tanner managed to force the word despite the utterly numbing effect of the question.

'You're too good at what you do with too many short cuts and not enough discipline. You lied about most of the ships you've been on.' He paused, but Tanner didn't know what to say. At sea the captain had unchallenged power, and there was nowhere to run and no way to fight. 'If you're about to deny it your explanation better be a good one.'

'I'm no pirate, sir,' Tanner managed to say.

'A smuggler then.'

'There's no warrant for me,' Tanner answered with a rare degree of honesty. The captain's manner softened a little.

'How long has it been?'

It was the opening Tanner wanted. He humbled himself and let sadness creep into his voice. 'I give it up for her. My wife,' he clarified. 'I promised her I'd leave the sea, you see, she didn't believe I'd leave the smuggling. Unless she had me on dry land she'd worry what I was up to.' He hung his head, not raising his eyes to meet the captain's.

'This importing business—was it legal?'

'Yes, sir.' Tanner raised his head, a look of fierce indignation on his face. 'Yes, sir, it was.' He lowered his voice. 'They were proper gentlemen and I was doing a good job for them too.' He shuffled his feet and bowed his head again—it was the only approach he could think to use.

'I don't appreciate being lied to.' The statement came with force.

'I only lied about the ships, sir, the ones I sailed on I mean, nothing else.' Tanner prayed silently that Buchanan had not caught him in any other lie.

'And you've done with the smuggling?'

'With God as my witness, sir.' It was an easy oath for Tanner to make, for smuggling was not a trade to which he intended to return.

Buchanan spent a moment or two considering Tanner's words, then he suddenly relaxed, sinking into his chair and regarding Tanner across the top of his desk.

'What led you to the smuggling in the first place?' There was a perceptible change in his attitude that told Tanner he was safe, and his respect and gratitude to the man prompted Tanner to be honest.

'A year on a slave trader, sir.' The emotion in his voice, which no trick could have created, touched the corners of the captain's memory and their minds met with a deeper understanding than words could ever have produced.

'That will be all, Tanner,' Buchanan said roughly. Tanner turned towards the door then halted. 'The girl, my brother, they don't know . . .'

'Nor will anyone outside this room.' The captain watched him leave then took a bottle of gin from his cabinet. He was normally a temperate man, but this night he would get drunk wishing that it was he who had chosen to break man's laws instead of God's.

As Tanner left Buchanan's cabin his mind was reeling from the closeness of the call and a growing realisation of what might happen if the full extent of his deceit was discovered. He was still trying to get over the shock as he turned the corner and found himself face to face with Davis. Davis was standing too close and had too keen an eye to miss the concern on Tanner's face.

'Trouble with the captain?' The hint of insolence in his voice put Tanner on his guard.

'Captain's concerned about me working a passage for my niece, worried I might try to jump ship even though I got a wife back in England. Wanted to let me know what he'd do to anyone who tried.' The expression on Davis' face soured and Tanner knew he'd had a small victory. He moved on, leaving Davis to ponder the possible repercussions of his own plans to remain in Australia.

In fact, so great was Davis' faith in his plans that the captain's threat had only momentary impact. More interesting to him was the news that the pretty girl installed with the old dragon was not some fine lady far beyond his reach, but the niece of a simple seaman.

Davis walked slowly to the rail. The sea was becoming rough and the night was closing in more quickly because of the gathering cloud. He remembered Tanner coming aboard with the girl—if he'd thought about it he might have made the connection. He gazed out at the sea. The ship was running with the wind, her ease of movement belying the true height of the waves.

'There's a storm coming up.' Davis jumped at the sound of the boatswain's voice—for a big man, he moved very quietly. 'They'll be at us soon to rip the sheets down.' Davis looked up at the rigging. That was the trouble with the sea, he thought, always too much wind or not enough.

It was not long after Davis had rejoined his fellow sailors that the boatswain's whistle signalled all hands on deck. Even as the men scrambled to the deck the ship began to pitch and turn, screwing round as if being hit from two different sides at once.

'Storm's come up on us faster than I thought,' someone yelled, but their voice was lost in the tumult of wind and wave. Tanner moved automatically to lend a hand with a rope that had snarled.

'No!' the boatswain barked at him. 'You and you two,' he indicated Joey and Davis, 'get below, see none of that cargo breaks loose.' Tanner's body responded immediately but his mind balked at the order. It was the type of job given to new chums, Smithy's nephew should be down there with Joey and Davis, not him.

It was dark and airless in the hold, and eerie with the sound of groaning timber and the unnatural shapes of the cargo.

'Check every rope by hand, don't just look at them, and be careful with those lamps,' Tanner shouted at Davis, who had reached up to light the swinging lamps that were fixed to the roof of the hold. 'Those barrels are filled with cooking oil— one of them breaks open, you drop the lamp . . .' Tanner left the rest to Davis' imagination.

'God!' The ship rolled unexpectedly and Joey pitched forward on to his knees. 'God, I feel sick.'

'Storm's moving past us.' Tanner's voice was forced. 'It's not going to be much of a blow. Let's check these ropes and get out of here.' Joey didn't move and Tanner grabbed him by the coat, dragging him to his feet and pushing him in the direction of the boxes. 'Check the ropes.' He turned to find Davis watching him, a slow smile spreading across his face.

'Aye, aye, sir,' he said, and made a mock salute.

In her cabin on the upper deck Amy sat silently on the bed. In the weeks since they'd left England, the fear and depression that had dogged her since her blindness had subsided. The ship was small and the places to which she had access limited, she managed to find her way around easily and with confidence. Tanner was there whenever he could be, making her laugh, teaching her about people, and she loved him with the simple devotion of youth. She lifted her head to listen, hoping for the sound of his foot fall, though all logic told her that he would be far too busy in a storm to come to her. She relaxed again.

'Ye though I walk through the valley of the shadow of death . . .' Miss Sharpe wailed above the noise of the storm. Her voice came from somewhere near the floor and Amy assumed that she was kneeling. 'Thy rod and thy staff . . .' Amy felt a sudden stab of frustration. All the praying in the world had not cured her blindness, and if the ship was going to sink, it would sink despite Miss Sharpe's supplication.

The ship lurched and shuddered. Miss Sharpe screamed and began reciting 'The Lord's Prayer'. Amy caught a whiff of something as she regained her balance—it was only the lamp burning, she knew that, but it filled her with terror. After her blindness, every time Auntie had dragged her from her bed and sat her by the hearth she had been afraid of the fire. She had listened to it hissing and crackling, trying to guess where the sparks might fly, always sniffing the air searching for a hint of smouldering wood or burning cloth.

'Miss Sharpe.' There was no answer. 'Miss Sharpe?'

'Oh, do be quiet child.' The voice came at last. 'Pray to the Lord for your salvation.'

'We should put the lamp out.'

'No!'

'In case it falls or spills, in case it starts a fire.' Miss Sharpe didn't answer, but Amy could hear her making a strong noise, the result of her praying and hyperventilating at the same time. Amy felt her way around the room until she located the lamp, leant forward, and blew it out. Miss Sharpe screamed and Amy had the impression that she'd thrown herself face down on the floor. The contempt she felt for the older woman was overpowering. It wasn't fair that Miss Sharpe, who would revel in blindness—playing the martyr, making everyone dance attendance on her—should have all her faculties while she, Amy, who had dreamed of the day she'd be free, who had wit to achieve more than most

37

people ever tried was trapped in useless darkness. Miss Sharpe gave a strangled scream.

'My hands,' she gasped, 'I can't move my hands.' Amy edged her way towards the panting, choking noise, feeling along the bed until she found Miss Sharpe slumped beside it. She cupped her hands and put them over Miss Sharpe's mouth. The woman let out a hideous scream and pushed her hands away.

'I've seen the doctor do this when Mrs White was having her baby. Doctor said she'd breathed too much air and she had to breathe her own air again to make it right.' Miss Sharpe stopped her feeble protest. 'Now, breathe slowly.'

Inside the ship's hold the effects of the storm were less obvious. The roar of the sea and wind were muffled and the biting cold of the salt spray and rain did not penetrate. Yet Tanner would gladly have swapped the pitching, turning, suffocating hold for the icy rigging or the slippery deck, for in the hold seasickness ceased to be a case of mind over matter.

Tanner had finished checking most of the cargo—the boatswain was a thorough man and it would take a bigger storm than this to strain the ropes he'd ordered on most of the crates and barrels. Tanner moved to an abnormally large box stacked upright against the hull. It was as wide as a man is tall, a man and a half long and twice a man's height. It had only two ropes on it and Tanner decided a third would not go astray. He bent to select one from the pile and instantly felt ill. The ship lurched and the cumbersome box fell forward against its bonds. Tanner didn't notice the box's movement. He secured the rope to the hull on one side of the box, then moved across the face of the box to secure it on the other side, but before he could do so the ship twisted and pitched, rocking the box back and then forward again, snapping the ropes. From where Tanner stood directly in front of the box it seemed to fall slowly, almost gracefully, but not slowly enough for him to get out of the way. He braced himself and took the full weight of the box, leaning against it with his shoulder and trying to force it back with his hands.

'Davis!' His voice came with amazing strength considering the force with which the box had hit him and the fact that his face was pressed against it as he tried to manoeuvre his shoulder to take the weight more evenly. 'Davis!' His whole body began to tremble, and soon his knees would buckle or his back would snap from the strain. '*Davis!*' His teeth were clenched and the sound seemed to die in his throat. He was losing his strength and was in danger of being crushed beneath the box. The ship rolled and he staggered under the shifting weight. Desperation took hold of Tanner as he felt the power go out of his joints, leaving the raw bone to take the full pressure. He tried to call again but no sound came.

'I've got it, I've got it.' Joey sounded almost childlike as he clambered across the hold, pushing his bulk close to Tanner's, taking the strain on his massive chest.

'No,' Tanner gasped, 'the rope.' But Joey was holding half the burden and Tanner couldn't have taken it all again for anything. He took a deep breath, the trembling seemed worse now that part of the weight was gone. 'Can you hold it while I get the rope?' He couldn't see Joey's face, but he took the muted groan to mean 'Yes'. He tried to edge towards the corner, still taking part of the weight of the box, but his body was unwilling to respond and his movements were jerky and unco-ordinated.

'I'll get it.' Davis sounded totally unconcerned.

'Where the hell have you been?'

'Topside. Wondered what was keeping you two.' He placed the rope across the front of the box above head height and passed it through one of the rings attached to the hull. 'When I say heave,' he said, 'heave.' They braced themselves. 'Heave.' Slowly the box began to lift, then without warning the ship listed and threw the box forward again. 'Get out!' Davis screamed. 'Get out!'

It was not strength that moved Tanner—he had none left—and it was not humanity that made him push Joey clear—he was simply in the way. The box crashed to the floor, the wood splintering as it fell and a dull metallic clunk issuing from inside. Tanner stared at the box for a moment; it looked so harmless lying there. He stumbled forward and sat on it. His trembling had stopped and the pain had not yet begun, but he felt an awful numbness and a total inability to control his limbs. He looked at Joey, who was still staring dumbfoundedly at the crate, then at Davis who was leaning back against the hull, his face so pale it was frightening. He slid down into a sitting position and turned his hands palm up, a crooked smile creasing his lips as he lowered his hands for them to see.

The rope burns had cut deep into Davis' hands, although Tanner didn't realise how deeply until he got Davis out of the hold. He had never seen worse—the palm and fingers of both hands were torn open, and in some places the sinew and bone could be seen through the raw flesh. The captain himself came to see Davis' hands and to hear first-hand the account of what had happened. He nodded, his face drawn with obvious sympathy.

'I've seen the likes of this before. Don't bandage it too tight and give it gentle exercise or else the hand will heal crooked. It will take a while and if we see a homeward bound we might transfer you to it.'

'No, sir.' Davis spoke before he thought and the words came with too much feeling. 'I signed on for the round trip, sir. Mum's counting on me having the work. Hands will be all right, sir.' The captain smiled and patted him on the shoulder.

'We'll see, we'll see. Meanwhile, as soon as you're able you start work in the galley.'

'Thank you, sir.' Davis sounded sincere and Tanner had no doubt that he was, for being off-loaded on the next homeward bound would certainly put an end to his plans.

CHAPTER 6

++++++++++++++

TANNER WENT to visit Amy the morning after the storm. It had not occurred to her that he might have been in danger, and as he told her what had happened in the hold the old fears began to reassert themselves. He was her only friend and protector, and without him she'd be lost. He understood her fear and gently took her hand.

'Nothing's going to happen to you, even if I'm dead tomorrow. My brother will take care of you.'

'Why would he?'

'My brother's as soft-hearted a man as you'll meet anywhere, just tell him what happened.'

'Why should he believe me?' Tanner didn't answer. 'You could write him a letter.' Tanner shook his head.

'Too much of a risk with Miss Busybody about.' He thought for a moment. 'I'll be back.' He left and returned a few minutes later. 'Here.' He handed Amy a silver chain with a silver cross and a gold wedding ring on it. 'They were my mother's. Your grandmother's,' he added as Miss Sharpe entered the room. 'Flo kept them for me. I want you to have them in case something happens to me.' She fingered the cross and the ring.

'Can I wear them?' she asked. Her face was alight with happiness, as delighted as any other woman might be by a piece of jewellery.

Tanner smiled at her. 'Of course, it would bring my mother great joy to see you wearing them.' It was the truth, for it would have given Tanner's mother great joy to see any evidence of the humanity she knew her son possessed. He kissed her hands. 'I've got to go back to work.'

'Should you be working?' Miss Sharpe's voice cut across the warmth of the moment. 'I'd heard you were hurt.'

'It's better to work, stops me from stiffening up.' Tanner's shoulders still felt as if they were tearing whenever he put pressure on them, and his back felt as if he'd been stabbed. Still, he did not complain, as compared to Davis he was well off.

The pain on Davis' face as he forced his hands to move was almost tangible to those watching. They flexed their fingers with him and clenched their teeth with determination. Davis' head fell back against the wall.

'Leave it go,' Joey implored. 'It's too soon, let them heal first.'

'Hands'll heal useless if I don't keep at them.' Davis smiled at Tanner with the old knowing smile, not the weak, forced one of the past week. 'Think I'll go for a walk.' He steadied himself as he stood up, then climbed slowly to the deck. The deck officer watched his approach. 'Beg pardon, sir, Mr Tanner asked if I could look in on his niece seeing as I'm good for nothing else right now.' He indicated his hands and the young officer nodded.

It was a warm, clear day with a stiff breeze to gladden the sailor's heart. Davis felt good in spite of the pain in his hands, and he curled and straightened his fingers as he walked. He smiled as he came in sight of the cabin—the only pretty girl on the ship his for the taking, and her uncle too much in his debt to do a damned thing about it. He knocked on the cabin door, which was opened by Miss Sharpe.

'Beg pardon, ma'am, Mr Tanner asked me to look in on his niece seeing as I've got time on me hands so to speak.' He held forward his hands for her to see. They were a mess, with raw flesh, open sores and scales. He'd left the bandages off deliberately, but Miss Sharpe's horrified look made him wonder if it had been wise and whether Tanner's niece would react with revulsion or sympathy. Miss Sharpe recovered herself and was immediately overcome with a sense of propriety.

'Well, I supose it would be all right if the three of us took a turn around the deck.' Amy, having heard the conversation, joined them at the door. 'There you are my dear.' Miss Sharpe never quite managed to sound kindly no matter how hard she tried. 'This is Mr, er . . .'

'Davis,' he supplied.

'Of course, Mr Davis. He's the man who saved your poor uncle during the storm.' Amy's eyes were averted, her head downcast, and Davis took it to mean that she was shy.

'Your uncle thought I might look in on you seeing as I'm not up to working and him working harder because of it.'

'That's very kind of you, Mr Davis.' Amy found it odd that Tanner hadn't told her Davis was coming. 'Are we going for a walk?' She stepped past Miss Sharpe, reaching out in Davis' general direction. He extended his arm and her probing hand found his sleeve. She altered her grip so that her hand was through the crook of his elbow, the whole movement giving no hint of her blindness. They walked along the deck, Miss Sharpe at their heels. 'I'm glad to have the chance to thank you for helping my uncle. He said you were quite badly hurt.'

Davis turned his hands palm upward, and to his surprise she didn't react. 'It wasn't that bad,' he said to cover his confusion. She turned her head in his direction and smiled.

'My uncle's been so wonderful to me, I'd just die if anything happened to him.' Davis looked into the beautiful, smiling face, but their eyes didn't meet and for the first time he had some inkling of her disability. He raised his hands in front of her face and waved them back and forth, but her eyes didn't even follow the movement. He felt like a man who'd bought a perfect apple then cut it in half to find it full of worms and his first reaction was to throw it away. He removed her arm from his and stepped back. She lifted her head, smiling, inhaling the fresh air.

'It's a beautiful day.' She half turned to Miss Sharpe. 'We should spend more time outside before the heat of the tropics makes it impossible for us to be comfortable anywhere.'

Davis recovered himself, his initial shock being replaced by a morbid fascination. 'You've been through the tropics then?' he asked.

'Er, yes, when I came to England,' she hesitated, 'and when we first went to Australia, but I was just a baby then.'

'What's it like, Australia?' he asked, and any aversion he still felt for her melted away in his desire to learn all he could about the place in which he intended to thrive.

'Well,' she started cautiously, trying to recall all that Tanner had told her, 'I've been blind for a long time. I mean, I can't tell you the way things look, just the way they are, if you know what I mean. It's hot there in the summer, very hot but not like the tropics, and the flowers are different and the birds, too. There's one there that really laughs at you.' She was telling Davis things he already knew.

'What's your father do?' he interrupted.

'Well, at the moment he's prospecting.'

'Has he been doing it long?'

'Ever since they found gold.'

'And he'd know a bit about it then?'

'I suppose so.' The sudden intensity of Davis' manner unnerved Amy, and her mind raced back over the conversation to see if she'd said anything she shouldn't have said.

'Then you'll be going to the goldfields?' Davis persisted.

'Yes.'

'How will you get there?'

'I don't know. My uncle will arrange something or my father will come for me.'

'Is is far?' Amy felt rattled. His questions came too quickly, unexpected questions for which she had no prepared answer. 'I mean from Melbourne, is it far?'

'I don't know.' She worried about her answer, then realised it was the right one. 'Gold hadn't been discovered when I left.'

Davis didn't speak. A contact, any contact, on the goldfields would be useful and, however far away they were, she wouldn't be expected to walk. It wouldn't be unreasonable to expect them to give him a ride. He looked up suddenly, aware that his thoughts may easily be written on his face, but she was gazing past him with unseeing eyes. He smiled—there might well be an advantage to having a woman who could not see. He took her hand and placed it on his arm again.

'I'd best be getting back now. Let me take you to your cabin.' They walked in silence, Amy's mind in a whirl. She'd never had to think so quickly before, never known anyone to be so interested in her conversation or so aware of its meaning. Tanner was grateful for her quick mind, coaxing her and encouraging her to use it, but this man had challenged her wit, forcing her to use it. She found it exciting.

They stopped at the door to her cabin. 'Tell my uncle I'm glad he sent you,' she said, although she was sure he had not. 'I wanted to thank you and I'm glad he's given me the chance.' There was a mischievous twitch in the corner of her mouth and Davis suspected that she had guessed the original reason for his visit.

'Your uncle didn't tell me you were blind.'

'Perhaps he doesn't think of me that way.'

'Then neither shall I, miss, neither shall I.' Davis nodded to Miss Sharpe and turned to leave. 'I'll see you again,' he called over his shoulder. Amy stepped back into the cabin, to her Davis seemed such a confusing young man, so different to all the other people she had known.

'What's he look like?' she asked Miss Sharpe.

'That young man?' Miss Sharpe's tone was caught somewhere between outrage and reproach.

'No.' Amy had been referring to Davis, but after hearing Miss Sharpe's reproval she cast about for an alternative. 'My uncle.' He was the only person she could think of, although something in her baulked at hearing a description of Tanner.

'Your uncle?'

'Yes, I've never seen him.'

'Looks are not important, my dear.'

'No, of course not, I shouldn't have asked.'

'Still, you should be able to describe him in case you ever become separated. Let me see—he's very tall.'

'I know that.'

'And quite solid too.'

'Yes, I can tell that much.'

'His hair is brown, so are his eyes, and quite deep set. He has a tanned complexion, a square jaw—I suppose those who judge such things would call him handsome. Of course, he's not a boy any more, but then you must know his age.' Amy didn't speak—her face had become blank and pale. 'Is there something wrong dear?'

'No, no, he's just different to what I expected.'

'Really?'

'Yes, I thought he'd be more like my father.' It was a halted explanation but it satisfied Miss Sharpe. Amy made her way to the bed, lay down and pulled the covers over her.

'Are you all right my dear?'

'I'm just tired, that's all.'

Amy turned her face to the wall and lay still, waiting for one thought or feeling to emerge from the churning mass of ideas and emotions. *It wasn't Tanner.* The thought came suddenly, terrifying her. Tanner wasn't the man who had blinded her. She had suspected it from the moment he first held her to him, when she'd felt his size. The man she'd seen had been much smaller, but she'd convinced herself that there hadn't been much light and that distance and speed could mar one's perception of height. She drew an unsteady breath, realising that eyes didn't change colour and grey hair didn't turn brown.

From deep within her mind came the memory of a face she'd could never forget, hair so grey it was almost white and eyes the brightest blue she'd ever seen, sparkling in the light from the inn door so full of anger. He'd shouted at her and she'd tried to duck behind the crates.

Amy forced her fingers in her mouth to stop the involuntary sob. It hadn't been Tanner! He'd come later, running, stumbling into the crates, burying her beneath them as she lay unconscious on the ground.

A tear trickled down her cheek. Ever since Tanner had promised to care for her she'd locked the memory of that night away, refusing to think about it, trying to pretend that she'd misinterpreted the expression on the grey-haired man's face, that his cane was not raised ready to strike her, that he had just bumped into the crates. Her tears were uncontrollable now as memories of the pain and the terror came rushing back. Tanner wasn't the grey-haired man, he wasn't responsible at all.

Relief came with this knowledge. She loved Tanner and she hadn't wanted him to be the one who'd blinded her, deep in her mind she'd always known the blow had been deliberate. But knowledge brought fear, too. Guilt was her only hold on him— he didn't love her, not the way she loved him. She fumbled for her handkerchief. He wouldn't dump her even once he knew the truth, but things would change—the gentleness, the tenderness in his touch, the half apology in his voice, they would all vanish. There would be a grudging acceptance of the situation and only their current circumstances would hold them together, then when the circumstances changed he'd be gone. The handkerchief was sodden and she dared not rise from the bed to get another. She buried her face in the pillow and feigned sleep to avoid Miss Sharpe's inquisition. Finally, sleep came.

She made no decision not to tell Tanner, but equally she made no decision to tell him. It may happen in the course of conversation that she would have to tell the truth or lie, and if that happened she would not lie but she would not seek out the opportunity to tell him. It was easy to believe that omission of the truth was somehow different to lying.

As Davis left Amy's cabin he found himself smiling. It wasn't often that a woman surprised him, but that one certainly had. He remembered the first time he had seen her, Tanner carrying her bag, Miss Sharpe looking for all the world as if she was her servant. He'd thought she was a lady, someone far beyond his reach, and he'd never wanted a lady—ladies could put a man down with a look or a word, and even if he was a rich man he wouldn't be good enough for one of them. Davis moved on again, but the bitterness of his thoughts sapped his concentration and he missed the step as he descended to the lower deck. He extended a hand to save himself, then drew it back screaming in agony as his fingers were pushed painfully back.

It was Tanner who came to his aid. 'Are you all right?'

'Yes,' Davis answered breathlessly. Tanner helped him to his feet and waited until he was steady before releasing his hold. There was concern on the older man's face, the look of one who felt responsible for another's pain. Davis smiled. 'Now, that was an unfortunate end to such a pleasant day.'

'Pleasant?'

'Yes. I was just talking to your niece. Made me forget all about my hands having such charming company.' The two men watched each other for a moment, then Davis smiled again. 'You didn't tell me she was blind.'

'Does it matter?'

'Yes,' Davis said cautiously, 'and no.'

'She's just a child.'

'Are you telling me not to see her again?'

'That's up to her.' There was a warning in Tanner's voice, but it was a gentle warning, for he owed Davis and he had no real basis for his growing mistrust, besides which the girl was not his despite all their pretence.

'But you'll be watching?'

'Like a hawk.'

As soon as Tanner had some time free he went to see Amy. He stood behind her as she leant against the rail, facing into the warm wind that whipped across a sea so bright that it hurt Tanner to look at it.

'Be careful of Davis,' he said.

'Why?'

Tanner took time to answer, partly for effect and partly to be sure his meaning was clear. 'He's a healthy young man, you're a pretty girl, the attraction is bound to occur, and passion takes the edge off judgment and discretion. You must never forget that we're living a lie.' Amy stiffened, remembering that she was living two. 'What's more, he's like me.'

'Like you?'

'An observer, a mishandler of the truth. He lied to get on this ship just like we did and he plans to leave it in Melbourne.'

'A kindred spirit.'

'No.'

'Why not?'

'He's more ruthless than I am, more ruthless than you can imagine.' The remark was unfounded and Tanner knew it weakened his case. He looked down at her—she had turned to face him, the wind blowing wisps of hair across her face. Amy had heard what he'd said and understood it, but she didn't believe it or, if she did, she didn't understand its significance.

'He saved your life.'

'Yes, he saved my life and I owe him, but don't let him use that to make you do anything you don't want to do.'

'Then I can still see him?'

'It's not my decision. I have no legal hold on you, I can't force you to do anything.' The corners of her mouth pulled down into an unwilling pout. He put his arm around her. 'Play his game if you must but be very, very careful.'

Davis came to see Amy several times during the next week. At first he told himself that she was nothing more than his ticket to the goldfields, but then he admitted that he was intrigued by her, by the blindness, by the contradiction of perfection and imperfection, vulnerability and strength. Slowly he became aware of an idea that was growing at the back of his mind, not so much an idea as a vision, a vision that would not be complete without her.

He longed for a chance to court her as he had so many other women and at last the opportunity came. They were alone on the deck, Miss Sharpe having been called upon to look after the baby while the vicar and his wife took tea with the captain. It was a fine day but cold with a stiff breeze, and Miss Sharpe considered it unwise to take the infant out. Davis led Amy to the rail, then took both of her hands in his and turned her to face him.

'It's very kind of you to take me out, Mr Davis.'

'Davis, just Davis, no Mister.' His voice was hushed and intimate. 'And it's my pleasure to take you out.'

'Well, thank you anyway, Davis.'

He was standing very near to her, holding her hands close to his chest. 'You're beautiful,' he said, his voice not quite producing the same expression of appreciation that showed on his face. 'Your hair is like black satin and your skin is like moonbeams.' Normally at this point he would describe the eyes, but this time he couldn't find the words. Not that they weren't attractive, a deep blue-grey framed in long black lashes, but to mention them would be a cruel reminder of her blindness. He moved on to the mouth, studying the pink lips held, not as he'd expected in a coy smile, but tightened against a derisive smirk. 'I'm making a fool of myself, aren't I?'

Her lips broadened into a smile. 'Tell me,' she whispered, 'what do you look like?'

'Me?' he stammered. 'I'm, I'm . . .' Women were usually all too aware of his looks and he relied on them more than he realised. 'I'm tallish.' He found his voice.

'Not as tall as my uncle, nor as broad.'

'No, but I'm younger and . . . Do looks really matter that much to you?'

'No, but they do to you. It was my looks that drew you here and my looks that brought you back in spite of my blindness. Did you think it would make me more gullible, more willing to swallow your crumbs of compliments, easier to entice into your arms?' She stopped, mainly because she'd run out of words, and it was a moment before Davis spoke.

'I'm sorry,' he murmured, but he didn't sound sorry. 'I thought you'd like the compliments. I never imagined you'd be so defensive.'

Amy didn't believe she'd been defensive, still, she cast her mind back over the conversation, hoping to reassure herself and searching for a way to respond. 'You didn't answer my question,' she said at last.

'Question?'

'What do you look like? Is your hair like black satin? Is your skin like moonbeams? Are your eyes . . . You didn't mention my eyes, is it hard to look at them? Do you—'

'They're beautiful,' he interrupted, 'and my hair is black and my skin unblemished and my eyes are blue, a truer blue than yours. Do you remember the colour of your eyes?' She nodded and reached up to touch his face. He put his hands on her waist— it was the right moment to draw her to him, to kiss her, but he refrained. She was unlike any woman he'd ever met, coquettes and termagants, virgins and whores, he'd known them all in his short life, yet none had confounded his thoughts and feelings as she had.

'I'm going to be a rich man, Amy, richer than you can imagine. I'll have a fine house and servants and you'll want for nothing. There will be maids to run after you and fetch your things and do your hair, carriages to take you anywhere you want to go and it'll be "Yes, sir, and no, ma'am" wherever we go and they'll treat you like a lady 'cause I'll be able to buy and sell them as I see fit.' His voice had changed in a way that frightened her, and had she been able to see his face it would have frightened her even more, for his single-minded ambition and utter ruthlessness were patently written there. The feelings that he erased from his features in the presence of others he let manifest themselves in the face of her blindness, not realising they would carry to his voice.

She had dropped her hand from his face as he started to speak and they rested limply on his chest, feeling its erratic rise and fall give emphasis to his words. She did not speak even when it became obvious that he had finished.

'You think I'm mad,' he said at last.

'No,' she murmured. She had some inkling of how he felt— she'd lain in that wretched room above the stables and dreamed of being rich with fine clothes and food and no auntie to take it all away from her, but hers had been dreams, distant and unattainable. With Davis it was different.

'Will I see you again?' He'd let go of her waist and taken her hands in his.

'Miss Sharpe—'

'Will be there,' he finished for her. 'I know and we'll play our little game and be distant and polite, but fate will give us another day like this, you wait and see.' His soft persuasive voice disconcerted her—it was too much in contrast to his earlier tone. She moved towards her cabin.

'Miss Sharpe will be suspicious if we don't get back soon.' Even as she spoke, Amy wondered what it was about Davis that troubled her.

Inside her cabin Amy found herself alone. Miss Sharpe had gone to the vicar's cabin to try to settle the child. She felt her cheeks, wondering if they were flushed. He was gone, and without the power of his presence her objectivity began to return. Tanner had warned her it was a game, and perhaps all that talk had just been part of it. When flattery had failed he'd simply employed a different tactic. She lay on the bed, holding tight to the logical thought, but the emotion she'd sensed from him had seemed so real and if he meant what he said, if it was the truth, then what she'd begun to feel for him would not be wrong.

CHAPTER 7

✦✦✦✦✦✦✦✦✦✦✦✦✦✦

T HE *LADY ANN* was hove to for Christmas services, although the order need hardly have been given as there hadn't been a breath of wind for three days, and there wasn't a sailor on board who wouldn't have traded his Christmas respite for a stiff breeze.

The captain made a surprisingly long speech. Surprising, not only because of its length but because of its content, for it dealt not with the Christmas story and its accompanying joy but with man's inhumanity to man.

Repeatedly he stared at Tanner, yet when their eyes met the captain diverted his, only to return his gaze a moment later. Eventually Buchanan handed the service over to the vicar who, feeling somewhat challenged by the lengthy oratory, extended his sermon to match the last, however much of his dissertation was lost amid the shuffling of feet and the clearing of throats.

After the benediction the passengers and crew gratefully dispersed, Tanner and Miss Sharpe leading Amy back to her cabin.

'I'm sure Miss Sharpe can do that by herself.' Buchanan's voice was clear rather than loud. He moved away from the small knot of sailors left on the deck and Tanner obediently followed him. 'Perhaps you would like to join them later for Christmas dinner.' The captain's voice still carried to those interested enough to listen. 'A family should be together at Christmas.' His voice level slowly dropped and with it the tight rein he kept on his features, so it was a tired and troubled face that he turned to Tanner.

'When I was in the navy we used to hang smugglers like you.' Tanner's throat contracted and his body became cold and distant, paralysed by the thought that Buchanan had put him in. It was the reason for the furtive looks and the haggard demeanour. 'Good men some of them, good sailors like you.' Tanner swallowed, trying to find his voice and the words that might still save him. 'You said there was no warrant for you.'

52

'None that I know of, sir.' Tanner's heart sank as he spoke, for it was more than possible that if Carstairs and his fine and proper friends had been caught then there would be a warrant for him.

'I wanted you to know it doesn't matter either way—I wouldn't put you in and I'd do my damnedest to see you're not caught.'

'Why?'

Buchanan smiled at Tanner's utter astonishment. 'I admire you Tanner,' he said. 'I admire the way you sacrificed your business in the vain hope of restoring your niece's sight.' He paused, and the tiredness in him seemed to grow. 'And I'd admire any man who'd risk the noose for smuggling rather than work the slave trade.'

'I don't understand.'

'I spent five years on those bloody ships.' The strength went out of the captain as he spoke, and at last Tanner understood the reason for the strange sermon and the averted stares. 'Five years of telling myself it was legal. Five years of telling myself it was what I had to do if I wanted the captaincy of a good ship and a share in her profits.' He glanced at Tanner. 'I bought my share of the *Lady Ann* with the deprivation of other human souls and I—'

'Captain, sir . . .' The mate sensed he'd interrupted something despite the rapid return of the captain's habitual facade. 'Er, the vicar . . .' The mate switched his gaze to Tanner, whose face revealed nothing. 'Might I relieve you of some duty, sir, while you take tea with the vicar?'

Buchanan smiled. 'Tell the vicar I'll be along to drink his whisky in a minute.' He turned to Tanner. 'We'll talk again. Merry Christmas.'

'And to you, sir.' Tanner watched the captain leave. It troubled him that he had the trust of such a man, troubled him more that he'd abused it.

'Getting cosy with the captain are we?' Davis was standing not an arm's length from him, partially concealed by the steps leading up to the bridge.

'Two old seamen talking about the sea.' Tanner spoke nonchalantly, but if such an insensitive soul as the mate had recognised the intensity of their conversation, then one as perceptive as Davis could not have missed it.

'You and him got a lot in common then?'

'A long time at sea, that's all.'

'A lot of the crew's spent a long time at sea. Captain doesn't spend much time chatting to them.'

'Ship ahoy, off the starboard bow.' The watch's voice rang clear in the breathless air. Tanner smiled.

'A homeward bound—how's your hands?' Davis dropped his gaze to his hands, the purple scars, the few remaining sores, enough to keep him from full duty. He looked up at the horizon and back at Tanner, but Tanner was gone.

'Captain said I could take my Christmas meal with you.' Tanner had knocked and entered the cabin in the same movement, and Amy brightened noticeably at the sound of his voice.

'I'm glad.' She moved towards him. 'Wasn't that a long service. I thought they'd never finish.' She linked her arm through his, guiding him to the table. 'And did you hear the vicar's wife? If she said it once she said it thirty times.'

' "Who'd've thought it could be so warm on Christmas Day?" ' they chanted together.

'There's a ship.' Miss Sharpe sailed into the room, looking as close to pleased as she ever managed to get. 'A homeward bound and,' she added importantly, 'a steamship.'

'Aye, there's a few around.' Tanner had no idea why he resented them, but he did. 'Noisy damn things.'

'Come along dear.' Miss Sharpe took Amy's arm. 'You don't want to miss seeing it.'

Amy jerked her arm free. 'I've seen steamships before,' she said angrily.

'Oh, I am sorry.' Miss Sharpe was sincere. She believed that the likes of Amy should be cloistered, protected from any reminder of their loss. She smiled apologetically at Tanner and left. He waited a moment to make sure she was gone.

'Where the hell did you see a steamship?'

'In London, of course.'

'In London,' he said sarcastically, 'but you've been blind the whole time you've been in London, blind before you left Melbourne, blind so long you don't remember what the city looks like or the landscape or your own damn parents either.'

'Or the colour of my own eyes,' she said softly, and he could see from her face the significance of the remark.

54

'What's happened?' he demanded.

'Davis,' she stammered. 'Davis wanted to know if I remembered the colour of my own eyes.' Tanner groaned. 'I told him I did. I'm sorry.' Tears prickled at the back of her eyes and her heart beat with an odd type of panic.

'Why Davis, of all people, why Davis?'

'I'm sorry,' she said again. 'I didn't think . . .' She swallowed to stop herself from crying. 'He won't put us in.'

'No,' Tanner agreed angrily. 'He won't put us in. Why should he when he can use it to trap you into saying more or pressure you into doing something you don't want?' He could tell by the slight stiffening of her shoulders that she rejected the idea. 'Well, if he does, just you remember that he lied to get on to this ship too, and that he intends to jump ship in Melbourne, so if he spoils our game we can spoil his.'

'You don't know that he lied to get on to the ship or what he intends to do in Melbourne.' Tanner's mistrust suddenly seemed so unwarranted to her.

'Do you remember the first night we were together, when you fell asleep in the tavern?'

'The night you stole the cape and bag.'

Tanner raised his eyebrows and sighed. Of all the things that happened that day, why did she choose to remember it by that? 'Joey and Davis were in the tavern, they were talking about their plans. That's how I heard about this ship.'

'So we owe him for that too,' she snapped.

'You don't owe Davis for anything.' Tanner was angry now, angry because of her sudden devotion to Davis, angry because of her attitude to the theft, angry because it was for her that he'd lied to Buchanan. He didn't need to settle in Australia, he could sail on this ship for the rest of his life. As long as he didn't stay in England those fine and proper gentlemen would be satisfied. It was all for her. He exhaled heavily. 'I owe Davis and I'll pay him in my own way. You owe him nothing. Do you understand?'

'Yes.'

'The tavern was called the King's Head and it was on Olde Pier Road, but don't tell him unless you have to, unless he threatens you. That information damns us too, you know.' There was still no kindness in his voice. 'And be careful what you say from now on, not just with him but with everyone. Believe me, if we're found out they'll dump you in Melbourne and make me work the return trip, and when I get there there'll be people waiting, people who'd stop at nothing to get rid of me.'

It was an exaggeration and Tanner instantly regretted it—he doubted he could have hurt her more if he'd struck her. Her lips were trembling and tears rolled down her cheeks.

He put his arms around her and she clung to him as she had that night in the tavern. He patted her hair and kissed the top of her head. 'It won't come to that,' he murmured as Miss Sharpe entered. 'Steam ships are terrible things,' he raised his voice, 'noisy, dirty, smelly things they are, flouting the wind with their great pall of smoke and hell fire in their belly. They've no care for God or man and you've missed nothing by not seeing one.' Miss Sharpe looked suitably penitent. Tanner held Amy at arm's length. 'Now, I've really got something for you to cry about. It's Christmas and I've no present.'

She threw her arms around him again. 'You've done so much for me,' she sobbed, and it was almost too much for Tanner— first Buchanan's approbation and now Amy's. A man of honour and an innocent child, he'd lied to one and taught the other to lie, and yet he'd no wish to hurt either of them. He was just trying to survive in a life that had left him few options. He didn't want their high opinion, just their acceptance of his limitations. He disentangled himself from Amy's arms.

'Tell me, Miss Sharpe, did you enjoy the service?' He led Amy to the chair.

'I thought the vicar spoke beautifully,' Miss Sharpe enthused. Tanner smiled wickedly.

'And who'd've thought it would be so warm on Christmas Day.'

There was not one part of the ship that had not been scrubbed, not one inch of the rigging that had not been checked a dozen times. All the crew were edgy and Tanner found it difficult to hold his temper with Davis. It galled him that he owed this man his life, and the way Davis always alluded to it, never saying it out straight, made it even worse. There was an arrogance about Davis, a contempt for everyone and everything, that made it almost impossible for Tanner to speak civilly to him. Yet he found himself following Davis, watching him, counting the number of times he went to see Amy, how long he stayed and whether or not Miss Sharpe was there. He listened in on Davis' conversations with Joey and watched to see if he did his fair share of the work. Tanner could not fault him there, though whether he'd still be working so hard if he wasn't threatened with a trip home was doubtful, at least to Tanner's mind.

Tanner was not alone in his vigil—Joey was watching too, and he saw what Tanner's ignorance could not perceive and his prejudice prevented him from interpreting. Davis had changed. So imperceptible was the change that at first Joey was not sure when it began, yet he instinctively laid the blame on Amy. Davis' conversation had always been dominated by his plans for acquiring wealth and the weaknesses of his fellow men and women. The topics had not changed, but had subtly begun to have focus. No more half-plotted roads to riches open to endless variation—he was going to the goldfields to make his fortune there. No more nebulous dreams of idle debauchery in lavish hotels with endless companions—he wanted a fine house and servants and Amy. To Joey she seemed to be the centre of the change, the change that was forcing he and Davis further apart.

He attempted to talk to Davis about it, clumsily trying to revive Davis' interest in their former fantasies, but Davis steadfastly turned the conversation back to Amy until, in exasperation, Joey blurted out: 'But she's blind.'

Davis turned on him with such viciousness that Joey thought he was going to strike him. 'Blind, is she? Well, she sees more with no sight than you see with your half wit.'

Joey made to respond, but Davis swung away from him, so he spoke the words to the empty sea and darkening sky. 'And I see more with my half wit than you see with two sharp eyes and a wit to match. You're changing Davis, it all matters too much to you now.' Joey shook his head at the futility of the appeal, for even if Davis had been listening he wouldn't have heard.

Joey resolved to watch Davis, although he didn't know what he expected to see or what he could possibly do. Tanner, on the other hand, knew exactly what he expected. He expected Davis to try to seduce Amy and he expected to be able to stop him. It was, however, Joey and not Tanner who saw Davis' dark silhouette disappear on to the deck. It was Joey who saw him secrete himself in the pale moon shadows, edging his way past the watch. He didn't see Davis reach the cabin, but he'd seen Davis with women before and his imagination did the rest.

Amy woke to find Davis' hand over her mouth and his voice whispering soothingly in her ear. 'It's all right, it's just me, Davis. Outside, shhh.' He took her arm, urging her gently towards the door, then guided her along the deck into the shadow of the long boat.

'I shouldn't be here,' she murmured.

'The old dragon never leaves us alone. I think your uncle's asked her to keep an eye on us.' Amy doubted it—she was sure that it was her own eagerness for him that had invited Miss Sharpe's attention. 'It's so much harder now I'm back on full duty.' Davis pulled Amy to him, but refrained from any intimacy that might startle her. 'It's not like I can write you a note asking you to meet me.' His voice was breathless and constrained. 'Would you meet me, Amy? Could you, if I could send you a message?'

'Of course.' She felt the same exhilaration she'd experienced when she and Tanner had plotted the deception that had earned them their berth, the same realisation that it was wrong and the same willingness to do it because of what she felt for the man who suggested it.

'Would you meet me at night, could you manage that?'

'It's always night to me.'

'I'm sorry.'

'Actually, I can tell the difference. The sounds, the smell, no heat from the sun or cool from the shade, but the fact that it's night makes no difference to me. If anything it will make it easier to escape Miss Sharpe.'

'Are you sure?'

'Yes,' she laughed. 'What kind of message? A signal of some kind when we meet, a phrase, a word?'

'No,' he halted her. 'Next time I come I'll bring a string with a couple of beads on it. I'll tell Miss Sharpe that I'm carving them to help strengthen my hands and I'll give one to you each time we're to meet. If I can't get away I'll give it to someone else to bring to you.'

'That's brilliant.' She was beaming at him and the temptation to kiss her was too strong. As they parted he studied her face. She looked pale in the watery moonlight, but there wasn't a trace of apprehension, no suggestion that she regretted the embrace.

'Here's the best place,' he said. 'Can you get here by yourself?'

'Of course.' She was nestling close to him, thrilled by his warmth and her own daring. 'What time?'

'Same as now, at the change of the watch.'

'You had this all worked out, you knew I'd come.' Deep in her mind Tanner's warning stirred.

'No . . . yes.' He held her tighter. 'No, I didn't know you'd come but yes, I'd worked it all out hoping, praying you'd agree. It's been driving me insane, not being able to see you alone.' His voice was breathy and soft, inaudible to anyone but Amy. 'We belong together.'

'And what will happen when we reach Melbourne?' she asked.

'I'll never leave you.' It wasn't exactly an admission that he intended to jump ship but it still unnerved Amy, for it meant that either he was lying to her to win her trust or he'd lied to Buchanan to get his job. 'I mean it.' Davis had interpreted her slight withdrawal as doubt.

'I know,' she said, 'but I have to get back.'

'Why?' He pulled her down on the deck beside the long boat. 'I've such wonderful plans for us, Amy.'

So their meetings began and so continued. Each time Davis slipped from his bed to meet her, Joey lay awake waiting for his return. He would have followed them, but he was afraid that his clumsiness might somehow precipitate their discovery, and it would go hard on Davis if he was caught seducing a passenger even if she was just a seaman's niece.

CHAPTER 8

✦✦✦✦✦✦✦✦✦✦✦✦✦

MISS SHARPE walked slowly along the deck, fanning herself with a handkerchief. 'This is ridiculous, absolutely ridiculous,' she panted. 'We're past the tropics, so why on earth is it still so hot?'

'It would be hot even if we were in Melbourne.' Amy had asked Tanner the same question and she repeated the answer for Miss Sharpe. 'It's summertime there now, you know.'

'Oh, I can't stand it, I really can't stand it.' Miss Sharpe leant listlessly against the rail.

'It's mostly a dry heat in Melbourne,' Amy consoled, 'not as draining as this.'

'Oh, I must lie down.' Miss Sharpe lurched in the direction of the cabin. 'Come along, my dear.'

'No, I'd sooner be out here where there's a bit of a breeze.'

'Are you sure?' Miss Sharpe didn't wait for an answer but headed determinedly in the direction of the cabin.

Joey stood at a distance watching the exchange, and it quite surprised him to find her left alone. He edged slowly towards her, his curiosity overcoming his caution. There was a softness in her face that he had not expected, she was so different to the brassy beauties that usually hung on Davis' arm. Joey moved slightly, trying to see more of her face.

'Who's there?' There was tension in her voice. Joey shuffled a few steps closer. 'Who is it, who's there?' The tension turned to fear and Joey was astonished to realise that he was the cause of it. 'Miss Sharpe!' She started back towards the cabin.

'N-n-no, it's—it's me,' Joey stammered. She stopped and turned to face the voice.

'Do I know you?'

'Joey,' he said, 'Davis' friend.'

She relaxed and smiled the way no woman had ever smiled at Joey before. 'You helped Davis save my uncle's life.'

He nodded then, realising she couldn't see, said: 'Yes.'

'I'm so grateful to you both.' She moved closer to him as she spoke, and there was no cruel twist to her lips, no hint of a taunt in her words, so different to any other girl he'd tried to engage in conversation. 'My uncle said that if it hadn't been for you nothing Davis could have done would have saved him.' Joey was oddly flattered by the remark—most people had forgotten his part in the rescue. He stared at her face, now quite close to his, gazing right into her eyes and slowly coming to terms with the fact that she really couldn't see.

'Did I frighten you?' he asked.

'A little,' she admitted. 'It's awful feeling that people are watching you and worse if you end up stumbling around, calling out for someone when there's no one there.'

'I'm sorry.' He raised his hand to touch her, but withdrew it before he made contact. He could see why Davis, or any man for that matter, would be attracted to her. She was beautiful and kind and she smiled at him, a warm and earnest smile.

'Don't worry about it,' she said. 'Just remember to say something next time.'

'There won't be a next time.' Joey was suddenly struck with the import of what he was doing.

'Why not?'

'Davis wouldn't like it.'

'Don't be silly.'

'No.' Joey stared at her perplexed face. 'Please, miss,' he begged, 'please don't tell him I came.'

'Why not?' She could tell he was serious although she couldn't imagine why.

'Well,' he said slowly, 'I wasn't too keen on him seeing you, that's why.' She was waiting for him to say more, but he could hardly tell her that Davis had changed and that he believed she was the cause. 'I mean, meeting you at night the way he does.' Amy still said nothing and Joey fumbled for words. 'It'd go hard on him if he were caught up here with you at night, it'd go hard.'

'But we only talk.' Amy finally found her voice.

'Don't tell him I came, miss, I don't want no trouble.' He sounded so worried that she reached to comfort him, but he retreated from her. 'Be careful, miss, be very careful,' he said, then he was gone.

Amy leant against the rail. Joey had used Tanner's words, in a different context of course but they still held the same dim prophecy of disaster, not only for her but for Davis as well.

The next time Amy was with Davis she asked him about Joey.

'He's a stupid, blundering oaf.' Davis laughed at her.

'But he did help save my uncle's life.'

'That's what your uncle would like you to believe, but if it hadn't been for me they'd both have been squashed flat.'

Amy found his egotism unusually annoying. 'I'd like to meet him,' she insisted, but the tension in his body and the way he slowly inhaled told her that he was about to deny her request. 'If you brought him up to meet Miss Sharpe, introduce him as the man who helped save my uncle's life, then he could bring the message for you when you aren't able to come yourself.' He exhaled and relaxed and she knew she'd won her point.

'All right,' he said, 'but Joey's got no subtlety in him and he'll look as guilty as hell every time he hands you the bead.'

'Does he know what the beads mean?'

'No,' Davis smiled, 'and what he doesn't know he cannot tell, even unwittingly.' He kissed her then held her at arm's length, trying to discern her features in the inky light of the moonless night. She was everything he wanted. She wouldn't spoil his plans with oafish stupidity the way Joey did and she wouldn't just hang around for as long as his money lasted. Other men wouldn't want her because of the blindness—they wouldn't realise how the affliction bound a woman to a man. She was beautiful and bright and she could pass for a lady any time.

'Will you take Joey with you when you jump ship?' she asked casually.

'I'll have to. He'd follow me anyway.' It didn't surprise Davis that she'd guessed his intention, because he'd said he'd never leave her and for that to be true he would have to stay with her when she left the ship.

'It's been your plan all along, hasn't it, to leave the ship in Melbourne?'

'My plans,' he said, 'ah yes, my plans.'

They were sitting on the deck beside the long boat, the usual venue for their meetings, hidden, quiet. Davis took her hand and began to stroke it; she'd become accustomed to the gesture and to the soft persuasive voice that always accompanied it.

'I've always had plans, big plans, all my life, but I never really thought any of them would work until I heard about the gold. Then I knew I'd found what I'd been looking for—a place so far away from England that who I was and what I did before wouldn't matter, a place where I had the same chance as everyone else, maybe better.' He stopped stroking her hand and squeezed it gently. 'Then I saw you and it was like a sign, an omen, saying, "This time, Davis me boy, you've got it right." I go over it again and again in my mind, picturing how it will be. I never told anyone, Amy, for fear they'd laugh, but I always wanted to be a proper gent with a fine house and servants, an office in the town and carriages to take me back and forth. I'd even go to church on Sundays and you can have everything you want.' His voice droned on and on, quiet, wistful, almost hypnotic in its effect. Amy leant back and closed her eyes. He painted such a beautiful picture.

It was a few days later that Davis brought Joey to be introduced. Miss Sharpe made all the appropriate comments, but declined to join them on the deck because of the heat.

Joey stuttered and stammered as they made their way along the deck, while Amy wondered how Davis failed to guess that there was something between them. Their conversation was awkward and their progress along the deck was practically impossible, with Joey initially walking beside Davis, then beside Amy and finally staggering backwards in front of them. Amy could almost feel him staring at her face, trying to divine what she might have said to Davis.

It occurred to Amy that Davis had not been entirely correct when he'd said that Joey lacked subtlety—what Joey lacked was the ability to lie. She reached forward and took his arm and he stiffened, the way a child stiffens when holding eggs or a man with a newborn babe.

'Look what Davis is making for me.' She reached in her pocket and pulled out the string of beads. Joey didn't speak. 'They're beads,' she continued. 'He's carving them himself and every time he finishes one he gives it to me and I string it on the thread with the others.'

'Very ingenious.' Amy jumped visibly at the sound of Tanner's voice.

'Uncle John.' She turned to face him, wondering why on earth

Joey hadn't warned her he was there. Of course, Joey didn't know they were discussing a secret.

'Very nice workmanship.' He took the beads from her. She had regained some of her composure and was smiling at him.

'Davis made them.'

'So I heard.' Tanner switched his gaze to Davis. Their eyes met and the barest smile crossed Davis' lips.

'Perhaps when I finish the next bead you could deliver it for me. I don't get up here as much as I used to, now that I'm on full duty.'

Amy felt her heart racing—how could he take such a risk, Tanner scarcely tolerated him as it was, and if he found out he'd been treated like a fool, used in their deception . . .

'Something wrong, Amy?' It was Joey who asked. The others were too intent on their rivalry to notice her discomfiture.

'No, it's nothing,' she lied, for she felt utterly miserable. She hated the dishonesty and the antagonism that made it necessary.

'Are you sure?' Joey's voice was warm with concern.

'Yes,' she said, but her shaking voice belied her words and she searched an excuse for her behaviour. 'It's just that everyone's been so kind to me.' She took the beads back from Tanner. 'So very, very kind.'

Joey delivered the next message. He was so formal and polite when he came to the cabin that even Miss Sharpe was impressed. He made quite a show of presenting Amy with the bead, and when he escorted her around the deck he was so stiff and proper that it almost made her laugh. She didn't tease him, instead she tried to make him relax. She liked Joey, she admired him, he was so guileless he made her ashamed of what she had become.

They talked about his home, a tiny farm in the north of England that he had been forced to leave because as third son he stood no chance of inheriting. They talked about Davis and how they met.

'The village fair it was, just after I left home. There was a bit of a fight and I ended up on Davis' side.'

'You saved him?'

'Orr, Davis give a good account of himself, I just evened up the numbers.'

'And you've been together ever since?' Amy sounded surprised and for the first time Joey thought to question his friendship with Davis.

'A man needs friends,' he said thoughtfully, 'and I've never had that many. People aren't drawn to me the way they are to Davis. Davis always seems to have people around him but they never seem to stay.' Joey frowned with disapproval. 'You call a man a friend, you should stick by him.'

Amy smiled vaguely—honesty and loyalty were traits upon which her father had placed great value, yet loyalty to the likes of Davis or Tanner often made honesty impossible and she wondered which of the two was the greater virtue.

When Joey had returned her to the cabin and had taken his leave she retrieved the bead from her pocket and threaded it on the string. It had been so exciting at first, sneaking out to meet Davis, hiding in the shadow of the long boat, listening to his soft voice weaving its magical fairy tale, but now she was reluctant to go, uncomfortable with the deceit and Joey's unwitting involvement. That night she tried to explain her feelings to Davis, but he brushed them aside with a kiss on the lips, a squeeze of her hand and a softly murmured. 'I love you.'

The next two messages Davis delivered personally and Amy found that she was disappointed by Joey's absence. Then the weather curtailed their activities, heavy squalls and choppy seas making it impossible for them to meet. Once Davis came to the cabin, but Miss Sharpe was loath to let him in.

'It's one thing for a young man to take a lady for a turn around the deck, but quite another for him to come to her sleeping quarters even in the presence of a chaperone.'

CHAPTER 9

✦✦✦✦✦✦✦✦✦✦✦✦✦✦

THE NEXT day Tanner came to visit her. It was quite late in the evening; the rain had stopped but the decks were still wet and there was a dampness in the air.

They walked for a short distance then he asked: 'Is it too cold for you?'

'No.'

'Not as bad as that night in London?'

'No.'

'Is something wrong?' She wished she could say 'Yes', she wished she could explain in a way that would overcome his prejudice.

'No, of course not. Why?'

'You seem very quiet, that's all.'

'I'm tired of all the lies,' she said honestly.

'Me too.' She was surprised by his weary tone, and in the long silence that followed she searched for words to comfort him. Finally he took her arm and led her back to the cabin. He opened the door for her but made no attempt to enter. 'By the way,' he said, 'Davis asked me to give you this.' He took her hand and placed a bead in it. He felt her stiffen as she recognised the shape, but her expression remained calm and casual.

She smiled. 'Another bead for my collection.'

'How soon before it's finished?'

'I don't know. I suppose I'll tie it off when Davis gets sick of making them.'

'May I see how it's progressing?' Amy's hand was trembling as she drew the string of beads from her pocket. Tanner looked at them for a moment. 'I didn't realise he'd made so many.' Amy returned the beads to her pocket.

'I'd best be going in now.' She hesitated, then stepped forward, reached up and kissed him on the cheek before turning abruptly to enter the cabin. She shut the door behind her. At first she felt nothing, then slowly the anger began to take hold of her.

How could Davis have been so stupid? How could he have the affrontery to ask Tanner to carry the message? It was bad enough that he involved Joey, but to scorn Tanner's intelligence was stupid, utterly stupid.

'Is something wrong, dear?' Miss Sharpe interrupted her thoughts.

'No, it's nothing.'

'You seem a little upset,' she persisted. Amy was accustomed to this form of inquisition—apparently being young and blind meant that she didn't even have the right to the privacy of her own mind.

'It's this awful weather and being shut in the cabin all the time.' It was the wrong answer for Miss Sharpe. 'And I'm afraid to go out with the deck so wet and slippery lest I should fall.' She sighed deeply, hoping that some part of the explanation would satisfy Miss Sharpe.

'There now dear, would you like me to read to you?'

Amy didn't always decline such offers, as it was far better to have Miss Sharpe reading than preaching. 'Perhaps when we're in bed you could sit up and read to me.'

'That's a splendid idea.' It was too—nothing made Miss Sharpe drowsier than reading out aloud, and when Amy heard the strain come into her voice she would pretend to be asleep. Then Miss Sharpe would douse the light and be asleep within minutes.

Amy lay awake listening to Miss Sharpe's rhythmic breathing and occasional snore. She heard the ship's bell toll the hour and at the appointed time she rose and stole quietly on to the deck. As she moved towards the long boat she thought she heard footsteps, she froze, waiting for the sound to continue. There was nothing, only the waves slapping against the hull and the wind calling in the rigging. She moved on again, stopping at their usual meeting place. It was too wet to sit on the deck so she clung to the long boat straining her ears for the sound of Davis' footsteps.

'I wondered where you two were meeting.' Tanner's voice shot through her like a bolt, making her jerk upright. 'Ingenious those beads and so many of them too.' He had moved close to her and she could feel the power of his presence.

'How did you know?' she managed to ask.

'Observation.'

She nodded her response, then turned vaguely in the direction of the lower deck. 'Davis,' she murmured.

'Davis isn't coming, I misappropriated one of the beads.'

'I see,' she said defensively, 'but that's just it, isn't it? I don't see and that makes me stupid and incapable of making up my own mind, vulnerable to anyone who shows me any kindness.'

'I have never equated your blindness with stupidity, never.' His voice was cold and so angry it was frightening. 'Blindness limits you, it makes everything you do harder, but everyone faces limitations and believe me, fear and prejudice, honour and duty, ignorance and guilt can cripple a being more effectively than withered limbs and sightless eyes. What limits you here is not a lack of sight but a lack of experience. You're only fifteen.'

'Sixteen.'

'Almost.'

'No, sixteen just before Christmas.'

'All right, sixteen, but Davis is still the first man to pay any attention to you.' His tone was still insistent but the anger had left it. 'I know how special he makes you feel when he tells you you're different to any other woman he's ever known, when he tells you he loves you and that he can't bear to be away from you, when he tells you that it drives him insane not to be able to touch you and hold you. He tells you you're beautiful with skin like moonbeams and hair like silk.'

'Satin,' she corrected, 'he said my hair was like satin.' Her voice was hushed—Tanner's words had been so like Davis' that it frightened her.

'He'll hurt you, Amy.' He spoke quietly now. 'He'll take your youth and innocence and then he'll leave you.'

'No,' she cried desperately, 'he wouldn't hurt me.'

'What makes you so special? Do you think him incapable of lying, incapable of deceit?' He waited, not expecting an answer. 'Do you think him so honour bound as to be incapable of seducing any woman? If he's capable of doing it to anyone then you're not so special that he wouldn't do it to you.'

His words stung her and she cast about in her mind for some way to retaliate.

'Maybe he is as infatuated with you as you are with him, but infatuation is all it is. When it wears off, when we reach Melbourne where there are other women, there'll be nothing to hold him to you.' The word 'hold' released a spring in Amy's mind.

'So I've no hold on him the way I have on you, no guilt to bind him to me. Well, what if I was to tell you . . .' She stopped, aware of the possible repercussions of what she was about to say. She cared for Tanner and the truth about her blindness told now, in anger, could drive them apart forever.

'Tell me what?' She had been facing Tanner squarely when she began her tirade, and the moon had come out from behind a cloud to reveal her face bright with anger and the glint of tears in her eyes. It was a moment before Tanner prompted her again. 'Tell me what?' She blinked and the tears fell.

'Nothing . . . it was nothing. I was going to say something that would hurt you.' She spoke slowly. 'And I don't want to hurt you.' She reached out to touch him, but he made no move to respond. 'I didn't want to lie to you, there just seemed no other way.' Her voice was shaking and she swallowed in an attempt to control it. 'We didn't do anything wrong, we hardly even kissed, only when we met and when he parted. Mostly he just held my hand and talked.' She was struck by the utter innocence of their encounters and by the injustice of Tanner's assertion. 'He wants to marry me but not until he's rich enough to build me a fine house with servants and carriages. And he's never asked me for anything, not anything at all.' She had regained control of her voice, and the dignity and certainty with which she spoke were not lost on Tanner. Still, he couldn't let the matter drop.

'He asked that you meet him here at night, alone, without anyone knowing.'

'I came because I wanted to.'

'And if he asked you to make love to him, would you want that too?' Her lips trembled—she wanted to tell him that Davis wouldn't ask, that his plans for them went far beyond the moment. Yet, if Davis did ask she didn't know what her response would be. 'I know men like Davis, they make you think that they want what you want and that you want what they want. Then when it's all over they tell you that you misunderstood.' His voice was soft and gravelly, and it occurred to Amy that it held the same hypnotic charm as Davis'. 'You're the only woman on the ship that he can have, but when we reach Melbourne there'll be others and you won't be so special any more, or do you still think that he didn't lie to Buchanan, that he plans to make the round trip?' She shook her head. 'I see.' He looked at her face—she was hurt, but unrelenting. 'And he made it sound as if he was going to jump ship just to be with you.'

'No.' She jumped at his sarcasm. 'All his life he's dreamt of being something better and he planned this trip the moment he heard about the gold and he's not a man to give up on his plans. Now I'm part of those plans and he won't give up on me either.' She spoke with great certainty, but she had been deserted too many times not to feel that her words were tempting fate.

'Amy.'

'No.' She raised her hand to forestall his next words, then rested them hesitantly on his chest. 'I won't see Davis any more.' She felt his sigh of relief. 'Not like this. It would go hard for him if we were caught, and I'd always have it in my mind that it was you that put him in.' She felt him draw breath to repudiate her statement. 'This way there'll be no doubt in my mind or his, but after we get to Melbourne, when all the lies and games are finished, if he still wants to see me then you'll let him.' Tanner was reluctant to argue with her quiet determination, but Melbourne may be too soon.

'You know as well as I do that I've no real say in what you do, but if I am to have a say and he's telling you the truth, then we're all bound for the goldfields and I'd sooner you left your reunion until then.' She nodded, and in the awkward silence that followed she began to feel terribly alone.

Her hands still rested on his chest, but he seemed a million miles away and her contact seemed unwelcome. She started to withdraw her hands then stopped, leaving them raised a few inches above his chest. She was about to drop them to her sides when he caught them in his own strong grip.

'I'm sorry,' she cried.

'I'm sorry, too.' And sorry he was, not just for the argument or for the fact that he'd blinded her, but because no matter how much he cared for her and for all his wit and wisdom he could not protect her from this.

Tanner returned Amy to her cabin and waited silently outside until he was certain that she was safe in bed. He'd had it in mind to take the beads and throw them in Davis' face but it was better this way, better for Amy to end it herself and on her own terms.

Tanner's progress along the deck was slow. It was a pleasant night, the clouds had parted to admit the full brilliance of the moon and even though the air was damp it wasn't cold. Below deck was dark and airless and Davis would be there, sleeping the untroubled sleep that he didn't deserve.

Tanner skirted the watch but stopped before he reached the lower decks. The thought of Davis angered him, and for the first time that anger seemed irrational. They were just two young people stealing a few moments alone together—he would have done the same at Davis' age. In fact, in many ways Davis was a youthful reflection of himself and yet Tanner didn't credit him with the same basic decency that he himself possessed.

Tanner sighed. In the past, few had credited him with any decency and perhaps he was being as unfair to Davis as all those pompous gentlemen, pious fools and irate fathers had been to him. The term 'father' struck a chord in Tanner's mind. Was that it? Had Amy become the daughter or sister he'd never had? He shook his head—no, he had disliked Davis from the moment he saw him. He'd disliked him for the way he treated Joey and the look on his face when he talked about the gold. That was the day he first met Amy, the day when he would have handed her over to anyone who'd take her. He shook his head again, no. By the time he saw Davis he'd already begun to accept responsibility for Amy.

Tanner was so preoccupied by his thoughts that he didn't notice Joey come on to the deck. Joey watched him for a moment, reading the confusion on his face.

'Don't put him in.' Tanner started at the sound of Joey's voice. 'Please, it'd go hard on him and he's done nothing wrong, she was willing, don't put him in.' Joey stared anxiously at Tanner's face.

'It would certainly curtail your plans for Melbourne if Davis was in irons, now wouldn't it?' Joey's jaw dropped in astonishment. 'She didn't tell me, she didn't have to. You two talk too loud and too often. It's a wonder half the ship doesn't know.' Tanner continued explaining, but Joey's mind was elsewhere.

'It'd stop him, wouldn't it?' he said suddenly. 'Being in the brig when he was in Melbourne, it'd stop him.'

'You don't want to jump ship?'

'Much as I hate the sea, I'd sooner be working the round trip.'

'You don't have to go with him.'

71

'But he's my friend.' Tanner studied the big, sullen face.

'It's hard to stop a man like Davis getting what he wants and I expect it's dangerous to try, even if you are his friend.' It took Joey a moment to grasp his meaning.

'I wouldn't put him in.'

'No, but now you wouldn't mind if I did.'

'I'm still asking you not to.' Joey's voice had lost its earnest appeal and gained a strength that surprised Tanner.

'I won't put him in, but not because of you or because of her, either. I owe Davis for what happened in the hold and this will make us even and he'd better realise that, for I'm not a man to be crossed either.' Tanner could see that Joey was impressed, but he doubted if Davis would be. 'I still owe you for what happened down there.'

'All I want is that there be no trouble.'

'No, what I owe you must be for yourself, not for Davis.' Joey was unaccustomed to such consideration and it made him regard Tanner in a different light.

'It must be a worry having the responsibility of a young girl, a blind one at that.'

'It does tend to make one ever vigilant,' Tanner smiled. 'Which reminds me—how did you know I found out?'

'I saw you take the bead.'

'You knew about the beads?'

'Not at first. Not when he asked me to take them to her, but later, him sneaking out the way he did, it was the only thing that made sense.' A silence fell between them and they both glanced unwillingly at the entrance of their sleeping quarters. 'It'll be hard for you to leave her in Melbourne.' Tanner didn't answer Joey, he didn't want to lie to him. 'I suppose you've never thought to leave the ship and stay with her.' Tanner should have said that he had a wife back home; instead, he opted for an answer that wasn't entirely untrue.

'I like the sea.'

CHAPTER 10

◆◆◆◆◆◆◆◆◆◆◆◆◆◆

T HE NEXT day the skies had cleared completely. The breeze was brisk, but not strong enough to create white caps on the rolling waves. The empty sea and sky merged to a distant blue void, and had Tanner been in a more appreciative mood he would have been touched by its immensity. However, he was too busy cursing himself for his stupidity.

He had left the bead with Amy instead of replacing it amongst Davis' things. He wondered how long it would be before Davis noticed, whether he would have time to retrieve it and put it back. He twisted the rope in his hands to check the splice, then coiled it deftly and returned it to the locker.

'Where is it?' The muffled sound of Davis' voice drifted from below decks. 'Don't lie.' The voice rose and fell again as Tanner made his way to its source. 'I know you've been watching me, sneaking around after me, you bastard, now give it back.' Joey's mouth was open as if he intended to speak, but no sound came out. 'Give it back.' Davis punctuated his words with a blow. Joey grunted and fell back, but made no attempt to defend himself.

'There's a fight,' someone yelled, and Tanner moved quickly to interpose himself between Davis and Joey.

'Deck officer's coming.' Davis didn't seem to understand him. 'Fighting's one thing Buchanan won't tolerate.' Davis dropped back a couple of paces, then turned his attention to his kit spread everywhere in the frantic search that had preceded his attack on Joey.

'What's going on here?' The young midshipman's voice broke into a falsetto.

'Nothing, sir.' Tanner's tone conveyed the kind of respect young officers liked to hear. 'Davis here thought he'd lost something, got into a bit of a panic about it, that's all, sir.' The young officer surveyed the scene. Davis, standing to one side, his kit spread about him half packed, half unpacked. Joey, his face blank

73

rather than concerned and Tanner attentive and polite.

'What's missing?'

'Nothing really, sir, Davis made a necklace for my niece, very pretty it is too, sir. I forgot to tell him I'd given it to her and he thought it was lost.' Tanner watched Davis as he spoke and only the slightest intake of breath indicated his surprise. 'Quite upset he was, sir, and after all the hard work he put in that's understandable.'

'One of the men said there was a fight.'

'Bit of yelling, sir, that's all.' The midshipman was unconvinced, but he knew he'd get short shift from Buchanan if he hauled men up before him without any proper proof.

'Get this place cleaned up,' he barked, turning smartly on his heel and leaving.

Tanner moved close to Davis, out of earshot of the rest of the crew who had come to see the fight.

'I don't owe you anything any more.' His voice was hushed but it carried an amazing amount of force. 'I'll keep my mouth shut about your midnight visits with Amy, I'll keep my mouth shut about your fight with Joey and about your plan to jump ship. I think that about makes us even.'

'I won't stop seeing her.' Davis' voice was equally soft and equally as determined.

'You will until she gets to the goldfields, then it's not up to me.' Davis regarded the hard lines in the older seaman's face. It was pointless to oppose him in direct confrontation, perhaps even dangerous, but there might still be a way around him and if there wasn't, well, Melbourne couldn't be more than three weeks away and after that Uncle John would be out of his way forever.

'I want to see her alone once more before we reach Melbourne.' Davis calculated that Tanner still owed him that much. Tanner nodded. It was better for Davis to hear it from Amy, more final.

'This evening we'll go together. I'll keep Miss Sharpe busy.'

Davis signalled his agreement but made no comment, then as Tanner went to leave he said: 'We didn't . . . I want to marry her.'

'She's just a child.'

'Not by much and not for much longer. I'm going to be a rich man one day and when I am I'll come for her and not you nor anyone else is going to stop me having her.' They held each other's gaze for a moment, then Davis turned away, pleased with himself for having had the final word, convinced he'd made his point. But Tanner had hardly heard his words, his thoughts had been dominated by the look on Davis' face for it bore the same expression it had when he talked about the gold.

The weather deteriorated over the next few days as if to reflect Davis' disappointment. He had accepted Tanner's opposition to his relationship with Amy, he could even accept the possibility of not seeing her again until the goldfields, but he couldn't accept Amy's willingness to comply with the restrictions. She said it was for the best but surely, if she felt just a fraction of his passion, if she perceived just a glimmer of his vision, she would have taken any risk, defied any authority to be with him.

The weather kept the passengers in their cabins and the crew busy. Both Tanner and Joey were too seasick to pay much attention to Davis, so the gradual shift in his mood from disappointment to frustration to resentment went unnoticed.

An improvement in the weather brought an improvement in nearly everyone's outlook. Melbourne was less than a week away and the excitement of journey's end even touched Miss Sharpe.

'I shall be so glad to set foot on dry land again,' she enthused, 'even if it is the Antipodes. If I never see another ship as long as I live it will be too soon.'

'You intend to settle in Australia, then?' Amy asked absently.

'Good Lord no, England will always be my home.'

'Then how will you get back there, if not by ship?'

Miss Sharpe ignored the question. 'God has brought me here to do his work and I shall not fail.' She began to hum tunelessly, the same fragment of melody over and over again, probably a line from a hymn but not one Amy could remember. The sound of a footstep outside alerted Amy and she was half-way to the door when the knock came. She opened it, half expecting Tanner.

'Hello Amy.' The sound of Davis' voice so surprised her that for a moment Amy couldn't speak. 'I hope I haven't come at a bad time?'

'No, no, not at all.' She still made no indication that he might enter, nor did she move to join him on the deck.

'Mr Davis.' Miss Sharpe appeared at the doorway. 'We haven't seen you for a while.'

'No, ma'am, the weather's been against it.' There was an

uncomfortable silence while Davis stood on one side of the door and the ladies remained on the other. 'Well,' he said at last, 'what I came for was your address, Amy, if you don't mind giving it to me. See, I thought I could write to you, a sailor likes to have someone to write to.'

'I can't,' Amy said slowly. 'I mean, I don't know it, my parents moved to the goldfields.' She stumbled over the explanation, painfully aware that she was lying to him, that she'd lied to him all along and that, to the best of her knowledge, he'd never lied to her. 'Uncle John wrote all the letters, you'll have to ask him.' There was a sadness in her voice and Davis took it to mean that Tanner had forbidden her from telling him where she'd be.

'Don't worry, I'll see your uncle.' He took her hand in a very formal gesture, then nodded to Miss Sharpe.

He heard the door close behind him as he left and he felt a surge of anger rise and fall. If Tanner wanted to play games then so be it. He'd stick to them like glue once they got off the ship, there'd be no sneaking off without him. The anger surged again—he'd given his word that he'd stay away until they reached the goldfields and he'd kept it. Tanner had no right to deny him knowledge of where Amy would be on the goldfields. He calmed himself again and set out to look for Tanner; he found him talking to Buchanan. They could often be seen deep in private conversation, and there wasn't an officer or man on board who wasn't puzzled by it.

'Will your brother be waiting for you when you arrive?' Buchanan asked.

'I doubt it, sir.'

'Then you'll want time to contact him?'

'Is that a problem, sir?'

'That homeward bound we met the other day, captain said there was trouble in the port, sailors jumping ship and running off to the goldfields, said the only way he could get a crew was to take convicts from the gaol. My partners have arranged for a group of mercenaries, off-duty soldiers probably, to prevent our sailors from jumping ship, but I still want to be in and out of the port as fast as I can.' He looked at Tanner for reaction but there was none. 'You'll get another ship back easy enough, if you miss the *Lady Ann*.'

'You'd let me go, sir?'

76

'You may be the best sailor I've ever had, but you're not indispensable.'

'No, I meant—'

Buchanan halted Tanner's explanation with a smile. 'I know what you meant, our agreement that you'd work the round trip, your pledge, your word, honour and duty.' His expression became introspective, as it did so often during their conversations. 'You've let your duty to your brother and your compassion for his child outweigh your duty to your business and your love for your wife. Surely it must outweigh the duty and friendship you've offered me.' Tanner silently cursed the captain. He liked and respected him more than any other man he'd ever known and it galled him that their friendship was predicated on a lie. 'I know the vicar would take the girl until your brother came, but I suspect you'd not be satisfied unless you see her delivered safe and sound, besides which it would be a shame to come all this way and not see your brother. I had it in mind to hold the *Lady Ann* over a day or two to give you time but now, the way things are—you understand.'

Tanner nodded. He should be grateful that Buchanan would never know that he'd been duped, but it seemed an insult to the man to let him continue to labour under the misconception. 'I'm most grateful to you, sir.' Tanner moved uncomfortably. He needed to get away from Buchanan before the overwhelming desire to be honest, which was beginning to overtake him, made him make a mistake. 'I'd best be getting back to work, sir.' Buchanan nodded his assent.

Tanner started to make his way back to the group of sailors working on the forward deck but, as he pushed through the narrow gap next to the stairs leading up to the bridge, a hand came from nowhere, gripping him around the throat, forcing him against the wall. He struggled, grabbing at the hand and trying to force it away, then he felt the point of a blade thrust against his chest and his struggle ceased.

'I kept my word, you bastard,' Davis hissed in his ear, 'now you try not keeping yours.'

'I don't know what you're talking about.' Tanner tried to move, but the knife dug into his chest and the grip on his throat grew tighter.

'I never tried to meet with her at night, not since we agreed.

Now you tell me where she's going to be once we've landed.'

'I don't know.'

'Liar!' A jab with the knife emphasised his words and Tanner felt the sting as it pierced his skin. Slowly Davis increased pressure on the knife, pushing it further into Tanner's flesh. Tanner cried out, but the sound was strangled by the grip on his throat. He could feel the pain as the knife gradually advanced and there was no way he could escape it.

'No,' Tanner cried desperately. 'My brother's got no address, just care of the post office.' The gradual advance of the knife halted. 'I've got a letter in my bag, you can see for yourself.' Tanner's voice was hoarse as it rose against the pressure on his throat. Davis pulled the knife slowly back from his chest.

'How will you contact him?' For a moment Tanner couldn't think. He'd made no plan to contact his brother, he was just going to go to the goldfields and look for him there. He pushed at Davis' hand still tight around his neck.

'Can't talk,' he gasped. The pressure lessened. 'I'd planned to leave a message at the post office and leave it up to him to contact me.'

A few seconds elapsed, during which Davis thought and Tanner gasped for air, then Davis said: 'We'll make a place to meet once I get off the ship and you'd better be there.' Tanner didn't answer and Davis slammed his hand against Tanner's neck. 'Agreed?'

'Yes.' Tanner could barely force the sound through his aching throat. Davis stood back from him.

'I'll see that letter.' Tanner nodded. He couldn't speak, he could hardly catch his breath. 'If it's as you say, we'll meet at the post office.' Tanner nodded again, but Davis was too absorbed in his own thoughts to notice. 'And if you cross me I'll get you, even if I have to come back aboard the *Lady Ann* to do it.' Davis studied the older man as he leant limply against the stairway still gasping for breath. He waited until Tanner looked at him, until he was sure he knew and understood his determination, then he lurched away.

At first Tanner was too shocked to think. He reached inside his shirt and felt the trickle of blood. The wound wasn't all that deep and it wasn't the injury that shocked him. It was Davis that shocked him, because he'd acted not in the heat of passion but coldly and deliberately.

Tanner looked down at his hand and the bloodstain that was spreading across his shirt. All this was for Amy and, if nothing else, it proved that Davis would not lose interest in her once they reached Melbourne. Tanner took the shirt off, rolled it up and pressed it against the wound. If nothing else it proved that Davis was capable of violence, unwarranted violence against anyone who thwarted him.

Tanner glanced at the group of men working on the forward deck. He could call to them for help, he owed Davis nothing now and if Buchanan found out all the better, it would be a fitting punishment for Davis to be in the brig when they landed in Melbourne. It would be a fitting punishment for him to have Amy know exactly what kind of a man he was. Tanner looked again at the wound, it wasn't that bad, and as they were almost at Melbourne there was no point in causing trouble, no need to land Davis in the brig, not now that there would be mercenaries to keep him on board. He moved slowly and carefully, heading in the direction of the lower deck. There was no point in telling Amy, not when she'd never have to see Davis again.

By the time Tanner had reached his quarters the bleeding had slowed. He threw his stained shirt in a wash bucket and searched in his kit for a clean one and something old that he could use as a bandage.

'Tanner.' Joey lumbered amiably towards him. 'What're you up to down here?' Tanner kept his back to Joey while he put on his shirt; there was no time for the bandage. Suddenly Joey's strong hand caught him by the shoulder and swung him round. Joey stared first at the cut on Tanner's chest and then at his face, and Tanner didn't need to ask if he knew who was responsible. Joey dropped his hand from Tanner's shoulder and stepped back a pace or two. 'You won't put him in?' It was a question, this time, not a plea. Tanner shook his head. 'Because of what you owe him?'

'I owe him nothing.' Tanner spat out the words then paused, regarding Joey thoughtfully. 'I owe you though.' He managed a smile. 'And, seeing as we'll be going our separate ways once the *Lady Ann* docks, I've not much time to pay. So I'll give you the benefit of the one thing I have, a lifetime of experience with people of all kinds.' The smile vanished. 'Get clear of Davis, get clear before —'

'He's changed,' Joey interrupted, 'ever since we come on this ship, ever since he heard about the gold and that niece of yours, she changed him.' Anguish gave way to anger. 'And you, you never gave him a chance even after he saved your life. You always expected the worst of him and if you expect the worst then that's what you'll get. You never had no time for him, not since we come on board. You've been down on him right from the start.'

'That's a lie.' The element of truth in Joey's accusation made Tanner all the more defensive. 'I'll admit I don't like him nor trust him neither, but I've treated him no different to any other man.' Joey's open disbelief was more articulate than words. 'All right, but I've a young girl to care for.'

'He cares for her, too.' Joey hesitated. 'He cares for the gold and being rich but she's part of that, part of the dream.' Joey had seen Davis with women before and he knew Amy was different. 'He'd never hurt her.'

'So long as she remains what he wants, so long as she fulfils his ideals, but what happens when she fails? Just remember that the higher you put someone up the more chance they have of doing just that. Amy's only human—she can't live up to a dream.' Tanner waited for Joey to speak, challenging him to refute the statement. 'There was no need for this.' He touched the wound on his chest. 'I didn't tell him where my brother lived because I don't know, but he did this to me before he even asked me to explain. What happens when Amy makes that kind of mistake? What do you think he'll do to her?'

'Nothing,' Joey exploded. 'I'll never let nothing happen to her.'

'You think he'll keep you around once he's got the gold and Amy too?'

'Don't try to drive a wedge between us, Davis is my friend.'

Tanner recognised unswerving loyalty and knew better than to argue with it. Anyway, soon it would be all over, he and Amy would be off the ship and Davis would be trapped aboard. He sighed resignedly. 'I've given you my advice, you don't have to take it but, if ever I'm proved right, don't say I didn't warn you, don't say I didn't pay my debt.'

CHAPTER 11

++++++++++++++++

T HE NEWS of guards on the dock spread like wildfire amongst the crew, along with word that their leave had been cancelled. Buchanan's promise of a bonus and extra rations of rum did little to relieve the crew's agitation, and the job of unloading the *Lady Ann* was carried out amid frayed tempers by tired and unwilling hands.

Tanner was to be allowed to disembark with the other passengers and was, therefore, excused from the unloading operation. He packed his bag desultorily. It was a strange way to leave a ship, no mates to get drunk with, no one to welcome him home, no one to say goodbye.

'You knew!' Davis burst into their sleeping quarters, sweating and covered with dirt from the hold.

'How?' Tanner felt no fear despite their earlier confrontation.

'Buchanan told you.'

'How would he know?' Davis had the look of a man who had lost everything and needed someone to blame. 'Buchanan didn't know, I didn't know, nobody made this happen.'

'Don't lie to me.'

'I'm not lying and even if I had known, even if I'd told you, what difference would it have made?' Davis' shoulders slumped as he accepted the truth of it. 'Life seldom works out the way we plan, the trick is to make the best of what comes along. Look, by the time you get back to England you'll have a pay worth having, and if you're determined to come here then you can get another ship. I've seen gold rushes before and you can take it from me that nine months from now there'll be plenty of disillusioned settlers and penitent sailors more than willing to take your place on a ship to work their passage home.'

'And where will all the gold be then?'

'If there's any real gold it'll still be there for those with the heart to dig, and if there isn't then it's a waste of time going even now.'

81

'And what about Amy?'

'If what you feel for each other is genuine, if she knows you're coming back, she'll wait. If not then your life together is doomed anyway.'

'No, I mean what happens to her now? What happens to her when you sail?'

'I'm leaving the *Lady Ann*.' Tanner spoke cautiously, almost unwillingly. 'I'll get another ship back.' Davis didn't respond, and for a long time he remained deep in thought.

'We could be married,' he said at last. 'Her and I, we could be married. Buchanan could do it or the vicar. You could sail and I could go ashore.' Tanner shook his head. Strangely, the only thought that occurred to him was how easily Davis had dismissed Joey. 'Why not?' Davis demanded.

'It's not up to me.'

'Your brother should be glad to have her married off, to have someone who loves her and wants to care for her in spite of her being blind.' The mention of Amy's blindness touched Tanner on a raw nerve.

'Amy's a beautiful, clever, kind-hearted girl and I'll not see her passed off to the first boyo who thinks he can forgive her her blindness.'

'That's not what I meant.'

'Go away Davis, go back to England and find some other get rich scheme and some other girl to go with it.'

'No!' Davis screamed and the power of his voice surprised Tanner. 'You don't understand.' There was pain in his face but his shoulders no longer sagged. Beaten he may have been, but not any more. 'All my life I've taken what they've handed out and tried to make the best of it and I've ended up with nothing. This time I know what I want and nothing and nobody is going to stop me.'

'Don't be a fool,' Tanner said, but the look on Davis' face prevented him from saying more. They held each other's gaze a moment more, then Davis turned and all but ran up the steps.

Tanner finished packing, then joined Amy on the upper deck. She stood a little apart from the others, her chin tilted upward, her face into the wind. She wore one of Flo's dresses, which she filled out much better now. It wasn't just the regular meals or the fresh sea air that had added a firmness and plumpness to her small frame, and even Tanner couldn't deny that she had

82

matured, at least physically. He smiled as she cocked her head to listen to his footsteps.

'Uncle John.'

'All packed and ready?'

'Yes, Miss Sharpe helped me.'

'The gangplank's up, I see. I'd like a word with the captain before we leave.'

'I think we've all got to wait for him, something about him escorting us off. Are there really guards?'

'Yes.'

Amy's face clouded with concern. 'What about Davis?' she whispered.

'He still thinks he can get off, but I don't like his chances.'

'Oh God,' Amy murmured, 'I don't want him hurt.'

'It's too late to worry about him now. I warned him not to try it and that's all I can do.'

'All ready I see.' Buchanan looked stiff and uncomfortable. 'All your luggage is ashore, Vicar, but I'm afraid you'll have to arrange to have it loaded on the carriages yourself. I don't want my men wandering around the dock lest some overly enthusiastic guard makes a fatal mistake.' The vicar looked less than pleased but said nothing. 'Your pay.' He handed it to Tanner.

'It's a full pay.' Tanner stared at the packet in surprise. 'I never expected —'

'Take it,' Buchanan insisted. 'Perhaps some day we'll meet again. I hope so, you're a good sailor.' He extended his hand and Tanner took it. 'And a good friend.' He released his grip and, without another word, headed for the gangplank, leaving the passengers to scoop up their hand luggage and scurry after him.

Buchanan stopped when he reached the guards, spoke a few words to the man in charge then motioned the passengers on. Tanner faced him squarely, acknowledging his parting gesture. He watched as Buchanan made his way back to the ship, part of him thanking God that the captain had never found out the truth and part of him regretting it, for he could not sail with Buchanan again, not while the lie still lay between them.

Tanner moved off slowly, carrying Amy's bag and his own. Suddenly Amy tripped, grabbing him for support as she fell.

'I'm sorry,' he said. 'You used to get around so well on the ship I forgot what it's like on the land.'

'It feels funny, as if we're still going up and down.'

'It takes a few days to get used to the land again.' He linked her arm through his. 'It's not far to the end of the wharf and then there are some steps down to the roadway. There's a seaman's hotel on the other side. We'll go there to get some directions.'

'What's it look like?'

'The hotel?'

'No, everything.'

'Well, the dock's got more ships on it than it can hold and there are dozens more waiting to land. There are people everywhere, Chinese, European, some Negroes too, more likely from the Americas than from Africa.' He looked around. 'There must be at least three ships with nothing but passengers. Mind the steps, there are about a half a dozen. The road's fairly wide. There aren't many permanent looking buildings but there are new ones going up everywhere, carts and carriages everywhere, dust everywhere.'

'I can taste the dust.'

'Last step.'

'FIRE, FIRE.' The voice came from behind them. 'FIRE!'

'I can smell it,' Amy murmured. Tanner turned in the direction of the voice.

'Fire on the *Lady Ann*, FIRE!' A sick horror gripped Tanner. 'Fire on the *Lady Ann*.' He took Amy by the shoulders and pushed her behind the steps leading up to the wharf.

'Stay here.'

'No.' She clung to his arm. 'Don't go, please.' The thought of fire terrified her and the thought of losing him terrified her even more. He tried to extricate himself from her hold, but as fast as he broke one grip she gained another.

'Amy, stop it!' He shook her.

'No, I won't let you go.' He pushed her and she fell, landing on the soft ground next to the wharf. Her final desperate cry reached him as he ran up the steps but he hardly heard her. He had only one thought in mind—Buchanan.

Tanner ran, as everyone on the dock ran, but there was little evidence of the fire, just a small column of black smoke rising from the hold. The smoke had billowed into a cloud by the time Tanner reached the ship. He could see Buchanan on the deck directing men with buckets. There was hardly any sign of a flame as Tanner climbed the gangplank. Then, in an instant the whole ship was alight. Fire climbed the masts and ran along the rigging. It seared the deck and twined itself amongst the superstructure. Screams of men and timbers filled the air, lingering for a second before the roar of the fire engulfed them, too.

Tanner's momentum carried him onto the deck, then the heat struck him like an impenetrable wall. He staggered back against its force, shielding his face with his arms and gasping air that was too hot to breathe. He took a few steps along the deck then faltered, the sheer power of the fire overwhelming him. High above him something cracked, loud and sharp as if a thunderbolt had struck. He looked up to see the top of the mast topple and fall. It was like a majestic bird with wings of flame, and for an instant he was enthralled by the sight. Then a subconscious reflex sent him sprawling along the deck. The mast shattered as it struck the deck, sending sparks and burning debris flying in all directions. Tanner scrambled away from his would-be pyre, swatting at the sparks and cinders that ignited his clothes and scorched his skin. He clambered to his feet, cowering against the rail.

'Jump for it. Jump for it, all of you.' The voice seemed hoarse and distant. 'Abandon ship.' The boatswain's whistle piped the order, then the man himself appeared, his face red and blistered, his eyes mere slits in swollen, black sockets. He raised the whistle to his lips again and they cracked and bled as he blew. 'Get off,' he yelled at Tanner as he advanced on him through the haze. 'Jump for it man.'

'Buchanan?' Tanner didn't recognise his own voice, which was little more than a whisper. 'Where's Buchanan?' The boatswain looked back along the burning deck towards the hold. He shook his head, a hopeless, empty look upon his face.

'Save yourself.' Tanner pushed past him, but the deck seemed to be crumbling under his feet. He stayed close to the rail, hoping that if the worst happened he might miraculously fall to safety.

His advance was perilous and slow, and with each step he became less certain. The heat had penetrated his boots and deep blisters had formed on his feet. His hands and face were pitted with burns and he could barely see or breathe.

At last he saw Buchanan, who was slumped against the rail on the opposite side of the ship. Tanner tried to gather his strength, for he knew the only way to cover the intervening distance was in one short dash. He searched his reserves for a burst of power, but all energy seemed to have deserted him. Even as he watched the flames were upon the captain. Writhed and twisted, trying to pull himself upright on the rail, and in that instant Tanner found his strength. He ran, oblivious to the flame, driving at Buchanan, using his own impetus to take them both over the side into the river below.

He held on to Buchanan despite the flames that engulfed them both. The water hit Tanner like a stinging slap, then it folded around him with icy fingers that made him want to gasp for air. He kicked his legs, clinging to Buchanan's limp body, trying to overcome their downward surge. His kicking became erratic, he didn't know which way was up and it struck him as terribly funny that he'd saved Buchanan from burning only to have him drown. He wanted to laugh out loud but every time he opened his mouth he started to choke.

Something tugged at his shirt and for one insane moment he thought of himself as a tuna being caught on a gaff. The tug came again and again, then air, half a breath, then more choking water.

'Let him go,' someone yelled, but Tanner didn't know what they meant. His grip on Buchanan had become part of a subconscious instruction that he had given his arms, and his conscious mind didn't have the power to countermand it. There was air all around him now and someone nearby was holding him up. 'Let him go.' The voice was familiar, one that Tanner liked and trusted. He couldn't see the face, his eyes wouldn't open. Other hands caught him, buoying him up. The familiar voice came again. 'It's me, it's Joey, let him go, I've got him.' All the strength went out of Tanner's limbs and he felt Buchanan floating away from him and strong arms holding him up, pulling him through the water, then other hands lifting him and then pain.

'It's not too bad,' he heard someone say and he wondered how much pain he'd feel if it was bad. He tried to open his eyes, but they stung unbearably and all he could see was a blur. He felt his clothes being cut away and his boots being pulled off, taking the skin with them. 'Not too bad at all.' The same person spoke again, and if he'd had the strength Tanner would have hit him. Instead he struggled to a sitting position and forced his protesting eyes to open. It was then that he noticed the pain in his chest. He tried to cough but his lungs screamed in agony. 'Easy now.' Tanner's eyes focused on a middle-aged man in a suit, his clipped, professional detachment labelling him as a doctor.

'Buchanan.' Tanner's voice made surprisingly little sound considering the amount of effort and pain needed to produce it. 'Buchanan.' He tried again with only marginally more effect. The doctor inclined his head towards a bundle of blankets a short distance away. Tanner stared at it, then at the doctor.

'Unconscious, best way to be, with any luck he'll never wake up.' Tanner felt sick, a miserable sickness that banished the pain, the same sickness he'd felt when he found Amy under the crates. He lay back on the pier and closed his eyes. What had he done? Buchanan would have wanted nothing more than to die on the deck of his ship, and he'd dragged him away to die in agony on the shore.

'Uncle John, Uncle John.' It was Amy, searching his face and chest with her fingers, setting every burn screaming again. He grabbed her hands and felt the blisters on his fingers burst.

'I'm all right, don't worry, Doctor says it's not bad.' Tanner looked around for the person who must have brought her to him, hoping they could take her and comfort her, but there was no one to be seen. 'Who brought you here?' She didn't seem to understand the question. 'How did you get here?'

She took a moment to come to her senses. 'I used a stick to feel my way along the wharf. It's made of planks laid straight in line, I just had to follow the cracks.' She sobbed, so he drew her to him and despite the discomfort he held her.

CHAPTER 12

++++++++++++++

I T TOOK three men to carry Tanner to the hotel and the publican was less than enthusiastic about having him until he learnt that Tanner was the only man on the ship to have been paid. He found them a small room near the downstairs rear exit, and Tanner guessed that it was usually reserved for family.

Amy proved to be a remarkably adept nurse, her sensitive touch rarely leaving a bandage too loose or too tight, and within a few days Tanner was able to hobble to the dining room to take his meals. It was a dark and dreary place, functional at best but cleaner than one might have expected. Seaman were encouraged not to linger there but to do their drinking and carousing in the bar. So Amy and Tanner often found that, in a hotel that was bursting at the seams, the dining room became a quiet haven. Amy smiled at him.

'The burns are healing well.'

'How can you tell?'

'By the smell. Things that are poisoned smell . . .'

'I know how they smell.'

'Anyway, yours don't smell that way and you're grumbling more. My father always said that was a sign that you were getting better.'

'You know, I've had your father quoted to me so often I almost feel as if he really is my brother, and I don't grumble.'

'My father was wonderful.' Amy's face was alight with the memory. 'He taught me to read and took me to see plays and operas. You'd have liked him, and you do grumble.'

There was a joy in their banter, a joy that had been missing since the destruction of the *Lady Ann*, a joy that deserted Tanner the moment he saw Joey's dismal face.

'What's wrong?' Tanner asked. 'Is it Buchanan?' Joey shook his head.

'Uncle John?'

'It's Joey and there's no news.'

Joey sat down, looking tired and worried. 'I can't find Davis,' he said hopelessly. 'I've looked everywhere, even at them bodies they brought up from the hold.' He looked appealingly at Tanner. 'Did you see him? You was the last one off the ship.'

Tanner shook his head. 'I saw the boatswain and Buchanan, that's all.'

'Boatswain broke his leg jumping off, I talked to him at the hospital, he . . .' Joey stared despairingly at his hands as the words failed him. 'Davis . . .' he tried again. 'Davis was working in the hold before the fire and no one's seen him since.' Amy extended her hand, feeling across the table hoping to find Joey's arm. He responded to her gesture by taking her hand in his.

'Maybe he jumped overboard,' she said. 'Maybe he's searching the hospital and hotels looking for you.' There was a quiet desperation in her voice. 'Maybe he's lying somewhere hurt and he can't come to us.'

'No,' Joey said forlornly. 'I searched all along the dock, in every warehouse, I knocked on every door. He's dead.' There were tears in Joey's eyes and Amy's face betrayed her grief. Only Tanner felt nothing. Perhaps he should have felt relief—now that the *Lady Ann* was gone there was nothing to stop Davis doing as he wished, but he didn't even feel that. Joey shifted his chair closer to Amy and put his arm around her. It was a clumsy, self-conscious gesture unlike Davis' fluid movement. She cried and Joey didn't know how to comfort her. He looked to Tanner for support. 'I don't know what I'll do if Davis is gone.'

'You can come with us.' The words were out before Tanner had time to think about them. 'That's if you don't want to go back to sea.'

'I don't like the sea, I've not got the stomach for it.'

'Then stay with us.'

'Please Joey.' Amy squeezed his hand.

'I've got no money,' he said, and Tanner smiled.

'At last I can do something for you. I got paid, and seeing as you've now saved my life not once but twice the very least I can do is to stand you your room and board. The hotel is crowded but they can put a cot in with us, if that's all right with you.' Joey indicated that it was. 'However, I do have one favour to ask.' The smile vanished from Tanner's face, and the sadness that replaced it made Joey willing to grant him almost anything. 'I have to see Buchanan and I need your help to get to the hospital.'

'They say he's pretty bad, pneumonia or the like, not up to talking or recognising anyone.' Joey had seen Buchanan and he would spare Tanner that if he could.

'It doesn't matter. I just have to see him.'

'He's not a pretty sight.'

'I know that. Will you arrange a carriage?'

'Prices are mighty high here for everything.' Joey glanced at Tanner's face—there would be no changing his mind. 'I'll ask the publican, he's got a trap, and he might loan it to us for a price.' Tanner sighed with relief. Joey was a strange man, he wasn't as simple or stupid as people believed and he cared for people more than most of them deserved.

The publican did indeed have a trap, but the cost of renting it was prohibitive. The alternative was a decrepit draft horse with no saddle or bridle, only a halter. Amy and Tanner sat on its bony back while Joey lead it through the streets to the hospital. It was Tanner's first sight of the city and it sickened him to find a place so new already polluted with sewage, and for all their marvellous width the streets were nothing but rutted dust baths overcrowded with people. Even the buildings held no appeal for Tanner, though some had been built with the permanency of the ages in mind and others seemed to have been thrown up overnight. None had the fine lines, the utter grace and beauty of a sailing ship and Tanner knew where he'd rather be.

The Melbourne Hospital, one of the more permanent buildings, had been built before the recent influx of immigrants and its facilities had already been stretched to the limit before the disaster of the *Lady Ann*.

Buchanan lay on the cot nearest the door, a fair indication of his condition. He was unrecognisable and Tanner found it difficult to accept that this pitiful wretch was the man he'd come to know so well. He forced himself to overcome the horror and draw near the cot. Buchanan's breathing was laboured and erratic. Suddenly it stopped, then the captain shook himself back to life. He gasped, then his eyes opened and stared fixedly ahead. Tanner knelt beside him.

'I'm sorry.' Buchanan didn't seem to recognise him. 'I thought to save you. I didn't know it would end like this.'

Buchanan's eyes fought to focus on Tanner's face. 'Tanner,' he whispered.

'Yes, sir.'

'Fire,' he murmured. 'Fire.' His eyes glazed slightly, then he found the strength for one last word. A word that Tanner was not certain he'd heard correctly, a word that may have been no more than the sound of the expulsion of air. A word that explained how a man as careful as Buchanan could lose his ship to fire. And the word was: 'Arson.'

Buchanan didn't die that day, nor for several days after. His death came in the early hours of the morning, and he died alone without any further moments of consciousness. He was buried on the land beside the five crewmen who had lost their lives in the fire. The entire ship's complement attended the funeral with the exception of those who were too badly injured and the three who were still missing. The vicar spoke too long and with little reference to the man as Tanner knew him. Then he spoke about the sea with even less knowledge. Although Tanner could not have said what he expected from a funeral, this one left him with little satisfaction.

'There be no stone for Davis.' Joey observed sadly as they trudged across the cemetery grounds to the road.

'For all we know there may be no need of one.' Tanner was tired of the depression Davis' disappearance had caused. 'Surely if he was dead someone would have found a body by now.'

'Unless he's at the bottom of the river.'

'Well, we can't go and look for him there,' Tanner said irritably, 'and we've looked everywhere else. I even went to the post office where I promised to meet him. If he's alive he's long gone from here, and if he's dead then there's nothing we can do.'

'Not even put a stone to mark his grave.'

'A lot of sailors end up at the bottom of the sea with nothing to mark their passing.' Tanner instantly regretted the sharpness in his voice. 'Look, if he's dead he's past caring and if he's alive he's not in this city. My guess is that if he escaped the fire he headed straight for the goldfields, and that's where we should be going too.' They had reached the roadway where the horses and carriages had been left. They had borrowed the publican's trap for the day and Tanner helped Amy into the seat. Joey drove—he had a way with animals, natural and relaxed, and they responded to him automatically.

'It don't seem right just leaving without knowing,' he said. 'My pay isn't going to last forever and it could take some time to find my brother.'

'But surely he'd be expecting you. I mean you wrote and told him you were bringing Amy home, didn't you?' Tanner glanced at Amy, her head was downcast, her face expressionless.

'No, I didn't write my brother, he isn't expecting me and Amy isn't his child.' Joey was waiting for an explanation, but Tanner didn't know where to begin. 'You see, I . . .' He stopped, then started again. 'There was an accident, it was my fault.' He paused. 'That's how Amy came to be blind. There was no one to care for her back in England and the only way I could bring her with me was to say that she was my niece, otherwise people might have thought there was something between us.' It wasn't the whole truth but as near to it as Tanner was prepared to get. Joey nodded understandingly.

'And your brother's not expecting you and you're not quite sure where he is and your money's running short. I can see why you have to go, but maybe I should stay here and keep looking for Davis.'

'No.' Amy extended the word into a cry. 'Please Joey, please come with us.'

In his heart Joey remained undecided, but years of Davis' domination had made him accustomed to abiding by other people's decisions and in any case Amy's appeal was impossible to resist.

CHAPTER 13

✦✦✦✦✦✦✦✦✦✦✦✦✦✦

T HERE WAS much to be heard by rumour about the goldfields, but very little in the way of hard fact. As the publican pointed out: 'Everyone keeps on going there and nobody's coming back.' One notable exception to this rule was the teamsters, the men who carried supplies to the goldfields, and everyone that Tanner asked agreed that if you wanted to know about the goldfields you asked the teamsters, and if you wanted to find the teamsters you tried the pubs, and if you wanted to find them sober you tried the merchants. After a few inquiries Tanner was given the name of a merchant who supplied the goldfields and whose premises were not far from their hotel.

The premises consisted of a large yard with wooden buildings on three sides and a fence, gate and office across the front. The buildings were mostly open-fronted stores from which employees of the yard were supposed to load goods onto drays as per the sales dockets. That was the theory, but the massive exodus of labourers to the goldfields meant that most of the teamsters did their own loading under the watchful eyes of a few supervisors.

Tanner looked conspicuously out of place as he entered the yard in his seaman's clothes. Everything was foreign to him, from the smell of the horses and bullocks to the language of their drivers, and the fierce activity of the yard accentuated the uncertainty of his movement as he traversed the quadrangle.

'You want something?' bellowed an angular-looking supervisor.

'Information about the goldfields.'

'You want the goldfields, just follow the crowd.'

'No, I'm looking for my brother.'

'Ha,' the man laughed, 'best of luck to you.'

'My brother went when they first discovered gold, when there weren't so many people.' The man shook his head. 'I got a letter, it said the name of a place but I can't quite remember it. I lost the letter but I know the place he went to was discovered not long after the first strike.

The man continued shaking his head. 'There's been dozens of strikes, hundreds of prospectors.' Tanner tried to think—he'd read his brother's letter so many times when he was in gaol, he thought he knew every word by heart.

'My brother was one of the first to go, surely someone would remember him.' The man was becoming irritated. 'Just mention the names of a few of the places, maybe that would jog my memory.'

'Ballarat,' the man suggested, but Tanner shook his head. 'Buninyong.'

'No,' Tanner said vaguely.

'Look, I can't help you, why don't you ask Ugly?' Tanner looked in the direction indicated, where there were about half a dozen teams with drivers and loading crews. He walked casually towards them and approached the first man in his path.

'I'm looking for Ugly.' The man pointed to a figure standing by the furthest dray. Smaller and thinner than most of the men, the figure moved with a grace that told Tanner it was a woman even before he caught a glimpse of her face. He approached her from behind, moving to her right as he drew near. Her profile, though strong, was hardly ugly and Tanner wondered why she was so named. As he spoke to her she turned to face him and he had his answer. Her left cheek and neck were scarred, horribly scarred, but more horrific to Tanner than the scar was the realisation that it had come from a burn. It set every one of his own half-healed sores and blisters tingling. Tanner was not quick enough to mask his feelings, but Ugly had seen the look too often to let herself be offended by it.

'You want something?' Her voice was gruff, but there was a soft sensitivity in her eyes that made Tanner regret his lapse of control even more.

'I'm sorry.'

'For what?'

'For the way I looked at you.'

'Beats having to pay money for a side show.'

He smiled at her self-derision. 'I had no right, it's just that I have a horror of burns.' He hesitated. 'A friend of mine died that way recently.' She studied Tanner as he proceeded with his halted explanation. 'I wasn't staring at you as if you were a freak,

94

please believe that.' She might have brushed him aside with another tarty remark, but her searching eyes had found an explanation more eloquent than his words.

'They be burns on your face too.'

'They're not too bad.' He fingered the few sores still remaining on his face.

'Are you one of the sailors off the *Lady Ann*?'

'Yes.'

'Captain was killed, I hear.' Again Tanner was too slow to hide his feelings from her. 'Were you the one that tried to save him?'

'I should have let him die.'

She raised her eyebrows philosophically. 'Not an easy decision to make.'

'No,' he agreed.

'Particularly when there's no time to think and your mind and body's all set to keep him alive.' He looked into the dark intensity of her eyes and it was easy to forget the scar and see only the deep perception of her mind. 'You save someone's life and that life's not worth living then they'll find a way to die, but if you let someone die then you never know what might have been.' He smiled at her, and it was as if a curtain passed across her face, hiding the warmth and humanity and leaving only the scar. 'Now, what was it you wanted to see me about?'

He continued smiling. 'I was hoping you might be able to help me find my brother.'

'Do I know him?'

'Perhaps, he was one of the first to go to the goldfields.' She began shaking her head as the angular young man had done. 'If I could just talk to some of the early prospectors one of them might remember him.'

'Even if I could find some of them, even if they knew your brother, there are so many people in and out of the goldfields every day they'd have no idea where he is now.'

'Bob isn't the type to keep moving about, he'd stake a claim and stick at it until it paid off.'

She laughed at him. 'Mining doesn't exactly work like that.'

'All right, but I've got to start somewhere. I got a letter from him and in it he mentioned the place he was headed, but I've lost the letter and I can't remember the place.' He closed his eyes, trying to picture the page. 'It was two words.'

'Forest Creek,' she suggested.

'No.'

'Mount Alexander.'

'Yes.' He beamed at her.

'Well, that is the way that I go but there are thousands of miners up there and I doubt I'd know your brother even if I'd seen him.'

Tanner frowned as he realised that she wasn't deliberately being difficult. 'You say that's the way you go.' She nodded. 'When would you be leaving?'

'As soon as I've finished loading.'

'Could we come with you?'

'We?'

'Myself, a girl, a young man. Girl would need a ride.'

'Oh, why's that?'

'She's blind.'

'That don't affect her legs.'

'It makes everything harder, even walking.' His defensiveness surprised Ugly, but she didn't let it annoy her. 'Joey and I would work for you to pay our way.'

'You're right about that and you'll buy your own supplies and you won't come crying to me when you can't find this brother of yours.'

'It's a deal.' He smiled at her. 'How long will it be before you're ready to leave?'

'A couple of hours the way this lazy lot are working.' She indicated the two youths who were half-heartedly loading the dray.

'I'll be back in two hours.' Tanner headed for the gate feeling oddly light-hearted.

Ugly looked after him, wondering why she had agreed so easily to him coming with her. New chums were worse than useless on the road, sailors were hopeless around animals and the girl was blind. She shook her head at her own stupidity. She was used to being alone and she liked it that way. There was no sense in getting close to people, doing them favours, calling them friends, knowing all the time that she'd never quite fit in. She turned back to the dray, bellowing at the lads who were loading for her, slow and lazy they were, only interested in earning enough money to kit themselves out for the goldfields.

Joey stared openly at the scar on Ugly's face—he didn't have the guile to hide his fascination.

'He said you'd work.' Ugly faced him squarely. 'And work you will. Get your back into loading the rest of these sacks. You other lazy louts,' she yelled at the boys who had been working for her, 'you're finished, here's your money, now get out. You, what's your name?' She addressed Tanner, who was helping Amy onto the dray, and he turned and extended his hand.

'Tanner, what's yours?' She ignored his hand and his question and began checking the yokes and harnesses on the bullocks.

'I'm heading for the new diggings at Golden Gully. I can leave you at Forest Creek if you like and you can start asking for your brother there.'

'All right.'

'It's about a seven-day journey provided the weather stays dry, not that we've had much rain these last two years. Hot as hell it was last summer, there was a bush fire, "Black Thursday", they called it, thought the whole city was going to burn. Anyway, if it does rain we'll be up to our axles in mud, all this dust goes like glue when it's wet.' Ugly could hear herself talking, prattling on and on, it happened sometimes when she'd had a few drinks or when someone started her off. It was like a flood gate opening, letting all her thoughts and feelings pour out with such force that she was unable to stop them. 'If your brother's the type to stick at a hole he might still be up at the Mount Alexander diggings, but to be honest with you he could be anywhere by now.' She finished checking the harness and found Tanner standing in front of her. She looked up at his face and the flood gates closed. 'You finished yet?' She yelled at Joey, who was standing stroking the lead bullock's ear. He nodded. 'You, what's your name, girl?'

'Amy.'

'Hang on. You two walk behind the dray.' She picked up the whip and cracked it over the head of the lead bullock. 'Move up there Willie, you lazy bastard!' Her language was colourful and the crack of the whip punctuated every phrase, but it never connected with any of the beasts and Tanner could hear past the string of invectives to the genuine affection she felt for the animals.

Walking was not an exercise to which Tanner was accustomed, and his feet were still tender as the skin had not yet regrown.

It was hot despite the fact that it was officially autumn and the dust was stifling. The full width of Swanston Street was taken up with carts and drays, horses and carriages and pedestrians of every class and colour. Tanner caught up to Ugly, who was walking beside the lead bullock still screaming abuse at him even though he'd not put a foot wrong.

'Is it always like this?'

'Gets worse with every boat load.' She looked at him. 'Haven't you been up here before?'

'No, we went up Elizabeth Street to the cemetery.'

She studied him for a moment. 'Ah yes, for the captain.' He nodded. She continued watching him for a few more minutes. 'Are you having trouble walking?'

'I'll be all right.' He wouldn't say anything that would make her regret her decision to take them with her.

'You sailors are a soft-footed bunch.'

'Burnt feet take a while to heal.'

She flinched visibly. 'You can ride up there with Amy if you like, going's easy for the animals here, out further you'll have no choice but to walk.' She moved off before he could thank her. Amy touched his hand as he climbed up onto the dray to reassure herself that it was him.

'She sounds awful,' she said.

'She isn't. She's just got a hard life in a hard country.' He squeezed Amy's hand. 'Think of it this way—she's got nothing to gain by giving us a ride. Maybe it's even costing her something, slowing her down.'

'So why is she doing it?'

'Out of the goodness of her heart,' Tanner said facetiously, but he'd seen the loneliness in her eyes and he'd known the need for companionship.

They passed along Albion Street, then up Mount Alexander Road to the Moonee Ponds Creek, the usual first-night stop on the way to the diggings. Tanner set up the camp while Ugly tended the animals, and Joey took unnecessary care of Amy. The meal would have passed for stew and dumplings it if had cooked a little longer, but no one complained. Tanner and Joey were too physically tired to care and Amy's senses were so attuned to the smells and sounds about her that even a poor meal couldn't spoil her enjoyment of the experience.

'On the way here,' she spoke to no one in particular, 'there was a sound very high pitched, always the same note.'

'A bellbird,' Ugly supplied.

'What do they look like?'

'Don't know, never seen one.'

'And you burnt something before, it smelt wonderful.' Ugly came and sat beside her. She picked up a few dry gum leaves and threw them in the fire.

'That it?'

'Yes.' Ugly picked some green leaves, crushed them in her hand and gave them to Amy. 'Oh,' Amy exclaimed.

'Gum leaves.' Tanner and Joey gave up tending their aching feet and moved closer to the women.

'What's your name?' Amy asked.

'Most people call me Ugly.'

'Good Lord, why?' Ugly took her hand and rubbed it against the rough scarring on her cheek. Amy recoiled and Ugly let her hand go.

'That's not your real name.' Tanner had moved so close to Ugly that his voice made her jump. 'When you were born they'd've given you a proper Christian name.'

Her face and body were set hard as she turned to meet his eyes. 'I doubt I was christened any more than my parents were married.'

'People haven't always called you Ugly.'

'For as long as I can remember.' She went to move away, but he pulled her back and her shock at having a man's hand on her was evident from her expression.

'I won't call you by that name.'

She jerked herself free from his grip. 'Catherine, if you must know, it's Catherine.' He smiled at her, and for an instant confusion rivalled anger for a place in her expression. Then all feeling faded and the impassiveness she wore like a mask reasserted itself. 'Time we got some sleep, we'll be up before dawn.' She took the dishes to the creek to wash them and left the others to settle to sleep. Tanner had it in his mind to wait for her return but hard work, fresh air and a full belly made him an easy victim for sleep.

CHAPTER 14

++++++++++++++

U GLY ROUSED them before dawn and the sun was barely colouring the distant mountains by the time they were underway. Tanner rode in the dray on the flat and walked or pushed on the hills. They reached a small creek around noon, where they stopped to water the bullocks and have a meal, which was no more than hard biscuits and water for there was no time to light a fire for tea.

'You seem in a hurry,' Tanner observed. 'Shouldn't you rest the animals?'

'So now, seaman, you're an expert on animals.'

'No,' he smiled at her and she found it disarming. 'Joey's the farmer, not me.'

She glanced in Joey's direction. 'He does have a way with them.' She continued studying the man and the animals he was tending. 'He's a good help, more than I expected he'd be.'

'Not like me?' Tanner teased.

She looked in his smiling face and the unaffected corner of her mouth twitched with amusement. 'You're not exactly what I expected either.'

'I'll take that as a compliment.' The twitch became a smile.

She moved away from him towards the team, collecting her whip on the way. 'Come on Willie, you lazy bastard.' The whip cracked, the team moved, and the journey resumed its slow, relentless pace.

By the end of the second day the track had lost any resemblance to a road. It was no more than wheel ruts twisting and turning amongst the gum trees. In some places the ruts were so numerous and deep that it was easier for Ugly to pull the bullocks off the old track and forge a new one of her own.

They had crossed several dry creek beds during the day and, when they had not found water by sundown, Ugly elected to carry on by the light of the moon until they reached the next creek. It was little more than a trickle, but enough to water the animals.

'What would you have done if this creek had been dry?' Tanner asked.

'I carry water with me,' she said, 'and I'd see you go thirsty before I'd put them at risk.' She indicated the team.

Tanner scanned the moonlit sky. 'Doesn't look much like rain,' he observed.

'Rain's the last thing we want, it'll turn this dust to a quagmire.'

'It's got to rain sometime,' he said, then let the subject drop, content just to watch her as she fussed about the dray. He was smiling at her and Ugly found it unnerving, and his presence without conversation made it even worse. She endured the silence for a few minutes then, finding no chore to offer her escape, she cast about for a new topic.

'The girl's your niece, then?'

'No,' he answered truthfully.

'What then?' She glanced towards the fire, where Amy and Joey were sitting, then back to Tanner. She couldn't quite see the hardening of the lines around his mouth or the sadness in his eyes, but she sensed that subject disquieted him in the same way as everything he said disquieted her. 'I mean, if she isn't your niece, why does she call you Uncle John?'

'To stop people prying.' Ugly accepted the rebuff as she'd accepted many others, but it hurt all the more because it came from him. She walked away from him to where the lead bullock stood. He nuzzled her for the piece of hard biscuit or bread she usually brought him. 'Catherine.' She didn't answer. 'Catherine.' She turned back towards the camp but he blocked her path. 'I didn't mean you.'

'You've a right to your privacy.'

'I'm responsible for her being blind.' He couldn't bring himself to say more, he couldn't bear going through the whole story again.

'And Joey?'

'A shipmate, tagged along with us after the *Lady Ann* burned.'

She nodded, then smiled her strange, crooked smile. 'A lot of men wouldn't have cared if they'd blinded a girl. A lot of shipmates wouldn't have treated a stray girl so proper.' She looked again in their direction. 'It's not spoiled her looks, the blindness.'

'Nor her temperament neither.' A second rebuff in such a short time was too much for Ugly, and she pushed past him without further word.

Joey watched her as she walked back to the camp. He was not usually given to philosophical thought, it would never occur to him to question why Amy should be blind or Ugly scarred, or why he had been less blessed in appearance, but as Ugly passed by him he wondered if she lived this life by choice or if society had cast her out. He touched Amy's hand. What kind of a society was it that had no place for anything less than perfect? All their religions and teachings said that the body was nothing but a temporary abode for the soul and that it was only the immortal part of man that needed to seek perfection.

Amy responded to his touch, squeezing his hand in a warm and trusting way. He knew now what Davis saw in her, although he still couldn't understand why he wanted to shower her with gold.

'You'd make a good farm wife,' he said suddenly.

'Really, why?'

'Man and his wife work together on the land. He'd be there to be your eyes and you'd be there to be his extra pair of hands.' He lapsed into silence again, a clear vision of Amy as a farm wife dancing before his eyes. 'Farmers are what they need out here, wheat, barley, oats—you know they import flour from America—and all this good land going to waste.'

'Is that what you'll do if we find gold, buy land, start a farm?'

Joey had never really thought about it before, going for the gold had been Davis' idea. 'Yes,' he breathed huskily. 'That's what I'd do.' A smile crossed his gentle face. He'd never really wanted anything before but to have a farm of his own, to work his own land. Now *that* was something worth wanting.

Tanner walked past them and bedded down without so much as a word.

'Uncle John,' Amy murmured.

'He's gone to his bed.' Amy felt a pang of what might have been fear, loneliness, or loss. The charade was over, there was no need to call him 'Uncle John' any more and once they reached the goldfield she wouldn't be able to do so. She wondered what she should call him, 'Mr Tanner' or simply 'John'. He had promised that he wouldn't leave her, but if his brother and sister-in-law were willing to take her how could she refuse to let him go?

Without warning her mind brought forth the vision of the courtyard and the gray-headed man. She should tell Tanner the truth and end all the pretence once and for all. She shuddered at the thought.

'Are you cold?' Joey asked.

'No.' She reached out for his hand. 'I'm just tired. Would you mind showing me to the tent?'

Although there were many travellers on the road, Ugly and her party saw only a small percentage. They had been passed by several men on horseback with pack animals, a couple of carts and a team of draught horses. The only vehicle that they had passed was an overloaded cart which had tipped sideways into a ditch. Only empty drays appeared from the opposite direction.

By late afternoon on the third day they could see a thick pall of dust rising like a flag, indicating the position of another vehicle on the road ahead. It was almost dusk before they saw it, another bullock dray moving marginally slower than they were. They lost sight of it soon after but Ugly pressed on, even after dark, until she reached the creek where the other teamster had camped.

'I thought 'twas you I could see behind me.' The teamster was a huge man with the look and sound of all Ireland about him. 'How far do you reckon you were behind, four hours?'

'Closer to five the way those lazy louts were loading.' Tanner began to unpack their camping gear while Joey helped Ugly with the team.

'No, no,' the burly Irishman called, 'come set up over here.' Tanner looked at Ugly for confirmation.

'That's Paddy O'Shea,' she said by way of introduction.

'Regan Thomas Frances Xavier O'Shea, but these ignorant bastards call every Irishman Paddy.' He moved to help Tanner with their gear. 'I'd like to think that it's you that's been making time,' he called to Ugly, 'but by the number that's passed me I think it's me that's been falling behind.'

'What are you carrying?' She had finished with the bullocks and was moving to the campsite as he answered.

'Passengers and their gear mostly.' Ugly stopped short at his words and visibly stiffened at the sight of them. The man was bald with a long, thin face and a gangling body to match. The woman beside him was short and round rather than plump with flaxen hair and blue eyes. She was pretty and bright and both

Joey and Tanner smiled at the sight of her.

'Well, now, I thought there wasn't a woman to be seen for miles up on the goldfields and here I've the company of one already.' She beamed at Amy, who clung unsteadily to Joey's arm.

'Two,' Tanner corrected, glancing at Ugly. They all turned to look at her and she received their gaze like an assault. There was a momentary silence while the newcomers stared at her, then the lanky man stood up.

'Allow me to introduce myself. I am Ezekiel Cohen.' His manner was theatrical and his accent American. 'And may I present to you Miss Loretta Singleton, the songbird of the south.' The woman stood up, made a short bow and sat down again.

'I'm Tanner, this is Amy, Joey and Catherine.'

'Catherine is it?' Paddy exploded with laughter and too late Tanner realised his mistake. Pain flashed across Ugly's face, then hatred as she caught Tanner's eye, then nothing. 'Well, I never, and how long has it been Catherine?'

'All my life.' Her voice was softened by the effort of controlling her emotions.

'Well,' Paddy continued boisterously, 'if you're going to call her Catherine you can bloody well call me Regan.' He chortled to himself as he drew a bottle from inside his bag. ' 'Tis a shame it isn't whisky, but rum's far easier to come by here. Still, I suppose it's what you're used to.'

Tanner's clothes marked him as a sailor. He took his swallow from the bottle then passed it to Joey, who barely put it to his lips before passing it to Zeke. Paddy took the bottle and offered it to Ugly, who declined though normally she would have accepted. Rum made company easier to tolerate.

After dinner Loretta sang, her sweet soprano voice lending itself to every request until Paddy got drunk and drowned her out.

'Get the piano,' Paddy roared.

'Piano?' Tanner queried.

'That's what's on the dray and all the makings of a stage.' It was Zeke who answered. 'I've been on the goldfields before and miners will pay anything for a pretty girl who thinks she can sing and when she's got a real voice like Loretta, well, we can name our price.' He beamed at everyone.

'Are women really such a rarity at the diggings?' Tanner asked.

'They most certainly are,' Paddy rallied, feeling that the question required his expertise. 'Hardly a dozen I've seen at any one of the diggings.'

'Then a man with a wife and children would be easy to remember.'

'My word yes.'

'I'm looking for my brother, he was one of the first to go prospecting, took his wife and two children with him.' Paddy began nodding. 'His name is Robert Tanner, his wife's name is Mary.'

'Aye, pretty woman she was too.' Paddy shook his head sadly. 'Just sort of wasted away, sad it was, goldfield's no place for a woman, a decent woman I mean, no place to raise littl'uns.'

Tanner's features remained unchanged, in fact they were frozen, his body numbed while his mind fought to assimilate Paddy's words.

'Seems to me I do know your brother.' Ugly squatted beside him. 'I just didn't recognise the name. He's at the new diggings at Golden Gully, I can take you right to him if you like.' He stared at her blankly.

'Uncle John.' Amy edged her way around the fire to where he was sitting. 'Uncle John.'

'Here.' Ugly took her hand and guided her to him.

'Oh, Uncle John, I'm so sorry.' She sat beside him, searching his face with her sensitive fingers, holding herself close to him. He drew an unsteady breath and put his arm around her.

'It's all right,' he said and his voice betrayed the emotions that his expression still concealed. Slowly the truth had dawned on Ugly.

'You didn't know,' she said, and the emptiness in his eyes confirmed it.

Tanner took another deep breath. 'Come on,' he said to Amy. 'I'll put you to bed.' They walked away together arm in arm and there was no need for words between them.

They left early next morning. It was hotter than the previous day, the wind had gone round to the north and it seemed to drive the dust before it. Conversation was impossible and Tanner walked more than he needed to, using the physical exercise to relieve the tension of his mind.

The day passed into night, the night into morning and the next day dawned as unpleasant as the last. The dust was like a massive, choking cloud that enveloped everything. At noon Ugly stopped the team and gave them water from the barrels she carried on the dray. She checked their eyes and hooves and the places where sores might be caused by yoke or harness while the others sat in the shade trying to wash down hard biscuits with warm water. Finally she doffed her hat and tipped the dregs of the water bucket over her head. Tanner got to his feet, taking a few biscuits to offer her. She refused, pouring herself a mug of water instead.

'You said you knew my brother.'

'I never knew his name, I hardly ever spoke to him. He had a claim up at Mount Alexander and then at Golden Gully. I only remember him because . . .' She stopped, unwilling to mention the woman.

'Because of Mary,' Tanner supplied.

'I sold her a bolt of calico once, cheap because it was water stained. She said she wanted it to make clothing for the littl'uns, though that lad of hers is hardly little now.' Ugly stopped, and if Tanner had looked at her face he would have seen more compassion than he ever expected to find in those crooked features. 'Anyway, I can take you right to him.'

He smiled at her. 'How much longer?'

'We're making good time in spite of the wind, give it the rest of today and tomorrow to make Forest Creek, then two days more to Golden Gully.'

Joey and Amy joined them. 'Are we ready yet?' Amy asked.

'Aye.' Ugly gulped down the last swallow of water.

'You've not had much rest.' Tanner stepped close to her and she automatically retreated a step.

'As much as I need.' She picked up the whip. 'Come on Willie, you lazy bastard.' She flicked the whip and the team moved on.

If the road to Forest Creek was bad, then the one to Golden Gully was non-existent and more crowded as prospectors came from other diggings to the new strikes along the Bendigo Creek. The language amongst the teamsters as they rivalled one another for position was enough to make a sailor blush, and Joey was visibly shocked every time Ugly opened her mouth.

'Do you need to talk like that?' Amy asked.

'It's the only language them dumb bastards understand.'

'I don't imagine bullocks really understand any language at all.'

'I didn't mean the bullocks.' Ugly let forth another string of abuse as she walked to where Tanner was toiling up a slight hill. 'We'll head for Kangaroo Flats first.'

'Why?'

'Well, for one thing I sell most of my supplies there and for another you and Joey'll have to get a licence each.'

'A licence for what?'

'To dig gold. If you're going to work with your brother you'll need a licence, and even if he isn't here you'd be well advised to spend a month at the diggings to make the trip worthwhile.'

'And a licence is really necessary?'

'It is.'

'How much?'

'Thirty shillings or half an ounce of gold.'

'You're joking!'

'You'd get more for your gold in Melbourne or even Forest Creek, but it's the inconvenience of leaving your mine and the merchants around here aren't willing to part with their paper money.'

'No, I meant the price. Three pounds for the two of us, it's near all I've got left.'

'You'd make that back in less than a week on a good claim but be warned, everything from a swallow of rum to a sack of flour can be ten times what you'd pay for it in Melbourne.' They had rounded the bend and Kangaroo Flat lay before them. Ugly pointed to a small group of huts. 'It's there that you get your licence,' she said. 'I'll take Amy with me to the store. Meet us there when you've finished.'

Ugly was still arguing with the merchant when Tanner and Joey arrived.

'I'll take the whole bloody lot and sell it in Golden Gully meself,' she threatened.

'All right, all right, but they're getting a lot more than three pound per ounce for gold in Melbourne.'

'In Melbourne, yes, but you're not allowing the miners more than two pounds fifteen shillings, so you're still making a nice, tidy profit.' He mumbled inaudibly as he weighed out the gold. 'And I'll keep one of them sacks of flour and a few of the fresh vegetables for the trouble of having to argue with you, you bloody thieving bastard.' She collected her gold, turned to leave and found Tanner smiling at her. 'I take it my language doesn't offend you?'

'I've heard worse. How much longer?' He looked weary and Ugly felt sorry for him.

'I'll take you now. I've saved the sack of flour and the vegetables for your brother. I'll be cheaper for him buying from me.' They walked together to the dray, where Amy was talking with Joey.

'What's it like?' she asked.

He looked around as if seeing the place for the first time. 'Well, there's the commissioner's camp, where we got the licences, no more than a few huts and tents with a flagpole stuck out the front and there's the store here and one a bit further away, if you can call them stores, just wooden frames with canvas on them. Over near the commissioner's hut there are a couple of waterholes marked for drinking only, but all the rest's got miners all round them with wooden cradle things that they use to wash the dirt away from the gold. There are carts everywhere full of dirt.' He looked further afield to the dry hills that surrounded them. 'There are little clusters of tents all over the place. I suppose they all get together around a spot where someone's found gold. There are all kinds of people, all different races, gentlemen some of them too.' He scratched his head, trying to think what else to tell her. 'I've seen a few women among the new arrivals and some with children too.' He stopped again and frowned. 'Everyone's working hard, fast as if they've got to get the gold before it all runs out.'

Amy lifted her head. Even through the general ruckus that surrounded the store she could hear Tanner's quiet voice. 'Are we going now?' she asked as he drew near.

'Right now,' Ugly answered for him.

Their progress to Golden Gully was slow, impeded by many smaller carts making their way to and from the waterholes. More than five hundred camps were dotted along the right bank of the gully and many of the claims were right up against each other, making it nigh on impossible to get the team to the area in which Tanner's brother had his claim.

As Tanner walked with Ugly between the camps he began searching for his brother. Not until that moment had he realised how anxious he was to see him, to commiserate with him, to listen to him talk about Mary and to tell him about Amy and Buchanan. He was still searching the sea of faces when Ugly came to an abrupt halt. Before her were a group of Chinamen working in a pit, and she made an effort to communicate with them but with little result.

'What's the matter?' Tanner asked.

'Blasted Chinese, so many dialects.' She yelled a few words in Chinese and a small man appeared from a nearby tent. She continued in a mixture of Chinese and English, the little man smiling and nodding all the time. He spoke a few words, then the other Chinamen all joined in. Tanner was irritated by the delay.

'What's going on?' he demanded, and the conversation immediately stopped.

'Your brother's not here, he abandoned these diggings and went to White Horse Gully, I think, I mean with them not being sure where he went and me not being sure what they're saying, White Horse Gully's my best guess.'

Tanner sighed loudly. 'How long before we get there?'

Ugly glanced heavenward—already the last rays of the sun were casting long shadows across the valley floor. 'We'll go back to the creek, camp there for the night and start looking for him in the morning.'

'No.' Anger and frustration showed in the long extended sound of the word.

'We'd never find him in the dark, that's assuming he's in White Horse Gully.' Ugly remained reasonable. 'And even if he is there, even if we can find him, how's he going to cope with the three of you landing on him for the night?'

Tanner smiled. 'Four of us.'

Ugly surveyed his tired grin, then turned on her heel. 'I can take care of myself.'

CHAPTER 15

++++++++++++++

T ANNER HAD trouble sleeping; to be so near after coming so far and still to have to wait was too much a test of his patience. He sat up and looked across at Amy's slumbering form and then at Joey—neither one of them stirred. He crawled out of the tent to the fire where Ugly slept. He sat watching her. She was lying on her left side so that the scar was concealed, and in the combination of moonlight and firelight he caught a glimpse of what her face was meant to be. Now in repose her features were quite soft, her jaw line was fine now that it was slackened by sleep and her body was not as large as the men's clothes made it appear.

The moon dipped behind the cloud and a slight breeze rustled the leaves. It was cool and Tanner considered returning to the tent or poking some life into the fire, but his thoughts didn't translate into actions and instead he wandered to the dray, where he sat facing the east waiting for the first signs of light.

It was mid-morning when they reached the diggings in White Horse Gully. The scene was typical: tents and shanties bunched together, men at their windlasses, carts full of wash dirt. As they moved further up the gully most of the claims were temporarily deserted, a large crowd having gathered around one of the mines. Ugly and Tanner abandoned the dray and as they approached the crowd there were cries of 'Get the commissioner.'

From the back of the crowd Tanner was barely able to see the source of the disturbance—a young boy standing by the mouth of a pit obviously confronting the two men at the head of the crowd. A younger girl stood beside him, lending him support but lacking his fire and determination.

'No law says I can't have a claim.' The boy lifted his head in a gesture that was oddly familiar to Tanner. He tried to move closer to get a better view, but too many burly miners blocked his way.

'Claim was your father's, boy, not yours.' One of the two men advanced on the boy, who stepped back and raised his shovel.

'What was my father's is mine now.' There was a familiarity in his stance, too, and in the inflection in his voice. Suddenly Tanner was gripped by a feeling of panic, and he tried to get nearer the boy.

'Now, come on lad, be reasonable, you don't want us to have to get the commissioner.' The second man now joined his companion.

'Get anyone you like, just get off my claim.' Tanner tried to push his way through the crowd, but none were willing to give up their vantage point. He shoved one man too hard and the man pushed him back. Tanner shoved him again, grappling with him, for the innate sense that usually made Tanner avoid fights had been overridden by a feeling of fear and urgency. The man turned on Tanner and several of his friends besides. One raised his fist, but the crack of a whip not inches from his ear brought him up short. The crowd turned to look at Ugly and the men closest to her moved away.

'We're looking for Robert Tanner.' The crack of the whip had silenced the crowd and her voice rang clear in the stillness.

'He's dead,' someone yelled, and it was as if all the strength went out of Tanner. He stood limply, still hanging on to the man with whom he'd been struggling.

'This is his brother.' Ugly still held the crowd's attention, but slowly their eyes turned to Tanner. Then the men began to move aside, making way for him to walk to the mine, and he followed the path they made until only the two men at the front stood between Tanner and the boy. He pushed past them. The boy was leaner than his brother had been and one day he'd probably be taller, his hair was lighter but his eyes and the expression round the mouth marked the boy as his brother's son.

'Bobby,' was all Tanner managed to say.

The boy lowered the shovel. 'Uncle John?'

'What happened?' Tanner's voice still held a note of disbelief, that last unremitting hope that would finally give way to grief.

'We heard someone at our wash dirt late one night. Dad went out to see who it was. There was a scuffle and the sound of someone being hit, then nothing.' There were tears in the boy's eyes but he would not let them fall. 'I called but he didn't answer,

111

so I went to see. I couldn't find him, I looked and I called.'
He stopped and took a deep breath, then all the emotion drained
from his face and a cold hardness replaced it. 'Then I looked
down the mine and he was there all covered in blood.'

'We wanted to take him to Forest Creek.' A man to Tanner's
left began to speak. 'There's a woman there good at tending the
sick.'

'He wouldn't let us though,' another man chipped in. 'Wouldn't
leave his claim, kept ranting about how he'd caught someone
fossicking in his dirt, stealing a nugget the size of your fist, delirious
he was.'

'Aye,' the first man agreed. 'He's been digging dead there for
more than a week.'

'Still, that makes no difference.' The second man spoke. 'He
believed it and he wouldn't let us take him, fought us off when
we tried.'

'He passed out in the end.' The first man resumed the story.
'But by the time we got him to Forest Creek it was too late.'

There was a short silence before Tanner spoke. 'When?'

'Be a week since it happened, five days since we took him to
Forest Creek, three days since we buried him.' The man paused
as if to reconsider his calculations.

'Three days,' Tanner murmured. 'We were there three days ago.'
He looked at Ugly for confirmation.

'All this makes no never mind.' One of the two men who had
been confronting the boy had grown impatient. Tanner was a
new chum, shocked by his brother's death, maybe easily bluffed.
'The man who owns the claim is dead and I say that makes it
open land.'

'What name is on the claim?' Tanner's voice carried well even
though he spoke softly.

'Your brother's name, but he's gone now and this claim should
belong to the first man who can stake it out.'

'What name?' Tanner insisted.

'Robert Tanner, I suppose.' The man could feel that he was
being tricked, but he didn't know how.

'And what's your name, boy?' Tanner asked his nephew.

'Robert Tanner,' the boy said triumphantly.

'Would seem my brother put the mine in his son's name.'

'He's only a child,' the men protested, but they were drowned

112

out by the laughter of the other miners. For them the decision was made—they could see the humour and justice of it, but the two men and their supporters were not so easily beaten. They began to manhandle Tanner out of the way and again Ugly's stock whip brought an end to the conflict.

'Why don't you all go up to the commissioner's office and you two gentlemen can explain to him how you think you've more right to the claim of a man bashed to death by claim jumpers than his son and brother have.' Ugly stood tall, the whip twitching in her hand, the scarred side of her face turned towards them. Even to Tanner she looked threatening.

The two men conferred, then retreated. Ugly joined Tanner and his nephew. 'If I was you I'd get across to the commissioner's office and get it all recorded. Once he says the claim is yours that'll be it once and for all.'

The boy was reluctant to move. 'What happens to the mine while I'm off at the commissioner's?' he asked.

'Most of the miners were on your side, none of them would try anything, and me, well, I make more on the road than you'll ever dig out of this hole and this will take care of all the rest.' She flourished the whip. The boy was placated rather than impressed, and he put down the shovel and gave his sister a shove.

'Go get the horses.' He turned to Tanner. 'How do I know you're my uncle?'

Tanner reached inside his coat and deftly slipped the forged letter out of the envelope as he took it from his pocket. 'Your father sent this to me.' He handed it to the boy. 'I lost the letter when the *Lady Ann* burned but you'll see it's your father's hand. He told me you were going prospecting, that's how I was able to find you.'

The boy took the envelope and studied it. It was such a flimsy piece of proof. He had no memory of his uncle, and when his father had spoken of him he had talked as if he was still young, not at all like the man who stood before him now. The girl returned with the mounts, unsaddled cart horses with makeshift bridles.

'You must be Jilly,' Tanner said kindly. She dropped the reins and ran. Tanner looked at the boy for explanation.

'She's been like that ever since Mum died.' He handed Tanner one set of reins. 'Don't worry, she won't go far.'

It wasn't until he returned to the mine that the full import of his brother's death dawned on Tanner. As expected the commissioner had signed over the mine to him, but before doing so he asked for Tanner's undertaking to care for the children. Tanner gave it without thinking, although in retrospect he knew there was nothing else he could do. It still shocked him to realise what he'd taken on, to realise that his brother was never coming back.

Jilly had retreated into the shanty and refused to come out for anyone. She hid from Tanner and screamed hysterically when Ugly went near her. As Ugly emerged from the shanty Tanner took her arm.

'I had no right to ask you to try with her,' he apologised.

She shrugged. 'I'm used to the way children look at me, pretending I'm a witch or a devil, daring each other to get close to me, laughing, taunting me then running away.' The emotion had built in her voice and the final words seemed to catch in her throat.

He was still holding her arm and he tightened his grip. 'I'm sorry,' he said hopelessly. He looked exhausted, emptied of all physical and emotional strength, and Ugly resisted the impulse to pull away from him.

'It's not your fault.' Tanner loosened his grip and walked with her to the dray. 'This land's not quite what you expected,' she said, and he laughed weakly.

'I had no expectations of this land, except that my brother would be here. I thought he might help me with Amy.' He sat down next to the wheel of the dray and pulled her down beside him. 'You want to know something funny?' he asked. 'If I'd been gaoled for assaulting her I'd probably be a free man by now.'

'That wouldn't make her less blind or bring your brother and his wife back to life or make these children less alone. It'd just excuse you from having to do anything about it.'

He made no comment and it occurred to Ugly that her remark was unkind. He wasn't the type of man who needed an excuse to get out of doing something he didn't want to do, people's opinion didn't matter that much to him. She frowned as her logic deserted her. Earlier he'd said that he'd blinded Amy and just now he'd mentioned assault. It didn't seem possible, not when they cared for each other so much. Ugly had hated and feared the man who'd scarred her, he'd never cared for her nor shown any remorse for what he'd done.

She glanced at Tanner's expression, but it was unreadable. 'Why did you assault her?' she asked.

'I didn't.'

'But you said . . .'

'It was an accident.' He sighed deeply—he didn't want to go through it all again, yet he wanted her to know. He leant back against the dray, angling his head so that she dominated his view. His face became blank and the voice in which he told the story was a monotone.

'So that's how she came to be with you,' Ugly said when he finished.

'That's how it started. If there'd been anyone else, any other place . . .' He left the sentence unfinished.

'Even your brother and his wife.' She spoke before she considered the harshness of her response.

'That's not why I came here.'

'Why did you come?'

'The people I was smuggling for were afraid I'd involve them, so they got me a good lawyer on the understanding that I'd leave the country if he got me off.' He paused thoughtfully. It still didn't make sense. He roused himself from his deliberation. 'Any other questions?'

Ugly glanced up at him, half expecting that he was mocking her but he wasn't. 'There is something that puzzles me.' She shrugged uncomfortably. 'It's probably none of my business.'

'Ask.'

'What was in that letter you took out of the envelope before you handed it to the boy?'

Tanner smiled. 'You've a sharp eye.' He took the letter from his pocket and handed it to her, but she didn't take it.

'I can't read,' she admitted. 'I know what some of the signs say and I can write my name, but no one ever took the time to teach me.'

'Then I shall.' He pointed to the words as he read them to her. 'I wrote this so Buchanan would let me work a passage for Amy. Since they found gold here most captains are scared of losing their crews and a man working a passage for someone would be a pretty bad risk, so I thought to play on his sympathy.' There was no regret or apology in his voice, just the sadness the memory of Buchanan evoked.

'But the boy took it as your brother's writing.'

'The envelope was, he'd written to me, as I said, but I'd switched the letters. The last contact I'd ever have with him and I burned it for fear it would incriminate me.' During the long silence that followed the sun dipped behind the hills and the cold shadow of dusk fell upon them. The chill brought Tanner back to the needs of the moment. 'It's time I got some sort of a meal.'

'You'd best leave that to me.'

'Why, don't you trust my cooking?' He stood up and offered her his hand. She was surprised by the gesture but accepted it, and he pulled her to her feet.

'There's no food in that shanty,' she said. 'I'll leave you the sack of flour, a couple of cabbages, onions and potatoes but you'll have to buy meat at the store. I'll have a word with Amy, see what she needs to set up here, then I'll bring it up from Melbourne next time I come.' He was smiling and as usual she found it disconcerting. 'What's so funny?' she asked.

'You remind me of a very soft-hearted woman that I once knew.'

'You think so, well, there's no care in me for man or beast,' she said tartly, 'except, perhaps, for old Willie there.' She indicated the lead ox.

'What about me?' Tanner asked, and the directness of his question caught her off-guard.

'If there was a being that I could care for it would be you.' Having realised what she'd said she added, 'But there isn't.' Her words didn't diminish his smile, nor did the haughty way she stepped past him to make her way back to the camp.

'Uncle John, Uncle John.' Amy's voice reached them and its urgency made them run. 'I'm sorry, it's my fault, I was only trying to help.'

'What's happened?'

'Jilly's run off,' Bobby answered disgustedly. 'She'll just be hiding somewhere, forget about her and she'll come sneaking back when she thinks we're not looking.'

Tanner ran his fingers through his hair. The last thing he needed was for the child to go missing. 'Bobby, you stay here with Amy. If she's going to come to anyone it will be you. The rest of us will spread out and look for her. We'll keep in touch by —'

'No,' Ugly stopped him mid-sentence. 'If it's as the boy says and she's hiding, looking for her will only drive her further away. We'll wait, carry on as usual, bed down early, chances are she'll come back.'

'And if she doesn't?' Tanner turned on her.

'She will.' Bobby added his weight to Ugly's argument.

'I don't know,' Tanner said hopelessly. 'Why did she run off like that?'

'It was my fault,' Amy said. 'We decided it would be best if I slept in with the children and you and Joey had the tent. I thought that if I got to know the inside of the shanty it would be easier. Joey was helping me, he spoke to her but she didn't answer, so I started talking to her, telling her how we were going to stay here and look after her, how I wanted to be her friend. All of a sudden, she just screamed and ran off. I'm sorry.'

Tanner put his arm around her. 'It wasn't your fault.' He scanned the nearby camps, hoping for some sign of Jilly. 'Don't worry, she'll be all right.' He spoke to comfort himself rather than the girl. 'Let's leave her for now, get our meal and act like nothing's happened.' He took Amy's arm and led her back to the shanty.

'So, Amy, what do you think you'll need from Melbourne?' Ugly asked, as they finished dishing up the meal.

'I don't know, I think we could use some milk and eggs. A cow and some chickens,' she corrected.

'A goat would be more use to you here,' Joey interrupted, 'and it's no use getting chickens now, they'll be going off the lay soon. You're better to buy layers in the spring, have eggs all summer and chicken soup in winter.' Amy looked deflated. Joey took her hand. 'Don't worry, we'll make a farm wife of you yet.'

'It's decided then is it?' Bobby said abruptly, and everyone turned to look at him. 'Those two are in with us are they?' He waited, not expecting an answer. 'And how will we be dividing up the gold?' he demanded. 'Even shares for the new chums and to hell with all the work Dad and me put in before you came?' The boy's face was hard with determination. His parents had sacrificed everything for the gold and it wasn't fair that he should have to share it with outsiders.

'Settle down,' Tanner said. 'Let's see if there is any gold before we start dividing it up.'

'No,' Bobby said emphatically. 'That's not the way it's done here, you decide how it'll be divided before you start digging.' He faced them with the same fearless resolve he had shown to the two men earlier that day.

'That miner said you've been digging dead for more than a week. Does that mean what I think it means?'

'Sometimes it happens that way.' He looked to Ugly for support. 'The surface gold goes and then you have to dig dead for a while to get into the main seam.' Ugly didn't speak—it was true, but there was a vast difference between digging dead for a few days and not getting anything for more than a week. 'It's true,' he insisted, 'we had a claim at Mount Alexander and after we left it the Chinese moved in and got more gold out of it and the same thing happened in Golden Gully, and Dad said we weren't going to let them do it to us here.'

'The Chinese are more efficient,' Ugly spoke at last, 'more patient, less greedy. They buy a hogshead, cut it in half and wash the dirt in it, sometimes they'll put the dirt through twice or puddle in the barrels to get the extra gold. They settle for dust when everyone else pushes it aside looking for nuggets.'

'They let the white men do the digging then move in when their back's turned.' Ugly laughed at him and the ridicule was the final straw. 'This is my claim and I'm not giving it up to anyone, not to a bunch of Chinamen, not to them two this morning and not to you.' He walked defiantly to the bundle of blankets that substituted for a bed and threw himself down on it.

Tanner went outside, leaving the others to tidy up. He searched the darkness in the vain hope that Jilly might be there. The nights were cold and the dress she was wearing was so thin. He walked to the mine and peered into the blackness of the hole—surely she wouldn't be hiding there. A movement by the dray caught his attention, but it was only Willie wondering why Ugly hadn't brought him his usual treat. Tanner strained his eyes to see further into the night. The child hadn't eaten and there was no meat on her bones, no reserves to keep her going. At the sound of a footstep Tanner turned, it was Ugly.

'There's no sign of her,' he said.

'If she's anything like I was at her age she won't be far away. Too hurt to come back, too scared to keep going.' He walked with her to the dray, where she gave Willie his damper.

'Why is she like this?'

'A man loses a woman, sometimes he doesn't know what to do with the children. A boy, a youth, can be a mate, but a little girl . . .' She paused, and if Tanner had been less preoccupied he may have noticed the bitter sadness and the strain. 'A little girl just doesn't belong.' Joey emerged from the shanty carrying the lamp, then headed for the tent. 'If she's not back in the morning I'll help you look for her.' She touched his arm, a clumsy and unnatural gesture. 'Go, get some sleep, there's naught else you can do.'

She watched him leave then made up her bed under the dray. Ugly rarely had trouble sleeping. There were nightmares, of course, bitter memories that would not die and she woke easily to any disturbance, but seldom did she lie awake waiting for sleep to come. Therefore, she was unaware of the rustle in the bush beside the dray or the small figure crawling past her to get to the camp. It wasn't until the child's hand brushed her face that her eyes shot open and she found herself gazing into Jilly's terrified face. They both remained frozen, each afraid that any movement might startle the other. Finally, the child sat back on her haunches, leaning against the wheel of the dray. Ugly twisted round slowly so that she could still see her. The child studied Ugly's face, not just the scar but the whole face.

'My mummy's dead,' she said suddenly, and Ugly didn't know how to respond. 'She's not coming back.'

'No,' Ugly murmured.

'Is your mother dead?'

'I don't know, she went away when I was a bit younger than you and I never saw her again.'

'Is that why you used to hide?' Ugly realised that Jilly must have heard her conversation with Tanner.

'Yes, that's why I used to hide.'

The child crept closer to Ugly. 'Amy can't see,' she said.

'No, she's blind.'

'Is her mother dead?'

'Yes, I think so.'

The child considered this answer for a moment. 'Amy's going to live with us.'

'I like Amy.' Ugly tried to sound encouraging. 'She's very nice.'

'My mother said you were nice.'

'Did she?'

'You gave her the material to make my dress, see.'

Ugly recognised the rough cotton that had been made up into a dress. 'I remember.' The child toyed with the blanket that Ugly had wrapped around herself. 'Are you cold?' she asked, and without further invitation the child climbed in beside her. Ugly was nothing like her mother. She was hard where her mother had been soft, tense and uncertain where her mother had been supple and sure, but she was warm and somehow separate from all the things the child wanted to escape.

Ugly lay rigid and absolutely still. She had no idea what to do and she wished with all her might that Tanner would come. Jilly cuddled closer to her and awkwardly Ugly put her arm around her. She'd never held another human being before. The child went from being freezing cold to boiling hot in a matter of seconds, and Ugly wondered if she was ill. But in the same instant the child was asleep, breathing deeply and naturally.

The hours passed slowly and painfully for Ugly. She watched the descent of the moon and saw the ashes in the fire lose their glow. She longed to sneak away and tell Tanner that she'd found the child, but she dared not for fear of waking her. Sometime between midnight and dawn she heard footsteps approaching. They stopped, then began to retreat.

'Tanner,' she hissed. The footsteps stopped again. 'Tanner, for heaven's sake come here.' The footsteps came towards her again. 'Tanner, I've got her.'

He squatted down beside the dray. 'Is she all right?'

'I think so, she just climbed in here with me and went to sleep.' Tanner peered under the dray, but all he could see was a dark bundle lying on the darker earth.

'How did you know it was me?'

'Who else would have reason to be roaming around here in the middle of the night. Tanner, what am I to do?' she asked desperately.

'What you're doing looks all right to me.'

She couldn't see his face, but she knew he was smiling. 'Be sensible,' she pleaded. 'I don't know anything about children.'

'Neither do I. I'm a sailor remember, the only time I've ever held a child was at Bobby's christening.' He stood up.

'Where are you going?' Her voice held a note of panic.

'To bed.'

'Please don't leave me.'

He squatted down again. 'It's too cold to stay here and if she wakes up and sees me it might frighten her.'

'What am I to do if she does wake up?'

He considered the problem. 'Find her something to eat.' He stood up again and walked away before Ugly could make any further protests. He was smiling, his one regret was that he hadn't taken a lamp with him so that he could see Catherine with a child in her arms. The smile deepened—she would have looked beautiful.

CHAPTER 16

++++++++++++++

U GLY PUT in the few remaining hours to dawn lying flat
on her back listening to Jilly's regular breathing. The sky
had scarcely paled when she disentangled herself from the child
and set about starting a fire and cooking a meal. Bobby rose
soon after. He hardly acknowledged Ugly and made no inquiry
about his sister, but moved straight to the mine.

'Jilly's come back,' Ugly called after him, but he didn't answer.

One by one the others appeared and finally Jilly came skirting
the main group and making her way to Ugly, nestling close to
her, twining her fingers through a tear in Ugly's jacket. From
then on Jilly followed Ugly everywhere, and it was some time
before Ugly could get away from the child to have a quiet word
with Tanner. He had been left at the mine while Bobby and Joey
took the wash dirt to the waterhole. Bobby had taken charge
and the men had allowed it in deference to his experience. Tanner
climbed out of the mine, having filled the bucket, and began hoisting
it to the surface.

'I've got to be going now, Ugly said.

'Why?' He all but let the bucket fall.

'Once the weather changes it will take three, maybe four, times
as long to make the trip from Melbourne, that's if I can get
through at all. I've got to make as many trips as I can before
then.'

He faced her without speaking. He had no right to ask her
to stay, no matter that he needed her knowledge and experience
or that she was the only one that Jilly trusted or Bobby respected.
He sighed. 'I'll miss you.' He smiled, and for the first time in
her life Ugly found herself blushing.

Tanner did miss Catherine during the weeks that followed, and
the passage of time did not diminish his feelings for her. Amy
missed her, too—it had been nice to have another woman to help

her with the personal things that men seldom understood, and with her gone so much more responsibility fell on Amy. Caring for the shanty took little effort, but preparing meals was a chore. Although she learnt to measure, chop and mix ingredients by touch, the fire still terrified her and even her keen sense of smell couldn't always tell her when the food was cooked. Damper in particular proved to be her downfall. Jilly was worse than useless, deliberately moving things, refusing to answer, staying quiet so that Amy wouldn't know where she was.

Joey also regretted Ugly's absence—she had been the voice of reason in the midst of so much emotion. She had remained logical and knowledgeable in the face of ignorance and grief.

Bobby alone was unaffected by Ugly's departure. She like everyone else was just an adjunct to his life, a life that didn't extend beyond the mine. He worked in it unceasingly, not even stopping for meals, rising before dawn, eating leftovers from the night before then working without a break until after dark, and he seldom thanked Amy for the meal she always saved for him.

At first he tried to oversee every facet of the operation, wishing to be both the man digging and the one operating the windlass. He wanted to go with the wash dirt to the waterhole, and when he did he berated the man left behind for not digging more. When he stayed at the mine he rebuked the others for not getting more gold out of the wash dirt, although his own efforts were usually worse than theirs.

Finally, Joey suggested that Amy could help with the washing, rocking the cradle and pouring the water while one man separated the clay and collected the gold. Bobby agreed, but took the precaution of sending Jilly with them to watch for pilfering, and he began searching their personal belongings while they slept, looking for the gold he was sure they were stealing for that was the only explanation he could accept for their lack of results.

They were supposed to take it in turns to go to the wash pools, but Bobby virtually refused to leave the mine and it was usually Joey who took the girls and made his way amongst the camps and claims to the waterholes.

Joey smiled at Amy sitting beside him on the cart. The trip was a glorious respite and even Jilly's sullen face couldn't lessen his enjoyment of it. They stopped by one of a group of stores, or rather, shanty shops that had sprung up en route. They called it a butcher even though it only carried hindquarters or fore-quarters of mutton or two tooth, or the occasional piece of kangaroo meat. The bulk of its supplies were made up of every other type of goods from picks to cigars, from rice to rum (under the counter, of course).

'How much have we got?' Amy asked.

'I'd guess about half an ounce.' He passed the chamois leather pouch containing the gold from one hand to the other, testing the weight as he did so.

'If you can't get a hindquarter a fore-quarter will do, but I definitely want some salt and some oatmeal. I can't face damper for breakfast any more.' She made a sour face.

'I don't mind doing the cooking,' Joey said.

''No, I can manage, it's just that the damper's got the better of me.'

'It would be easier if you had a proper stove.'

'That it would. Couldn't you do something with that fireplace inside?' Joey made a disgusted noise that gave Amy her answer.

'Do you want to come with me, Jilly?' Jilly didn't speak, but she climbed down from the cart. 'She's coming,' Joey said. 'Would you like to come too?'

'No, but don't let them give you less than that gold is worth.' She liked Joey, she felt protective towards him and at the same time protected by him. The sound of his footsteps on the soft earth vanished quickly in the noise of the diggings.

For a moment she listened—occasionally one voice would ring out above the rest, often a strange accent or a foreign tongue. She inhaled, testing the air, but the dust of Kangaroo Flat obliterated any other scent. The sun was warm but not burning and Amy relaxed, letting herself absorb all the sensations that surrounded her.

'I've been from Buninyong to Mount Alexander asking everyone if they've seen a blind girl with hair like ravens' wings, skin soft as swans' down and eyes like a dove, and here you are just sitting by the road waiting for me.'

'Davis,' she whispered. There was a prickling in her eyes and a tightness in her chest. She wished that she knew the sight of him and that she could see him now. He climbed onto the cart beside her and her fingers searched out the shape of his hands and face. 'Davis,' she murmured again, and tears rolled down

124

her cheek. 'We thought you were dead.' She put her arms round his neck and pulled his face close to hers. 'We searched everywhere.'

'Oh, yes,' Davis laughed. 'I bet your uncle searched every little nook and cranny hoping to find me.'

'Not Uncle John,' she gulped, 'me and Joey.' As she spoke his name she remembered that he was only a short distance away. 'Joey.' She raised her voice. 'Joey.'

At the sound of her cry he dropped everything and ran. He'd taken one pace through the door before he saw the man beside her and two paces more before he realised it was Davis.

'Davis!' He clambered up on the cart, hugging Davis then holding him at arm's length. 'We thought you were dead.' He slapped him on the shoulder. 'We looked everywhere. Where the hell have you been?'

'Ballarat, Mount Alexander, every gully and flat where they're mining gold. I knew I'd find my girl somewhere.'

'What happened to you after the fire?' Amy asked.

'I was long gone before the fire started.'

'But I thought you were working in the hold.' Joey's brows knitted with perplexity.

'That's what I wanted everyone to think, but I swam ashore while she was being moored.' He gave Joey an affectionate punch in the ribs. 'I'm sorry I didn't take you with me, but it was too much of a risk with all them guards. I didn't want you getting hurt and I knew in your heart you didn't really want to come.' He beamed at Joey.

'Why didn't you meet us at the post office?' Amy asked.

'Don't tell me your uncle actually turned up?'

'Several times,' Joey answered for her. 'I was with him.'

'Well, I'll be damned.' Davis looked suitably surprised. 'I must have missed him.'

'That's possible,' Amy said thoughtfully. 'We didn't go anywhere the first week because Uncle John was still too sick.'

'Sick?' Davis queried.

'Burns.'

There was a moment's silence before Davis spoke. 'You weren't still on the ship when the fire started?' He sounded shocked.

'No, Uncle John went back to try to save the captain.'

'I heard he died.'

'And it didn't occur to you that we'd be at the funeral?' Amy had no doubt that he was pleased to see her, but after all Tanner had said she couldn't help but doubt that he'd really been looking for her.

'I was halfway to Ballarat before the papers caught up with me.' He gave her a hug and put his other arm around Joey's shoulder.

'I thought you said you went to the post office?' Amy insisted.

'Only the first day, then when you weren't there I figured your uncle had persuaded you that I couldn't get off the ship and had taken you straight home. I bet your parents were glad to see you. Whereabouts is their claim?'

'They're dead,' Joey answered before Amy could speak. For some inexplicable reason he didn't want Davis to know that Amy had lied to him.

'I'm sorry,' Davis consoled.

'They weren't really my parents.' Amy spoke slowly, trying to think of a way to tell Davis the truth without making Joey look a fool. 'My real parents died when I was twelve.'

'Then Tanner's not your real uncle.'

'No, he only said he was to stop people thinking the wrong thing about us travelling together. He was bringing me here to live with his brother and sister-in-law, they were going to adopt me, sort of.'

'Sort of?'

'Well, I am sixteen, too old for adoption.'

Davis sensed that Amy was being too cautious with her explanation. 'Now, why would they want to adopt a child all the way from England when there must be plenty of needy ones here?'

'Uncle John arranged it because he felt responsible for my blindness. He wasn't, of course, he was just in the wrong place at the wrong time. I had no one else to care for me so he took me on.'

'Very noble.' Davis still wasn't entirely satisfied, but he knew better than to push too hard. He smiled and punched Joey again. 'What's this, a load of wash dirt? I'm down here for the same reason myself—I've thrown in with three others. We've got a claim in Eaglehawk. Where did you say your claim was?'

'White Horse Gully,' Joey answered.

'Now, why don't I ride back with you when we've finished

and see for myself where it is, say hello to your uncle?' He climbed down from the cart before either Amy or Joey could say anything. 'Don't leave without me.' He walked backwards, waving to them as he went.

Amy sighed. The elation Davis' return had brought had departed with him, and now she felt shaken and a little deflated.

'I can't believe he's really alive,' she murmured.

'Nor I,' said Joey. He was staring after the vanishing figure. 'We'd best get on with what we came for.' He picked up the reins.

'Jilly,' Amy said suddenly.

'Oh Lord, and the meat.' He climbed down from the cart, returning a short time later with the child and the supplies.

Joey could not settle to his task; his attention kept wandering to the groups of miners coming and going to and from the wash pools. He searched for Davis, illogically needing reassurance that he had truly come back. More than once Jilly's sharp eyes caught sight of gold that Joey had missed. She looked at him curiously— despite his clumsy appearance he rarely made so many mistakes.

'Who was that man,' she asked, 'the one that made Amy scream?'

'He's a friend,' Joey answered her. 'He was on the same ship as your uncle and me. We thought he'd been killed when she burnt.

She continued studying Joey's distracted face. 'Did you want him to be killed?'

'Good Lord, no, child, what a terrible thing to say.' Joey was genuinely shocked and offended, but there was the slightest hint of guilt in his reaction too.

Davis returned before they'd finished and stood watching them for a while. 'You don't seem to be getting much,' he observed.

'Sometimes you've got to dig dead for a few days before you hit the main seam.' Joey repeated Bobby's words.

'And who's this little lady?' He reached out to Jilly, who shrank back from him.

'It's Tanner's niece.'

'His real niece.' Davis was still smiling at the child. 'And how do you like having Uncle John to look after you?' Jilly drew closer to Joey, putting him between herself and Davis. 'Very good at being an uncle he is, had a lot of practice. He'll keep the likely lads away from you.'

'That's enough, Davis.' It was Amy who cautioned him. 'I'm glad you're alive and I'm pleased you're here, but if you're going to start a fight with Uncle John I'd rather you didn't come back to the camp. He's had enough misery lately.'

'I promise I won't put a foot wrong.' He put his arm round her and kissed her in a possessive gesture that made Joey turn uncomfortably to his work. Davis helped them pack up, then went to fetch his horse, one he'd managed to borrow on the pretext of being interested in buying it.

Tanner climbed out of the hole and blinked at the brightness of the light. The boy made no move to help him.

'They're a long time,' Bobby said.

'They've got to go to the store.' Tanner got himself a drink of water from the bucket that should have been in the shade of the hoist but wasn't. The water was warm with dust sitting on the top and sediment on the bottom. Tanner couldn't force himself to swallow the second mouthful, so he spat it out and emptied the rest of the pannikin over his head.

'We've not got water to waste,' the boy admonished him.

'They'll bring more back with them,' Tanner said patiently. 'When they turn up.'

'What's the hurry? We haven't got another load ready for them yet.'

'Aye, and if they time it right they won't have to do more than load up and go back.' Tanner sighed in frustration. 'Aren't you going back down?' the boy asked.

'No, it's your turn.' At first he'd tried to work harder than the boy, but Bobby's lack of appreciation coupled with the lack of results left Tanner feeling that the extra effort wasn't worthwhile. In fact he was beginning to think that none of it was worthwhile.

The boy climbed down the hole. Tanner lowered the bucket to him, then leant against the windlass listening to the dull thud of the shovel. He let his eyes lose focus, and the shimmering heat and the dust reduced everything to a yellow-brown blur. A cart materialised out of the blur. Tanner watched its progress for a moment or two, then a tug on the line demanded his attention. He hoisted the bucket to the surface, emptied it on to the pile, then lowered it to Bobby. He leant against the windlass as before and again his eyes wandered to the cart. He could make out three adult figures and a horse tied at the rear, a fair indication that it wasn't Amy and Joey, yet the cart still held his attention and the closer it came the more convinced he became that it was their cart.

Bobby tugged on the rope, but Tanner ignored the signal. The figures had begun to take shape: Joey, definitely, and Amy, and there was something uncomfortably familiar about the third. Bobby repeated the signal but Tanner didn't even notice it, for suddenly he felt as if he'd taken on a massive burden, his shoulders sagged and he had a great need for extra air. It was Davis. Bobby emerged from the pit. 'What's the matter with you?' He scrambled to where his uncle stood, and even one as self-absorbed as Bobby couldn't fail to see that something was wrong. He followed the direction of Tanner's gaze, then studied his uncle's troubled face. 'What's wrong?'

'Davis,' Tanner murmured. The boy had seen the fourth person on the cart and he realised that that was who Tanner was referring to.

'What's he want?'

It was a moment before Tanner answered. '*Everything*.'

By the time the cart had reached the diggings Tanner had regained control, and he even smiled at Davis, a weary smile, one of acceptance rather than greeting.

'Tanner.' Davis beamed at him. 'I bet you never thought you'd see me again.'

'I never believed that you died in the fire.'

'Never dared to hope, eh?' Davis swung down from the cart.

'No, it's true.' Joey followed him. 'He said all along that you'd got clear and gone to the goldfields.' Tanner and Davis exchanged a glance, and Tanner thought he detected a hint of apprehension in Davis' eyes.

'You know, I think I really will buy this horse. It's not that far from here to Eaglehawk on a good horse.' Davis helped Amy down, then turned to face Tanner. 'And there's nothing to stop me seeing you now, is there Uncle John?'

Tanner could tell by the inflection in Davis' voice that he already knew that Amy was not his niece. 'You've a mine in Eaglehawk, I gather,' Tanner said.

'Me and three others.'

129

'And these partners of yours, they won't mind you leaving them with all the work?'

'We make enough out of our claim to let us take a little time for ourselves now and then.' Davis looked contemptuously at the pile of wash dirt.

'And you can trust these partners of yours?' Bobby put in for he resented Davis' implication.

'As much as you can trust yours.' Actually Davis would have trusted Joey and Tanner far more than he trusted his current partners, however, he had found the boy easy to read and the remark was contrived to discomfort him. He walked to the load of wash dirt. 'Do you want me to help you load this?'

'No,' the boy snapped at him.

'You can help me.' Amy moved cautiously towards Davis. 'There are supplies in the cart and water too.' He took her extended hand, collected the supplies from the cart and went with her to the shanty.

Joey lifted out the clean water and followed them while Tanner and Bobby began shovelling dirt into the cart.

'Happy little family,' Davis quipped as he deposited the supplies on the table.

'Their parents are dead and they're landed with me, how do you expect them to act?'

'They don't have to be landed with you,' Davis said seductively. She drew breath to argue, but he didn't give her the chance. 'Anyway, I meant your uncle, not the children.'

'How can you expect him to be happy with what happened on the *Lady Ann* and his brother being dead and him being left with two ungrateful children and a mine that's not worth—' She stopped suddenly, unwilling to confide more to him.

'That doesn't mean you have to suffer with him, in fact, it might be easier for him if you came with me.'

'Do you really think so?' she asked sarcastically.

'He wouldn't approve of course, but in the end it might be the best all round.' The silence that followed was broken by the clatter of plates as Joey began preparing a meal. Davis frowned at him. 'Leave that Joey.' He inclined his head towards the door, indicating that Joey should go.

Joey complied, pausing outside the shanty door. Bobby was at the windlass so, presumably, Tanner was in the mine. Joey

130

had no wish to talk to the boy—he was tired of the endless snide remarks and ill temper. He walked further up the valley wall to a small copse of trees that had survived the ravages of the diggers. Joey started collecting fire wood, as he would need a reason to be away from the diggings. He laughed mirthlessly. Here he was, a grown man accountable to a thirteen-year-old boy and so afraid of trouble that he had to have an excuse to steal a few moments alone.

He sat down beside the pile of sticks he'd collected. He felt miserable and it didn't make any sense. Davis was back, he should feel happy, soon he and Davis would be doing all the things they'd planned. Even as the thought occurred to him he knew he was no longer part of Davis' plan. He rested his elbows on his knees and his head in his hands. Amy—Davis had come looking for Amy, not for him. Davis would take Amy and go and he'd be left behind. Joey felt as if he was going to cry. They were the two people for whom he cared most in the world and there was no place in their lives for him.

'Is your mother dead?'

Joey jumped at the sound of Jilly's voice. She had crawled close to him, close enough to see the tears in his eyes. 'No.'

'Then why are you crying?'

'Davis is my friend. I thought he was dead and I'm crying 'cause I'm glad he's alive.' Joey choked on the words, for as much as he may have wanted them to be the truth they were not.

She sat beside him. 'My mother's dead and she's never coming back.'

Joey put his arm around her. 'I know,' he said. 'Your mother and your father both, it's a sad thing but we'll look after you.'

She put her tiny arms around his broad chest. 'I like you,' she said, 'you and Ugly.'

'What about Amy?' Joey couldn't imagine anyone not liking Amy. 'Your brother and your Uncle John,' he added as an afterthought.

'Bobby's mean.' Her eyes narrowed. 'Uncle John's all right, but I don't like Amy or that other man. They made you cry.' She got up and ran away before he could speak, before he could deny it, before he was forced to lie.

Davis returned next evening just before tea, bringing fresh bread and four of the smallest roasting birds that anyone had ever seen.

131

He had bought the bread from a woman at a claim near his. She was earning more from her bread-making than her husband was from his mine. Nobody asked where he had obtained the chickens.

He insisted on doing the cooking himself and the aroma of the meal he prepared was delicious. However, the tiny bundles of flesh that he dished out were far less inviting.

'Have you heard about the singer?' Davis asked between mouthfuls.

'What singer?'

'Some singer that's touring the goldfields, the songbird of the south, probably can't sing a note but—'

'She can,' Tanner interrupted.

'That's right,' Amy agreed. 'We met her on the way here, she has a lovely voice.'

'Well, they're setting up on Kangaroo Flat for a concert tomorrow night. You'll come, won't you Amy?'

'Why don't the three of you go?' Tanner suggested.

'Why don't we all go?' Amy asked.

Tanner smiled. It was tempting, to listen to Loretta's sweet voice and spend some time away from the oppressive atmosphere of the mine, to be able to keep an eye on Amy and Davis, but he shook his head. 'No, I'll stay here with the children, but say hello to Zeke for me.'

The concert began a little after dark. The stage was a small wooden structure raised six foot above the ground, with a canvas canopy over the top. The piano that Zeke played was in the middle of the stage, and all above and around it were strings of lanterns. Loretta appeared from under the stage just as the crowd became restless. She looked stunning: her golden hair was held in place by a dozen red ribbons and she had a single ribbon at her throat. Her bare shoulders were framed by a ruffle of black lace, the dress was red with a frill of black lace around the bottom and the bodice was of brilliant gold brocade and bows of similar material dotted the skirt. The crowd was immediately silent.

Zeke struck a chord and Loretta sang, her clear, sweet voice carrying easily in the still night even to those furthest from the stage. She sang for about twenty minutes, ending with 'The Ballad of Bold Jack Donohue'.

'Did you like that?' Zeke yelled as the last notes died away.

His answer was thunderous applause. 'Would you like to hear more?' More loud applause. He produced a small pannikin. 'Can you see this?' He held it up. 'Can you fill it with gold?' As one the miners reached into their pockets for their gold.

The cup was soon full and Loretta was singing again, but this time she sang for only fifteen minutes before Zeke moved amongst the company again. So it continued with shorter and shorter intervals between each collection until Zeke announced that Loretta was tired and that perhaps they would play to this delightful audience again sometime.

'One more song,' a voice near Davis boomed. 'We'll fill the cup for one more song.' Zeke moved through the crowd towards the sound of the voice. 'Over here at the back.' Amy could hear the crowd shifting as Zeke approached, the sound of the gold being placed in the pannikin, Zeke's deliberate movement amongst the miners' shuffling steps.

'Hello Zeke,' she said as he passed. 'And hello from Uncle John, too.'

'Well now.' He grinned at Amy and Joey while the miners poured gold into his cup. 'Why don't you two come on up the front, Loretta would just love to see you.' The crowd parted before Zeke as he led Amy back to the stage.

'Up here,' Loretta greeted her warmly then Zeke led her to the piano. He showed her a combination of four notes by placing her hands on the keys and pushing each finger in sequence. She got the idea quickly.

'I have an assistant,' he announced to the crowd then began to play, tapping Amy every time she should join in. The result was greeted with applause and cries of more. Loretta shook her head and touched her throat. Zeke nodded.

'Joey,' he called. Joey climbed obligingly onto the stage. 'Dance with Loretta.' Joey didn't have time to protest before Zeke started to play a polka and Loretta swung herself into his arms. He danced stiffly but in time to the music. After a few rounds Loretta caught Amy by the hand and in one deft movement exchanged places with her. While they continued to dance to the clapping of hands and the stamping of feet, Loretta disappeared beneath the stage.

Amy clung tightly to Joey at first, the whirling, turning dance making her dizzy. Slowly she relaxed as she started to anticipate Joey's movements and to match her own to them. She lifted her head confidently—her face was alight with joy and exhilaration. Davis caught sight of her expression—he'd never seen her look more alive. He smiled to himself as he edged towards the stage. He started up the steps, but a massive arm caught him across the neck and chest and threw him to the ground.

'No one on the stage.' Paddy stood between Davis and the steps. He smiled cheerfully. 'Sorry, no one on the stage.' Davis nodded and made a show of getting slowly to his feet, then in one quick movement he side-stepped Paddy and vaulted onto the stage. He was caught mid-flight by a group of miners who had witnessed the exchange. They dragged him to the ground and the more he struggled the more fiercely they restrained him.

'Leave him,' Joey shouted, deserting Amy and rushing to Davis' aid. 'Leave him.' He pushed the men aside, dragging them off Davis. The men retaliated and the incident threatened to escalate into a full scale brawl, but Zeke's voice rang out above the melee.

'The songbird of the south!' Loretta reappeared wearing a long black shawl that covered her head, shoulders, the gold bodice and much of the skirt. Most of the miners fell silent immediately and those who didn't were quickly brought to task by the others. Zeke played a single note and Loretta sang 'Ave Maria' in her pure soprano voice. The hushed crowd stood motionless even after she'd finished, enraptured by the utter beauty of her voice. She sang several other hymns, ending with 'Rock of Ages'. As she descended beneath the stage Zeke turned out most of the lanterns. The aura, the magic was gone and reluctantly the crowd dispersed.

Amy tinkered with the piano while Joey, Paddy and Davis sorted out their differences. Gradually she began to pick out a tune, one that she'd heard as a child.

' "Greensleeves" '. Zeke recognised it. 'Now where did you learn that?'

'I just remembered it.' Amy smiled.

'You've never had lessons?' She shook her head. 'Well, you should have.'

'How much for the piano?' Davis asked.

'More than you can afford.' Zeke laughed. 'Come on,' he slapped Paddy on the back, 'let's get out of here.'

'You'll have a piano one day.' Davis helped Amy down the steps. 'Lessons too. The best of everything and anything you want.' He was patting her hand, the same compulsive gesture he'd employed on the ship. 'Come with me Amy, come with me now.'

'I can't.'

'Why not? I'm making a fortune out of my mine, and soon I'll be able to give you all I promised.'

'I can't.'

'It's Tanner, isn't it, he's found some way of stopping you.'

'You don't understand.'

'Come on, Davis, we need a hand,' Zeke called. 'We've got to be clear of this valley by sunrise.'

CHAPTER 17

✦✦✦✦✦✦✦✦✦✦✦✦✦✦

T HE PRE-DAWN chill woke Tanner, who was half sitting,
half lying by the ashes that had once been a fire. He stared
at the lifeless coals then up at the stars, calculating the time from
his knowledge of the heavens. He got stiffly to his feet and walked
to the shanty. He was about to enter when he heard the tinkling
of a piano. He hesitated and again the sound came, this time
accompanied by a chorus of voices. Tanner looked in the direction
of the sound and the shape of a dray appeared. He watched as
it came towards him.

'Well, if Mohammed won't come to the mountain . . .' Zeke
yelled as Tanner became visible to him.

'Uncle John, listen.' Amy played the first nine bars of
'Greensleeves', ending with a strangely dissonant sound.

'It wasn't your fault, honey,' Zeke consoled. 'The way she gets
jolted and jostled around I've got to tune her before every concert.'
The dray came to a halt beside Tanner and Joey climbed out.
He reached up to help Amy down, but Davis edged between them
and lifted her down, then, holding her close to him he turned
the action into an embrace.

'Hold on there you two,' Loretta teased, 'you're not married
yet.'

'Not yet,' Davis replied.

'There'll be no wedding 'til I get back,' Paddy bellowed, 'for
I love to toast the bride.' He unfurled his whip and all moved
back to give him room.

'There will be a wedding,' Davis murmured, and the remark
might easily have been lost in the calls of 'goodbye' except that
Tanner's slight reaction told Amy otherwise.

'Please, Davis, not now.' Amy eased herself out of his arms.

'You'd be better off coming with me.'

'I can't.' Amy felt a tightness in her chest, the awful feeling
that always possessed her whenever Davis and Tanner were together.

'I love you, Amy, and my claim will make me rich.'

'Rich claims don't guarantee a home nor passion a marriage.' It was Tanner who responded.

'And the fact that you gave your word on the ship doesn't guarantee it will be kept now we're here on the goldfields.'

'I've not broken my word.'

'Then Amy can come with me.'

'If that's the choice she finally makes, but she has a home with me for as long as she wants it and she doesn't have to go anywhere or do anything because of some agreement you and I made on the *Lady Ann*.' Tanner stepped past Davis, taking Amy by the arm and turning her towards the shanty.

Bobby blocked their path, glaring at everybody then addressing his uncle. 'Ready for work are you?'

'It's still dark.'

'Aye, and it'll be morning soon and this lazy lot will be wanting to sleep.'

'That's right,' Tanner said, 'so you and I will finish this load once it's light, then we'll take it down to the water holes and they can get a couple of hours' sleep while we're gone.'

'That'll put us almost a load behind.'

'Behind what? We're not working to any schedule here.'

'I see, I see.' The boy shook with temper, his eyes flashing from one person to another. 'I work while they take time to do as they like.'

'We work,' Tanner corrected, 'and if you'd like some time to do as you like by all means take it.' The boy stood facing the man, knowing that he had neither the wit nor the strength to defeat him. Slowly he turned and walked to the mine.

'So this is what you'd have her refuse me for,' Davis' voice was soft and even, 'to work a worthless mine for a selfish brat who'd deny her even a moment's pleasure.' Davis waited for Tanner to face him before he continued. 'This isn't the ship, she doesn't need you or your lie any more. It isn't her parents who are dead nor her inheritance that's invested here. She's a right to go some place else, some place where she'll find a little happiness, for sure as God she'll never find it here.'

'No.' Tanner's voice was hoarse as if he was controlling his emotions. 'There's no happiness here. My brother and his wife are dead and nothing I can do will make this mine produce gold,

137

no matter how much the boy wants it, and I can't make Jilly smile or give Amy back her sight or raise Buchanan from the dead either.' His voice had built steadily to a crescendo, and when he stopped it left an expectant silence during which Tanner's mind embarked on an odd train of thought.

Bright images of the fire forced themselves into his mind, then words and phrases from different conversations. Joey had said Davis was in the hold, Davis had said he was on the shore and Buchanan had said 'Arson'. The image of the dying captain faded from Tanner's mind, leaving him face to face with the very real Davis. 'When did you get off the *Lady Ann*?' he asked quietly.

'I told you.' Davis seemed less surprised by the question than he should have been.

'You told us you climbed overboard and swam ashore and I'm asking you when?'

'I'm not sure of the time.' Davis sounded evasive, at least to Tanner's ear. 'Right after I talked to you.'

'Ah yes, our conversation when you offered to marry Amy and take her off the ship, leaving Joey and me to sail back to England together.' He glanced at Joey, but for once his face revealed nothing. 'Let's see, I'd all but finished packing when we spoke, I went up on deck, waited perhaps a minute for Buchanan, went ashore, said goodbye, walked to the end of the wharf, then somebody shouted "Fire".' He looked contentiously at Davis. 'In that time you got off the ship without any of the crew seeing you, got on shore without any of the guards seeing you and got so far away from the *Lady Ann* that you didn't see the smoke of her burning or hear the screams of her dying.'

'That's right,' Davis said impassively.

'It's a shame you didn't wait a little longer, fire makes a very good diversion.' They held each other's gaze for a moment before Davis laughed derisively, and to Tanner it seemed a contrived response.

'I know you don't like me,' Davis said, 'and that you'd do anything to keep me from Amy, but surely you're not suggesting that I had anything to do with that fire?'

'Why not? You had no time for Buchanan and burning the ship was as good a way as any to make sure you didn't have to sail on her.'

Davis laughed again. 'Oh, for heaven's sake,' he said.

'You could have gone back to the hold after you left me and started the fire then,' Tanner insisted.

'Anyone who was in that hold when the fire started would've been burnt.'

'How do you know that?'

'It was all the talk in Ballarat.'

'You could've started the fire before you came to see me, used something that would take a while to ignite.'

'You and Amy were well off the ship before the fire started.'

'And how do you know that? Was that all the talk in Ballarat too?'

'Amy told me.' Davis had answered all Tanner's questions good humouredly and with just the right amount of incredulity to portray innocence, and as the two men stood facing each other Tanner realised he had no basis for his accusation. He turned wearily towards the mine, but Davis called him back.

'That's a hell of a thing to do to a man, call him a murderer in front of his friends. That is what you're saying isn't it, that I started the fire that killed five of my shipmates and the captain too?' He waited a moment, not expecting an answer. 'What have you got against me, Tanner? What did I ever do to you to make you lie to me and about me?' There was anger in his tone and indignation. 'You told me Amy was your niece and she wasn't. You told Amy I'd seduce her then desert her and I haven't. And now you're telling Joey that I set fire to the ship and left him on it to burn. Why?' he demanded. 'I saved your life and this is how you repay me.' Tanner drew breath to speak and if Davis had said no more he might even have apologised, but Davis had sensed victory and wanted it to be absolute. 'It's Amy isn't it? It's all because of Amy.' He didn't give Tanner time to answer. 'You can't bear me being near her, can you? Why not, eh? Do you want her for yourself, is that it? Or have you already had her? Is that why you've got to keep me away so I won't find out how you've been using her all the time she's been calling you uncle?' Tanner sprang at Davis, grabbing him by the throat.

'No!' Joey yelled, traversing the short distance between them with amazing speed.

'Or is it because you blinded her!'

Joey had grabbed Tanner, pinning his arms to his sides, but

it was unnecessary. Davis' last words had already sapped all the power from his body.

'Are you frightened that she'll tell me how you did it?' Davis continued. 'Tell me, was it a beating, or was it something more subtle?'

'Stop it!' Amy stumbled towards them. 'Stop it.' It was Davis that her groping hands found, Davis that she clung to as she spoke. 'It was an accident, my being blind was never Uncle John's fault, never, and all those things you said about him aren't true, you know they aren't true.' She was crying and Davis knew he'd overplayed his hand. 'I know you didn't burn the ship, and I know we lied to you and that you never lied to us, and I'm sorry.' Sobs punctuated each phrase. 'But you had no right to say those things, no right to make me sound like a whore.'

'Amy, no, good Lord, no, I never meant that.' He held her to him. 'You're my lady, my fine, fine lady.' He held her tightly, looking foolishly at Tanner for reassurance.

Joey released Tanner and moved cautiously towards Davis. 'It's been a long night and we're all tired, losing our tempers and saying things we don't mean.' He gently took Amy's arm. 'I think we could all do with a bit of sleep.' He began to usher her forward, but Davis pulled her back.

'Come with me now, Amy.'

'I can't.' Amy's voice shook as she spoke, but she was determined not to cry any more.

'Why not?' Davis demanded. 'Surely to God you don't want to stay here.'

'Please, Davis, you don't understand.'

'If you're waiting for his blessing you're wasting your time. He'll see us in hell before he gives us that.'

'I don't want to talk about it now.' She stumbled over the words as her mind searched for a way to end the conversation, the argument, the anger. 'I'll talk to you later.'

'When?'

'At the water holes, this afternoon.' It was Joey who answered.

'Yes.' Amy removed Davis' hand from her arm. 'We'll get some sleep now and talk later.' The effort of controlling her emotions made her voice hushed, and each phrase was produced with great difficulty. 'You go now, please. We'll talk later.' She touched him gently on the chest. 'Please.'

'Davis hesitated for a moment, then turned angrily towards his horse. Amy listened to the sound of it galloping away.

'Joey.' She reached out for him. 'I've sort of lost my bearings. Could you take me to the shanty?'

Once inside the shanty Amy broke down, sobbing heartbrokenly, and none of Joey's clumsy attempts could console her.

'Why? Why are they doing this?' she demanded. 'Why are they saying such terrible things when they know they aren't true? Why does Uncle John hate Davis so much? Why does Davis keep on goading him? Why?' She stopped to regain control of her breathing. 'If they both care for me as much as they say, why can't they get on together for my sake? Why are they forcing me to choose between them?' She choked back another sob. 'I don't want to get married yet, I'm only sixteen, I'm not ready, I can't, I can't.' Her voice was strained by crying and her throat ached from controlling the tears. 'I want to go out with Davis to concerts and dances and for walks in the evenings. I want him to come here and sit down and talk with us, like a proper courtship. I don't want to get married and find we're still strangers. I don't want him to find out too late that I'm not what he thought I was.' She held her breath while she fumbled for a handkerchief.

'No man could ever be disappointed with you,' Joey said earnestly.

She touched his arm gratefully. 'Oh Joey, what am I to do?' She looked so abjectly miserable and appealing that Joey couldn't resist the temptation to put his arm around her.

'It'll be all right,' he said. 'Things have a way of working themselves out.' He guided her to the bed. 'Now you get some sleep, things won't seem so bad after.' She lay down. 'Would you like a drink of water or some tea?'

'No, thank you.' She took Joey's hand. 'It was such a lovely night, why did it have to end like this?'

Joey didn't know how to answer her. All he could do was hold her hand gently and watch until her erratic sobs eased to the rhythmical breaths of sleep. He watched her for a long time, even after he was certain she was sleeping. Propriety told him he should leave, that he should not be alone with her while she slept, but a stronger instinct made him remain until sleep overtook him too.

Sometime during the argument Bobby had climbed out of the

mine and had begun loading the wash dirt onto the cart. When Tanner joined him he seemed oblivious to all that had happened. They finished their task and drove to the wash pools with not so much as a word passing between them. The load yielded no more gold than usual and they returned in the same stony silence.

'Still sleeping they are,' Bobby said as they entered the deserted camp, but before he could begin his usual tirade Joey appeared from the mine. He observed them but said nothing, preferring to get on with the job of hauling the dirt to the surface. The boy got off the cart and into the mine without another word to anyone. Tanner moved less enthusiastically, taking the fresh water to the shanty first then joining Joey at the windlass. Tanner endured the uncomfortable silence for a few interminable minutes, then threw caution to the wind.

'I know Davis is your friend and that you don't want to believe anything bad about him but . . .'

'You're driving her away.' Joey turned on him with such viciousness that Tanner was dumbfounded. 'You're making it so she has to choose between you, making it so she has to go with him just to prove she doesn't believe your stupid stories.' He was yelling and his face betrayed the depth of his feeling. 'She doesn't want to get married, she's just a child, she should be going about and having fun the way the young ones do, not having to choose between this dreary place and your unreasoning hatred or Davis with his demands for marriage.' The torrent of words ended as quickly as it had begun and the anger faded from Joey's face, leaving only the sadness.

Tanner was still too stunned to speak, and by the time he found his voice the truth of Joey's words had started to dawn on him. It was true, the more he attacked Davis the more she would defend him. Tanner moved almost unwillingly towards the shanty. When Davis had reviled him she had been drawn to him to protect him, so, logically the more he vilified Davis the more she would align herself with him. Tanner hesitated at the shanty door. Amy had been asleep when he'd taken the water in, and perhaps it would be unwise to wake her.

'Joey,' she called. 'Joey, is that you?'

'No, it's me.' Tanner answered her as he entered. She didn't respond. 'I came in before but you were asleep.' Still no answer. 'I want to talk to you.'

142

'Strike while the iron's hot, eh, Uncle John?'

He ignored the acrimony in her voice. 'I was wrong to accuse Davis.'

'Wrong to accuse him.' She jumped at his words. 'Not wrong about his intentions towards me, not wrong about him burning the ship, not wrong about him dumping Joey, just wrong to have made your feelings public.'

'I can't help what I believe.' It was a gentle persuasive tone and it made her even angrier.

"Do you know what my father used to say? He used to say that if you tell a person they're evil often enough they'll believe they're evil, and if they believe they're evil they will act accordingly.' She moved closer to him, facing him squarely, certain that she commanded his full attention. 'That's what you're doing to Davis, isn't it, driving him until he does what you expect of him?'

Tanner would have liked to argue, but his own experience had taught him that, at least in part, she was correct. All his life people had told him he was nothing more than a liar and a thief, and no matter how hard he tried it had always come back to that.

'You've always hated him, right from the first time you saw him.'

'That's an exaggeration.'

'Is it?'

'I've always mistrusted him.'

'Why?'

Tanner groped helplessly for an answer. 'You didn't see the way he looked when he talked about the gold. You don't see the look on his face when he senses victory.'

'I don't see anything,' she said bitterly, and it hurt him more deeply than she could possibly know for she had forgotten that he still carried the full burden of guilt for her blindness. 'I wish to God I *could* see, then I wouldn't have to depend on you or Davis or anybody.' It was the culmination of all the frustration of the last few months and once the great catharsis began it could not easily be stemmed. 'Do you know what it's like to be trapped everywhere you go, to be limited to the space you can explore by hand and commit to memory? Do you know what it's like to be afraid to be alone, to be afraid to take a step, to wake up and not know if it's day or night, to smell fire and not know whether it's safe or not, to have someone stand right in front of you and not know whether they're there or not? Do you know what it's like to be shut in by great walls of darkness that reduce the greatest vista to the stretch of an arm or the width of a pace? Do you know what it's like to have every hope or dream curtailed, to have every decision revolve around your limitations?'

Tanner could have argued that everyone faces limitations and that few people ever reach their full potential let alone realise their hopes and dreams, but he was too shaken by the bitterness of her attack.

'Do you know what I'd do if I could see? I'd go to Davis and I'd live with him, not as man and wife but as friends, that'd be my terms and I'd leave if he didn't accept them, but if I went to him like this, blind and helpless, then he'd own me as surely as you own me now.'

'I don't own you.' Tanner found his voice at last.

'Don't you?' Amy laughed mirthlessly. 'You've owned me since the day Auntie walked off and left me with you. Yours to leave on the streets to starve, yours to put to the workhouse, yours to bring to Australia whether I wanted to come or not. I'm not saying you haven't been kind to me, you have, even if it was only out of guilt.' She stopped, finally aware of the effect her words must be having on him.

'Maybe it was guilt at first.' His voice was hoarse and the pain it expressed made Amy feel ashamed. 'Maybe was guilt,' he repeated, 'but not now, not for a long time. I just don't want to see you hurt.' He stumbled over the words, and if Amy could have seen his face, the pain and anguish it reflected would have broken her.

She took a deep breath. 'I don't want to talk about it any more,' she said. 'I don't want to say things I'll regret.' She felt a familiar tightness in her throat and a prickling behind her eyes, but this time she was determined not to cry. She made for the door. 'I'll get some lunch.'

The noise of the argument had woken Jilly, who sat on her makeshift bed wide-eyed and too afraid to speak. Amy's departure left only Tanner in the room and she shrank from him. Her slight movement caught his attention. He came towards her, towering above her, grim faced and menacing. She scrambled to her feet.

'It's all right, Jilly.' His voice rasped as he spoke and she cringed under the advancing hand. Before he could touch her she bolted past him out of the shanty screaming for Joey. Joey sprang from the mine, dropping to his knees as he reached the child. She threw her arms around his neck and buried her face in his filthy shirt.

'What the hell's the matter with you?' Bobby yelled at her. 'Go on, get out of here. We're too busy to waste time with your stupid screaming.' He walked over to them. 'Go on, get.' He went to grab her arm, but Joey pushed him away.

'Leave her,' he warned.

'I'm getting lunch.' Amy called. She wasn't quite sure what was going on, but she'd had enough argument for one day.

'Lunch, is it?' Bobby said scornfully. 'I suppose soon you'll be wanting tea and drinks, like they have at the cricket.'

'There's some bread left from last night—' Amy ignored the boy, '— and a bit of cold stew we can spread on it. I'll make the tea.'

'It's an easy life for some, isn't it?' The boy continued with his heated sarcasm. 'Out all night having fun, sleep all morning, then it's up in time for lunch. No one wants to work in the mine, but you're happy enough with the meal it provides.'

'Shut up.' The force and strain in Tanner's voice shocked everyone. 'Just shut up.' He appeared from behind Amy and advanced on the boy as he spoke. 'We are all sick and tired of your smart, snide remarks, we're sick of your self righteousness, self pitying, self indulgence. We all work here, even though we'd all gladly chuck it in and start afresh someplace else, but we don't, we keep on working in this useless pit because of you, because we don't have the heart to shatter your dreams despite all your rudeness and ingratitude, but not much longer, my boy, not much longer, I'm warning you.'

At first the boy had been shocked by the sudden anger and the power of the man, but as his speech continued the old resentment reasserted itself, his eyes narrowed and he drew himself up straight to face the man.

'My father died for this mine,' he said with great dignity.

'Then your father was a fool.' It was the cold, hard truth from which Tanner could no longer protect the boy. Robert Tanner had died fighting over a worthless hole in the ground, and the giant nugget he saw was a mere hallucination, the result of concussion. A look of pure hatred crossed the boy's face before he turned and stalked back to the mine, and Tanner knew that if a wish could kill he would now lie dead at the boy's feet.

Bobby had vanished from sight before Tanner found the strength to move. He headed in the direction of the fire, but as he came closer he could see no place for himself amongst the others. He walked past them to the same copse of trees to which Joey had gone for solice.

He pushed between the bushy wattle that surrounded the stand of trees and into the cathedral-like heart, where the trunks of the gums stood in semblance of columns and the branches and leaves cast the same eerie shadows as stained glass windows. Unlike Joey he didn't make the excuse of collecting wood, he simply sat in the grass leaning against one of the tree trunks and, unlike Joey, he wasn't surprised by the arrival of another for he heard the sound of approaching footsteps. She made her way between the trees, the golden sun at her back like an aura around her silhouette.

'Catherine,' he murmured. She looked a little surprised to see him.

'Every time I come here I expect to find that some fool miner's found gold here and they've torn this place apart like they have everything else.' She halted when she reached him. He was looking up at her, but there wasn't a trace of a smile on his face. She'd seen him when he heard of his sister-in-law's death and his brother's death too, she'd seen the sadness and the pain, but she'd never seen him like this. He had the look of a man beaten. 'What's wrong?' She squatted beside him.

He gazed blankly at her face, there was a hint of a smile, warmth and gentleness, qualities rare in Ugly's usually guarded expression.

'Everything,' he sighed.

She slid sideways into a sitting position, not quite facing him. 'Mining too hard for you, is it?' she teased.

He shook his head slightly. 'There's no gold.' He looked at her. 'You knew, didn't you?'

'I guessed as much but it wasn't my place to say. Still, now you've found out for yourself there's nothing to stop you trying someplace else.'

'Boy doesn't believe it,' he said laconically, 'thinks we're not trying or holding out on him.'

'Tell him it's not so.' She shrugged. 'Tell him you're moving and that's it.'

'He hates me,' Tanner said flatly. 'He resents me and he hates me.'

'No.'

'Yes. His parents sacrificed everything for the gold, their home, their security, their few possessions, even their lives. If there's no gold then that sacrifice was for nothing. If there is gold then he has to share the fruits of their sacrifice with us. Either way he resents us and he hates me, every day we continue with this useless digging he hates me more, but if I were to make him give it up he'd never forgive me.' He looked at her hopelessly. 'Damned if I do and damned if I don't.'

'He'll come round,' she said.

Tanner shook his head. 'Jilly's terrified of me.'

'Give her time, it's only been a few weeks.'

'She adores Joey and you, you've only known her those same few weeks.' He sighed. 'She tolerates Amy, ignores Bobby, but she's terrified of me and I'm frightened to try to get close to her in case she runs away like she did before.' He lapsed into silence and Ugly found herself wanting to reach out to touch him, to reassure him and convey the fondness she felt for him, but such gestures were alien to her and she combated the impulse.

'They're only children,' she said at last. 'Their parents are dead, they need time to get used to the way things have changed.' His face remained immobile and Ugly couldn't think of how to comfort him. 'You've still got Amy and Joey, and me,' she added, but the last words were lost in Tanner's derisive laughter. He noted her puzzlement.

'Things have changed now Davis is back.' Ugly waited for him to clarify the remark. It was obvious from his voice, his face and even the slump of his shoulders that Davis' return had contributed greatly to his problems.

When finally Ugly realised that he was going to say no more she asked: 'Who's Davis?'

He looked up into her eyes, astounded that the one person he still felt close to didn't know who Davis was. He laughed, more genuinely this time.

'Davis,' he said, 'you want to know about Davis.' His eyes ceased to focus as all the events of the last few months came vividly to mind. 'I first saw Davis in a tavern in London. He was trying to persuade, no, not trying, he was persuading Joey to join the crew of the *Lady Ann* with the intention of jumping ship here and going prospecting.' He paused. 'You know that look some men get when they talk about gold?' She nodded. 'Well, he had that look and it's really all I've got against him.' He went on with his story, trying to include the tiny nuances of expression, the odd words and gestures that had made him mistrust Davis. '. . . while his hands were healing he got to know Amy, then he persuaded her to meet him secretly at night.'

'Did he . . . were they . . .' Ugly didn't know how to phrase the question, but her meaning was clear.

'No, and the meetings stopped when I found out about them, but by then Amy really cared for him.' He studied her face, trying to gauge what effect, if any, his words were having. 'Later he pulled a knife on me because he thought I'd planned to take Amy off the ship and not tell him where we were going.'

'Does Amy know that?'

Tanner shook his head. 'It didn't matter at the time and I doubt she'd believe me now.' Tanner resumed his story, but stopped when he came to the day of the fire. He closed his eyes, forcing himself to recall clearly his last meeting with Davis aboard the *Lady Ann*. 'Davis came to my cabin while I was packing. I felt sorry for him at first, but he wouldn't admit defeat, he wanted to marry Amy there and then, leave the ship with her and to hell with Joey. I said it wasn't possible, but there was no reasoning with him, he was like a cornered animal and nothing and no one was going to stop him.' He took a breath. 'Then the *Lady Ann* caught fire and Davis was missing.'

Ugly had no need to ask Tanner if he thought Davis started the fire, the implication was clear. Instead she asked: 'Have you heard his side of it?'

'Oh, yes.' Tanner laughed sardonically.

'You told him that you suspect him?'

He snorted at the question. 'Him, Amy, Joey, even Bobby could've heard.' His eyes clouded with fatigue and frustration at his own stupidity. 'And not a shred of evidence, so not one of them believes me.' He looked at her appealingly. 'I'm so afraid she's going to go with Davis just to prove to him that she doesn't believe my accusation.'

'And you're certain that would be a bad thing?'

'He'll hurt her.' Tanner still couldn't give substance to his groundless fears. 'He's cunning and he's cruel and if Amy ceases to be what he wants, if she thwarts him . . .' He left the rest to Ugly's imagination.

'You're a good father,' she said.

'I'm not even her uncle.' He looked at her. She was smiling that strange, crooked smile of hers. 'I worry about her so much, I never worried about anyone before. I've cared for people but I've never worried about them, not like this.'

'You're a good father,' she repeated, and he understood.

CHAPTER 18

++++++++++++++

TANNER WALKED with Ugly to the camp, and all but Bobby were delighted by her return. Jilly accepted Ugly's gift of sweets, her tiny face beaming with pure pleasure. She hugged Ugly, touching her face and hair as if to make sure she was real, and then she took the lollies and hid them in the shanty.

'That's the first time I've seen her smile,' Tanner mused.

'Give her a chance.' Ugly turned to Amy. 'I've got that goat for you and a couple of hens.' She glanced at Joey. 'It's true they're not laying well, but they're young so you'll have eggs aplenty in the spring and a couple now and then in the winter too.'

'Are you going to bring the dray up here?' Tanner asked. 'Spend the night with us?'

'I should be getting on.' She looked at Tanner and the little brightness that was left in his face faded, leaving him looking grey and old and tired. 'Still, I suppose another day won't make that much difference.'

He smiled. 'I'll give you a hand.' He took her arm as they walked down to the dray, the way a gentleman might escort a lady, and although she looked surprised she didn't pull away from him.

He walked beside her as she guided the team back to the camp, listening to the tongue-lashing she was giving old Willie.

'I bet he wouldn't recognise a kind word if you said it to him,' Tanner observed.

'That's assuming I'd know one to say.'

'I could teach you a few,' he said. Her features tensed, holding firm her expression for fear he would see how strongly he affected her. So often his words made her see her life as it might have been, as it should have been, and at such time the feeling of deprivation was overwhelming.

'I'm glad you're staying.' Amy drew Ugly aside when they returned to the camp. 'Joey and I have got to go to the wash pools now but I want to talk to you later.' The sound of Joey approaching terminated their conversation. He led Amy to the cart.

'They're meeting Davis at the wash pools.' Tanner had appeared at Ugly's elbow.

'Joey,' she called, 'I've a mind to ride down to the flat with you.' She turned to Tanner. 'You don't mind do you?' He shook his head.

Davis joined them before they reached the wash pool, and one might have been excused for thinking that he'd been waiting for them. He stared at Ugly's scar but maintained an expression of indifference.

'Are you here to give Joey a hand?' he asked optimistically.

'No, that's Amy's job.'

'I was hoping to have a private word with her,' he persisted.

'Amy?' Ugly glanced at the girl.

'Would you mind?'

'Not if that's what you want.' Amy nodded, and before she could say any more Davis leant across the cart, grabbing her round the waist.

'Hang on,' he said, lifting her onto the horse. At first she gasped, then laughed with exhilaration as she realised what was happening and warmed to the thrill of the experience.

Ugly marked their course and after she'd helped Joey set up she took one of the cart horses and rode to the spot where she'd seen Davis and Amy dismount. She could hear Davis' voice as she crept silently through the bush—it was soft and enticing. She caught the words 'gold' and 'fine lady' then Amy broke in, her voice sounding loud after Davis' hypnotic whisper.

'It's not the money,' she pleaded. 'I don't need a fine house, I don't have to be a fine lady. I don't want to be looked after and protected. I want to have worth.'

'You'll always have worth to me,' he murmured.

'As what?' she demanded. 'What do you see in me?'

'You're beautiful.'

'Ha,' she laughed. 'Is that it? Well, accidents happen you know, I wasn't always blind. Another mistake and I could look like Ugly.'

'It wouldn't matter to me.'

'Wouldn't it? I heard the way your voice changed when you

saw her face, the coolness in your oh so polite words.'

'You're imagining it.'

'I bet there wasn't a flicker of expression on your face, that's why you think no one would notice, but I could hear it in your voice.'

'Don't be stupid,' he scolded, moving closer to her. 'I love you, I want to marry you and one day we'll have a fine house and —'

'What if we don't? And if you end up with nothing but hard graft and a bunch of littl'uns with naught but a blind wife to look after them?'

'Amy,' he said enticingly.

'No.' She pulled away from him. 'Maybe you will have a fine house one day and, if it means that much to you, maybe you'd be better off looking for the gold without me tagging along.'

'And when I find the gold?'

'I'm not making any promises.' She laughed suddenly. 'A year ago, in London when I still had my sight, I'd have jumped at the chance to marry you, I'd have loved you for all your compliments and promises of gold, but I've changed and there's so much more I want now, things my father tried to show me when I was too small to understand, music and poetry, stories, beliefs, he loved them all.' She touched Davis' hand. 'He wasn't so unlike you, he wanted to escape, "the oppression of poverty" he called it, and what you seek to do with wealth he sought to do with knowledge.' She curled her fingers over his hand. 'I care for you, you've made me feel things that I never knew I could feel, but I'm not sure that's enough or that it will last, so I can't make any promises for the future.' She tightened her grip on his hand. 'And I can't leave Uncle John, not now.'

'Why not?' Davis wrenched his hand from her grip.

'He needs me and I owe him so much.'

'For blinding you.'

'It's not his fault I'm blind, I told you that.' Davis made a guttural noise that expressed his disbelief. 'It's true Davis, I . . .' The words stopped coming, some force more powerful than her desire to be honest prevented her from telling him that she'd allowed Tanner to believe he'd blinded her even though she knew that it was someone else. 'I have to be sure he knows that I don't blame him. I have to stop him blaming himself.'

'And then do you think you'll be free of him?'

'Perhaps not, but he'll be free of me.'

'That's not what he wants. He'll never set you free, he'll use your blindness to imprison you and never let you have a man.' There was a chance that he was right, but she doubted it just as she doubted all of the things Tanner had said about him.

'I won't leave him now. Please don't make me choose. I don't want to lose you again.'

'And how do you plan to prevent that?' he said peevishly. 'What if he won't let us meet any more?'

'He will.'

'What if he doesn't? This isn't the ship, you can't just slip away into the night and we can't rely on Joey to help us either.'

'I'm sure we could rely on Joey.' Something about Davis' attitude to Joey had always annoyed her. 'But it would hardly be fair to him, in fact none of this is fair to him. He came to Australia because of you, then you just went off and left him on the ship. He searched for days when you were missing and he helped take care of me, then you turn up and tell him you've got other partners. Now I'm supposed to walk off and leave him with Uncle John and those two wretched children and that worthless hole in the ground.'

'Joey can take care of himself,' he cajoled. 'He's like one of those great, floppy hounds who'll follow anyone who whistles. If you could see that great, soppy face —'

'That's just it,' she cut in angrily. 'To my eyes you and he look the same and I think you should take me back to him now.'

'And if I don't?' he said impulsively.

'Then he and Ugly will come looking for me.'

'And if they can't find you?'

'They'll go back to Uncle John and he'll organise a search. There were plenty that saw you take me off the cart and you know what they do to a man that takes a woman against her will.' He'd forgotten the keenness of her mind—in his idyllic memory she had been more pliable.

'When will I see you again?' he asked.

'Whenever you like,' she said, but they both knew the difficulties that would cause.

'We can't go on like this forever.' Davis had helped her to her feet.

'I doubt if Uncle John can cope with the children and the mine much longer, things have to change.'

He led her to the horse. 'How will they change, Amy? How will they change so we can be together?' She didn't answer, and he kissed her as if to emphasise his point. She responded and it seemed to take away his doubts. 'I'll ride over every night after dark and we'll sit by the fire and to hell with Tanner.'

Ugly arrived back at the wash pool moments after Amy and Davis. No one asked where she'd been and she guessed that Joey knew and that Amy and Davis didn't care. She helped Joey pack up while the others said their farewells.

'Were they . . .' Joey said suddenly, 'I mean, did they . . .'

Ugly smiled. She'd had trouble with the same question. 'Your friend Davis is too smart for that. It's what Tanner expects him to do, what Tanner's told Amy he'd do.' The relief that flowed across Joey's face told Ugly more than words ever could. He saw the perceptiveness of her look.

'It's just that she's so young,' he said.

When they arrived back at the camp each turned to their habitual task, with Ugly helping Amy prepare the meal.

'You wanted to talk,' Ugly said as soon as they were alone.

'Yes,' Amy said slowly, 'but I don't know what to say, there's so much that you don't know and I'm so confused.' She looked so pathetic that Ugly overcame her natural reticence and put her arm uncomfortably around the girl. 'I love them all.'

'All?'

'Davis, Joey and Uncle John and I don't want to lose any of them. I lost my parents when I was twelve and I was so alone.' Her voice was strained but she wasn't crying. 'Do you know what it's like to have no one, no one at all to care if you live or die?' Ugly knew only too well, but she didn't answer. 'It's awful, really awful, that's why I don't want to lose any of them, that's why I don't want to have to choose.' She lapsed into silence.

'Is that what you wanted to tell me?' Ugly asked.

'Uncle John will listen to you, you can make him understand. Tell him Davis didn't start the fire, tell him there's no harm in us being together.'

'I can't make him believe Davis didn't start the fire and he already knows that he was wrong to accuse him, and I can't make him believe that there's no harm in you being together but I doubt he'll interfere.' She noted Amy's despondent face. 'I'll try to make him understand.' She hugged Amy's shoulder before she moved away. 'Now, we'd best do something with this meal.'

The meal was surprisingly good, though neither woman had any culinary talent they seemed to complement each other's shortcomings. Jilly manoeuvred Joey and Ugly into sitting together during the meal, then promptly fell asleep sitting between them. Bobby was last to eat and first to bed, and when Amy announced that she was tired Joey retired also.

Tanner took the lamp and walked with Catherine to the dray. He sat down beside her, studying her face in the odd patterns of the lamplight. She was beautiful. He smiled at her, but she was too deep in thought to notice.

'It's none of my business what's happening here,' she said at last.

'Did Amy ask you to speak to me?' She nodded. 'So speak.'

'Well, for a start I suppose you already know you're a fool to stay here, a fool to let those children act as they do.' He didn't answer. 'And you were a fool to accuse Davis or to try to stop him seeing Amy.' She paused, but he didn't respond. 'And I suppose you know all this is tearing her apart and that it's not just you and Davis she's got to choose between.' She stopped again, but he seemed more intent on looking at her face than listening to her words. 'There's Joey to consider too.'

'Joey?' he scoffed.

'Yes, Joey,' she said defensively, 'poor, pockmarked, beady-eyed Joey, near as ugly as me he is, but not to her. To her he looks as good as you or Davis and he's twice as considerate and half as domineering.'

Tanner smiled suddenly. 'Well, I'll be damned.'

'You mark my words, as long as Joey stays with you she won't leave either and I doubt if she even knows why.' The thought of Joey and Amy together pleased Tanner immeasurably. She was still too young of course, but Joey was a man he trusted. Tanner gazed into the blackness that extended beyond the circle of light surrounding the lamp. He could tolerate Davis if deep down he knew that Amy was more attached to Joey.

He looked back at Catherine, who was rubbing absently at the scar on her face.

'Does it hurt?' he asked.

'What?'

'The scar.'

She shrugged. 'Mostly it's numb but sometimes it feels sort of tight.'

'How did it happen?' he asked and his words cut her like a knife, ripping away the hard callouses of the years and opening up the old wounds. He saw her body stiffen but she faced him squarely, speaking evenly, almost offhandedly.

'My father was too lazy to get off his backside to fetch the whip, so he threw boiling oil at me.' She saw him flinch, the muscles in his neck contracting in an involuntary spasm. Tanner had prepared himself for a horrible accident, not a deliberate act of cruelty.

When at last he spoke his voice was hoarse and barely audible. 'How old were you?'

'Jilly's age.' Catherine watched, fascinated, as he fought to regain control.

'Did your mother not try to stop him?'

'She'd gone by then.'

'Who nursed you? Who treated the burns?'

She shrugged. 'I remember running to the stream and lying face down in the water 'til someone dragged me out. I remember being sick. I remember lying in the dray with him cursing me and hitting me and calling me ugly. I remember there was pain.' She stared at him curiously as she spoke, her voice was flat and unemotional, yet he responded to every word as if it evoked some deep understanding of her pain.

'What happened to him?'

'My father?' Tanner nodded. 'He laid into me once too often, got falling down drunk once too often. I took the team and left.'

Tanner reached out with an unsteady hand to touch the scar, but she pushed his hand away. He looked hurt by the rebuff, but persisted in his attempt. Catherine drew back against the wheel of the dray, only allowing his hand to reach her when she could retreat no further. The scar was rough and hard, the skin shrivelled by the burning oil. His hand moved across the scar to touch the unaffected side of her face. She was trembling and the look in her eyes was one of panic.

'I wouldn't hurt you,' he said.

'You hurt me.' Her voice was caught somewhere between a

156

sob and a laugh. 'You hurt me more with your kindness than all the others with their cruelty.'

He leant forward and kissed her full on the lips, and the look of surprise on her face when they parted made him laugh. He took her hand and held it and she was too stunned to pull away.

'I would never hurt you.' He gripped her hand and she smiled weakly.

'You'd not mean to,' she conceded, 'but what seems like an ordinary act of kindness to you is something rare and precious to the likes of me, and we're apt to put too much store by it, to think it means something it doesn't.' Her voice was strained and breathless.

'If you think it means I care for you or that I want you with me everywhere I go for everyone to see, then you've made no mistake.'

She stared at him in disbelief. 'You're tired and lonely, and you think the world's against you. You need to get away from here, go further up the valley, there's plenty more places to dig. The boy will soon come round once he sees you getting gold. Or give it all up, go back to Melbourne, there's all sorts of jobs, high up in the government some of them. Go back before the rush is over and you'll have your pick.'

'Would you come with me?'

'There's no place in polite society for me.'

He gazed at her uneven face. It was true—those fine, upright citizens, protectors of public morality and pillars of the church would laugh at her behind her back or even to her face, they'd exclude her and ignore her.

'Do you know what I'd do if I found gold?' he asked. She shook her head. 'I'd buy a ship and we'd sail away together, you and I.'

'Oh, yes,' she laughed, 'and what would I do on a ship?'

'I'd teach you to read and write, to navigate and sail.'

'You're starting to sound as fanciful as Davis.'

'We're not so different, he and I. We were born into the same poverty. We lied and cheated to get ourselves out because that is the only way out. If there's any way out at all,' he added wistfully, his thoughts turning to the endless plots and schemes that had failed to rid him of his background. 'I'm as good a sailor as they come and I can captain a ship, in fact I did during my smuggling days, but I couldn't do it legally, I've not got my papers you see, and I could never get them for there's no place for a poor man's son on the officer's deck.' There had been bitter resentment on his face, but it vanished as he smiled at her. 'But if I owned the ship I'd be telling the captain what to do.'

'Well, you won't find gold digging in that hole.'

'True,' he said, then asked: 'How much longer will you stay?'

'I go tomorrow.'

Tanner would have liked to argue, to beg for one more day, but he didn't. 'How long before you'll be back again?'

'Two and a half, three weeks, if the weather holds, if not . . .' She shrugged.

'Will you stay longer next time?' He looked so sad that she didn't have the heart to say no.

'I'll see.' They said little else to each other. Tanner sat for a while holding her hand. He was almost too tired to crawl into his bed, but the dampness and the chill made him go.

Catherine left early the next morning. The valley was still in darkness although the sky was light. Tanner watched the dray until it faded from view, then turned wearily to his work.

Davis came that evening and every evening from then on. He arrived after the meal and stayed until past midnight. Tanner usually retired early, finding it easier to lie in half sleep listening to their conversation than participate in it. Joey, too, was often driven to bed early by Davis' attitude to him, and Tanner began to detect an irritation in Amy's tone when she spoke to Davis following Joey's departure. Tanner resisted the temptation to create more trouble, but it gave him much pleasure every time Davis made the mistake of belittling Joey.

CHAPTER 19

++++++++++++++

I T WAS exactly one week after Ugly's departure that Davis stayed much later than normal. Tanner didn't hear him leave, but he heard him return less than an hour later. He arrived at a gallop, screaming for Joey.

'You've got to help me.' He blundered into the tent, groping for Joey. 'I can't take them by myself. You've got to get a gun and a horse.' Tanner lit the lamp. Davis' face was wild with desperation, he was shaking Joey and shouting in his face. 'You've got to get a gun, you've got to help me stop them.'

'What the hell's the matter with you?' Tanner asked. Davis spun round to face him, staring uncomprehendingly. 'What's happened?'

'The gold, they took the gold.'

'Who?'

'Martin and Baker.' He could see the answer meant nothing to Tanner. 'Two of my partners, they snuck out while old Tom was asleep, took the cart horses and the gold, all the gold. I've got to stop them.'

'Have you thought of getting official help?' Tanner asked calmly.

'Old Tom's gone to the commissioner but they won't do nothing, they won't leave the goldfields for fear there'd be trouble while they're away. Write a report, that's all they'll do.' He turned back to Joey. 'We can run them down, you and me, we can get it back.' It was a plea, an urgent and desperate plea.

'How much gold was there?' Tanner asked, and the strength seemed to go out of Davis' body.

'Thirty pounds, maybe more.'

'What?'

'We've been saving it up, planning to take it to Melbourne ourselves, you get near a pound an ounce more there.' Despair threatened to engulf Davis, but he shook himself free of it. 'We can catch them if we start now. Get a gun, Joey, and a horse.'

159

This time it was an instruction, not a request.

Tanner stood up. 'Come on.' He guided Davis out of the tent.

'Where are we going?'

'To wake the others. Joey, get the cart horses, both of them.'

'You're coming too?'

'Yes,' Tanner answered, and moved off before Davis could ask him why. Tanner woke Amy and Bobby and explained what had happened.

'And you're going to take my cart horses and go after them, is that what you think?' Bobby yelled.

'That's what I think and that's exactly what I'll do.' The boy opened his mouth to protest further, but Tanner didn't allow him the chance. 'We'll be gone three days, no more, because if we can't find them in that time we'll never find them.' He pre-empted Davis' objection. 'You'll have to be careful with the water while I'm gone and there'll be no point in digging.' The look on the boy's face was one of blind hatred tinged with exasperation. 'Try fossicking on the surface.' Tanner began packing supplies into a canvas bag. 'Are you going to be able to manage, Amy?'

'You've left it a bit late to ask.' She smiled.

'What about a gun?' Davis asked.

'You're not taking my father's gun.'

Tanner ignored Bobby. 'I don't much fancy shooting anybody.'

'They're armed.'

'Then again, I don't much fancy being shot.' He took the gun from behind the makeshift cupboard. His brother would have been useless with it and he wasn't much better.

'Horses are ready.' Joey appeared in the doorway.

Amy kissed each man goodbye and told them to be careful, but her last embrace was for Tanner and her last words were 'Thank you'.

They rode across country, towards Forest Creek, reasoning that Martin and Baker would have done the same, being anxious to get rid of the gold as quickly as possible. The two men would also expect to have a good headstart as, under normal circumstances, the disappearance of the gold would not have been discovered until morning. They hadn't allowed for Davis' obsession with the yellow metal, which had compelled him to have one last look at it before retiring. They would be moving briskly but not pushing their horses too hard.

160

Tanner, Joey and Davis arranged whistle signals then spread out, covering as much ground as possible at a pace that was less than safe on a moonless night.

The sun rose, spreading orange fingers through the clouds of dust that hung in the still air. It was hot, hotter than it should be at that time of year, and Tanner's horse was blowing like a steam train. He eased it to a walk, scanning the bush about him for some sign of the thieves, but there was none. He brushed the flies away from his face. It wasn't inconceivable that they'd missed them as they careered through the night, but it didn't really matter. It might even be preferable to face them in Forest Creek rather than the bush. Tanner came to a small stream and whistled the others to join him. He didn't bother lighting a fire, but set out some cold rations.

'What are we stopping for?' Davis demanded.

'Horses are exhausted.' Tanner noted that Davis' horse seemed to have suffered more than his own despite the fact that it was younger and fitter and that Davis was a lighter man. Joey's mount broke through the dense scrub and Joey all but fell off it. Tanner smiled wryly at Davis' obvious disgust. 'We'll probably beat them to Forest Creek,' he said.

'If that's where they're going.' Davis agitation was obvious.

'Where else?'

'Melbourne, along the back road.' Tanner nodded thoughtfully. 'Possible.'

'And if that's the way they've gone we haven't got a hope in hell of finding them.' Davis turned on Tanner as if it was his fault.

'You're the one who decided to come this way,' Tanner retaliated.

'And what if we've missed them in the dark?'

'Then we'll be waiting for them when they reach Forest Creek.'

'And what if they're still ahead?'

'Then we'll catch up with them. There's no way they'll be pushing their horses as hard as we have.'

'What if they are?' Davis paced irritably.

'Then we'll find their horses dead and them on foot.' Davis swung round about to continue the argument, but Joey intervened.

'He's right, Davis, them cart horses of yours were older than these and not as hardy or as well cared for.'

'And they're carrying that extra weight,' Tanner added. Davis looked confused. 'The gold,' he clarified.

They continued as before, stopping again about noon and arriving in Forest Creek late in the afternoon. The officials were sympathetic but unhelpful, only offering to place a description of the men on a flyer to be dispatched to all commissioners. The bank had not received a deposit of the size Davis described, but the men could have made several small transactions or even traded with the merchants. With each setback Davis' anger grew, and when they had exhausted all possible avenues of inquiry he stood before Joey and Tanner whitefaced with rage and frustration.

'What are we going to do now?' he challenged them. 'What bright ideas can you two come up with now?' Joey tried to think, but Tanner's attention had been captured by a small country church and, beyond it, not quite hidden from view, a graveyard. 'They've gone to Melbourne, that's where they are,' Davis exploded. 'Sitting in some digger's hotel, lighting fat cigars with money that should have been mine.' Neither Tanner or Joey spoke. 'I'm going after them, going to get back what's mine.'

'I don't think that's such a good idea,' Joey said. 'Feelings different in the city to what it is here. It might be hard to prove the gold's really yours, you start pointing guns at people and it might be you that ends up in trouble.'

Tanner was only half listening to the conversation. 'If they get to Melbourne you'll never find them,' he said. 'They could be on the first ship out or on their way to one of the new settlements. We should stay here another day, in case we missed them on the way, then head back.'

'Head back?' Davis yelled. 'You expect me to go home and forget all they've taken from me?'

'You can do what you like, but we're going back for I'll not leave those children alone any longer.'

'So, you're speaking for Joey too, now, are you?' There was a sneer on his face and derision in his voice.

Tanner smiled at his artful attempt to divide them. 'Joey can do what he likes, but the cart horses are coming with me.' He began to walk away, but Joey's warning cry made him turn to find Davis facing, his gun aimed and cocked.

'It was all show, wasn't it?' Davis yelled at him. 'All show for Amy, jumping on your horse, galloping into the night. You don't want to help me find the gold, you don't want me to be able to come and claim her. You just didn't want her to think you wouldn't help me when I was in trouble.' Davis had advanced on Tanner until the barrel of the gun rested on his chest.

'You may be right,' Tanner said evenly, 'or maybe I just wanted to have you in my debt. I didn't think about it at the time, it just seemed like the right thing to do, just like going back is the right thing to do now.'

'I'm going to Melbourne,' he prodded Tanner with the barrel of the gun, 'and I'm taking one of them cart horses for Joey.' Tanner looked along the barrel of the gun to Davis' remarkably steady hand. He looked into his eyes and had no doubt that Davis would like to kill him or that he was capable of it, but he doubted that he would do it.

'Joey can do what he likes, but I should like to remind you both of the penalty for stealing a man's horse.' He retreated slightly from the gun. 'If I were you I'd camp near where the Bendigo Creek road enters the town. If we've missed them on the way that's the one place they'll be sure to pass when they arrive.' Tanner turned slowly and walked towards the church.

'Where are you going?' Davis called after him.

'To look for my brother's grave.'

It was early morning when Tanner found Joey and Davis. He'd located his brother's grave, an unmarked plot in a dreary corner of the cemetery. He'd spent the night making a wooden cross and carving his brother's name on it and, because he didn't know where or how Mary had been buried, he added: 'Beloved husband of Mary (deceased)'. The vicar had come to talk to him while he worked, offering platitudes that couldn't banish the pointlessness of his brother's death or alter the profound and permanent effect it had had on his own life.

Joey rose to meet him as he rode into the camp. 'Where have you been?' he asked.

'Carving a marker for my brother's grave.' He dismounted and sat by the fire. 'You know that bastard nephew of mine didn't even go to his father's funeral, didn't go with him when he was dying. There was no one with him at the end but a couple of miners who didn't even know his proper name.'

Joey rummaged among the supplies. 'I'll make you some tea.' Davis stirred. 'He's been up most of the night, no sign of them.'

It was late when Davis woke and together he and Joey roused

Tanner, who had fallen asleep. By the time they'd eaten and ridden into town it was mid-afternoon. They repeated their circuit of banks and officials and it soon became obvious, even to Davis, that Martin and Baker had not been there and were not coming.

'I'm sorry, Davis, I've got to start back now.' Tanner was genuinely sorry. Davis had pinned all his hopes and dreams on gold and Tanner knew what it was like to have such hopes and to see them dashed.

'I'm going to Melbourne,' Davis looked at Joey, quite expecting him to say he was going too.

'You'll never find them,' Joey said uncomfortably, 'Melbourne's a big place to search. I know, I looked for you when you were missing.' He frowned, realising his words were having little effect. 'For all you know they mightn't be in Melbourne, for all you know they might've spent the gold by now. It's a waste of time, Davis.'

'You're not coming with me?'

'What if you find them? How are you going to get it back—it's just your word against theirs. What if it comes to a fight?'

'You gutless, snivelling bastard,' Davis spat the words at him, 'cringing and grovelling in front of everything and everyone. You're nothing, Joey, and you'll always be nothing.' Tanner could have spoken up to stop the tirade, but in a way it pleased him that Joey should see Davis at his worst, see what he was like when someone crossed him.

'I'm sorry, Davis,' Joey said, 'I can't.'

'Bastard,' Davis swore as he mounted his horse.

'Leave it be, come back with us, there's plenty more gold,' Joey implored.

Davis laughed bitterly. 'Like all you're getting out of that worthless pit of yours.' Joey rested his hand on the neck of Davis' horse.

'Leave it go, Davis, for Amy's sake.' Davis put his foot in the centre of Joey's chest and kicked him to the ground. It was a slow, deliberate kick, an act of cold anger and brutality rather than spontaneity.

'Tell Amy I'll be back,' he said as he turned his horse towards the Melbourne road.

'Come on.' Tanner helped Joey to his feet. 'If we start now we'll be home before tomorrow night.' Joey was staring after

Davis. 'You couldn't have stopped him.' He slapped Joey on the shoulder. 'If you'd gone with him he would only get you into trouble.' Joey reluctantly climbed on the back of the cart horse and it plodded on behind its mate, which Tanner guided along the Bendigo Creek Road. They'd ridden for about an hour before Joey spoke.

'That's why you came, isn't it?' Tanner shot Joey a questioning glance. 'To keep me out of trouble,' he clarified.

'I came because it seemed the right thing to do,' Tanner inclined his head thoughtfully, 'but now that you mention it, if I hadn't been half afraid you might follow Davis into hell I wouldn't have tagged along.'

CHAPTER 20

++++++++++++++

A MY GREETED them warmly when they arrived, holding them and touching them.

'Where's Davis?' she asked.

'Gone to Melbourne.' Tanner saw her recoil at his words. 'We couldn't stop him, he still thinks he can find them and get the gold back.'

'You should have gone with him.'

'And leave you alone?'

'But surely —'

'There was no way of stopping him and no sense in going with him.' Tanner could see she was unconvinced. 'Our being there might easily have made things worse, and what would have happened to you without the horses to get water and supplies?'

'I should have gone with him,' Joey murmured.

'No.' Amy took hold of his arm. 'No, Uncle John is right. Davis would find it easier to admit he was wrong and turn back if he was alone.' She fidgeted with Joey's sleeve, twisting it in her fingers. 'I tell him the gold doesn't matter but he never listens to me.' She wasn't crying, but so close to it that she might as well be.

'I should have gone,' Joey repeated.

'No,' Amy tightened her grip on him. 'I couldn't bear to lose you both.'

'So, you're back are you?' Bobby burst into the shanty.

'I said three days.' Tanner was determined that the boy's belligerence wouldn't upset him.

'I've a load of wash dirt ready.'

'So I see, but I thought I told you to fossick on the surface.'

'It wasn't worth it.'

'Did you even try?'

'Yes, he did,' Jilly interrupted, and on her face was a look of pure spite, 'and he found lots of gold and he's hidden it.'

166

Tanner looked at the boy—there was no sign of repentance, only disgust for his sister's disloyalty.

'Let's have it.'

'No!' the boy shrieked. 'It's mine, I'm the one who worked for it.'

'We're partners in this mine and we need that gold just to stay alive.'

'This claim is mine, the shanty's mine, the picks and shovels, the cart, even the horses you stole, they're all mine.'

'Fine,' Tanner said sarcastically. 'That makes us labourers, so you can pay us a labourer's wage for this last month and we'll be on our way.' The boy's eyes burned with hatred, but he didn't speak. 'If you've not got the money we'll take it in tools and supplies, then we'll take what's ours and stake our own claim further up the gully. Jilly can come with us and you can do what you like.' The boy wouldn't say the words of capitulation but he knew he was beaten, so he closed his mind to his uncle's words and took refuge in the only thing that mattered to him, the mine. Tanner slumped against an empty crate that served as a chair or table. Amy put her arm around him.

'I can make you some tea, we've got a little water left.'

Jilly had retreated to the furthest corner of the shanty during the argument. Now she came forward, her eyes fixed on her uncle. She stopped a short distance from him and her incessant stare finally drew his attention. He smiled, and for once she didn't run away. Slowly she raised her hand—in it was a torn piece of calico folded into a pouch. Tanner opened it. Inside were flakes of gold, two ounces or more.

'Bobby found that much in three days?' Tanner asked.

Jilly nodded uncertainly. 'You said it was everyone's, but you can have my share for the new claim. You said you'd take me.'

'Of course we'll take you.' Tanner held back from the impulse to touch her. 'We'll look after you, no matter what happens.' She moved cautiously next to Joey and buried her face in his coat.

'Will you really stake a new claim?' Joey asked.

Tanner looked thoughtfully at the gold in his hand. His brother's mine was situated on the very edge of his claim, which was directly adjacent to his neighbour's. A spur of gold ran across his neighbour's claim, but petered out soon after it reached his. When Tanner had first arrived the mine had been approximately six foot by four foot by eight foot deep, with occasional shaft dug horizontally to follow the seams of gold. Now the mine was two foot longer and twice as deep and Tanner realised that what little gold they'd found had not come from the greater depth or even from the lateral tunnels, but from the extended length. Once they'd exhausted the spur the only gold to be found was in the topsoil.

'We'll take the first couple of feet of soil off the entire claim, forget about the mine.'

'What about the boy?'

'He can dig in the mine if he likes. I don't care any more.' Amy returned with the tea and some damper. 'The shanty's partially on the claim, we might have to move it.'

'What's going on?' she asked.

'We're going to strip the surface soil, see if there's any gold in it, and then we're getting out of here.'

'What about Bobby?'

'I don't care about Bobby.' Actually Tanner cared a great deal for the boy and he would have done anything he could to mend the rift that lay between them, but the more he gave in the worse things became and he could take no more of the mine and its empty promise.

'We're going to have a new mine.' Jilly appeared from behind Joey.

'Are we?' Amy smiled.

Tanner slipped from his seat and squatted in front of Jilly. 'Would you mind very much if we didn't have another claim? Would you mind if we went back to Melbourne and I got a job and we lived in a proper house and you could go to school?' The child didn't speak and Tanner was struck with a sudden fear that she might run away again. 'You tell me if you don't want to go.'

'Can I have a proper bed?' she asked.

'Of course.' Jilly smiled, then crept back into her own quiet corner. Tanner stood up.

'You wouldn't really leave the boy?' Joey asked.

'No, he wouldn't leave the boy,' Amy answered for him. 'And what about Davis?'

'Davis would be well advised to cut his losses too,' Tanner said. 'Anyway, I'm sure he'd manage to find us in Melbourne. He found us here didn't he?'

'God, I hope he's all right,' Amy said. 'I hope he doesn't do anything stupid.' Her young face furrowed with care and Tanner thought it cruel that she'd been forced to grow up so quickly. He walked to the door and saw that the boy was hitching the horses on to the cart, which he had loaded with wash dirt.

'I found the gold you'd hidden.' Bobby spun round to face him. 'I didn't think you'd mind me searching your things, seeing as you've searched mine so often.' Tanner had no qualms about lying to the boy, particularly if it protected Jilly from his wrath.

'And if I had minded, would it have made any difference?'

'Not any more.' Tanner knew that nothing he said would change things now. 'We're going to strip the topsoil to see if there's any gold in it, and if there isn't or when we're done we're going back to Melbourne.'

'And if I refuse to go?' The boy's voice was as steady and determined as his uncle's.

'You'll have a while to think before you make that decision, and if I was you I'd think very carefully.'

The topsoil near the mine yielded well, not by comparison with other claims but by comparison with their previous efforts. The boy continued to work in the mine, insisting that there was no way of telling whether the extra gold had come from the topsoil or the mine. Tanner didn't argue with him, he couldn't be bothered any more. He longed for the sea, yet he knew that even at best his plans offered him no chance of returning to it.

With each passing day Amy became more concerned for Davis. She seldom expressed her fears, as Joey was all too willing to take the blame for anything that may have gone wrong. Tanner was also sensitive about the subject, feeling that Amy somehow thought less of him for not going with Davis. So the tension grew, and the silence, and the misery.

At first Jilly remained the one happy exception, the prospect of a new life burning brightly in her imagination, but slowly she realised that Joey wouldn't be part of that new life and she became more withdrawn and uncommunicative than before. By the time Davis returned even Tanner was glad to see him.

He arrived mid-afternoon on a sweating horse that was barely a shadow of what it had been before the trip to Melbourne. Joey embraced him in a giant bear hug when he dismounted, only releasing him when Amy arrived. Then without one question about the gold he took the horse to care for it, a look of anger and disgust upon his face.

'Thank God you're back.' Amy hugged him. 'Thank God you're all right.' She felt his face and shoulders as if she expected him to have changed. 'I was so worried.' Her voice faltered and she buried her face in his chest.

'I'm all right.' He patted her shoulders. 'I'm sorry I made you worry.'

'Did you find them?' Tanner asked, although he already knew the answer. Davis' return would've been a more triumphant one if he had the gold.

'No, no one's seen hide nor hair of them between here and Melbourne.' He kissed the top of Amy's head. 'We were so close,' he said, 'the way we'd been going, a few more months and we'd have been set.' He let Amy go suddenly, almost violently. 'If I ever find them I'll kill them, I swear to God I'll kill them.'

'No.' Amy reached for him. 'Forget them, Davis, just forget them.'

He took her hand and squeezed it. 'How about getting some food for a hungry traveller?' He watched her make her way back to the shanty. 'Where's Joey?' he asked.

'Tending your horse.'

'I've got to talk to you, both of you.' Davis headed in the direction Joey had taken and Tanner followed him. He was curious but cautious, for something in Davis' manner made him uneasy. Joey was on his way back and they met him not far from the camp.

'You damn near rode that horse into the ground,' he berated Davis.

'I just wanted to get home,' he explained, and Tanner couldn't help but feel that the slightly piteous whine in his voice had been put there by design.

'What are you doing here?' Davis' eyes flicked across the excavations.

'Stripping some of the topsoil.' Tanner settled himself by the fire and Davis took a seat next to Amy, who was battling with the damper.

'No gold in the mine?' he asked. Tanner shook his head. 'I thought as much.' He remained quiet for a few seconds as if taking one last moment for consideration. 'I've been thinking about it all the way back from Melbourne,' he said at last. 'See, there were four of us, so we could stake a claim twenty-four foot by twenty-four foot, instead of twelve by twenty-four as it is for two or three men.' He glanced round the faces to see if there was any reaction. 'Now, with Martin and Baker gone there's only old Tom and me, and they won't let us keep a full twenty-four by twenty-four. There's gold all over that claim, we've taken near fifty pounds and there's plenty more there.' He paused once again, assessing their faces for reaction.

'What are you suggesting?' Tanner had had enough of Davis' salesman spiel.

'Come in with us, the two of you. Old Tom won't mind, he'll be glad not to have to start over again.' He paused to let them assimilate his words. 'You'll take more gold there in a day than you've dug out of this hole since you've been here.' It was an exaggeration but, in terms of profit, probably closer to the truth than Davis realised. 'How much are you getting out of the topsoil and how much longer do you think you'll be getting it?' The yield from the topsoil had been reasonable at first, but the further they moved from the original strike the lower the yield became. Tanner moved uncomfortably—Davis had obviously thought it all out very carefully and everything was to his advantage, two new partners that he knew he could trust and Amy right there at his side. 'You can't stick at this hole forever,' Davis persisted, and Tanner knew he was right and he also knew that any objection he raised to Davis' scheme would be seen as bias.

'Uncle John, you said we were going to move on.'

'I said we were going back to Melbourne.'

'It might be easier to persuade Bobby to try someplace else rather than give up altogether.'

'I don't think Bobby was being offered a share in this partnership, was he Davis?' Tanner could almost hear Davis trying to work out what answer would be to his best advantage. Tanner smiled— Davis had assumed that he would dismiss the boy as easily as Davis dismissed people he didn't want or need.

'We'll have to talk to old Tom, but I don't think a small share would be unreasonable if he was willing to do the work.'

'The boy's a good worker,' Joey said.

'Well, what do you say?' Davis looked earnestly into Tanner's face, but behind the boyish grin Tanner sensed a coldly calculating mind. Still, he wasn't outwitted yet. Bobby wouldn't settle for less than a full share, that is, if he was willing to go at all, and old Tom might not be willing to carve up the shares any smaller.

'We'll talk to your partner first and then to the boy, if everyone's agreeable . . .' He left the sentence unfinished.

'Oh, Uncle John,' Amy stood up, her hands extended for him to guide her round the fire. 'Uncle John, I'm so pleased.' She hugged him. He looked across the top of her head to Davis, their eyes met and Davis couldn't erase the hint of victory from his expression.

'We'll ride over to Eaglehawk after tea.' Davis relaxed, turning his attention to the damper Amy had left to burn in the fire.

'Not on that horse you won't.' Joey's voice was unusually cool and determined. 'That horse is going no where 'til tomorrow and then at no more than an amble.'

'All right,' Davis said amiably.

'Did you not think to feed it?' Joey yelled at him.

'It grazed at night when I stopped.' Davis looked mildly surprised and amused at Joey's outburst.

'On what? There's not a blade of grass growing in this drought.' Davis opened his mouth to speak but Joey didn't let him. 'And what about in Melbourne, did you just tie him up someplace without food or water?'

'I didn't stop the whole time I was in Melbourne. You don't know what it's like trying to find someone in that place. All I did the whole time I was there was to search for them, I didn't eat, I didn't rest —'

'And neither did he,' Joey interrupted.

'I was in a hurry.'

'And did you think beating him would make him run the faster whether he had the strength or not?' Amy gasped and Davis knew that such behaviour was unacceptable to her.

'You're exaggerating,' Davis said calmly.

'The hell I am.' Joey stood up and marched off in the direction of the horse. Davis glanced at Amy. She looked shocked and hurt, and there was no doubting she believed Joey for he was incapable of lying and Davis knew that it would not be easy to discredit him.

'What the hell's the matter with him?' Davis shook his head

disbelievingly, a look of astonishment on his face. The performance was perfect but wasted, for Amy couldn't see his face and Tanner had seen the horse.

Bobby emerged from the mine, but refused their offers of burnt damper and tea. He made his usual protests about their inactivity then went back to work.

Tanner stood up. 'Well, if you'll excuse me I've got some dirt to shift.' Davis offered to help and Tanner didn't refuse.

They left for Eaglehawk early next morning and Davis was careful not to let Amy near his horse in case her probing fingers found testimony to his mistreatment.

They rode slowly and the effort of self-control was almost too much for Davis. As they drew nearer his claim he urged his horse along faster, so that he arrived ahead of Tanner and Joey. A tall, thin young man was leaning against the windlass, while two equally youthful companions were hitching horses to a cart.

Davis sprang from his horse, yelling as he dismounted. 'Where's old Tom?' The young man looked puzzled. 'My partner, where is he?' The young man shook his head. 'Tom, Tom,' Davis yelled as a sense of panic suddenly gripped him, and he cast about for some sign of his partner as he advanced on the young man. 'The old man,' Davis yelled in his face, 'where is he?' This time the young man was too shocked to answer. Davis lunged at him, grabbing him by the shirt and pulling him away from the windlass. The young man broke free.

'Get your hands off me.' Davis grabbed him again, throwing him to the ground then landing on top of him, his hands on the other man's throat.

'Where is he, what have you done with him?' The two men by the cart came to their partner's aid, grabbing Davis and pulling him to his feet. In the same moment Tanner and Joey arrived. Joey tumbled from his horse, attacking the men who were holding Davis, dragging them away from him and flattening the only man who dared to throw a punch.

'Wait,' Tanner yelled as he dismounted. 'Wait, Joey.' He had no intentions of getting into a fight for Davis' sake. 'Wait, all of you, just wait.' The two men that Joey had dispatched regained their feet, but they were in no hurry to continue the fight now that the odds were even, especially as they didn't know what was going on. Davis, however, had other ideas. He threw himself at the man nearest him, but Tanner moved quickly for a big man, interposing himself between Davis and his victim. A fourth man had emerged from the mine and quite a large crowd had gathered to watch the fight.

'This is my claim,' Davis screamed at Tanner. 'They're bloody claim jumpers. Ask them what they've done with old Tom, ask them.' Tanner glanced at the man nearest him, who shook his head blankly.

The fourth man spoke up.'He must mean Mr Gibson.'

Davis spun round to face him. 'Where is he? What have you done with him?' He took two paces before Tanner pulled him back.

'Well?' Tanner asked the man who had spoken.

'I don't know where he went.' The young man looked hopefully at the crowd.

'You're a liar.' Davis tried to move forward again but Tanner maintained his grip. Davis faced him. 'They've taken over my claim, my partner's missing, for all you know they could have murdered him.'

'Now steady on there, Davis.' It was the voice of one of the miners who'd come to watch the fight. 'These lads bought the mine fair and square from your partners.'

'No!' Davis screamed as he wheeled round to face the miner, but his attention didn't rest on the agile little man, instead it was held by the two cart horses. The same two cart horses on which Martin and Baker had made their escape.

'Your partners said you'd taken your share and gone,' the miner continued. 'Seeing as they couldn't keep a twenty-four foot by twenty-four foot claim, just the three of them, they sold it.' Davis stumbled to the cart and horses, a low groan issuing from his throat. 'The commissioner's ratified the deal, you was gone over a week.'

Davis ran his hand over the back of one of the horses. It all made sense to him now. Martin and Baker had only ridden a short way from the camp, somewhere just off the road. As soon as they saw him ride away they'd come back. Old Tom hadn't gone to the commissioner to report the theft because he'd been in with them. They'd waited a few days, told everyone he'd walked off the claim, then sold it and everything along with it. He leant his head against the horse. It was all gone, he had nothing left, nothing but a half-starved horse. Davis closed his eyes and tried to swallow the lump in his throat and pain in his chest. It wasn't fair, no matter what he did or how hard he tried there was always someone waiting to snatch it all away from him.

'No!' Davis rebelled against the injustice, screaming as he ran toward the young men, bent on their destruction as his only means of compensation.

Tanner's punch caught him under the ribs—he ran into it and it had the full force of Tanner's strength. The punch bent Davis double and dropped him to his knees. He slumped to the ground, holding his ribs and gasping for air. Tanner looked down at him—the punch had been unnecessarily hard and Tanner despised himself for giving in to the enmity he felt for Davis. He jerked Davis to his feet but he couldn't stand, he was still gasping for air and unable to speak.

'Get the horses, Joey.' Tanner half dragged, half carried Davis to his horse, then took the reins and led it along at a walk.

'You'd no right to do that,' Joey said.

'I know.'

'Then why?'

'That I don't know.' It was true that Tanner didn't like him and that Davis had often pushed him to his limits, but they weren't the reasons for the assault. Tanner looked back at Davis still sprawled across the neck of his horse. Davis had been out of control. Even when he was in control Davis was capable of cold and deliberate acts of violence and out of control he may well have been capable of murder. Tanner turned his attention to Joey—that wasn't the kind of explanation he'd accept. Davis groaned and struggled to sit up. He looked pale and ill and obviously in pain.

Tanner watched him for a moment then said: 'I had no right to hit you so hard, I'm sorry.'

Davis made an effort to smile. 'Afraid I'll tell Amy?'

'I have no doubt you'll tell Amy and I wouldn't ask you not to. I'm just telling you that I know I was wrong.'

'Well, now, that makes me feel a lot better, hardly hurts at all now you've apologised.' Tanner ignored Davis' sarcasm. The apology had been for Joey's benefit and his own. Whether Davis accepted it or not didn't really matter.

Bobby was waiting for them as they rode into the camp. 'It's about time you got back with those horses.' He marched over to them, taking hold of the reins before they had a chance to dismount.

'Careful now,' Tanner cautioned, 'Davis is hurt.'

'How?' Amy cried as she edged her way towards them.

'I hit him.'

'What?' Amy halted at his words. 'Why?'

'To stop him getting into a fight with four men, but I hit him too hard and there's no excuse for it.' Tanner helped Davis down. Amy found them and put her arm solicitously around Davis, helping him to a seat.

'What happened?' she asked, and he told her with all the skill of a storyteller, using the right words to evoke her sympathy and anger.

Joey prepared a meal but Tanner didn't join them. He had no appetite for the food or for the company, and instead he loaded the wash dirt and went with the boy to the water holes.

CHAPTER 21

✦✦✦✦✦✦✦✦✦✦✦✦✦✦

THE GOLD yield had dwindled yet again and the boy's hostility and frustration was almost tangible. Tanner studied him as they trundled back to the camp, his young face was set and hard and Tanner could no longer pretend that there was something he could say or do that would persuade the boy to leave the mine. In the end it would come to a confrontation no matter how hard he tried to avoid it.

He sighed and stared in the direction of their camp, now barely discernible amongst the hotchpotch of tents and shanties. He would wait for Catherine then sell everything and hitch a ride back to Melbourne with her. The campsite came more clearly to his vision and he could pick out the three figures sitting almost exactly as they had been when he left. As they drew nearer the figures seemed to tense; Amy appeared more agitated than the rest and Tanner knew even before he saw the look on Davis' face that she had decided to go with him.

Tanner climbed slowly from the cart, his body felt leaden and he made no attempt to help Bobby with the water. He tried to arrange his features into a smile, but like the rest of him they were reluctant to move.

'Would you like some tea Uncle John?' Amy's voice quavered as she spoke.

Tanner sat beside her and watched with fascination as she made the tea. 'You've learnt a lot.' His voice was hoarse. 'I mean, ways of getting round the blindness.' Her hand was shaking as she handed him the mug, and Tanner wondered if he should make it easy for her, if he should tell her he knew that she was going with Davis and that he understood, but the words wouldn't come for he still clung to a hope that he might be wrong.

She took a breath. 'Uncle John . . .' she began but her voice faltered and tears welled in her eyes.

He put his arm round her. 'Come on now, it can't be that bad.'

'Uncle John . . .' She started again and again she could get no further than his name.

'Amy's coming with me.' Davis spoke for her.

'I asked you to let me tell.' She turned on Davis angrily.

'It's best said out straight.'

'I wanted to do it my own way.'

'No,' Tanner said steadily, 'Davis is right, it's best said out straight.'

'No,' she wailed, 'you don't understand, none of you understand.'

'Oh, I think I do,' Tanner said. 'You think I'm unjust to Davis and that he needs you more than I do, that he loves you and that you love him.' He said it simply and there was no mockery in his voice.

She took Tanner's hand, touching it and following the shape of its contours, committing it to the deepest part of her memory. 'Please,' she said sadly, 'there's something I want to tell you, something I wanted you to know before I told you I was leaving.' She drew an unsteady breath. 'I never wanted it said in anger, I never wanted to hurt you, I never meant to deceive you.'

They were all silent, and Tanner could tell from a glance that neither Davis nor Joey knew what she was about to say.

'It wasn't really a lie, not at first, you see I really thought it was you.' She stopped, aware that she was making no sense. 'The night of the accident . . . the night I was blinded.' She paused, then continued constrainedly. 'I was in my room, you remember, the one above the stable. I heard the police whistles and people running and I went downstairs to see what had happened.' The words came haltingly, unwillingly. 'There was a man with grey hair, almost white, and blue eyes. He was running across the courtyard, he had a walking cane with a silver handle and his clothes were so fine that I just stared at him. He yelled at me and I turned to run and he hit me, he hit me with the cane.'

'Carstairs.' The name came like a low hiss from Tanner's lips. So many things that had seemed so strange before suddenly made sense. He didn't see the girl behind the crates because she was on the ground. The expensive barrister wasn't hired to prevent him from testifying about the smuggling, he was hired to prevent Amy from testifying at all, for if she had described the man who had assaulted her not only would it have guaranteed Tanner's freedom, but it would have armed him with information that

178

he could have used to blackmail Carstairs for the rest of his life. It was no wonder they'd wanted him out of the country. Amy was crying and saying 'I'm sorry'. Tanner patted her shoulder. 'It doesn't matter,' he said.

'I thought it was you, I really thought it was you,' she sobbed. 'When Auntie left me, I was so frightened, you kept saying it was an accident and I got so confused.' Her voice faltered again, then regained its strength. 'You were too tall and your voice was wrong. Auntie said you used a lump of wood and I'd been so sure you'd used a cane that I thought maybe I was wrong about the other things too.' She shook her head hopelessly. 'I didn't want to think about it, I wanted it to be the way you said. I was afraid to think about it, you were willing to look after me and I needed you.' She stopped again, the confusion of their first few days together, the fear, the speed with which everything happened, these were her excuses and they seemed so inadequate now. 'After the *Lady Ann* sailed, a long way out to sea, I asked Miss Sharpe what you looked like. When she told me I realised that you weren't the man I'd seen, that you'd come along later just as you'd said.' Tears were running down her cheeks and she clung to Tanner's hand as if it was a lifeline. 'I should have told you,' she finished disconsolately.

'It would have made no difference,' Tanner said. 'It makes no difference now,' he added, but he knew he was wrong, for Amy, guilt was a powerful hold and although it had long since ceased to be her hold on him, it had become his hold on her.

'Uncle John —'

'I'm not your uncle,' he interrupted, and the words cut him as deeply as they cut her. 'If I was I'd forbid you from doing this.' He withdrew his hand from hers, then fought to regain some semblance of control. 'Where will you go?' he managed to ask.

'Not far, just up the gully, there's been some good strikes there.' It was Joey who answered and it gave Tanner some comfort to know that Joey would be going with them and that they were not going far.

'When?'

'As soon as possible,' Davis answered. 'I'd like to have found workable gold before the licences are due again.' He paused, but Tanner didn't speak. He was wondering how he'd come to care so much for Amy in such a short time and why he was so certain Davis would hurt her. He looked at them and it occurred to him that only a few hours ago Davis had been begging him to be his partner, but now he was being dismissed as easily as Davis had once dismissed Joey. He smiled at them. If he pressed the matter Davis would cite the punch as the reason, but Tanner knew as surely as he knew his own name that it was simply a matter of convenience.

'We've got a bit of a problem, though,' Joey said uncomfortably. He glanced at Davis, then cleared his throat several more times, ignoring Davis' encouraging looks.

Finally, Davis took over the conversation. 'We need a stake.' Tanner raised his eyebrows questioningly. 'We figure you owe Joey for all the time he's worked here.'

'The owners of the *Lady Ann* owe him a damn sight more and you as well for that matter.'

'Aye, but we'd have to go to England to get it.'

Tanner's remark had been intended to remind Joey of the fact that he'd supported him during their stay in Melbourne, but no sooner had Tanner said the words than he regretted them for he owed Joey more than money could ever pay.

'Take the tent,' he said, 'anything we brought with us from Melbourne, nothing that belonged to my brother.'

'Are there any picks and shovels in that?' Davis asked.

'No, but even half starved as that horse of yours is you'll be able to trade him for a broken down horse and cart and a few picks and shovels.' Amy's reaction was slight, but Tanner knew the thought that Davis had mistreated the animal must disturb her and he was glad that it was Joey who had made the accusation first.

'We had it in mind to stay here until we find a place to stake our claim, if that's all right with you,' Joey said.

Tanner nodded. 'Fine,' he said, then added, 'I'll move into the shanty with Bobby and Jilly and you three can set up in the tent.' He watched Amy as he spoke and it was clear that she'd given no thought to their future sleeping arrangements. 'Where is Jilly?' he asked.

'She ran off when she heard I was leaving,' Joey answered.

'And you didn't think to go after her, to tell her you weren't going far and that you'd come to see her?' Tanner stood up. It was late and he didn't like the child being off by herself, but he remembered Catherine's warning that searching for her would only drive her further away. 'I'll get some fire wood,' he said. 'Maybe one of you could do something about a meal.'

Davis watched him leave. 'He took that very well.'

'I wish he hadn't.' Amy got to her feet. 'I wish he'd yelled at me and screamed at me and called me a cheat and a liar. I wish he'd said that he hadn't saved me from the streets of London to see me prostitute myself here.'

Davis sprang to his feet and grabbed her by the shoulders. 'Stop it, stop it.' He shook her. 'I'll not have you talk about yourself that way. You're my lady, do you understand, MY LADY!'

'No.' She pushed him away. 'My father worked in the mill from the time he was ten, he taught himself to read and write and my mother never learned. We lived in a two-room house and I've never even seen the other side of London. When my parents died I lived with a drunken old whore who put me to work and took my pay and I was lucky I could get a job because if I hadn't she'd've put me to the street there and then. If Tanner hadn't taken me on it would've been the streets or the workhouse or the blind asylum and I'd've rather it be the street.'

'Stop it!' Davis screamed at her and there was an anger, a violence in his voice that was frightening.

'Joey,' she called instinctively, reaching out to him and he was there. The two men stared at each other for an instant then the moment passed, Davis' face relaxing into a smile.

'Now we'll have no more of this silliness,' he said gently. 'You got yourself all worked up over what Tanner would say and in the end there was nothing to it, he doesn't care so why should you?' Joey had been with Tanner when he learnt of Buchanan's death and that of his brother and sister-in-law too, and he knew Tanner wasn't a man to scream and yell over things he couldn't change.

'He cares all right,' Joey said, 'and you're lucky he's not a violent man.'

'Not violent?' Davis laughed, clutching his ribs.

'It's true he hit you too hard, harder than he intended I fancy, but you'd no right to be attacking those young lads and if he hadn't stopped you maybe I would have.'

'A damn sight more gently I'd wager.'

'He could have done you a lot more harm than he did, he'd beat you in a fair fight any day.' The emphasis Joey gave to the word 'fair' made Davis cautious with his reply.

'Well, it's not come to a fight has it? So let's get this meal he's asked for and start working out what he's giving us and what we have to buy.' Amy was still holding Joey's arm and they went together to the shanty, leaving Davis alone by the fire.

Tanner had gone into the bush ostensibly to collect wood. He wandered aimlessly, gathering pieces here and there as his mind struggled to maintain its rationality. He couldn't leave now, that much he knew, not until he was sure Amy would never want him or need him again. He knew something else too, he knew he couldn't stick at the mine any longer. The alternative seemed to be staking a new claim, hoping Bobby would settle for that. He shook his head—the boy was totally intractable as far as the mine was concerned. It occurred to Tanner that he might make a better living taking the cart and hauling wash dirt for pay, then the boy could do what he liked with the mine. Gradually, unconsciously, Tanner had been drawn to that small copse of trees where he'd once found solace in Catherine's company.

He slowed his pace as he drew near, his mind still focused on the boy. Then he heard it, a soft voice, a child's voice, chatting happily or scolding, rising and falling with the moods of her game. Tanner crept closer, the child too absorbed in her play to notice him.

'These flowers are all for Mummy,' Jilly said. 'There are none for Daddy today 'cause he hasn't been good. He didn't bring Mummy flowers at all so he only gets them on special days.' She had picked a small bunch of wattle blossom, which she was trying to tie with gum leaves. Finally she was satisfied with the result, she picked them up lovingly and moved from the main clearing to a smaller area off to the left. Tanner saw her kneel before two makeshift crosses. They were just bits of stick tied together with bark and leaves and they were badly in need of repair. She persevered with one for some time, oblivious to Tanner's approach. The sound of his footsteps reached her just as the cross fell apart yet again. She looked up at him and for an instant Tanner was afraid she would run away, but she tilted her chin at him defiantly, still holding the two pieces of twig.

'There's a cross with your parents' names on it in the cemetery in Forest Creek. I made it myself.' He squatted beside her. 'It marks your father's grave, but I put your mother's name on it too because I didn't know where she was buried.' He smiled at her. 'I'll take you there, if you like.' She looked back at the twigs in her hand and at the untidy bouquet.

'Can we take flowers?'

'Of course.'

She put the flowers and the twigs back in place. 'Joey's going,' she said, 'and Amy too.' She looked up at him. 'I wish Ugly would come back.'

'Catherine,' he said softly, 'why don't you call her Catherine?' There was a sadness in his voice and it occurred to the child that he missed Ugly too.

'Did you like my mother?' she asked.

'Yes, I did, very much.'

'Do you like Bobby?' Tanner didn't like the boy and he doubted if Jilly did either, but he felt a loyalty to him, the same loyalty that Jilly might feel.

'I think Bobby's very unhappy and angry because your parents never found the gold they wanted and because he can't find it for them.'

'They don't want it any more.'

'No, but what else could Bobby do for them, it's the only thing that he knows they wanted.'

Jilly thought for a moment. 'Mummy would want me to brush my hair and say my prayers and put flowers on her grave.'

'Your mother would be very proud of you.'

She stood up so that she was on eye level with him. 'Are we going to stay here forever?' she asked.

'No, one day when Catherine comes, maybe not this next time or the time after but one day, we'll sell up everything and go back to Melbourne with her.'

'Like you promised before?'

'Like I promised before.' She moved closer to him, peering into his eyes, and then she smiled. 'Do you want to come back with me?' he asked. She nodded and took his hand.

They made an odd pair scrambling down the side of the gully, and in spite of all that had gone wrong that day Tanner smiled as the trusting hand was thrust in his and the innocent smile beamed back at him.

CHAPTER 22

++++++++++++++

I T HAD begun several days after the others had moved to the new site. Although initially not enough to worry about, it had struck a sick fear in Tanner the moment he heard it. He had been lying in the shanty, stirred from sleep by the pre-dawn chill. At first he'd thought it was just the wind buffeting the shanty with dust and leaves, but the sound grew more rhythmical and the smell of it reached him and he knew it was rain. His thoughts turned to Catherine and the dusty road that she'd said would become a quagmire if it rained.

The next few days were fine, but then the weather broke with a vengeance.

Amy sat huddled in the centre of the tent while Joey and Davis tried to make the gutter large enough to cope with the torrent of water that washed down the side of the gully. Joey crawled inside the tent.

'That seems to have fixed it,' he said as he felt amongst their sodden blankets to see if water was still getting in.

'It's your turn in the mine,' Davis barked from outside.

'For heaven's sake, Davis, hole's full of water.'

'Yes, and it's going to get worse before it gets better, so let's make the best of what we've got.'

'It's Sunday,' Amy said plaintively. 'Most miners don't work on Sunday.'

'The Chinese do.'

'Aye,' Joey agreed, 'and Bobby never took time off for the sabbath.

'I wonder how Uncle John's managing,' Amy sighed.

'He's not your uncle.' Davis had crawled halfway into the tent.

'No,' Amy conceded. 'He's not my uncle or my lover or even the man who blinded me, but he's taken better care of me than any and never asked a thing in return.'

'Maybe you'd rather be with him than here,' Davis sniped.

'It's not that, it's just that it's so unfair, he's tried so hard and everything's gone so badly for him.'

'And it's not gone badly for me?' Davis retorted.

'You've got me and Joey.' Amy remained calm. 'All he's got are those ungrateful children.'

'And Catherine,' Joey added.

'Who?' Davis asked.

'Ugly,' Amy clarified, 'but you can't count her, she's hardly ever there.'

'Sometimes people don't need to be together when they . . .' Joey stopped, unwilling to intrude on Tanner and Catherine's privacy.

'When they what?' Amy insisted.

'When two people care deeply for one another they don't always have to be together, sometimes just knowing is enough.'

Davis burst out laughing. 'Come on,' he said, 'Tanner could do better than that, even out here.'

'It's true she's untidy and crude, scarred and uneducated, and we're taught such people are to be scorned or pitied at best, but I've never seen two people more deeply in love.'

'What about me and Amy?' Davis joked but Joey ignored the question, for beside Tanner and Catherine their bond looked no more than infatuation. Davis retreated from the tent still chuckling to himself.

'Are you sure, Joey?' Amy asked.

'Aye, but I doubt anything will come of it, her being so . . .' He hesitated, searching for the right word. '. . . frightened and him not being the kind to push.' There was a sadness in Joey's voice that touched Amy.

'I want to go to him,' she said. 'I need to talk to him.'

'Davis won't like it.'

'Please.'

'It's pouring rain. I take you out in this your uncle will kill me.' She felt round the floor until she found a piece of oiled cloth, she threw it about her shoulders and crawled to the entrance.

'Where are you going?' Joey demanded.

'If I keep heading downhill I'll be going in the right direction, and who knows—some kind soul might offer to help.'

Joey crawled after her. 'I know you don't mean it,' he said. 'I know you're just counting on me not taking the risk of you going by yourself.'

'Davis!' she called.

Davis appeared from the mine. 'Joey's right, it's hopeless trying to dig like this.'

'We're going to visit Uncle John.'

'Are you?' He shot an angry look at Joey.

'You don't mind, do you?'

'What if I do? What if I say you're not to go, will it make any difference?'

'Of course,' she said confidently. 'It will make me wonder if I might not be better off staying there, if I'm not free to come and go as I please here.' She had no doubt that Joey would take her even if Davis forbade it. 'Do you want to come with us?' she asked. Davis didn't answer and she took his silence to mean no. She could not see his face, the look he gave Joey, the implied threat.

Tanner and Bobby stood in the teeming rain, facing each other across the mouth of the mine.

'For God's sake, Bobby, use your head. It's raining, the mine's half full of water and there's no gold in it anyway.'

'That's what you say.'

'That's what I know.' They gazed at each other for a moment, then Tanner exhaled in frustration. 'Let's give it away, Bobby, let's try somewhere else.'

'No.'

'Please,' he said desperately. 'I want to do this with your agreement. I want to cut our losses and start building a decent life, either here in a new mine, in Melbourne with a new job, or with you two in boarding school and me at sea.' He wiped the rain away from his face. 'Those are the choices so make up your mind, because whether you want to or not we're giving up this useless damn hole in the ground.' Tanner finished angrily, but the boy had ceased to listen long before his last words. 'Don't go back into the mine, Bobby, it's too dangerous.' Tanner softened his tone. 'Fossick on the surface if you must but it's Sunday, the day of rest, a damn miserable one at that and my advice to you is to take the rest and think hard about what I've said, for I promise you I'll not stay in this place much longer.'

'What if I won't go with you?'

'Commissioner said this claim and everything else was mine to control as long as I provided for you and Jilly. What will you do if I take it all and move it further up the gully or sell it and go back to Melbourne?' The boy said nothing, but walked to the edge of the mine and stared at the inky waters in its depths. He turned and examined the rest of the claim, reduced to a sea of mud by their excavations.

'My father saw a nugget as big as his fist.' He spoke slowly, enunciating each syllable clearly the way a man might if he was in pain.

'Your father saw someone in his mine, someone who beat him to death, and in his last moments of consciousness his mind conjured up a vision of that which he most wanted to see.' Tanner's voice held such bitterness and grief that even the boy couldn't argue with him. Instead, Bobby made for the shanty, leaving Tanner alone in the mud and the rain.

He remained there even after the boy had reached the shanty, and it shocked Joey to find him like that, a solitary figure unmoving in the pouring rain.

'Tanner,' he called, and the figure turned slowly to face him.

'What's wrong?' Amy had recognised the sound of concern.

'Nothing.' Joey gently urged the horse forward.

'What brings you out in all this rain?' Tanner asked, and there was no warmth in his voice. Joey helped Amy down from the horse, and she extended her hands to Tanner, but he didn't take them. 'Perhaps we should go inside.'

'Are the children there?' Amy asked.

'Yes.'

'Then I'd rather talk out here for the moment.' Tanner glanced at Joey, hoping to glean some idea of what was going on from his usually expressive face.

'It's awful wet,' Joey ventured.

'Then you go in,' Amy said. 'It's best we talk alone.' Joey left and Amy reached again for Tanner's hands, and this time he responded. 'I wish you'd come and see me sometimes.' She squeezed his hand. 'The track to the water holes comes quite near here, you must know when Davis isn't there.'

'And if I didn't you could always get Joey to drop off one of those beads Davis made you to let me know the coast is clear.' She bowed her head and Tanner instantly regretted his words. There was an awkward silence, then Amy felt behind her neck and undid the chain from which hung the small cross and ring that Tanner had given her. She took Tanner's hand and placed them in it. She heard his sharp intake of breath and realised that he had misinterpreted her gesture. She maintained her grip on his hand.

'These belong to Catherine, not me.' She smiled at him. 'They meant so much when you gave them to me, a reassurance, a promise, and I know they'll mean the same to Catherine, perhaps more.' She waited for him to respond, wishing that she could see his face.

'Maybe the ring,' he said, 'but keep the cross.'

'No, it was your mother's, even Jilly has more right to it than I.'

'I'd sooner you had it.'

'I can't take it.'

'Do you want no part of me?' he asked bitterly, and her brave smile crumbled.

'I never meant to hurt you.' Her lips trembled. 'I wanted, I wanted —' She stopped, unable to explain.

'What do you want, Amy?'

'I want you to be happy, I want us all to be happy. I want you to get out of this mine and away from those awful children. I want you to be with Catherine and to be happy. I want you to be my Uncle John, I want to call you that and if I marry Davis I want you to be the one who gives me away.' Her voice faltered and ceased.

In the silence that followed Tanner could only think of one thing that she'd said, one phrase, one word—if she married Davis. 'If', not 'when'. He looked down at her standing before him in the icy rain, her hair sodden and matted clinging to her face and neck, her saturated dress hanging about her slight frame. Her face was raised up to him, but the rain made it impossible for him to tell if she was crying. He believed she was. She looked worse than she had that first day in London, a child miserably reaching out to the closest thing she had to a parent. Other things she'd said began to register in his mind. 'Those awful children,' a sign of jealousy perhaps, a kind of sibling rivalry, and her blessing for himself and Catherine. His grip tightened over the cross and the ring, a lovely gesture and one that he'd misread. It finally struck him how much the animosity between himself and Davis had hurt her, for if she had objected to Catherine the way he had to Davis it would have torn him apart. He put his arm around her.

'I'd be honoured to stand up with you if you ever get married and I couldn't imagine you calling me anything but Uncle John.' He guided her to the shanty. 'How did you know about Catherine?'

'Joey told me.'

'Joey,' he said thoughtfully.

'He said nothing would come of it because you weren't the type to push and Catherine was too frightened.'

'A very perceptive man, our Joey.'

'Why would she be frightened of you?'

'I don't think it's me in particular.' They paused at the shanty door. 'I think she's been alone too long, hurt too often, to let anyone close to her.' He ushered her through the door.

'Will the ring and the cross help?'

'They might.'

On the rear wall of the shanty was a fireplace. It had not been necessary to use it during the summer months, nor even desirable, for it smoked constantly and, although it gave off little heat, it would have made the shanty intolerably stuffy. Worst of all, it was totally impractical for cooking and no one could use it without getting burnt, least of all Amy. Necessity had forced Tanner to light the fire and he guided Amy towards it, scolding her mildly for coming out in such weather. Joey was already squatting by the hearth, attempting to get a billy to boil. He smiled at them.

'Might be an idea if Amy stays here for a few days, 'til we get a bit of dry weather.'

'No,' Amy began apprehensively.

'It'll be all right,' Joey interrupted.

'Davis won't like it.' Tanner shared Amy's misgivings.

'He'll understand,' Joey insisted. 'Our tent's running with water, the blankets are soaked, the food's ruined and the fire's out. I need a few days to build some bunks and a cook house where we can keep a fire going.'

Tanner looked at him sceptically. 'You think Davis will agree to Amy staying here while you do all that?'

'It's not up to him.' Joey glanced at Amy.

'Would you like to stay?' Tanner asked her. 'Just 'til things dry out a bit?'

'I should go back and talk to him first,' she said.

Tanner shook his head. 'You can't keep on traipsing about in this rain.' Amy moved uneasily, she looked cold and miserable, unwilling to leave but afraid to stay. 'Joey, would you mind going back and getting Davis? If your food's ruined and your fire's out he'll appreciate a hot meal, and maybe after he's had one he'll see the logic in Amy staying here for a while.' Joey nodded. 'Bring back the blankets and Amy's clothes, and we'll see if we can dry them out.' Joey made to rise. 'Have your tea first.'

Jilly brought the mugs, beaming at Joey as she handed them to him.

'I've missed you,' Joey said. She turned her head coyly and snuggled close to Tanner. 'Well, I'll be damned.'

'What?' Amy asked.

'He's stolen my best girl, whisked her away from under me nose.' Jilly giggled and Amy guessed that she had preferred Tanner to Joey. She smiled genuinely, pleased by the change in Jilly and more than willing to forgive her for her past transgressions. Bobby was another matter. She frowned as she thought of him. They were too close in age for her to accept the excuse of youth for his behaviour and too far apart in ethics, intellect and maturity for her to have any understanding of it. Jilly touched Amy's hand the way one might touch a deaf person to get their attention.

'Uncle John's going to take me to see Mummy and Daddy's grave.'

Amy didn't know how to respond but the child sounded pleased, so she said: 'That's nice.'

'We're going back to Melbourne and I'm going to have a proper bed.'

'That's nice,' Amy said again but with less conviction, for Tanner's departure was the last thing she wanted.

Joey and Davis returned sooner than expected, bringing armfuls of wet blankets and clothes. Davis dumped his goods down in front of the fire.

'I've brought what food I could salvage too.' He smiled at everyone. 'It's nice of you to ask us back here.' Tanner and Joey exchanged glances, but neither said anything. 'It'll only take us a day or two to fix things up.' He'd shed his wet coat and was sitting next to Amy, using her hands to warm himself. 'I wish I could get hold of a decent length of canvas, make a roof over the tent and extend it out like a verandah so that it covered the camp fire as well.' He looked round the shanty as if searching for items that might be of use to him. 'We could make the bunks out of sack stretched over wooden frames . . .' He talked on and on, his enthusiasm overriding any objection anyone might have to anything he proposed. He slept next to Amy on the floor in front of the fire, and Tanner found himself pushed to the furthest corner sharing a bed with Jilly.

The next day Joey and Davis left early for their claim and did not return until late at night. It was the beginning of a pattern that continued for the rest of the week.

Finally, the rain stopped and the weather cleared to a fine, cold day with an icy, southerly wind. Tanner helped Amy rig clotheslines to dry off the last of the blankets, while Jilly hung around their feet chattering about pink curtains and matching quilts.

'Where's Bobby?' Tanner asked, casually glancing round the mud pile that was their claim.

'In the mine,' Jilly answered.

'What?'

'In the mine,' she repeated, but Tanner was already on his way.

'Get out,' he bellowed at the boy.

Bobby was standing knee deep in water, digging a lateral tunnel at about waist height. Other lateral tunnels had been dug further up, most of them running back towards the adjacent claim.

'Get out now!' Tanner roared. He was more angry at being disobeyed than he was concerned by the potential danger, so his manner remained domineering rather than reasonable. 'Did you hear me?'

Bobby looked up disinterestedly. 'Water's not deep.'

'I don't care, I said to stay out of the mine.' The boy ignored him, turning his attention back to the tunnel. Tanner started down the ladder. He had an urge to shake the boy, to drag him out of the mine and into the cart and as far away from the diggings as he could get.

He didn't actually see it happen—he turned at the sound of Bobby's cry to see mud spewing from one of the lateral tunnels just above the boy's head. It showered over him, knocking him sideways, then another tunnel collapsed sending more mud down on him. The boy groped blindly to the ladder but he couldn't climb it, the pressure of the mud pulling him down.

Tanner stared at the wall in horror as he realised what had happened. The adjacent mine had been half full of water and mud and where their lateral tunnels had penetrated close to the mine the wall had been weakened and finally breached.

He climbed down the ladder, grabbing the boy's hand trying to pull him free, but the oozing mud made it impossible for him to maintain his grip. The tighter he held Bobby the more he slipped away from him. He could feel the boy's fingers bend and crush within his grip—they seemed so small and fragile and not part of a bitter, stubborn boy but part of a helpless, frightened child.

Tanner edged further down the ladder. The mud was up to the boy's waist. He tried to put his arm under the boy's shoulder to lift him, but his position on the ladder made it impossible. He looked about him hopelessly—he needed a rope. He started for the surface, but the boy grabbed hold of his legs, screaming.

'No! No!' There was a look of panic on his muddy face. Tanner stared at him, then back at the surface. There was a moment, a pause, a second of indecision, then Tanner jumped into the mud beside the boy. He bent down, lifting the boy under the crutch and easing him higher and higher up the ladder until the boy could get a foothold on his knee. He dropped lower, getting his shoulder under the boy's backside, then slowly and painfully he tried to straighten up. The strain was massive, and he felt his muscles begin to shudder as the mud dragged the boy back, sucking him down with greater force than quicksand. Bobby grabbed the ladder, pulling himself higher using Tanner's arms and shoulder, even his head as a stepping stone upon which to scramble to safety.

Tanner had sunk down into the mud as he lifted the boy, and his body refused to make the effort needed to force himself up. He breathed heavily, trying to summon the strength to grip the ladder, to pull himself up just one rung. Slowly, agonisingly, he moved his body, but it felt like it was being held back by a fantastic weight. He heard someone scream, a child's voice, high pitched and piercing. He lifted his foot, searching vainly for the next rung. He thought he'd found it, but as he put pressure on it his foot sank uselessly deeper into the mud. Someone was yelling, Amy perhaps, he couldn't make out the words. He tried again, the speed at which the mud was rising seemed to have slowed.

He made a gigantic effort and succeeded in hauling himself up one rung.

'Get a rope.' A man's voice—familiar. Tanner felt movement on the ladder above him and a rope being passed round his chest. He couldn't look up but he sensed that the man was Joey. He tried to speak but no sound came, then the man left and Tanner felt the rope become tight.

'Heave,' someone shouted, but the voice was drowned out by Jilly's scream. A large section of the wall between the two mines had collapsed, the dirt and mud engulfing Tanner and flattening him against the ladder with such force that it expelled all the air from his lungs. He gasped, trying to catch his breath, but dirt and mud blocked his nose and filled his mouth.

He didn't hear the clamour above, the screams of 'Get the horse', but he felt the burning pain of the rope as it dug into his chest and back, he felt the mud tearing at his clothes, his boots being stripped away, one ankle twisting painfully as if it would break, then numbness. All at once he was breathing and vomiting, his head and shoulders free of the mud. Then suddenly his whole body came free and he was dragged out of the mine, the ladder gouging him as he was pulled over the top of it onto the surface.

Water poured over his face, forcing him back to consciousness. His eyes wouldn't open, the dirt made them sting unbearably, more water doused him and he compelled his eyes to open despite their painful protest.

'Enough,' Joey yelled, kneeling down beside him.

'Joey.' Amy began feeling her way towards them.

'He's all right, now stay where you are.' He turned to Jilly. 'Get some blankets.' Joey used a knife to cut away the rope and the rest of Tanner's clothes. 'You're bruised up awful bad,' he said. 'I wouldn't be surprised if your ribs are broken.'

'Again,' Tanner murmured.

'What?'

'You saved my life again.'

Joey looked disgusted. 'What possessed you to go down in that mine?'

'Bobby,' Tanner murmured, 'caught in the mud slide, couldn't leave him.'

Joey eased Tanner into a sitting position.

'Did you not think to get a rope?'

'No time.' Jilly returned with the blankets and Joey wrapped them round Tanner.

'You know there's a fine line between courage and stupidity,' Joey said as he and another miner lifted Tanner to his feet. Tanner coughed non-committally and made the effort to take his own weight, but his legs buckled beneath him and he had an odd sensation as if his bones had been stripped out by the mud.

'Where's the boy?' Tanner managed to ask. Joey was all but carrying him and the shanty had never seemed so far from the mine.

'Don't know,' Joey grunted. 'When I arrived all I saw was Amy yelling her head off and miners running from everywhere.'

Bobby was inside the shanty, his clothes discarded in a filthy trail that led from the door to the fire where he crouched over a bucket of water washing the last of the mud from his body. He looked up as Tanner entered, then wrapped himself in a blanket and retreated to his accustomed corner. Joey seated Tanner by the fire.

'Where's Amy?'

'I'll get her.' Joey stood upright, his eyes fixed on the boy for a moment, but he left without comment.

Davis had returned by the time they'd finished cleaning Tanner up and plying him with tea and rum. He knelt down beside Tanner, studying the vicious wield the rope had made and the gash across his hip and thigh.

'Sorry I wasn't here to help,' he said, and Tanner had no doubt that he meant it for there was nothing Davis would have liked more than to have him in his debt again. 'You were lucky,' he added.

'Aye.' Joey joined the semi-circle that sat around the fire.

'How did it happen exactly?' Davis took up a position next to Amy.

'Boy was in the mine when the wall started caving in,' Tanner began wearily. 'Got him out, couldn't get myself out.'

'I told Amy.' Jilly said suddenly, 'didn't I Amy? I saw Bobby get out of the mine and I waited for you and when you didn't come I told Amy and we went to see and I told Amy about the mud.'

'Did you now?' Tanner said. 'You probably saved my life.' He smiled at her, then switched his gaze to Bobby, his expression souring as he did so, for it occurred to him as it had to everyone else that the boy had made no attempt to get help for him.

194

CHAPTER 23

✦✦✦✦✦✦✦✦✦✦✦✦✦

T ANNER SAT by the fire examining his swollen foot. It was twisted, not broken, but that didn't make it any less difficult to get about. His chest still ached and the gash on his hip showed no sign of healing. Amy had gone with Joey and Davis to put the finishing touches on the new camp, while Jilly played nursemaid and Bobby sat morosely in the corner.

'Anybody home?' a voice called from the door.

'Zeke.' Tanner made a half-hearted attempt to rise, then sank back into his place.

'Well, what have you done to yourself?' Zeke smiled broadly as he traversed the shanty. 'Buried alive I hear.' His face became more serious as he sat beside Tanner. 'I've seen men die that way.'

'The boy was trapped,' Tanner said irritably.

'So I heard.' Zeke began making himself a cup of tea. 'There's a difference between bravery and stupidity, you know.'

'So Joey says.' Tanner moved uncomfortably. 'Not that he's one to talk, he's saved my life three times and if it hadn't been for Davis he might well have been killed on the first occasion.'

Zeke raised his eyebrows thoughtfully. 'I heard the three of them have staked a new claim.'

'Yes, there wasn't much point in Joey staying here and Davis had to start again, he was cheated by his partners.'

'So I heard.'

'Is there anything you don't hear?'

'I don't hear that you've given up this useless hole in the ground.'

'I'm going to just as soon as Catherine gets back. I'm going to sell up everything and go back to Melbourne with her.'

'Never!' The boy sprang to his feet. 'I'll never go back to Melbourne, never.' He lurched for the door then halted, surveying the claim before heading towards the track.

'Either that,' Tanner continued patiently, 'or we'll start again somewhere else.'

195

'No,' Jilly wailed. 'You said I'd have a proper bed, in a proper house.' Tanner pulled her down beside him, shushing her as he did so.

'As you can see we are all in complete agreement.' Zeke smiled. 'Speaking of Catherine, I don't suppose you've seen her?'

Zeke shook his head. 'She could be anywhere, rain started in Melbourne before it did here, but according to Paddy if anyone can get through she can.' Zeke fished the billy gingerly from the fire. 'Stupid arrangement this.' He indicated the fireplace.

'My brother made it.' Tanner smiled. 'He never was much at building things, too much the dreamer.'

'Not a practical soul like you?'

'I know my limitations.'

'Oh sure, that's why you jumped into a hole full of mud and onto the deck of a burning ship.'

'They are my limitations.' Zeke looked perplexed. 'Taking too big a risk for too little reason.' Tanner leant his head back against the shanty wall and closed his eyes. He could see his brother clearly, not as he was the last time he saw him but as he had been they were younger. 'We were alike Bob and I, dreamers, too sickened by the life we were born to to face the reality of it, more willing to throw it away than to live it out as fate decreed, too soft-headed to know the type of sacrifice we'd have to make to change it, too soft-hearted to make it when the time came.' He accepted the tea Zeke handed him. 'I knew what I was, the way I'd probably end up, that's why I never took on a wife and children, but Bob thought . . .' He stopped. It didn't matter what Bob had thought, he'd taken his risk and lost his life, not for a friend or a child but for a useless hole in the ground.

'You've plenty of children now.' Zeke observed.

Tanner smiled at the little girl nestled beside him. 'And there's a wife I wouldn't mind having.'

'Catherine?' Tanner nodded. 'She wouldn't fit well in Melbourne society.'

'No, and I'm reluctant to leave Amy, but I haven't the heart to start again here.'

'So, what will you do?'

Tanner shook his head. Jilly had been listening to the conversation, and although she didn't fully understand its implications she understood that Tanner wanted to marry Ugly and that Ugly wouldn't want to live in Melbourne.

'We could live with Ugly on the road,' she said. 'If you got married, we could live with Ugly, it wouldn't matter if I didn't have a proper bed.'

'Well, there you are,' Zeke laughed. 'Little lady's got it all worked out for you.'

Tanner smiled non-committally, for Jilly's suggestion had more merit than Zeke imagined. Catherine may well accept him in her own environment, especially as a bit of brute strength wouldn't go astray at this time of the year. He would be able to check on Amy each time they returned here. The only stumbling block was Bobby. He smiled at Jilly.

'You're very kind, I'll keep it in mind.'

Mid-morning on the following day found Tanner alone in the camp. Joey, Davis and Amy had left early to take up residence in their new camp, and Tanner had sent Bobby off in the cart to get some supplies and to ask about for anyone who might want to hire them to haul wash dirt. At the last minute Jilly decided that she wanted to go too, and as the day wore on Tanner became more and more uneasy about his decision to let her go.

He leant heavily on the makeshift walking stick as he hobbled to the edge of the claim, peering out across the valley hoping for some sign of them. He continued walking until he arrived at the track that led up the gully, pausing to consider his position. His ankle gave him little pain, but it was still very weak and, although he might easily manage the climb down the side of the gully, he'd have no end of difficulties getting back. Of course once he found the children they could give him a lift back, unless they were in trouble and if they were he'd be more of a burden than a help in his present state and if they weren't then there was little point in him going. He went on arguing with himself as he made his way down to the valley floor.

The area was veined with watercourses, which were dry in summer and mud in winter. They joined together at the foot of the gully they formed a small creek, which ran through a small, ravine-like creek bed. In times of heavy rain the little creek overflowed with water, but it soon drained to a string of muddy puddles. As the inclination of the gully lessened the depth of the creek bed reduced, until it finally disappeared allowing its water to disperse across the flat, turning it into a swamp. It was here that the track met the little creek, and logs had been laid across it to stop carts sinking into the mud, but it was still an unpleasant, boggy hole and most pedestrians and horsemen chose to cross the creek further up, jumping or climbing across the narrow ravine.

Tanner hesitated on the bank, inspecting the yellow mud beneath him. He was at the narrowest point of the ravine and on a good day he might have jumped it, but not today. A little further down the gap was wider and the mud was broken up into puddles divided by slightly higher pieces of ground, one of which Tanner decided might hold his weight. He made his way to it, climbing cautiously down the bank, sliding occasionally but never actually losing control. He prodded the higher piece of ground tentatively with his foot—it seemed firm enough, so he risked it and arrived safely on the other side more pleased with himself than he should have been for there still remained the climb up the other side.

It was a steeper bank than the one Tanner had descended, and to make matters worse his ankle, which had barely been able to support him, would now not even lift him. He still carried the stick, which made him even more awkward as it left only one hand free to grab at the crumbling bank. He cursed himself for his stupidity as he fumbled from foothold to foothold until he'd almost reached the top. He threw his stick up onto the bank then lunged at a small sapling growing precariously on the edge of the creek bed. Tanner grasped the tiny trunk, hoping it would support his full weight, but as he began to drag himself up, the bank, undermined by weeks of rain, collapsed.

He fell back into the creek, screaming in agony as he landed on the same thigh and hip that he'd injured in the mine. He lay gasping in pain, dirt and mud all around him, the tiny sapling lying across his chest. His ankle ached unbearably and the welt on his back and chest stung enough to put tears in his eyes. As his breathing steadied he made a few half-hearted attempts to move before surrendering to his predicament. Other miners had heard his scream and come running, but stopped when they neared the edge. Tanner lay scanning the faces that peered back at him, wondering why no one moved to assist him. He closed his eyes and threw back his head, panting as he tried vainly to extricate himself from the dirt. It was this gesture that alerted the miners to the fact that he was hurt. One by one they began to clamber down the bank, slipping and sliding in the crumbling earth.

'Jesus,' one man yelled as he fought to control his descent. 'Christ, will you look at that.' The man next to him gawked at the stone in his neighbour's hand.

'It's bloody gold,' he said stupidly. Suddenly the bank was alive with miners crawling on top of one another, digging in the soft soil with their bare hands. More miners poured into the creek bed, scratching and tearing at the bank, and some arrived with shovels and picks, buckets and bags. The dirt and the small sapling that had fallen on Tanner were thrown off him in the frantic search for gold. He was trodden on, scrambled over and generally ignored by just about everyone. Finally, one miner attempted to stake a claim, another challenged him and a fight broke out with screams of 'Get the commissioner'. While the two men battered each other and a few more tried to negotiate a settlement, a large proportion of the crowd turned to watch, leaving only the die-hards still grubbing in the mud for by this time most of the nugget-size gold had been extracted from the soft surface soil.

Tanner moved cautiously—the shock that had taken possession of him after the fall and held him enthralled during the subsequent confusion was wearing off. The intense pain had diminished to a tolerable level and the discomfort of moving became preferable to the discomfort of remaining in the fetid bog. He eased himself into a sitting position. His twisted ankle was still buried under a pile of sloppy mud and stones. Carefully he began to dig it out, half afraid that the fall might have caused further damage. One of the rocks seemed abnormally heavy for its size, requiring both hands to lift it instead of one. Its surface had an unusual texture and for some reason Tanner's heart began to race with anticipation as he dragged it from the bog. He laid it on his lap and cleaned the mud off its surface, then turned it over and cleaned it again, still unable to believe what he was seeing. Gold— it must have weighed twenty pounds at least.

Tanner rolled to a kneeling position clutching the nugget to him as he tried to rise. He had never understood men's obsession with gold, the dreams or the greed it evoked. He had never thought it worth fighting for let alone worth dying for, in fact there had been times when he'd even doubted it was worth digging for, but now that he had the gold in his possession his determination to keep it was almost overpowering.

He struggled back to the bank down which he'd recently climbed, hiding the nugget in his shirt, clutching it to his side as he searched for an easy way out. Further up the valley the creek bed divided into several smaller gullies, all too narrow and deep. Further down the valley the creek bed became wider and filled with putrid mud. He glanced back at the miners still fighting and arguing amongst themselves. One man grabbed another's nuggets, screaming that the creek formed part of his claim, the second man grabbed a pick and wielded it threateningly, the first man brought up a gun and a stillness fell across the crowd. Tanner, too, was caught in immobility, for if this claim was worth fighting for then a nugget the size of a man's two fists was worth killing for.

The moment of paralysis passed with the cry of 'The commissioner's coming'. Tanner turned to face the steep side of the ravine. It seemed so much higher now, so much more sheer. There were no footholds and the parts of the bank that didn't disintegrate at his touch were too slippery or too steep to climb. Behind him he could hear a man yelling that the claim was his and that they were all thieves. His cry was answered with jeers and abuse but if it was true, if the claim was his, they were all thieves. Tanner tore at the bank with his free hand, kicking and pushing at the earth, ignoring the screaming pain in his ankle. He'd been a cheat and a liar all his life, but he'd never done anything like this, never had anything so valuable, never been so intent on keeping it. He lost his grip on the soft earth, his fingers grabbed helplessly at the mud and despite the pain he forced his feet to act as braces. The gold was his and there was no one to say otherwise, not until the commissioner came, and there were dozens like him who'd grubbed gold from the creek—surely they wouldn't be expected to give it back. He climbed blindly up the bank, mindless of how far he'd gone or how far he had to go.

Finally, he could see the top of the bank and with his free arm he grabbed at it, pulling himself up, first his shoulders, then his chest, then the gold. He lay still, enjoying the sheer relief of no longer having to support its weight. After a few moments he mustered his strength and dragged himself up onto the bank. It suddenly struck him as funny that such a simple climb almost proved to be insurmountable. He was grinning as he got to his knees, but a gunshot sent him sprawling.

'No, you don't, anyone leaves before the commissioner gets here and I'll shoot them.' Tanner turned his head cautiously—

on the far side of the bank stood a man with a gun. He was a tall man and his stance was set with determination. The gun was raised and aimed, but not at Tanner. His quarry was a group of men who were trying to return to their own claims.

'You shoot one of us and it'll be murder and you'll be strung up before the commissioner gets here.' There was the sound of general agreement. 'I say any man wants to leave leaves now, he can't shoot us all.' It was a thin, wiry man who spoke. 'And if you decide to make an example of one of us, you'd better be damned sure that he's carrying gold and that the gold's yours.' The wiry man turned and walked steadily away, then his companions followed him and one by one other miners plucked up their courage and left.

'No!' The man with the gun screamed, firing a shot in the air. No one even hesitated, and no matter what the commissioner said none of the gold would be returned.

Tanner laboured doggedly up the track. Every injury he'd received in the cave-in had been aggravated by the fall, and carrying the gold brought an exhaustion that accentuated every ache and pain. The last few paces to the shanty were the hardest. The gold had slipped so that he was clinging to it with weakening fingers, his side cramped every time he took a step and his ankle refused to take his weight at all. He sank to the ground just inside the shanty door, the gold falling from his grip as he did so.

How long he lay there was uncertain, but he came suddenly to his senses as if disturbed by some external influence. He had to hide the gold, it was an instinctive reaction rather than a logical decision, but even after reflection Tanner decided that it was the right one. He needed to know the commissioner's ruling before he told anyone, and even then he'd tell only a few. Given the way his brother had died, he'd not take the risk of attracting thieves.

He crawled to the fire, which had gone out, and removed the stones that formed the hearth. He dug down to a depth where the earth was cold and damp and buried the gold there. He replaced the dirt and stones, restarted the fire, then collected up the excess dirt and deposited it on the claim.

Tanner stared despondently at his dirty hands and equally dirty clothes. He'd obviously been doing more than admiring the scenery, and the effort required to clean himself up was more than he felt like making. However, by the time the children returned his clothes were out drying, the billy was boiling and the makings of a damper was ready to cook.

'You were a while,' Tanner observed.

'There was a big fight.' Jilly came close to him, waiting for the gesture of affection she'd come to expect.

'Was there now?' He patted her shoulder. 'What happened?'

'They found gold in the creek bed,' Bobby answered for her. 'One man said it was his claim, but the others just took what they liked anyway.'

'Was it his claim?' Tanner asked.

'Commissioner said not, but what else could he say with half the miners in the lower gully ready to riot if he said otherwise. Now there's a great rush to see who can stake it first and a great fight with men pulling out each other's markers. Commissioner's a fool.' Bobby's answer gave little doubt to where his sympathies lay, and Tanner drew back from mentioning the nugget. He gazed at the boy thoughtfully—of course he'd have to tell him soon, but perhaps it would be wiser to confirm the commissioner's decision first.

Bobby returned his even stare. 'Are you going to cook it or are we having it raw?' The boy's sarcasm jolted Tanner back to reality.

'Cook it yourself, I'm going to see Joey.' The boy made no reply and Tanner was almost out the door before Jilly spoke.

'Can I come too?'

'I suppose so.'

She trailed outside after him. 'Joey's at the wash pools, we saw them going when we were coming back.'

'Well, then, there's not much point in going to visit if he isn't going to be there.'

'We could see Amy.'

'Why don't we wait and go after tea when everyone's finished working. We'll be able to have a nice long visit then.' The child nodded agreeably. 'The notice about hauling wash dirt, did they let you put it up in the store?'

'Yes, but we couldn't get all the supplies, we didn't have enough gold. The man said near nothing was getting through and what was cost twice as much.' They had re-entered the shanty. 'Do you think Ugly will get through?'

'Catherine,' Tanner corrected, 'will get through, if anyone can.'

The afternoon passed incredibly slowly, time and again Tanner brought himself to the point of telling Bobby but each time he retreated from it. The boy had taken to moping about outside, contemplating the abandoned mine and its depths still half full of mud. Each time Tanner approached Bobby he was greeted with barbed comments or silent snubs. They ate their evening meal early and without asking Bobby to join them Tanner and Jilly took one of the cart horses and headed up the gully.

The new camp still left much to be desired. A tarpaulin had been erected over the tent and fireplace, thereby directing most of the smoke into their sleeping and eating areas. The raised bunks took up much of the available tent space, so most of their goods were heaped together under the tarpaulin leaving little room for seating. Amy and Jilly sat on a bunk just inside the entrance of the tent. Davis was seated on a crate just outside and Joey and Tanner occupied a log seat next to the fire. They sipped tea and Tanner waited for one of the others to introduce the subject of the gold find at the creek. It was Joey who obliged.

'Did you hear about the doings down the gully?'

'A gold strike,' Tanner prompted.

'Aye, a gold strike and damn near a riot as well. One damn fool pulled a gun.'

'Well, wouldn't you,' Davis interrupted, 'if you saw men raking out nuggets half the size of your thumb from land you thought was on your claim?'

'Was it on his claim?' Tanner asked.

'Commissioner said not and he paced it out to be sure.'

'And that damn near caused another riot,' Davis laughed. 'Everyone fighting over who found the gold first.'

'A thick-set, red-headed man with a beard,' Tanner said flatly.

'How do you know?' Amy asked.

'I was there, I was crossing the creek when the bank gave way, and he came to help me out.'

'Well, I'll be damned,' Joey swore.

'Tell me,' Tanner continued, 'what did the commissioner say about all the gold that was taken before anyone had a chance to stake a claim?'

'Belongs to whoever took it,' Davis answered. 'It was open

land until the markers were set and the names recorded.' His eyes narrowed, focusing intently on Tanner. 'What's it to you anyway?'

'I found a nugget there.'

'Oh, Uncle John.' Amy was delighted.

'Only one,' Davis scoffed.

'Only one,' Tanner confirmed, but the dignity of his speech and the amusement that played round his mouth alerted Davis.

'How big?' he asked.

Tanner held his two fists together and extended them for Davis to see. 'Twenty pounds, maybe more.' Amy gasped and Joey whistled.

A sly smile spread across Davis' face. 'And what would you have done if the commissioner had ruled in favour of the man who said it was on his claim?'

'Same as every other man there, same as you'd have done.' Davis nodded understandingly.

'What?' Amy asked.

'Taken it back to his own claim and pretended he found it there,' Davis answered.

'But that's dishonest,' Amy said aghast. Both men laughed at her.

'Dishonest and unlawful,' Tanner agreed smiling.

'It's wrong,' she insisted and Tanner remembered the King's Head Tavern, a wool cape and a green portmanteau.

'Don't start preaching morals at me,' he admonished her. 'There's little that's moral or just in this world and certainly not the arbitrary decisions of our mealy-mouthed officials.'

'You feel the same do you?' She turned to where she knew Davis was sitting, and the keenness in her face prevented him from lying.

'You don't understand the way of it Amy. Them that makes the laws set them up for their own advantage then make it morally wrong to disobey. A poor man's got no right to challenge, no way of changing things. Neither Tanner here or the man who said it was his claim can appeal the commissioner's decision. There's no justice in any of it, they charge us thirty shillings a month whether we find gold or not and do little or nothing to support or protect us. Money made by the gumption of those who come here to dig is being sent back to England for them that's too lazy to get out of their chairs to answer their own door or stoke their own fire. They take it openly and honestly and well within the law, and tell me where's the morality in that?' He finished acrimoniously and so suddenly that for an instant no one spoke.

'Well, it hardly matters does it?' Joey said at last. 'I mean, gold's Tanner's, commissioner said so, there's no need to pretend he found it anywhere else.'

'Just as well too,' Davis added.

'Why?' Amy asked.

'If he'd said the gold had come from the claim the boy would want his share.'

'Makes no difference,' Tanner said. 'Children will share in everything I have no matter where it comes from.' But it did make a difference and Tanner knew now why he'd held back from telling the boy. This gold was his, his alone, Bobby had no claim to it and no matter what he gave the boy the fact would remain that it was a gift from his uncle not a bequest from his parents or something he'd earnt by his own labour.

'Does that mean I can have my proper bed?' Jilly asked.

'Probably,' Tanner said cautiously, 'though it may not be in a proper house. You see, I've a mind to buy into a coastal freighter, a ship, and it might be that I have to take you with me.'

'Could I still have a pink quilt?'

'Of course.' He smiled. They lapsed into silence as each one realised that Tanner wasn't talking about some dim and distant dream but the possible and immediate future.

'What about Catherine?' Amy asked.

'I think she'd like the sea.'

'And Bobby?'

'Boarding school, I suppose.'

It was late when Tanner and Jilly arrived home; no light shone from their camp and it was with relief that Tanner realised that the boy was asleep. Before putting Jilly to bed Tanner cautioned her not to say anything about the gold to Bobby until he had a chance to speak to him.

He smiled as he tucked her up in the makeshift bed, but the smile faded as he sank down on to his own untidy bed. How to tell Bobby—that was his problem. How to do it without widening the rift that already existed between them? Tanner rolled on to his side. Why couldn't he let the boy think the gold had come from the mine? He turned on to his back: if Bobby thought the gold came from the mine he'd never give it up. He rolled on to his side again, there seemed no position in which he was comfortable. He closed his eyes and sighed frustratedly. How to tell Bobby?

CHAPTER 24

++++++++++++++

'D o so."
  'Do not.'
'Do so.'

The argument penetrated Tanner's unconscious state, although the voices seemed miles away.

'You stupid, troublemaking little brat, I ought to belt you.' Bobby moved threateningly towards his sister and she screamed.

'Stop it, stop it,' Tanner yelled. He forced his eyes open and dragged himself into a sitting position.

'I do know a secret, don't I Uncle John?' She nestled beside him, taking courage from his strength.

'Yes,' Tanner moaned as he prayed for some way to put it off until after breakfast.

'I told you I don't care about your stupid secrets.' Bobby crouched by the fire, throwing twigs and dried leaves on to the embers. 'I'm going to have a pink quilt.'

'Oh, yes, it'll look bloody lovely in this place.'

'It won't be in this place,' Tanner said softly.

The boy regarded him coldly. 'That again, is it? Well you gave me a choice and I choose not to go back to Melbourne, not to have any proper houses nor pretty pink quilts neither.'

'Things have changed.' The quiet tones of Tanner's voice were accentuated by Bobby's loud anger.

'Changed have they? I'll bet they've changed. You thought I wouldn't have the guts to start again. You thought I'd want to go crawling back to Melbourne or be so sick at heart that I'd leave it up to you.' Bobby had risen to his feet and was looking down at Tanner, shouting at him with such venom that Tanner was too surprised to be offended. 'Well, I'll not give up, I'll not go back to Melbourne. There's gold here and I'm going to have my share of it.'

Tanner got slowly to his feet. 'Bobby, listen to me —'

'No!' The boy bellowed. 'I've seen the gold, I know it's there. Yesterday they were digging nuggets out of the creek bed with their bare hands.'

'I know, Bobby.' Tanner's voice wasn't loud, but it was commanding. 'I found a nugget there too.'

'In the creek?'

'Yes, a big one, twenty pounds or more.' The boy shook his head vaguely. 'You see, I was the one who fell in the creek, the one they were pulling out when they found the gold.' The shaking of Bobby's head became more pronounced and his breathing became shallow and agitated. 'I found the nugget when I was climbing out.'

'I see, I see,' the boy stammered. 'You found it in the creek and it's yours, yours alone.'

'It makes no difference,' Tanner tried to interrupt.

'No difference, no difference at all, except if you'd found it in the mine there'd be a share for me, a share for Jilly.'

'I didn't find it in the mine.'

'I don't believe you.' The boy's nostrils flared with anger and his voice was tinged with hysteria. 'You found it in the mine.'

'Bobby—'

'When, when did you find it, eh? Was it before Amy and Joey left, did you cheat them out of their share too, or was it just before the rain, just before you warned me to keep out of the mine? Did you leave it hidden there? Did you rig the mine to cave-in on anyone who went down there? Is that why you came after me, to get your precious nugget?' The boy's voice had built steadily louder and louder until Tanner had to yell to be heard.

'Bobby, I told you —'

'Liar, liar, liar.'

'Stop it.' Tanner shook Bobby and raised his hand to hit him. The boy didn't flinch, and the look of triumph on his face as Tanner lowered his hand almost made him regret his self-control. 'I found the nugget in the creek bed.'

'Oh, yes,' the boy jumped at his remark, 'and what were you doing there, taking a leisurely stroll?'

'I thought you and Jilly might be in trouble, so I started walking down the track to meet you. I couldn't jump the creek so I had to try to climb across. The bank collapsed on me and when people came to help they found the gold.' Tanner spoke evenly, reasonably, but he knew his words would have no effect. 'Bobby, the whole point in looking for gold is to find enough to get yourself a better life. Your father didn't just want to own a gold mine, he wanted you to have a proper home and a decent education.'

'My father saw a nugget the size of his fist in that mine and you found one.' He spoke slowly, enunciating each word separately.

'I found the nugget in the creek.' Tanner responded in kind.

'LIAR!' The boy screamed.

'Bobby.'

'No.' The boy flew at him, flailing him with his fists. The punches were aimed in the general direction of Tanner's chest, but few connected. Bobby's blows were easy to anticipate and Tanner had been in too many fights not to be able to parry them. The punches became weaker and finally ceased as Bobby sank to his knees and elbows, sobbing with frustration, anger and pain. Tanner's arms stung from the blows and he'd no doubt that the boy's hands hurt even more. Jilly came close to her uncle, staring at her brother's prostrate form.

'Uncle John knew about the red-headed man and nobody told him.' Bobby made no movement, and his lack of response heartened the child. 'And I am going to have a pink quilt, so there.' She squeezed Tanner's hand and ran out of the shanty. Tanner knelt beside Bobby.

'Get away,' he sobbed, scuttling to one side, evading Tanner's touch.

'Let me see your hands,' Tanner said softly.

'I said get away.' This time the boy retreated to his bed.

Tanner made a billy of tea, took a cup for himself and left the rest for Bobby—fighting and crying tended to make a body thirsty. Tanner wandered outside, the morning was bright and clear. He rubbed his bruised arms—the boy had hit hard.

'Where's the little one going?' Joey emerged from the scrub.

'She's made a grave for her parents in the trees. I expect she's gone there to tell them about the gold.'

'Amy sent you some milk and eggs.' Joey handed them to Tanner, who took them to the hut and returned with a mug of tea for Joey. 'So what are you going to do now you're a rich man?' Joey asked.

'When Catherine comes, I'm going back to Melbourne.'

'What about Amy?'

'Amy must make up her own mind.' Tanner sounded weary. 'I can't stay here any more, I can't stake another claim and it doesn't make sense to try. I've got what most men come here for, a chance at a better life, and I'm not going to squander it out of greed or for —'

'A headstrong girl,' Joey finished for him.

'I was going to say an ungrateful brat and I didn't mean Amy.'

'You've told the boy then?' Tanner nodded. 'And you wouldn't look so down if he'd taken it well.'

Tanner almost laughed. 'He accused me of lying, said I found the gold here, got rid of you and Amy to avoid giving you a share, said I'd hid it in the mine and rigged it so it would cave-in on anyone who went down there, said I wasn't trying to save him, just getting the gold back, said I made up the story about finding the gold in the creek just to cheat him.' Tanner sighed hopelessly.

'Boy's upset,' Joey said, 'he didn't mean it.'

'He attacked me, kept hitting me until his fists hurt too much to hit me any more.'

'Did you hit him back?'

'I was tempted to, but after what happened with Davis, no.' They were both silent for a moment, each examining the tea in their mugs as if it might hold some hidden wisdom. 'I don't know who to tell about the gold or where to sell it,' Tanner said at last.

'Well, you'd best tell someone, if the boy starts spreading that story about might be some would believe him.' Joey frowned thoughtfully. 'Go to the commissioner—pretend you want to be sure the gold's yours to keep. Tell him what happened, tell him it was the red-headed man that found the gold first, then he'll be more than willing to believe you seeing as he decided in his favour.'

Tanner smiled. 'You're a more devious man than I gave you credit for.'

'Ah,' Joey scoffed, 'it's being with you and Davis, changed me it has, made me start wanting things and thinking of ways of getting them, terrible thing for an honest, hard-working man to do.' Tanner smiled. 'There's plenty that'd buy your gold, them that brings paper money to the goldfields and sells gold in Melbourne for one pound an ounce more than they pay for it here, and a nugget the size of yours could bring more than its weight value too.'

'Are you suggesting I take it to Melbourne?'

'You'd be taking a risk but it might be worth it.'

Tanner nodded thoughtfully. Joey hadn't told him anything he didn't already know, but it helped to have someone else say it. He glanced back at the shanty.

'Would you do something for me?'

'Surely.'

'Find Jilly, take her back to the camp with you. I don't want her left here with Bobby in the mood he's in.' Joey indicated his agreement. 'I think I'll visit the commissioner.'

'Good idea.' Joey stood up and cast the rest of his tea into the fireplace.

'And Joey,' Tanner also stood up, 'would you do something else? Would you catch one of those damned cart horses for me? Between the cave-in, the fall and Bobby I'm so bruised I can hardly move.'

The commissioner was courteous, interested and quite pleased to have a statement from the man who fell in the creek, especially as it confirmed his decision regarding the red-headed man. Naturally he promised discretion in the matter of the gold, but Tanner could tell as he walked from the office that the secret was already out. Miners pointed at him and stared, a few even came closer to have a better look at him.

Tanner clambered back on his horse. He wasn't much of a horseman and his body ached to distraction as he headed back to the camp. The sheer effort of riding coupled with his current preoccupation made him less observant than normal, and he might have ridden right by her if a high-pitched string of invectives hadn't assailed his ears.

'Your language is enough to make a poor sailor blush,' he said. Catherine swung round to face him, looking oddly embarrassed by his good-natured censure.

'I was on my way to see you,' she said, and it sounded like an apology. Tanner all but fell off his horse and hobbled lamely towards her. 'You're hurt.' She came to meet him and he put his arm round her broad shoulders. 'What happened to you?'

'Everything.' He leant on her, for he knew it was the only form of contact she'd accept. 'Marry me Catherine. Marry me and we'll sail away into the bluest ocean you've ever seen.'

She helped him to the dray. 'Whatever's happened to your body's addled your brain as well.' He prevented her from moving away and kissed her before she could object.

'We could be married in Forest Creek, or would you rather wait until we get to Melbourne?'

'You're drunk.' She went to leave him, but he caught her by the arm.

'How many children do you want?'

Her eyes misted with tears and in her face there was such pain that all the joy went out of Tanner. 'If this is your idea of a joke, I don't think much of it.' She tried to pull away, but he maintained his grip.

'It's no joke and I'm not drunk or insane.' Tanner realised his rather impulsive proposal had been a mistake. 'But I can well understand your refusing me.' She moved uneasily in his grip and he let her go.

'So what brought all this on?' she asked.

'I found gold.'

'In the mine?'

'No, in the creek bed, twenty pounds of it or more.' He grinned at her astonishment, which even the scar and the disciplined expression could not hide.

'If you found it in the creek bed,' she said slowly, 'then it's yours, not even Joey has a share in it.'

'Joey's not with us any more.' Her brows knitted. 'Oh, my dear Catherine, so much has happened since you left.' He moved along on the seat and she climbed up beside him, controlling the team from the dray as easily as she did from its head, although the progress was a little slower.

Words came easily to Tanner for he'd longed to talk to her, longed to let the story tumble out without restraint. He told her about Davis and his partners, about the way he'd pulled the gun and attacked Joey and the young men who'd taken over his mine. He told her the truth about Amy's blindness. He talked about the new claim and Bobby, about Jilly and her pink quilt, about the cave-in and the gold. Everything he'd done, everything he'd felt in her absence was laid out for her to see and he felt a joy, a relief as if a great burden had been lifted from him. He grinned at her and kissed her, then asked what she'd been doing. She laughed airily.

'I've been the same as you, up to me arse in mud, track's near a hundred feet wide in places, one dray pulls round a patch of mud and makes it wider then the next dray has to go further out.' She shook her head disgustedly. 'New chums with wrecked wagons everywhere and men that should know better bogged so they'll never get out. Paddy's stuck on the Forest Creek road, promised I'd give him a hand on the way back.'

As they came in sight of the camp the cart horse whinnied to its mate standing near the shanty door, bridled and laden with goods.

'What the hell's she doing here?' Tanner eased himself down from the dray.

'Looks like someone's going somewhere, food sacks, bed roll.' Catherine joined him and they walked together to the shanty. They stopped just inside the door and stared in disbelief. The interior had been demolished, ransacked by Bobby. He hadn't left one thing intact—he'd smashed the cupboards and crates, torn apart the bedding, spilt the eggs and milk and ripped open the sack of flour with a knife, spreading its contents across the floor. He was on his hands and knees in the middle of the debris, the knife still clutched in his hand, a low animal noise issuing from between his clenched teeth.

'It's not here,' Tanner lied. The boy got slowly to his feet, his eyes wild with hatred.

'Where is it?' he screamed.

'That hardly concerns you.' The look on Bobby's face frightened Tanner, for it precluded all hope of reaching him by reason. 'Now clean up this mess.'

'Where is it?' Bobby screamed again.

'I said clean up the mess.'

'No!' The boy shrieked, lunging at Tanner with the knife. Tanner moved deftly aside, catching Bobby by the wrist and twisting his arm until he dropped the knife. It fell to the floor and Catherine moved with amazing speed to retrieve it. Tanner twisted Bobby's arm behind his back and threw him face first into the mess of milk, eggs and flour.

'Clean it up or I'll hit you as hard and as often as you hit me.'

'No.' The strangled cry came from Catherine. 'He's only a boy,' she implored. Tanner grabbed her by the arm and pushed her

213

out the door. 'He's only a boy, please don't . . .'

He put his hand across her face to stop her saying more. 'I've no intention of hurting him,' he said when they were beyond the boy's hearing, 'but what would you have me do, meekly clean up after him?' She shook her head. 'I should have taken a firmer hand with him right from the start. I let him get away with too much because of all he'd lost,' he sighed resignedly, 'and now I've got to do something.' She nodded uncertainly. 'I'd not hurt him.'

'What if he doesn't clean it up?'

'I'll leave him there 'til he does. I expect all the edible food is right here on this horse, more than enough blankets, weather's cleared up, Jilly and I will camp with you.' He was smiling at her and as always she found it disarming.

Catherine brought the dray up closer to the shanty and took her animals together with the cart horses further up the gully to graze. Tanner had started a fire by the time she returned.

'How's Bobby?' she asked.

'Don't know, haven't looked.' Tanner found a billy, tea and a water bag amongst the things the boy had loaded on the horse. 'Can I interest you in some tea?' he asked facetiously. 'We don't seem to have any eggs and milk but I can make a flour and water damper to go with it if you like.' He made a show of dusting the log that had been set as a seat and guided her to it. 'I'm afraid 'tis a poor meal with which to court a lady.' His voice was theatrically loud and Catherine assumed that his attempt at humour was for Bobby's benefit.

'Where's Jilly?' she asked.

'With Joey,' his voice had dropped and he added, 'thank God.' He mixed up the dough and twisted it round a stick to cook in a fire still burning too brightly for the purpose. 'You know, if we get married, one of us is going to have to learn to cook.'

'It's a tiresome joke Mr Tanner,' she said coolly.

'It's not a joke.' From his pocket he produced the silver cross and gold ring. 'They were my mother's, I gave them to Amy so that if anything happened to me my brother would know —'

He was stopped mid-sentence by the sound of laughter and the sight of Joey leading the horse with Amy and Jilly on board. He returned the jewellery to his pocket.

'Catherine.' Joey greeted her and Jilly ran to her side, searching her pockets for the sweets she'd promised to bring.

'Just in time for some of my delicious damper,' Tanner offered.

'It smells burnt.' Amy wrinkled her nose.

'Only on the outside.'

'Aye, and raw in the middle.' Joey helped Amy down. The damper was as expected, burnt and raw. Amy threw hers away in disgust.

'Why didn't you use the milk and eggs?'

'Boy smashed them.'

'What?'

'Ransacked the inside of the shanty looking for the nugget.'

'Good Lord,' Joey murmured.

'Did he find it?' Amy asked.

'No.'

'There's a rumour you left it at the commissioner's.' Joey looked at him directly.

'Best place for it,' Tanner said, and the look that passed between them told him Joey knew it was elsewhere.

'What are you going to do?' Amy's voice was hushed.

'About Bobby? Leave him there 'til he cleans it up.'

'No, I mean about the gold. Everyone knows about it, and if Bobby would try to steal it then so would others. Even if you sell it to those men that come around they'd still rob you of the paper money.'

'I'd like to get it to Melbourne if I could, if not, at least to the bank at Forest Creek.' A long silence ensued while each of them contemplated the problem.

'There is a way,' Catherine said at last. 'You, Davis, Joey, you all take off together riding just far enough apart so they can't bail you up all at once and close enough so that you can keep an eye on each other.'

'We couldn't leave the mine long enough to ride to Melbourne,' Joey objected.

'You wouldn't have to, one of you could turn back at Forest Creek, the other a bit further on.'

'Then they'd know Tanner had it.'

'But he wouldn't have it, I'd have it. I've got the perfect hiding place built into the dray, sort of like a false bottom it is, I always put half my gold there in case I'm held up.'

'Why not all of it?' Amy asked.

Catherine laughed. 'Then they'd know I'd got it hidden away, wouldn't they?' She gazed impassively at Tanner, who was shaking his head.

'I'd not want you to take the risk,' he said.

She shrugged. 'I carry my own gold.'

'Don't be too quick to say no, Tanner,' Joey said. 'You've not got too many choices.' A slight movement by the shanty door caught Tanner's attention. How long Bobby had been standing there he didn't know, but he couldn't help feeling that the boy had been spying on them.

'Have you cleaned up the mess yet?' Bobby didn't answer him, turning instead to walk up the gully. 'Where are you going?' Tanner's voice held an air of authority that couldn't be ignored.

'To see the commissioner.' Bobby answered Tanner without facing him.

'Commissioner's in the other direction.'

'I've a right to a horse.'

'Don't make me get up to you lad.' Tanner's voice held the chill of a threat. 'I'm tired and I'm hurt and you've caused me no end of grief. Now, I don't care if you go to the commissioner, but I'll not have you riding off on one of those cart horses.' For a few seconds nothing happened, then Bobby turned and headed downhill.

'Is it wise to let him go to the commissioner?' Amy asked.

'Commissioner signed the mine over to me on the understanding that I'd look after the children. Boy'd have no claim on the nugget even if it came from the mine.' Tanner moved uncomfortably; his bruises hurt, his ankle ached and his head had begun to pound.

'Now would be a good time for us to clean up that mess,' Catherine offered.

'Boy's to do it,' Tanner said stubbornly.

'He'd rather take a beating than give in to you.' There was fear in Catherine's face, fear that he'd hurt the boy, fear and understanding too. 'He thinks he's right, people don't give up easily when they think they're right.' Tanner made no comment. 'Let Joey and me do it.' He still didn't speak. She stood up slowly, watching him for a reaction. There was none, and after a moment she turned towards the shanty. Joey joined her and Tanner got up too, groaning as he did so. Ugly halted at the sound of his voice, flinching as if in anticipation of a blow. There were no words he could say, no way he could reassure her.

Clouds began gathering not long after Amy and Joey left, and by the time Bobby returned the first heavy raindrops were falling. He stood irresolutely just inside the shanty door. Tanner regarded him coolly.

'What did the commissioner say?' The boy measured the distance to his bed then crossed it self-consciously. 'I asked you a question,' Tanner insisted. Bobby sat down on his bed and took a deep breath before speaking.

'Take your gold and get off my claim.' Tanner was going to say more, but the look on Catherine's face prevented him. He smiled at her—it was strange how he'd learnt to read her expressions, they were different to other people's, obscured or contorted by the scar.

'There's some stew here Bobby,' she said, but he ignored her. They sat in silence for quite some time while the rain pelted down on the roof. Finally it eased, and Catherine stood up. 'Come on, let's go for a walk.'

'It's raining.'

'Not so much any more,' she said. Tanner put on a look of deep forbearance and made a great show of getting to his feet. He threw a blanket around Jilly, but instead of lifting her he looked helplessly at Catherine, who scooped the child effortlessly into her arms. Outside the shanty Tanner peered at the dismal landscape through the curtain of misty rain. He shivered at the chill and hobbled down the muddy track after Catherine.

'I presume we are doing this so Bobby will eat,' he called after her.

She stopped and waited for him. 'He's afraid of you,' she said.

'He hates me.'

'That too.' They walked on together, drawn as usual to the tiny copse of trees. 'I remember what it was like at his age,' she said bitterly, 'to have nowhere to go and no one on your side.'

'When I was his age I was at sea and it was "Yes, sir" and "No, sir" and a damn good hiding if you disobeyed.' Tanner could see no parallel between the mistreatment he was sure Catherine had endured and the mollycoddling Bobby had received.

'I've heard the sea can be a hard life for a lad.'

'It wasn't so bad. The captain was a reasonable man and I

217

had my father and brother there.' He paused and a million memories flooded through his mind, bringing the sea so close that he could almost smell it.

'I've the money to buy into a ship now,' Tanner said. 'Remember what I told you last time you were here?'

'I remember.'

'Do you remember what else I said?

'We'd best be going back.' She turned in the direction of the shanty. 'Boy will have eaten by now and there's no sense in staying out waiting for the next shower.'

It was raining heavily by the time they reached the shanty. Catherine unwrapped Jilly and sat her by the fire.

'Look at you, soaking wet and filthy dirty. Has no one thought to wash you while I've been away?' Tanner watched as she cleaned the child and it occurred to him that, for someone who worked with filthy animals in mud or dust, Catherine was always remarkably clean. He remembered the nights on the road when she disappeared, presumably to check the animals, and he knew now she'd been bathing. He smiled at her. 'Is there any more stew in the pot?' she asked, glancing at Bobby now tightly wrapped in his blankets, sleeping or feigning sleep. Tanner checked—the boy had eaten.

'A little,' he said, 'enough for you and Jilly.'

'I'm all right, but this one better get some more into her.' Tanner watched patiently as Catherine fed the child and settled her to sleep. He began to speak, but she put her finger to her lips and moved quietly to the door. 'I'll see you tomorrow,' she whispered as she left. Tanner followed her, overtaking her before she could reach the dray.

'I want to talk to you.'

'It's pouring rain now. We'll talk in the morning.'

'Come back in the shanty.'

'It's late, Tanner, I'm tired. In the morning.'

'In the morning you'll make some other excuse.' Catherine faced him, her features set in that expressionless facade she wore so often. The rain trickled across her cheeks and down her neck, but she seemed unaware of it, unaware of any feeling, physical or emotional. Tanner allowed his own features to soften as if by doing so he might soften hers. 'I've spent all day trying to ask you to marry me.' She stiffened at his words. 'Please, Catherine.'

'No!' Tanner took the jewellery from his pocket. 'No!' The hardness was supplanted by panic. 'I can't marry you.'

'I know you care for me,' he said, and her expression confirmed it. 'Then why?' She mouthed the words that would not come. 'Why?' he appealed again, and from somewhere within her she dragged up enough anger to attack him.

'Marriage,' she laughed. 'You men, you make it sound such an honour, make it sound like a woman's nothing without it, a prize that she should want and be willing to sacrifice for. I've as much gold in the banks in Melbourne as you have in that nugget of yours, and if I marry you it'll be yours to do with as you please and I'll be yours to go where you choose and be treated as you like with no way out and neither God's law nor man's to protect me.' Her words hurt, but Tanner knew them for what they were, a defence, a shield to protect that part of her that was vulnerable to him.

'Then we'll not marry, I'll put the money aside to educate the children and I'll come with you on the road.' Her expression softened to one of despair and she shook her head sadly. 'Come inside, we'll talk.' He tried to guide her to the shanty, but she pulled away.

'Sit beside me and we'll talk, lie beside me and we'll touch and you're man enough to hold me down if I'm not willing and if you're not maybe you could get a few of your friends to help. You could take your turn and make your filthy jokes about what an ugly wretch of a being I am.' Her voice had increased in volume until she was shouting at his astonished face. Her speech ended abruptly and for an instant she stared at his bewildered face, then she dropped her gaze to the ground, too embarrassed and ashamed to face him any more.

'Do you really think that of me?' he asked gently.

The noise she made was caught between a laugh and a sob. 'I didn't think it of the man who did it to me either.'

Tanner drew breath as if he'd been kicked for, although he knew her life had been hard, nothing had prepared him for this. He rested his hands carefully on her shoulders. He moved slowly, cautiously, but still she flinched beneath his touch. He drew her to him and she raised her forearms, bracing them against his chest as if to push him away, but she didn't have the strength. He wrapped his arms round her and held her to him. Then they began, great, racking sobs that erupted from deep within her body with such force that she shuddered. He held her tighter and each sob was like a blow to him. Gradually they eased and Tanner rocked her in his arms, supporting her weight as she leant against him.

Eventually she regained control of her breathing and found the strength to support herself. Tanner loosened his grip and she stood upright. She was trembling and the icy wind and rain offered no comfort. Their eyes met but not for long—she couldn't stand the pity his expressed.

'There were four of them,' she said coldly, 'and for all I wash I can never get the filth of it off me.'

He touched her face, turning it so that she was compelled to look at him. 'I would still wish to marry you, it makes no difference to me.' She closed her eyes and there was such anguish in her face that he could say no more. He took her by the arm to guide her to the shanty, but she stood her ground. 'I'll not leave you out here, Catherine, it's cold and miserable and there's no warmth in that dray of yours.' She still resisted the insistent pressure on her arm. 'Trust me, Catherine, just this once.' He urged her forward and reluctantly she let herself be led into the shanty. He took off her wet coat and boots and wrapped her in a blanket, pushing her gently on to the bed. He lay down beside her but not touching her, still he could feel the fear and the tension that seemed to surround her like a wall. He closed his eyes—it would be easier for her if he was asleep, and finally sleep did come, a light unnatural sleep from which he was easily stirred.

The gentle touch that woke Tanner might have been from an insect or the rough edge of a blanket, but even in his semi-conscious state he knew it was Catherine. He could hear her breathing and it told him she was crying. Her fingers brushed across that part of his face that corresponded with her scar, then they slid down his neck and across his shoulder. He heard her swallow, gulping back the tears. Then the hand moved again, and avoiding the welt made by the rope it lingered for a moment on the scar Davis' knife had caused. The hand moved again, resting this time on a slightly larger scar, the result of another knife attack, then slowly it covered the full expanse of his chest. He felt the warmth of her breath and the wetness of her tears, then her lips on his cheek and he knew it was a kiss of farewell. As she withdrew from him he caught her by the wrist. She gasped and struggled until he let her go.

'It's all right, Catherine, it's all right.' He propped himself up, trying to see her in the darkness. She had retreated as far from him as possible and was crouched against the shanty wall, trembling uncontrollably, and Tanner realised that if the position in which he was lying hadn't prevented her reaching the door, she would have run from him. He sat up. 'I didn't mean to frighten you,' he said.

'You just startled me that's all.' Her voice belied her words.

'Where were you going?'

'Nowhere.'

'I thought perhaps you were kissing me goodbye, I thought that might be why you were crying.'

'I wasn't crying.'

'There's no shame in crying.' He looked at the place where her face should be, but the darkness concealed all expression. 'You must be cold.' He retrieved the blanket she'd lost in the struggle and put it round her. 'Would you like me to stoke up the fire, make some tea?'

'No,' she said but he ignored her, lighting the lamp first to dispel the darkness and the fear. He glanced at her several times as he fiddled with the fire, and measured a cup of water into the billy.

'You know,' he began conversationally, 'I've often wondered why you keep your hair so short.'

'It's easy to keep clean.' He waited, but she said no more.

'Why so interested in my scars?'

'There are so few of them.' The strain had eased from her voice and she'd moved away from the wall so that she no longer appeared to be cowered there.

'Is that why you'll not marry me?' There was a long pause before she answered him.

'I would marry you if I could.' The words came haltingly and he knew what it cost her to say them. He sat beside her, close enough to see her properly but not so close as to intimidate her.

'What prevents you, Catherine?'

She moved uncomfortably but not away from him. 'You deserve a proper wife, one you could be proud of.'

'I'd not be ashamed of you.'

'A woman who could keep your house and bear your children.' Her face held the same sadness it had when he'd mentioned children earlier that day.

'I've all the children, I need,' he said. 'More children than I ever thought to have and I don't recall saying anything about a house.' He put his arm around her; she was still trembling. 'Are you afraid of me?' he asked and she seemed to shrink beside him.

'I'd not wish to make you angry.'

'Why? Do you think I'd beat you?'

'Not so hard as some, but it would hurt all the more.' Tanner closed his eyes against the pain of frustration. 'It's not the beating so much as the things you'd call me and knowing that one day you'd not want me any more.'

Tanner pulled her close to him. 'I'd not beat you or abuse you or desert you.' He sighed hopelessly, nothing he said would make any difference. It was time, not words, that would make her trust him. He tightened his grip of her shoulder and kissed her before turning his attention to the tea. She crept closer to him as he worked, and by the time he'd finished she was sitting beside him.

'Would you really come on the road with me?' she asked.

'Yes,' he said simply.

'T'would be a hard life for the child.'

'Better than she's got now.'

'What about the boy?'

'He could do as he liked, boarding school, trade, I doubt he'd come with us.'

'And Amy?'

'I could see her each time we came back this way and if she ever changed her mind . . .' It was his habit to leave sentences unfinished and those who knew him understood. She shivered as she sipped the tea; he put his arm around her and she cuddled closer to him.

'You're warm, like Jilly,' she said.

'Most people are when you get close to them.'

'Not the ones I've known,' she said bitterly, and her words touched Tanner more deeply than she intended for he could imagine them, her father and the men who'd attacked her and the thought that there was no one there to comfort her made it worse. She could see he was shaken and she handed him the last of the tea. 'It troubles you, what they did to me.' He didn't need to confirm it. 'So how can you say it'd make no difference, when every time you'd see the scars you'd be reminded of it and every year I didn't produce a child you'd know the reason why?'

'Not looking at what they've done to you won't take it away and it would trouble me more to think that what happened to you in the past has denied you a future, denied us both the chance of something better.'

'I could never give you a son.'

'Until I met you I never wanted a wife let alone a son.' He put the cup down. 'Anyway, what makes you so sure you couldn't have a child?' He couldn't imagine her going to a doctor or putting herself in a position where she might reasonably expect to become pregnant.

'There were four of them that took me and no babe to show for it.'

'Is that the only reason, I mean, there's nothing wrong with you otherwise?'

'My body still has its cycles, if that's what you're asking, but there couldn't have been something wrong with all four of them, it had to be something wrong with me.'

He held her close and kissed her forehead. 'Oh, Catherine, we're not sheep or cattle, some people are married for years before they have a child. It may have been the wrong time for you or the brutality of their attack prevented it. I'll not accept that as a valid reason, nor the scars or anything else you've said. I want you for my wife, but I'm willing to settle for a lot less, and if you intend to refuse me at least tell me the real reason for it.' She crawled away from him, back to the untidy pile of blankets that constituted his bed. He followed her, sitting beside her and putting his arm around her again. 'Tell me you don't care for me or that you don't want me.'

'It's not that,' she said, and for a long time she said no more. 'It's hard to explain,' she said at last. 'The more I'm with you the more I fear the day when you'll not want me.' He went to speak, but she wouldn't let him. 'Let me finish.' She paused again, this time not in thought but in search of the right words. 'I knew a man once, so scared of dying that it ruined his life, he ended up a hermit living in a cave, afraid to eat or sleep or let another human soul near him. You can't escape death and when it finally took him he'd had nothing, worse off than a prisoner in a dungeon he was, the fear had robbed him of everything.' She looked up at Tanner and there were tears in her eyes. 'Even if you only stayed with me one day, I'd always have that, so if you want to come on the road with me . . .' The corners of Tanner's mouth creased into a smile. He gripped her shoulder firmly, then lay back on the bed pulling her with him. She made no attempt to resist and as he released her she turned to rest her head on his shoulder. 'I can't help thinking,' she murmured, 'that tomorrow you'll've changed your mind.

He kissed the top of her head. 'Go to sleep, Catherine, and tomorrow you can teach me how to swear at the bullocks.'

CHAPTER 25

✦✦✦✦✦✦✦✦✦✦✦✦✦✦

T ANNER WOKE suddenly; somewhere in his dream he'd heard
the sound of movement, and now that he was awake he
knew it was not part of his dream. He tried to rise but Catherine
held him back.

'Shush, listen.' The sound of footsteps faded. 'It was the boy,'
she said softly.

'I'll go after him.'

'No, he took no supplies and he's not headed for the horses.
He'll not go far.'

'Are you sure?'

'I expect he's gone to find a place to cry, away from you and
all the other prying eyes.' Tanner moved uneasily. 'I'll follow
him if you like,' she offered. 'He'll not see me, I'm good in bush.'

'No, let him have his time.' He hugged her. 'Go back to sleep.'
She did, but he couldn't and just before dawn he gave up trying.

Outside the shanty everything was still soaking from the previous
night's rain and the smoky fire that Tanner managed to light
in the fireplace offered little cheer to the cold, grey morn. Catherine
joined him before the billy had boiled and Jilly a short time later.
They'd eaten their breakfast by the time the watery sunlight touched
the valley, allowing Tanner to scan it for some sign of Bobby.
There was none.

'Joey, Joey.' Davis' voice echoed through the valley above the
early morning sounds of the diggings. 'Joey, wait.' Joey picked
his way through the camps and shrub, leading a horse. Tanner
rose to meet him.

'I hear you're willing to haul dirt for pay.'

'Oh, for heaven's sake, Joey,' Davis burst into the camp, 'with
a nugget the size he's got what would he want to haul dirt for?'

'For enough supplies to last me 'til I sell it.' The simple fact
that Davis didn't want him to haul their dirt was enough to
make Tanner want to do it. 'What's the matter, Joey?'

'It's nothing but a bruised hoof,' Davis said disparagingly.

'Horse isn't fit to work,' Joey insisted. Catherine examined the foot and nodded her agreement.

'Be two or three weeks at least.' She showed the injury to Tanner, but he was more interested in the track and the valley beyond.

'Well,' Joey said, 'can you help us?'

'When will you want to go?' Tanner continued his surveillance.

'We've a load ready now,' Davis answered.

'Do you mind looking after Jilly?' Tanner touched Catherine's shoulder.

'Of course not.'

'Joey, you know where the horses are. I'll be coming with you.' Tanner looked determinedly at Davis. 'You could give him a hand.' He put his arm round Catherine and waited for them to leave. 'I want to look for Bobby, but I don't want it to look as if I'm looking for him. I don't want him to run because he's scared of being punished. If I go with them I'll be able to search the gully and the flat.'

'And if you find him?'

'I just want to be sure he's all right, that's all.'

'What if he comes back?'

'Let me know if you can, but don't worry too much. I can't get back until Joey's finished at the wash pools.' He kissed her and limped to the cart.

It was still quite early when they finished loading the dirt. Tanner looked in on Catherine as they passed the camp, but the boy still hadn't returned. He searched amongst the faces on the track and watched the men moving through the camps, but still there was no sign of him. They had reached the end of the gully when Tanner saw him. He was on the far side of the creek bed moving quickly, stealthily between the camps, scurrying low to the ground looking over his shoulder.

'That's Bobby.' Joey had followed the direction of Tanner's gaze.

'I wonder what he's been up to,' Davis said, for it was obvious that he had something to hide.

'It's me he's hiding from and so he should be after the mess he made.' Tanner couldn't have said why he made an excuse for Bobby except that he, like Davis, recognised the attitude of one who'd done something wrong.

News spread quickly on the goldfields, carried by word of mouth across the diggings. Its importance could be measured by the number of temporarily abandoned mines and small clusters of men.

'Something's up,' Davis observed.

'Some poor devil caught without his licence,' Joey said.

'More than that.' They drew level with another cart returning from the diggings.

'What's all the commotion?' Tanner asked.

'Somebody broke into the commissioner's office, rifled the strong box, nothing taken.' The wagon passed on. Tanner and Davis exchanged glances, but neither voiced their suspicions.

'I heard a rumour your gold was in that strong box.' Davis broke the silence.

'It wasn't.'

'I also heard a rumour that you'd trust me to help you get it to Melbourne.'

'I would.'

'Would you now?' Davis laughed. 'Well, I'll be damned and I suppose it's true that you told Amy you'd be there to give her away when we got married?'

'If Amy told you that it must be true, because Amy wouldn't lie or suffer a man who did. A very moral soul, our Amy.'

'It's a wonder she put up with you as long as she did,' Davis quipped and Tanner smiled. There were many ways to lie—he'd been guilty of them all and not regretted any of them, yet he still thought himself a more honest man than Davis.

'Tanner.' The voice was clipped and arrogant, the sound of a gentleman addressing a subordinate and it offended Tanner. He hadn't been in the company of gentlemen since he left London nor had he affected their way, there'd been no need to in this country, but he could still copy their accent and ape their mannerisms and his clothes, which had once belonged to his brother, were those of a miner worn at the diggings by both rich and poor. He erased the smile that had begun to play about his lips before he turned slowly, surveying the two men coldly. One was clearly a fine and proper gentleman, the other his servant. Tanner smiled frostily.

'I am Jonathan Tanner,' he said in a voice that neither Joey or Davis recognised, 'and you, sir?'

'Braithwaite, David Braithwaite.' Tanner gave the servant a dismissive glance.

'And how may I help you Mr Braithwaite?'

'I was told you were a seaman.'

'I was,' Tanner said. 'I sailed on my father's ships for a while and later had a command or two of my own.' It wasn't exactly a lie, all sailors call the ships on which they sailed 'their ship', and he'd certainly been in command of the ships he'd used for smuggling.

'I am most terribly sorry, sir,' Braithwaite apologised. 'I seem to have handled this most clumsily, please forgive me.' He glanced around the crowded track and the muddy flat. 'Is there some place we could discuss business?'

'Business?' Tanner queried.

'The sale of your nugget.'

'Ah,' Tanner said offhandedly, but his heart was racing as he climbed down from the cart. He couldn't have chosen a better guise in which to sell the nugget to this man yet he feared the deceit, feared that it was already flawed by the way he'd stumbled into it, feared that providence might take away the luck that had brought him the nugget if he tempted it with a lie. 'You,' he addressed Davis for he knew Joey didn't have the guile to play the part. 'Pick me up when you're finished.' Davis nodded and urged the horses on. 'I'm afraid, Mr Braithwaite, there's little that's conducive to business in this place.' Tanner limped towards him. 'Perhaps your man could arrange some seating.' They stood together while the man tried to concoct a seat from blankets and sticks.

'What brings you to this Godforsaken place?' Braithwaite asked. Tanner could have argued that he'd seen places in England less in God's care than this, but instead he smiled.

'Opportunity.'

'Ah.'

'And you?'

'I'm a collector of sorts, arts, artefacts, coins . . . gold.'

'So, you wish to purchase my nugget.'

'If it's as large as I've been told.'

'I don't know what you've been told, but I can assure you it is in excess of twenty pounds.'

Braithwaite remained silent for a moment, more for effect than to consider what he was going to say next.

'The going rate out here is three pounds an ounce, isn't it?'

Tanner nodded. 'I shall pay you four.' Tanner pursed his lips thoughtfully—instinct made him cautious and experience had taught him that there was many a fine and proper gentleman more dishonest than he.

'Do you have the money here?'

'In Forest Creek, but I can send my man to get it.'

'For what purpose—I should only have to return there to bank it.' He watched Braithwaite as he spoke, for it was possible that Braithwaite might buy his gold to lull him into a false sense of security then rob him of the paper money.

'What do you suggest then?' Braithwaite asked.

'If we can agree on a price we meet in Forest Creek in, say, two days and conduct our transaction there.'

'I assure you four pounds an ounce is as good as you'll get anywhere.'

'In Melbourne I might get more, but your offer saves me the risk of taking it there.' Braithwaite almost smiled. 'However, I still have to transport it to Forest Creek,' Tanner returned the condescending smirk, 'and for that I'll need a good horse.' He switched his gaze to Braithwaite's mount.

'You're not serious.'

'There's a lot of gold about but not too many nuggets that size.'

'But if I give you my horse what shall I ride?'

'Ride your man's horse, he can ride the pack animal. Sell your pack at the store or trade it for a saddle, you'll have no need of it if you ride straight back to Forest Creek. I'll meet you there within two days.' Tanner smiled at Braithwaite's discomfort—obviously it was not the deal he'd thought to make, not the deal he'd make with a simple seaman, but with one of his own class . . .

'All right, I'll have my man fetch the horse.'

'No, tether it at the store when you go to sell the pack. I'll have my man collect it later. I'm sure I don't have to stress upon you the need for secrecy.'

Braithwaite nodded. 'Forest Creek, two days' time, four pounds an ounce.' His face distorted into what might have been a smile. 'And the horse.' He extended his hand and Tanner took it. Fortunately Braithwaite was wearing gloves, for Tanner may well have had the voice and manner of the gentry but he had the hands of a working man.

Tanner sat uncomfortably in the grass watching the horse as it waited patiently by the store. There wasn't much chance of anyone stealing it in broad daylight, but Tanner had nothing better to do while he waited for Joey and Davis to return.

'I take it your gentlemen friends are gone, Mr Tanner, sir?' Davis jibed as he halted the cart beside Tanner.

'Joey, can you do me a favour?' Tanner barely acknowledged Davis.

'Surely.'

'See that horse over there, the one that belonged to Braithwaite?'

'Aye.'

'Could you ride it up the gully for me, and tether it in that copse of trees just up from our claim.'

'Surely.'

'Why can't you ride it yourself,' Davis asked.

'Because I don't want anyone to know it's mine just yet.'

'Is it yours?'

'Yes, a deposit on the nugget. I've agreed to meet Braithwaite in Forest Creek and sell it to him.' Tanner returned his attention to Joey. 'Give Davis and me a head start then go into the store and buy something. When you come out get on the horse as if it was your own.' Joey looked like a man who'd just been asked to rob a bank. Tanner smiled and clouted him affectionately on the shoulder before scrambling up onto the cart.

He saw her as they turned on to the track that led up the gully. She walked towards them, straight and tall, her hair catching the few rays of sun that forced themselves between the patchy clouds. She was as he always imagined her, moving with that natural grace that many a lady would envy, her face emptied of all expression save the softness in her eyes.

'Catherine,' he called to her, and she waved and swung Jilly onto her back so that they'd make better time.

'Boy's come back,' she called as she neared the cart.

'I know. We saw him on our way to the water hole.'

'He seemed in quite a state.' She passed Jilly up to Tanner, then climbed up beside him.

'What's he doing now?'

'Back in bed, but he was white as a sheet when he came in and breathing like he'd run a hundred miles.' She studied Tanner for moment—clearly her news was no news to him. She glanced at Davis.

'Someone broke into the commissioner's office, looking for Tanner's gold or so they say.' Catherine gaped at Tanner, but he shook his head irritably.

'Boy ran away from the shanty because I was there, he took off up the gully when he saw me coming because he thought I was after him.' No one contradicted Tanner. There was no need to for it was obvious that even he did not believe the explanation.

'Anyway,' Davis said, 'lad might settle down now gold's been sold.'

'Sold?' Catherine looked to Tanner for confirmation.

'Just as soon as I can get it to Forest Creek.' He put his arm round her then smiled at the child. 'Jilly, how would you like to go with Davis, up to the new camp? You could wait there for Joey, maybe spend a day or two.' He glanced at Davis. 'I know Amy would like that.'

'No.' The child pouted. 'I want to stay with you and Ugly.'

'I have to go to Forest Creek for a few days.' The child's lip continued to protrude.

'I wouldn't mind —' Catherine began, but the sharp pressure on her arm told her to say no more.

'I'll bring you something from Forest Creek, some lollies and ribbons for your hair.'

'Can I have both?' Tanner nodded, and the child frowned pensively. 'But we're still going with Ugly, you'll still take me with you?'

'Of course, you and anyone else who wants to come.' He might easily have been referring to Bobby but Davis knew he meant Amy.

Davis deposited them as near to their camp as the track took him and they walked the rest of the way.

'I could have looked after her,' Catherine said.

'No, I need you to take the nugget as far as the Forest Creek Road. I want to ride around for a while to make sure I'm not being followed, then on to Forest Creek without coming back here first.'

'You're being mighty careful.'

'That I am. There's a bit of high ground just before the turnoff, it's got good cover. Do you know it?' She nodded. 'We'll meet there. It shouldn't be too much of a risk for you to carry it that far, there'll be a fair few people about until after dark.'

'What about the boy?'

'Joey and Davis will have the cart. Anyway, he wants this mine too much to leave it.' Without warning he embraced her, swinging her off her feet, groaning as his battered body took her weight, stumbling as his weakened ankle refused to support it. Initially she recoiled from him, but then she relaxed, laughing as he set her back on her feet. 'That's the first time I've heard you laugh.' He grinned at her shy embarrassment. 'What would you like?' he asked.

'What?'

'A present, anything you want, a goldplated stock whip.'

'A tent would be more useful.'

'No, something for you.' He kissed her and it was such a joy not to have to hold back with her, such a relief to be able to walk away from the mine.

She disentangled herself from his arms. 'You've missed lunch and it's too early for tea, but you'd best make some kind of a meal before we get on the road.'

'So it's decided is it? I'm to be the cook.'

'I was going to get the team,' she apologised, and the look on her face told Tanner that she wasn't ready for his sarcasm. He touched her face. 'You be the teamster and I'll be the cook.' She smiled uncertainly and he kissed her again.

Catherine returned with the team to find Tanner labouring over a smoky fire. He seemed unaware of the fine, misty rain that was drifting across the valley. Catherine hunched into her coat.

'Why are you cooking out here?' she asked.

'I've my reason.' She peered into the pot.

'What is it?'

'Potatoes and onions, I'm counting on you to supply some salt meat.'

Tanner saved a little of everything for the boy, and when they had finished their meal he collected the plate, and taking Catherine by the hand he led her into the shanty. He shook Bobby.

'Food.' He deposited the plate beside him. 'And now, my dear Catherine, allow me to show you your dowry.' He knew the boy was watching and he wondered if there was a malicious streak in his nature that had made him ensure the boy saw the nugget and its hiding place. In fact he had been forced to be open about taking the nugget by the simple fact that it was impossible to be covert.

As he pulled away the hearth stones he was struck with a terrible fear that the nugget may no longer be there. He could imagine how Davis felt looking in his secret hiding place and finding nothing there. The soil was easier to dig this time, and sooner than expected he felt the hardness of the gold.

'Fetch me a sack.' He indicated a cupboard by the door and Catherine obeyed. As he struggled to his feet he faced the boy so that he could see the full size of the nugget. 'You're my brother's son, Bobby, and I'll always look after you, you'll never want for anything while ever I can provide for you.' The boy stared at him impassively. 'I'll be back in a couple of days, we'll talk then.' Tanner put the gold in the sack and carried it to the dray, concealing it beneath the floor boards. He gave Catherine one last hug. 'Be careful,' he said. 'If you're challenged give it up. I'd sacrifice the gold for you any time, remember that.' She smiled and unfurled the whip.

'Come on Willie, you good-for-nothing, lazy bastard.'

Tanner stood watching as the dray lumbered slowly down the track until the fine rain grew heavy enough to obscure it. He faced the shanty, momentarily considering having one last word with Bobby, but instead he collected his pack and his brother's gun and ambled slowly towards the trees. He knew better than to move furtively, drawing attention to himself by the very act of being secretive. His thoughts turned to the boy scuttling back to the camp after the break-in at the commissioner's—such a stupid thing to do.

The horse was a joy to ride compared to the hard-mouthed, bony cart horses. Tanner guided it aimlessly off the track, looking for all the world like a man out hunting. It was well dark by the time he reached the rendezvous. Catherine had no fire and was sitting hidden amongst the bushes a short distance from the dray. Tanner didn't see her as he rode in and was instantly gripped with a fear that something had happened to her. There was no sound that alerted him to her presence, then he turned and she was standing right beside him.

'You move quietly,' he said.

'I told you I was good in the bush, years of hiding from my father.' She pulled out the floor boards in the dray, lifting the gold out for him. He fixed it firmly on to the saddle, then bent down to kiss her. 'How long will you be?' she asked.

'I'll be there tomorrow, back late the day after.'

'I'm going to help Paddy. It'll take near a day to get there in the dray and Lord knows how long to transfer his load and pull him out. If you come back along the Forest Creek road, I'll still be there.' Her voice trailed away as if she still couldn't accept that he wanted to be with her.

'Day after tomorrow,' he said, 'and we'll celebrate with Paddy.' He kissed her goodbye.

'Be careful.' She smiled impishly. 'I'd rather you than the gold any time.'

He rode parallel to the track for a time before turning off into the bush. He kept a steady pace, much slower than the breakneck speed at which he'd made his last trip to Forest Creek. He thought of Davis and the horse he'd nearly ridden into the ground, then his thoughts turned to Amy and he longed to take her with him, to get her as far away from Davis as he could.

Suddenly he reined the horse, willing it to be silent and still, and, holding his breath, he listened. Things moved in the bush at night, even the kangaroos, and the sound of a man could easily be misinterpreted. He waited, but the only sound was that of his own heart.

He rode on faster than before, the horse sensing his urgency. His mouth was filled with the bitter taste of adrenalin and he realised he was dragging on the reins. The horse slowed and stopped. Tanner sat still, forcing himself to breathe easily. He'd taken greater risks than this, done things that might have earned him the hangman's noose and his nerve had never been shaken. He urged the horse on again. This was different, this was his way out, his way to end the risks forever, and there were people who mattered now, Catherine and Jilly, people who needed him. He sprang from the horse, dragging his brother's gun from his pack. There was a horse coming, unshod perhaps, but a horse nonetheless. He leaned the gun on the saddle, using the horse as a shield.

The sound came closer—it was a horse, he was sure of it. The creature moved uncertainly between the trees. Tanner caught a glimpse of it as the moon broke through the clouds. The light vanished again and Tanner strained to catch the sound of its progress, nearer, nearer, then suddenly it was in front of him. It reared up at the sight and the smell of a man, and wheeling on its hind legs it galloped into the bush. Tanner leant his head on the saddle—it was nothing but a brumby drawn to him by the scent of his own horse. He would have laughed at himself, but he didn't have the strength.

Tanner mounted up again and rode on. He felt calmer, although he was at a loss to know why—perhaps the body and mind could only take so much groundless fear before it refused to react, or perhaps his natural self-possession had reasserted itself. He rejoined the Forest Creek road a little after dawn. Even at that early hour it was packed with carts and horsemen and people on foot. They were all heading for the diggings and he was like a man swimming against the tide as he made his way to Forest Creek.

He found Braithwaite at the hotel, and after a few polite words they made their way to the bank, where the transaction took place. The nugget weighed twenty-three pounds six and a half ounces and Braithwaite paid him the even fifteen hundred pounds. The dealings were conducted with the utmost cordiality, and the ease with which Braithwaite parted with his money, his indifference to what the gold cost in human terms, irked Tanner. The man was too much like those he'd smuggled for in England, and it was with much effort that Tanner maintained his gentlemanly facade until the deal was concluded.

He took a room at the hotel and a bath, as much to wash away the dirt of his deception as to wash away the mud of the road. There would be no more games and deceptions, he promised himself that, no more tricks and half truths—at last he was free from the need for it. Even though there was as much wrong with the rule in the colonies as there was with the rule in England, here he would fight to change it rather than try to circumvent it. Here there were those who would stand with him and they outnumbered those who believed in the aristocratic rule.

Tanner was too tired to eat, so he lay on the soft mattress gazing up at the ceiling, his body aching for comfort, but weeks of sleeping on the hard ground made it impossible for him to find it in a soft bed. He closed his eyes. It had been all right for him to dance around taking his risks and using his guile to get himself out of trouble, but what of those who had neither wit nor will to rise above the structure of the law? People like his brother who worked all their lives without bettering themselves and never knowing why. People like Amy and Catherine who society abandoned and the law failed to protect. The thought of Catherine's childhood haunted him, and he wondered what Amy's or for that matter Jilly's fate would have been without him. He twisted and turned, trying to find a position in which to sleep. Perhaps things would never change for people like Amy and Catherine, perhaps the fear of anyone who was different was too deeply ingrained to be washed away even in this place, where so many of the old prejudices had been forgotten.

Sleep came, a fitful and dream-laden sleep from which hunger finally woke him. He dined, and the sheer luxury of sitting at a proper table on a proper chair and eating a meal that didn't smell like smoke and taste like mud filled him with an almost childlike glee. He wished Catherine was with him and he vowed that one day they'd have a proper honeymoon in the best hotel in Melbourne. He retired early, rising again before dawn as had been his habit on the goldfields, and by the time the darkness of night had paled to a dull and overcast day Tanner was on his way home.

CHAPTER 26

++++++++++++++

THE LEVITY that Tanner felt as he embarked on his homeward route soon deserted him, the deteriorating weather and the overcrowded road making for an arduous journey. At first he rode harder than usual, ignoring the rain that ran down his neck and the biting cold that turned his hands purple, but slowly the sheer pressure of people slowed him down. He passed a dozen carts stuck in the mud and more than a couple of drays. He helped a man on foot get his family and possessions across a flooded creek, a creek that had not existed the first time Tanner rode along the track.

Paddy's dray was more hopelessly bogged than any. He had pulled the dray off the track while trying to cross a creek and it had sunk up to the axles. Water flowed around and over the dray, which still carried all the makings of the stage. The piano sat in the tent, having been manhandled on to dry land while Paddy sat under a wattle brush lean-to near a smoky fire. Tanner laughed at his dejected face.

'I never imagined you would look that miserable unless the colony ran out of rum.'

'Out of rum, out of luck, out of partners and out of friends.' Tanner crouched down beside him.

'Where are your partners?'

'Gone.' Paddy motioned despondently towards the road. 'We'll get help they say, then off they go and that was four days ago.'

Tanner laughed. 'Where's Catherine?' he asked.

'That's another fine one—don't worry, Paddy, I'll be back.' He snorted disgustedly.

'She should have been here by now.' Tanner automatically looked down the road in the direction from which she should have come. 'Yesterday, this morning at the latest.'

'Maybe she's bogged,' Paddy suggested mournfully.

'Maybe.' Tanner stood up, scanning the grey landscape. 'We

were to meet here to celebrate the sale of the nugget.'

'You've sold it? Damn, I wanted to see it. How much did you get?'

'Fifteen hundred pounds.' Paddy whistled. 'You must have got at least that much sharing with Zeke and Loretta.'

'Not all at once and most of what I got went down my throat.' Tanner walked back to the track, staring at the grey shadows moving in the misty rain. None were coming towards them.

'Well,' Paddy called after him, 'it's not going to be much of a celebration with nary a drop of rum.'

'I'll see what I can do.' Tanner remounted his horse and Paddy waved dejectedly.

Tanner rode slowly, searching between the trees in case Catherine had tried to forge a new trail of her own where the existing one became impassable. By the time he'd almost reached the place where he'd last seen her he was all but convinced that he'd missed her. Then he saw them, a crowd of people gathering, miners and prospectors, some running, some walking, all converging on the place where she'd camped. Tanner overtook one man, a teamster by the look of him.

'What's the matter?' Tanner called.

'Ugly's dead, murdered they reckon.'

Tanner felt a chill run through him and a sickness in his stomach that brought bile to his throat. He couldn't swallow it, he couldn't breathe, the whole world seemed to be reeling and he clutched the saddle to stop himself from falling. He leant forward over his horse's neck and it carried him to a small knot of people clustered round an inert, a blanket-covered form. He fell from his mount and stumbled to the crowd, pushing and dragging them out of his way.

'Dear God,' he prayed silently, 'not Catherine, please not Catherine.' He dropped to his knees beside her, pulling away the blanket and gaping in horror at what he saw. She had been beaten, her face was bloodied and bruised, even the scar had been torn open, her lips were stained with blood and her eyes were swollen closed. He felt an awful tightness in his chest and a stinging in his eyes, and he knew he was crying for the tears blurred his vision. He reached out with trembling hands to touch her—she was so cold, and the sadness that gripped Tanner was like a deep pain in the very centre of his being. Gently he bent down to lift her, to hold her one last time.

'No.' A firm hand gripped his shoulder. 'Don't move her, might be damage done inside.' Tanner gazed blankly at the man, the import of his words taking time to penetrate Tanner's shocked state. He looked back at her and noted for the first time the slight rise and fall of her chest. She was alive, barely, but still alive. Slowly his thoughts began to move again, and he wiped the tears from his face and the wetness from his nose.

'A doctor,' he managed to say. 'She needs a doctor.'

'There's one in Golden Gully,' the teamster said.

'He'll not come.' It was a miner who spoke. 'He's given up the doctoring to look for gold.'

'Tell him I'll pay anything,' Tanner insisted.

'That won't be necessary.' The teamster got to his feet. 'I'll have a word with him.' He was a short man, thickly set with a hardness about him against which few men would argue. Tanner nodded vaguely, his attention drawn again to Catherine's unmoving figure. Two miners pushed past the crowd carrying a stretcher improvised from blankets and sticks.

'We're taking her to the dray, out of the rain,' one of them explained. Tanner helped, cradling her head and shoulders in his arms. They lifted her carefully, but their progress was suddenly halted. Willie stood before them, his great nostrils flaring, his massive head lowered as if to charge. He lurched towards them wavering unsteadily. There was a great gash across his head and the blood that poured from it must have almost blinded him. They tried to move past him but he'd caught the scent of Catherine and he wouldn't let them take her.

'Willie, you good-for-nothing, lazy bastard, get out of the way!' Tanner bellowed at him. The bullock stopped his advance: the voice was wrong, but the tone and the words were familiar. Tanner pushed past him. 'Somebody get Paddy,' he yelled. 'He's about three miles down the road, up to his axles in a creek bed. Tell him to bring his team.' He threw back the covers of the dray. Confronting Willie had brought back his self-control; the shock and the grief were still there, but he could function again. He sat beside Catherine, piling more blankets around her. 'Somebody start a fire,' he continued, issuing orders. 'We'll need hot water, there are some towels and soap somewhere, one of you look for them.'

He started to remove her sodden clothes. She was soaked to the skin and it occurred to him that the attack must have happened the night he left, that she had lain there for two days in the pouring rain while he was in a bed too warm and soft for sleep.

He took her boots off then elected to cut away her remaining clothes. It was with infinite care that he removed her coat and shirt, so it was not until he finished that he noticed the full extent of the scar or the dozens of other scars that wracked her lovely body, all testament to the brutality she'd suffered throughout her life.

'Water's warm.' It was a woman's voice. 'Do you need any help?'

'No,' Tanner replied curtly. 'Just some dry blankets.' He washed away the dirt and dried blood, gently drying her and wrapping her in warm blankets. She still seemed so cold and her breathing was shallow and irregular, sometimes stopping altogether then starting again.

Paddy arrived before the doctor. He hitched his team to the dray, then organised some onlookers to look for Ugly's team. Finally the doctor appeared, stinking of rum and complaining loudly. He crawled into the dray, and pushing Tanner roughly aside he pulled back the blankets to reveal his patient.

'My God,' he gasped, his face softening with the compassion that years of hard experience had all but stripped away. The human moment passed and he turned to his task, poking, prodding and listening indifferently, answering Tanner's questions with a non-committal grunt. 'Ribs are broken,' he said at last, 'and there's fluid on the lung, but it could be pneumonia rather than blood. Jaw's not broken for all he's hit her. Bastard.' He glanced at her hands. 'She didn't fight.'

'Look again.' The doctor complied—it was true her hands were unmarked, but her wrists were deeply lacerated.

'Rope burn, the bastard.' He went to examine her internally and Tanner couldn't watch. He stared at the lifeless hand he now held in his own and thanked God that she was unconscious. 'Doesn't seem to have been raped, of course she was no virgin.' He covered her again, then shaking his head disgustedly asked: 'Why?' Tanner didn't answer. 'Was she robbed?' Tanner looked through her pockets and then in the hiding place.

'Yes, but there was no need for this. She'd've given up the

gold the moment he threatened her, it didn't matter that much to her.' The injustice and the cruelty of it overwhelmed Tanner again and his voice shook with emotion. 'She's such a sweet, gentle soul for all the hardness she professes, and there's no hate in her for all they've hurt her.' Tears ran down his cheeks. 'Will she . . .'

'Die?' The doctor finished for him. 'Probably. There's a chance not. If she's not bleeding inside. If she can beat the pneumonia.' He studied Tanner's disconsolate face and saw through the sadness to the desperation. 'It'll be a long, hard fight and if she starts passing blood or coughing it up then there'll be no hope for her.' He paused to study Tanner again. 'If not, and you keep her warm and propped up so she can breathe, get some fluids into her, sweet tea and salty broth—well, there's a chance. No promises mind, just a chance.' He hesitated, as if afraid of giving Tanner false hope. 'Those scars, they'll work for her this time, she's no stranger to pain or brutality so all this won't be such a shock and the shock goes a long way towards the killing. She's strong, a pampered pretty hurt like this would have no hope but this one,' and there was admiration in his voice, 'must be strengthened by what she's already survived.'

'Can we move her?' Tanner asked.

The doctor grunted. 'Well, you can't leave her here.' Paddy climbed up on the dray, peering under the hastily erected canopy that covered them.

'Well?' he asked.

'Doctor says she's got a fighting chance and we can move her to the shanty when you're ready.'

'My team's hitched up and ready now, but I can only find half of Ugly's team and I think I'm going to have to put Willie down.'

'No!' Tanner turned on him.

'He's got a bullet in his head.'

'I don't care, he's the only creature on this earth she cares for, he's got to survive.' Tanner could tell by the look on Paddy's face that he sounded irrational. 'Tether him here, I'll send Joey back for him.' He looked at the doctor. 'Is there anything else?' The doctor shook his head. 'How much do I owe you?'

The doctor smiled shrewdly. 'I'm told I could ask a pretty penny from you.'

'That you could.'

'But no, the teamsters are the lifeblood of the diggings and I'd not dare run foul of them.' He nodded to Paddy as he climbed down. 'Let me know how it turns out.'

It was dark by the time they reached the shanty but there were plenty to show a light, for a large crowd had gathered with offers of food and blankets, help and prayer. News travelled quickly on the diggings and the people there responded to disaster and with more generosity and concern than was to be found in the cities. Amy and Joey had built a fire and made a bed on which Catherine was carefully laid. Her breathing was harsh and audible; one moment she burned with fever, the next she trembled with cold. Tanner sat beside her holding her hand.

'I'll make some tea,' Amy said.

'Joey,' Tanner rallied, 'Willie's been shot. Paddy thinks he should be put down but if you could save him . . .' Tanner swallowed, surprised to find that his voice was shaking at the thought of Willie's death. 'She'll ask about him as soon as she's able and I don't want to have to lie.

Amy handed him his tea. 'How bad is she?' she asked. Tanner hadn't prepared himself for the question and he found it almost impossible to answer. He stared at the unconscious form and thought for the first time of the way in which the attack must have been carried out.

'By the looks of things,' he began slowly, 'he's tied her hands behind her back and hit her 'til she's fallen down, then kicked her.' Amy gasped. 'Her ribs are broken and God knows what else.'

'Why?' she exclaimed.

Tanner shook his head as he felt the grief engulfing him again. 'Maybe I'll ask him,' he said constrainedly. 'Just before I kill him maybe I'll ask him.'

Amy reached up to touch his face and found it wet with tears. 'Oh, Uncle John.' She threw her arms around him. 'I'm so sorry.' She clung tightly to him, as if to return some of the strength she'd borrowed from him in the past.

'You'll stay?' he managed to ask.

'Of course I'll stay and I'll look after you both. Davis and Joey can fend for themselves.' She hugged him. 'I'll make some food.'

Tanner didn't eat nor did he sleep. The next twenty-four hours passed in a blur dominated by Catherine's fragile form, interrupted by concerned faces, inquiring voices and hopeless attempts to force water between Catherine's dry and trembling lips. Tanner felt exhausted, emptied of all feeling and strength. He didn't notice the lamps being lit or the quiet that signalled the end of the day. Nor did he notice Jilly as she came into the shanty and crept silently to Catherine's side. She stared at the unrecognisable face and listened to the rasping wheeze.

'Ugly's going to die,' she murmured. 'Ugly's going to die.' Tanner looked up, seeing the child for the first time. 'Ugly —'

'Catherine,' he corrected.

'She is, isn't she?' Jilly sobbed. 'Ugly's going to die.'

'Catherine.'

'Ugly's —'

'Catherine.' He grabbed the child and shook her. 'Why can't you call her Catherine?'

'It's my fault,' Jilly sobbed, surrendering to Tanner's attack as if she welcomed the punishment. 'It's my fault.' Tanner felt the thin arms within his grip and watched the tiny form helpless in his hands. He let her go, horrified by what he'd done. 'It's my fault Ugly's going to die,' she sobbed. Tanner reached out tentatively, catching the child and drawing her to him.

'Did . . . did I hurt you?' he stammered.

'It's my fault,' she wailed.

'It's not your fault, it couldn't be your fault.' He held her carefully, still terrified he'd hurt her.

'Everyone,' she sobbed, 'everyone I love dies, everyone gets hurt.'

'No.' He extended the sound to belittle her words.

'Mummy died, and Daddy.' She looked directly at him, challenging him to say otherwise. 'I liked Joey and Amy made him cry and I liked you and you got hurt in the mine and Ugly was going to be my new mother and that's why she'll die.'

'No, no.' He held the child close, rocking her in his arms. 'That's a silly way to think.' He kissed her on the forehead. 'A silly, silly way to think.' Silly it may be but Tanner had embraced similar thoughts himself, for it seemed that in the last year he'd brought nothing but misery to everyone he cared about, everyone he touched.

'What's the matter?' Amy had heard the commotion from outside.

'Jilly's upset,' Tanner managed to say. 'I think I hurt her—get Joey to make sure she's all right.' He released the child, pushing her gently towards Amy. 'No more silly talk about Catherine dying or it being your fault, all right?' She nodded, and Amy led her out of the shanty. Tanner looked at Catherine again; she seemed to be fading away before his eyes.

'Where d'you think you're going?' Paddy's voice boomed from nearby.

'Please, must see Miss Ugly very important, must see.'

'I'm not having any bloody Chinaman anywhere near her!' Paddy yelled.

'Please, very important.'

'No, get to hell out of here.'

'It's all right, Paddy,' Tanner called. A moment later a small, round Chinaman entered, closely followed by Paddy. Tanner thought he recognised the man, although he couldn't fix the time or place of their meeting. The Chinaman bowed deeply to Tanner, then came forward to kneel beside Catherine.

'Miss Ugly have fever?'

'She's been beaten and she has pneumonia.' The man bowed again and produced a small porcelain container.

'I have medicine for fever and pain.'

'You're not giving her any of your damn opium.' Tanner was too tired to be either angry or polite.

'Not opium.' The man paused for a moment, searching his knowledge of English for the right word. 'In Western province of China grows tree, like your willow. We boil bark for medicine for fever and pain. Not like opium, just make well. Not like poppy,' he insisted, and Tanner understood. He accepted the bottle from the man, opened it and cautiously sipped the contents. It was exceedingly bitter.

'Thank you,' he said.

'You give to Miss Ugly, just a sip every few hours.' Tanner nodded. 'Not forget.' The man demanded assurance.

'I won't forget.'

'Miss Ugly show great respect for Chinese people.' He got to his feet as he spoke. 'In place where few people have respect, it becomes a great gift, now we can repay.' He bowed again to Tanner and to Catherine before leaving.

Amy entered as he left. 'What did he want?' she asked.

'He brought some medicine for Catherine,' Tanner answered.

'You're not going to give it to her?' Paddy sounded disgusted. 'Why not?'

'You don't know what it is.'

'Actually, I think I do. It tastes like the stuff the Chinese cook on one of my ships gave me when I had fever.'

'Did it help?' Amy asked incredulously.

'I'm not sure, we all had it. It got better, others died, but I think it made me feel better and it certainly didn't do any harm.'

'I doubt the doctor would approve.' Amy still wasn't convinced.

'What doctor?' Tanner edged closer to Catherine, gently propping up her head and shoulders. 'Doctor's not come near her again, nor is he going to.' He forced open her mouth and poured a little of the liquid in. She choked then swallowed, and he repeated the process a couple of times then let her rest. She looked so frail it frightened him.

Amy touched his shoulder, trying to find some way to comfort him. 'Willie's coming along just fine,' she said. 'Joey says the bullet went in at an angle, and that's why there's such a big gash. It's lodged in that bony bit between the horns.'

'Lucky it didn't split his skull,' Paddy added, but Tanner wasn't listening to them.

'Would you like something to eat?' Amy began, but her voice trailed away. She could feel the sag of his shoulders and she'd heard the heaviness in his voice. 'You should get some rest,' she said. 'I'll sit with her.' Tanner didn't answer. 'Uncle John,' Amy insisted.

'Leave him.' Paddy took her arm and led her from the shanty.

The night passed slowly into dawn. Catherine's fever lessened after each dose of medicine, but rose again a few hours later. At first the respites gave Tanner hope, but as the night wore on fatigue and disappointment eroded his optimism and by morning he was on the verge of despair. Mechanically he raised her head and forced the fluids down her throat, numbly he watched until it was time to try again. At noon Amy brought him a meal and the smell of it sickened him even though he'd hardly eaten in the last two days.

'What's this then?' Tanner had heard the whispers outside before the voice loudly addressed him. 'Trying to make yourself as sick as she is, are you? So it will be "Oh, poor Tanner" when you can't carry on for them children nor her neither.' Tanner's face made a movement reminiscent of a smile—there were few women with voices that strong or who'd dare to be that tarty.

Loretta knelt beside Catherine. 'You eat your meal and get some sleep. I'll watch her for a while.'

'I'm all right.'

'No you're not, and the last thing we want is two patients. Now off you go.' She pushed him slightly, indicating that he should go, but he didn't move. 'Go on, I meant what I said. Off you go.'

'I'm all right,' Tanner repeated.

'Look here, John Tanner, you're dead on your feet, and if I have to I'll have Paddy and Zeke come in here and cart you off. Now get some sleep.' She pushed him more firmly this time.

'I said I'm all right,' he yelled at her. Deep within her Catherine heard his voice—she knew he was yelling, but he seemed such a long way off. She forced her eyes open just enough to see, but her eyes wouldn't focus and her vision encompassed nothing but a blur. Soon the effort became too much and her eyes closed. Loretta stared at Catherine's twisted face, unsure of what she had seen.

'Catherine,' Loretta said firmly, 'Catherine.' There was no response. 'Yell at her,' she instructed Tanner.

'Catherine.' He spoke loudly, but with nowhere near the volume he'd produced before. He took her hand in his as if it could transmit the strength his voice now lacked. 'Catherine!' Her eyelids opened just a crack and her eyes moved slowly beneath them, searching the gloom for his familiar form. She found it and, satisfied, let her eyes close. 'Catherine!' He demanded confirmation and obediently she opened her eyes once more. Tanner was shaking as Loretta put her arm around him.

'Now she's conscious, will you get some sleep?' He ignored her, edging closer to Catherine and lifting her gently.

'You've got to drink this,' he said. 'It tastes awful.' He poured the medicine in her mouth and she coughed weakly at the acrid taste. 'Now water.' He made her drink as much as she could, then he laid her back on the bed.

'Fever's broken,' Loretta said. 'She needs rest now and so do you.' Tanner stared at Catherine: indeed the fever had broken, she was cool and still, and he wondered when it had happened.

'Did you hear me, Tanner?' Loretta insisted. 'Sleep.' He still didn't move. 'Damn you.' Catherine's eyes opened again and her lips moved noiselessly. Tanner leant close to hear her.

'Sleep here,' she whispered, and her hand slid down beside her to indicate the position he should take.

'What did she say?' Loretta asked.

'Sleep here,' Tanner repeated.

'Good idea.' Loretta got some blankets and made him a bed next to her. He lay there, holding Catherine's hand and listening to her breathing. Within seconds he was asleep.

Tanner woke with a start, and his eyes flew open to see nothing but darkness. He rolled on to his side, groping amongst the pile of blankets.

'Catherine,' he breathed heavily.

'She's all right.' It was Amy's voice, and in the faint glow from the fire he could see her silhouette. 'I gave her some warm tea just before, next time she stirs I'll try her with broth.' She felt her way round the bed until she was sitting next to him. 'Would you like something?'

'No.' He fell back, feeling nauseous and giddy. 'Did you give her more medicine?'

'The fever's broken,' Amy said uncertainly.

'It's for pain, too.'

'I didn't think she'd need it as she was sleeping so quietly.'

'You're probably right.' He closed his eyes and it only seemed a few minutes later that he opened them again, but the shanty was light and it was Loretta who sat beside him, not Amy. He opened his mouth to speak, but she pre-empted him.

'She's fine, eaten her soup, drunk her tea; a better patient than you are.' Tanner sat up cautiously, remembering the giddiness of the night before. Some of the swelling had gone out of Catherine's face and the bruises were less livid. He touched her hand, which was warm. 'I can make you some oatmeal, or there's some of Amy's world-famous damper.

'Anything, I'm starved.' Tanner stared at Catherine while he ate, and when his hunger and his concern for her were satisfied he rose unsteadily to his feet and ambled outside. He'd been out only a couple of times during the last three days, to answer a call of nature, but he hadn't really noticed his surroundings or the people who had waited with him through the long hours of

247

Catherine's fever. The dray stood in its accustomed position, with a tarpaulin rigged above it like a tent. Zeke sat on its seat, whittling a small doll from a piece of wood while Jilly watched in fascination. Paddy and Joey were making a futile attempt to hold Willie still while they examined his wound. Amy was nowhere to be seen. Tanner assumed she was sleeping and Davis was conspicuous by his absence. Tanner's attention finally rested on Bobby, who sat hunched in his coat gazing vacantly into the fire. His face was totally without expression, like one drugged or insane. Tanner moved closer to him, but he remained unaware of Tanner's presence.

'How is she?' Zeke called.

'Better.' Tanner faced him. 'Fever's broken.'

'She'll be all right then.'

'Perhaps.' Tanner glanced back at Bobby. 'I knew a man once got into a fight, he was fine for two or three days then he started haemorrhaging.' He took another look at the boy, vaguely remembering the bitterness that had passed between them. Fleetingly, he wondered if he was in some way responsible for the desolation that surrounded the boy, but then without warning his whole body began shaking uncontrollably. He tried to reach the dray and was barely able to make the distance. Zeke helped him on to the seat.

'Steady on there.' He reached into the dray. 'I got something here I've been hiding from Paddy, figured you'd need it sooner or later.' It was rum and Tanner had never known it to taste so good.

CHAPTER 27

✦✦✦✦✦✦✦✦✦✦✦✦✦✦

CATHERINE KNEW she was awake, although her eyes were still closed and vague visions and half dreams crowded her thoughts. What's more, she knew she was in pain and gradually she remembered why. She forced her eyes open far enough to confirm that she was in the shanty then she let them close, but movement in the room made her force them open again.

'Tanner,' she murmured.

'I'll get him,' Loretta called excitedly as she backed out of the shanty. Catherine felt her hold on consciousness slipping and she fought to maintain it. She tried to think, to remember, but the memories were all jumbled and distorted.

'Catherine.' The name had never sounded so sweet to her before, still she frowned rather than smiled as she opened her eyes. He looked terrible—he was tired, drawn and so worried that she knew instantly how ill she must be. She felt herself sinking into unconsciousness again and she grasped at any thought that might keep her awake a moment longer. Out of the confusion of ideas came a shot and a bellow of pain.

'Willie!' she wheezed.

'He's all right. Bullet bounced off that thick skull of his.' The relief that showed in Tanner's face only served to convince Catherine that she was worse than she felt.

'See him,' she whispered. 'Want to see him.' Despite the confusion Catherine could still reason that if she was that sick Tanner would lie rather than upset her and she had seen Willie fall.

'Don't you trust me?' he asked. Her lips moved and if it hadn't been for the swelling and the natural constraints of the scar it might have been a smile.

'With my life,' she said, 'but not with the truth.'

'I'm wounded to the quick,' he mocked, scrambling to the door. 'Joey, get that great ox in here.'

249

'In there?'

'Yes, in here. She wants to see him.' They could have brought any bullock to the door, the bright light outside made it impossible for her to discern more than the outline, but she was too hurt and tired not to be satisfied.

It was more than an hour before she regained consciousness again, but it was a more genuine form of consciousness. The pain was more acute and localised, and she was aware of the difficulty of breathing and the weakness that paralysed her body. She was aware of something else too—she was naked, and she knew intuitively that it was Tanner who'd made her so. It was something that she'd feared from the first time he'd treated her like any other woman, a fear that had intensified with every advancement in their relationship. A fear that one day they would reach the point of intimacy and he would see her, all of her with all the scars and disfigurement, and that it would drive him away, leaving her more alone for having known his company.

'You're awake I see.' He sat beside her and she noted that his colour had returned and that he looked less drawn.

'My clothes?' she asked.

'I had to cut them off, they were sodden, filthy.' He smiled at her doubting face. 'I'll buy you new ones, the best in Melbourne. The day we're married there won't be a more finely attired couple anywhere.'

'You don't have to marry me or come with me on the road, you don't owe me that.' Tanner knew her well enough to realise that it was the scars that made her refuse him now, just as they'd made her refuse him all along.

'Those scars don't matter to me.'

She closed her eyes and tears ran down her cheeks. 'You're such a clever liar,' she said.

'I've never lied to you and I swear before God that those scars make no difference to me.'

She shook her head. 'You don't owe me anything. It wasn't your fault,' she said, and Tanner knew instantly that it was his fault. He couldn't see how but an awful sinking feeling in the pit of his stomach, a burning cold that spread through his body, told him it was so. For a moment his mind was caught in immobility, then at last he had an answer for all those people who had asked him 'why'.

'You should have told them I was taking the nugget to Forest Creek.'

Her eyes flickered open, a faint smile creasing her lips. 'I'd not betray you.'

He watched her eyes close and her breathing slow as she succumbed to the exhaustion even a few moments of consciousness produced. It was his fault, somehow, someone had found out that he'd asked her to carry the gold for him. His eyes fixed on a deep purple gash along her jaw, so few people knew, Amy and Joey and, yes, the boy. Bobby had been listening when Catherine offered to take the gold. Bobby had seen Tanner take it from its hiding place and could easily have seen him put it in Catherine's dray. Bobby, who had resented him from the first day he arrived, who believed the gold came from the mine. Bobby, who'd left him to die when the mine collapsed.

Tanner's breathing quickened as he rose slowly to his feet. He turned for the door, and the anger that possessed him quickened his pace. The boy still sat by the fire, staring into the embers, and Tanner crossed the distance between them in a few swift strides. He dragged Bobby to his feet.

'Who did you tell?' He shook him. 'Who did you tell?' Even in his unreasoning fury Tanner knew Bobby was physically incapable of inflicting the injuries that Catherine had suffered. 'What did they promise you?' He shook the boy again. 'A share of the nugget, is that it?' He pushed Bobby to the ground, then dragged him to his feet again. 'Or did you just do it out of spite, as a way to get even with me?' He continued shaking the boy and pushing him, yelling in his face before throwing him to the ground then dragging him to his feet again. 'It wasn't enough to call me a thief and a liar, it wasn't enough to leave me to die after I'd saved your useless life, it wasn't enough ransacking the shanty looking for my nugget or breaking into the commissioner's hut trying to steal it. You had to betray us all, me, Catherine, Jilly, even yourself and all for a little revenge.' They reached the dray as Tanner dragged Bobby to his feet again. 'Who was it?' He slammed the boy into the side of the dray. 'Who was it? *Who was it?*' Each time he repeated the phrase he repeated the action.

'Tanner, for God's sake!' Zeke yelled at him but he lacked the courage to intervene, so it was left to Paddy and Joey to pull them apart. Zeke jumped down from the dray and helped Bobby to his feet, He was bruised and shaken, but far less injured than he might have been if Tanner had surrendered to the full power of his rage. Zeke looked up at Tanner. His chest still heaved with every breath and his muscles were still tensed, but the look of unbridled hatred had been replaced by one of shock. 'What exactly are you accusing the boy of doing?'

'The man who attacked Catherine did so because he believed she was carrying my nugget. Only Amy, Joey and Bobby knew that she'd offered to carry it for me. Only Bobby knew the exact time I took it from its hiding place, only Bobby had a motive.' Zeke turned his attention to the boy, who was shaking and still too shocked to speak.

'They're serious charges, son.' Zeke fixed him with an authoritative eye. 'What have you got to say for yourself?'

'I didn't . . .' The boy started, then bit his lip. They wouldn't believe him, they hadn't believed him when he said Tanner found the gold in the mine, they wouldn't believe him now.

Come on, son.' Bobby refused to look Zeke in the eye, 'Did you know Catherine offered to take the nugget?' Bobby compressed his lips, determined not to give them the satisfaction of an answer. 'Did you see your uncle take the nugget and give it to her?' The boy could envisage the nugget just as he'd seen it on that night, twice as big as he'd imagined, resting in his uncle's gloating hands. Zeke decided to alter his tactics. He put a friendly hand on Bobby's shoulder and altered his voice to match. 'Maybe you told someone by accident, just mentioned it in passing.'

'Who?' The boy wrenched himself free of Zeke's grip. 'Who would I tell? Who do I know? Who could I trust? They're all a bunch of thieves and killers, they murdered my father and stole his nugget then they couldn't wait to get their hands on this mine, but he got in first.' He spun round to face Tanner. 'I know what you're doing. You're trying to make them hate me so you can keep stealing from me, and they won't do a thing to stop you.' He gasped for air like a man drowning in his own emotion. 'My father found a giant nugget as big as his fist and you found one twice as big and I don't care what your friends down in the lower gully say or what the commissioner says, I know that nugget came out of this mine and it belongs to me.' He shrieked the last words, his voice breaking, his face crimson and his body rigid, like someone having a fit.

For a moment after the outburst nothing happened. Joey and Paddy had let Tanner go, and the three of them stood together gaping at the boy. Zeke was also too stunned to move. Bobby panted or sobbed, it was impossible to tell which, and he stood transfixed, his arms and head jerking spasmodically.

'Bobby,' Zeke said.

'No!' The boy screamed, and his voice came with such force that it seemed to have been ripped from his chest. 'No!' He wheeled round to face Zeke then headed down the gully, running, stumbling and crawling to get out of their sight, beyond their hearing.

'Hope we haven't come at a bad time.' Two men had entered the circle of their camp without being noticed, and it was hard to tell how much they'd heard.

'What do you want?' Tanner asked curtly. He recognised them as the men who had been confronting Bobby the day he'd first arrived.

'We've come to say how sorry we were to hear about your, er —' a look passed between them and a smirk crossed their faces, '— lady friend.'

'And to congratulate you on your excellent find,' the second man added. Tanner observed them coldly.

'Thank you,' he said insincerely.

'I hear you've already sold it.' The first of the two men took a seat by the fire.

'Yes.'

'And that you've given up the diggings.' He glanced round the claim. 'But you've not moved on.'

'Not yet.' Tanner was deliberately uninformative.

'Lucky stroke, finding that nugget in the creek.' The second man also sat down. 'Means the gold's all yours and only yours.'

'That's right.' There was a short silence before the second man spoke again.

'Boy doesn't seem to be taking it too well.'

'Bobby's still upset about his father.' For an instant Tanner toyed with the possibility that they may have been involved in his brother's death.

'Ah yes, his father, killed for a giant nugget, so they say.' Tanner regarded them speculatively—they actually believed there was a nugget which, if nothing else, proved they were not the men who killed his brother, for Tanner was certain that no

253

giant nugget ever came from that mine.

'My brother was bludgeoned—that's apt to make a man hallucinate.'

'Aye.' The men nodded their agreement.

'Still,' the first man said thoughtfully, 'two brothers, two giant nuggets, that's apt to make a man —' he paused as if searching for the word, '— suspicious.'

'No, no, no,' his companion objected. 'Only a third nugget would be suspicious. I mean, if you were to re-open the mine and find another nugget, well . . .' He spread his hands as if to indicate that his argument was proven.

'There is no gold in that mine,' Tanner said. 'Besides, it's half full of mud where the shafts have collapsed.'

'Oh, you couldn't work it now,' the first man agreed, 'but in the summer, when things dry out and people forget the boy and all his nonsense . . .'

'You know, I heard the boy complained to the commissioner.' The second spoke.

'Oh, the commissioner will forget, I'm sure.'

Tanner was tired of their innuendo. 'What do you want?' he snapped.

'There may not be another big nugget down there, but even if there is, there's no way you'll be able to hold on to it, might even cost you the one you've got if you try.'

'Two hundred pounds.' The second man spoke up. 'Two hundred pounds, you walk off, we walk on and you'll be long gone by the time we find anything.'

'The mine is worthless, gentlemen, I found that nugget in the creek.'

'If it's worthless then you won't mind selling it to us,' the first man insisted.

Tanner sighed frustratedly. 'I've had a hard few days, gentlemen, a hard few weeks, a hard few months and there's nothing I'd like more than to take your money and leave you with this mine, but there is no gold here.' He spoke slowly, emphasising each of the last five words. The two men glanced at each other then at Paddy, Joey and Zeke, who had stood silently throughout the conversation.

'We understand.' The first man smiled knowingly. 'We're camped on the other side of the track, where the gully starts to turn rocky, you could come by later if you've a mind to talk.' They stood up, nodded acknowledgement to the assembled company and left.

'You should have sold it to them,' Zeke said.

'It's worthless,' Tanner protested.

'Ah, well now,' Paddy wandered forward, 'it all depends on your point of view.' He sidled up to the dray, peeping into the place where Zeke had hidden the rum. 'Tell me—would the boy sell it for that amount of money?' He frowned as he found Zeke's posse empty.

'The boy thinks there's gold in it.'

'So do they.' Paddy glared at Zeke.

'Well, I know there isn't.'

'Oh, so now you're an expert are you?' Paddy continued his search. 'And how would you feel if you walked off the claim and they walked on and found gold?'

'Astonished.'

'Aye, and very foolish.' Paddy abandoned his search. 'And how would the boy feel?' Tanner gazed in the direction Bobby had taken. 'He'd feel cheated, but two hundred pounds is better than nothing.'

'I don't know,' Tanner said thoughtfully. The children had nothing left of their parents, even Mary's wedding ring was gone, and this would be something, a legacy, a price for their sacrifice. 'I suppose I could put it in trust for the two of them.'

'No.' Amy appeared from inside the dray. She had been awakened by Tanner's attack on the boy and had pulled Jilly into the dray, hoping to shield her from some of the violence of the argument.

'Why not?' Paddy asked.

'It's not honest.' All but Joey laughed at her.

'If I tell them I think the mine's worthless, then I'm not deceiving them. If they choose to think I'm a liar then they're deceiving themselves.'

'If you think the mine's worthless you should just walk away.'

'And what about the boy and what he believes?' Tanner watched Amy's face as it changed from fierce advocate to pouting child, and he was reminded again of a London tavern, a blue wool cape and a green portmanteau. She may have matured physically and grown more confident, but underneath she hadn't changed at all for all the deception she'd practised on the ship. Suddenly

Tanner felt angry as the vision of Buchanan materialised before his eyes.

'Uncle John, it's wrong,' Amy continued disapprovingly, 'and in the end Bobby won't thank you for it.'

'Just as you never thanked me for the wool cape that stopped you from freezing to death in London.' He turned on her angrily. 'But you didn't mind lying to Buchanan, stealing his trust and his friendship, you didn't mind deceiving me about your meetings with Davis or letting me think that I'd blinded you. No morals are broken unless there's property involved, is that what your petty morality dictates?' He saw her lips tremble and tears in her eyes, then his vision clouded and his head began to pound. He fought to steady himself before he turned to go into the shanty. As soon as Tanner was gone Zeke turned on Amy.

'How dare you judge him, how dare you deny him the chance to walk away from this mine with something for the boy. Do you know how few men would have picked you up off the streets, how few would have lied and stolen to protect you —'

'That's enough.' It was Joey who interrupted, his voice uncharacteristically loud and his face creased with unaccustomed lines of anger. 'Come along, Amy.' He took hold of her, half helping, half lifting her down from the dray. 'We've left Davis doing the work long enough.'

Joey led her up the valley at a rather brisk pace, and before they reached their camp she slipped and fell. Joey helped her to her feet, brushing her down and holding her near as she began to cry.

'There now.' He patted her back self-consciously.

'Zeke was right,' Amy cried. 'Uncle John's been so good to me.'

'That he has,' Joey agreed, 'and perhaps it wasn't the best time to go criticising him, but you were right, too. Maybe it wasn't your place to say anything at all, ever, but you were still right.'

'Do you really think so?' Amy brushed away the tears.

'Of course I do.'

Davis looked up as they entered the camp. 'What's up?' he asked, noting Amy's flushed cheeks.

'Things are getting a bit strained down there,' Joey answered.

'Oh?' Davis prompted.

'Aye, Catherine's conscious, she told Tanner the man that beat her was after his nugget. Well, seeing as it was only me, Amy and the boy that knew, he naturally assumed it was the boy that give her away.'

'Naturally.' A combination of experience and intuition told Davis they were holding back. 'What else?' Joey didn't answer—he suddenly seemed preoccupied. 'Well?' Davis insisted.

'Oh, they had an awful fight,' Amy answered, 'then these men came and offered to buy the mine.'

'Buy the mine,' Davis said with bemused surprise. 'I bet he jumped at that.'

'Not yet.'

'The damn fool, what sort of game's he playing?' Davis frowned thoughtfully. Tanner was many kinds of fool, but not that kind. 'Of course.' Davis' voice was hushed with admiration. 'He'll let them think the nugget's come from the mine, push the price up—the man's a genius. And Ugly's conscious you say?' He didn't wait for them to confirm it. 'Was she able to give a good description of her attacker?'

'I don't think anyone's asked her yet,' Amy said. 'She's still very groggy.'

'Should you two have come back so soon?'

'I wanted to come back.'

'To be with me?' Davis teased.

'Yes,' she said, and he knew it was a lie.

CHAPTER 28

++++++++++++++

NEWS OF Catherine's recovery spread quickly and the camp was immediately inundated with well-wishers. The Chinaman came, bringing a new medicine designed to alleviate congestion. The commissioner came too, but his visit was an official one. He made the usual polite inquiries before settling to his purpose.

'If you could just tell us exactly what happened.' Catherine hesitated for a moment; the memories were all still a little disorganised.

'It was not long after Tanner left that he came. I was just about asleep and I thought I heard something. I got up to see what it was and he was there with a gun.' She licked her lips to moisten them—the memories were falling into place. 'He asked me for my gold and I gave him what was in my pocket, then he hit me and asked for the rest of it. I got what was hidden under the floor.' She looked sadly at Tanner, but there was no way to spare him from the truth. 'He hit me again and asked me for Tanner's nugget. I said I didn't have it and he hit me over and over, then Willie started bellowing.' Her eyes fill with tears and her voice choked. 'I've had him since he was a calf, I was like a mother to him, he just wanted to protect me. God, he only had to yell at the damned, stupid ox and he'd stop, but he shot him.' She lay still, panting, waiting for her strength to return. 'I grabbed the whip and hit him, would be that what messed up his aim. I went to hit him again but he grabbed the whip and hit me with the butt of the gun.' She touched the purple gash on her jaw. 'When I came round he'd tied my hands and was searching the dray. He couldn't find anything so he started on me again. In the end he believed me.' She laughed sardonically. 'And that's when he really hurt me. God, I thought he was going to kill me.' Her last words were followed by an empty silence.

'Can you describe him?' The commissioner asked.

'Tall, not as tall as Tanner there but leaner and younger I

think. He'd covered himself up so I couldn't see him, gloves, strips of cloth tied round his face and a hat. He tried to make himself sound Chinese but he wasn't.'

'Are you sure?'

She made a slight shrug. 'I rather fancy his eyes were blue and I answered him in Chinese and he didn't understand me. Of course, there are so many dialects but most of them speak Mandarin.'

The commissioner frowned, it would have pleased him personally to be able to blame the Chinese. 'At the end, when he beat you uncontrollably, did he still have his accent?'

'It wasn't like that.'

'Like what?'

She shook her head irritably for she wasn't good with words. 'He'd not lost control, he was hurting me on purpose, almost out of spite, and he didn't say anything.'

There was a movement in the doorway, and Tanner looked up to see Joey's bulky form just before he withdrew. Briefly he wondered if Amy had come too, then Catherine began coughing, great rattling coughs that made her whole body shake and brought tears to her eyes. Tanner put his arm around her and reached thankfully for the Chinaman's remedy.

Joey wandered slowly away from the shanty. He was stunned by Catherine's description of the attack—for some reason he'd imagined a fight, her struggling and the attacker quelling her. Joey stopped by the fire, which was almost out; a combination of rain and neglect had left it lifeless. On the far side of the claim, next to the mouth of the mine, Bobby had built a small fire of his own. He sat on an empty box, a piece of oil cloth pulled over his shoulders. Such a lonely figure, Joey thought, not that he hadn't brought a lot of it on himself, but not this final punishment. Joey glanced in the direction of his own claim. He loved Amy more than life, he could admit that now if only to himself, but Davis was his friend who'd stood up for him when other men had mocked him. He glanced again at the boy, then started to infuse a little life into the fire.

'Joey.' Tanner joined him at his task. He glanced several times at Joey's troubled face before he continued. 'Tell Amy I'm sorry. Tell her I just couldn't take any more.' The fire began to burn and both men sat back on the log. 'Tell her it never mattered to me that she let me think I'd blinded her, that deceiving Buchanan was my idea and I know I left her no choice but to go along with it. As far as what she and Davis did, well, I expect it was Davis' idea and like me he gave her little choice.'

Joey nodded but he looked no less concerned. 'I'll tell her you were only thinking of the boy, trying to get him something for all this mine's cost him.'

Tanner looked at him curiously. Joey had heard his words and understood their meaning, but his mind was focused on a different level. 'So you think I was right and she was wrong?'

'No,' Joey said abstractedly. 'I think you were trying to do what was best, but she was thinking beyond that to what was right. Do you know what I mean?'

'Oh, sure, absolute right, the cardinal virtues, just fine for those who can afford to live up to them.' Joey frowned. 'Truth, honour, justice,' Tanner explained. Joey nodded thoughtfully. 'But even things like that can seem to be against each other sometimes,' Tanner said.

'You mean, like a soldier going into battle torn between loyalty and the sanctity of human life?' Tanner had never imagined Joey to be capable of such profound thought. 'Loyalty, aye,' Joey said, 'say, loyalty and truth, now how's a man supposed to choose between them?'

Tanner frowned—he knew Joey well enough to realise that this wasn't a purely hypothetical discussion, that it had some practical purpose and the look on Joey's face told Tanner it mattered a great deal.

'Well, the purists like our Amy would go for truth every time, for the object of loyalty may not be worthy of it. But myself, I've always supported that which was most likely to ensure my survival.'

Joey made no response and, even though he'd given the question reasonable consideration and been totally honest, Tanner began to wonder if he'd answered the question at all or if he'd even understood it. Joey stared into the fire, his bland face creased with unnatural worry lines. He rose slowly.

'A man can do the right thing for the wrong reason,' he said.

'Better than not doing it at all.' Tanner had the oddest feeling, a disquiet prompted by Joey's mood and fed by a series of disassociated ideas that began invading his thoughts. Joey left without saying more, but Tanner was too preoccupied to notice.

Loretta fussed irritably with Catherine's hair, which was short and unruly, and nothing Loretta could do would make it feminine.

'At least try it on.' She indicated a blue dress lying discarded at Catherine's side.

'Please, Catherine,' Jilly implored, 'it would make you look pretty.'

Catherine touched the child affectionately. 'I'd not feel pretty nor comfortable neither.'

'Fine,' Loretta said curtly. 'What are you going to wear?'

'There's trousers and a shirt in the dray. You'll have to ask Tanner what he did with my boots.'

'Tanner,' Loretta said disgustedly. 'I haven't been able to get two words out of him since the commissioner left.'

'I'd've given anything not to have to tell him it was his nugget they were after,' Catherine said, sadly.

Tanner was sitting by one fire staring at Bobby sitting next to the other while Paddy and Zeke hitched the team to Catherine's dray.

'Where are you going?' Loretta asked as she emerged from the shanty.

'To get our stuff off Paddy's dray. Thought we might set up on the flat, give a concert there.'

'Good idea.' Loretta located Catherine's clothes, then returned to the shanty.

'Do you want to come with us?' Zeke called to Tanner, but Tanner didn't respond.

'Where are you off to?' Joey had arrived in time to hear Zeke's offer.

'We're moving our stuff on to Catherine's dray.'

'I don't suppose you've got a couple of hours free?' Paddy asked.

'A couple of days more likely.' Joey's grin faded as he looked at Bobby. He took a few steps towards Tanner then stopped. His resolve had brought him this far but it could not push him any further, for he could see clearly the repercussions of his proposed action and Joey might have turned and left or joined Zeke and Paddy on their expedition if it hadn't been for the arrival of the commissioner. He was flanked by two of his troopers and wore that sour, official expression that men of duty wear when they are about to do something unpleasant.

'I'd like a word with the boy.' He addressed Tanner.

'Why?'

'A few questions.' He nodded to the troopers, who fetched the boy handling him as if he was a criminal. Tanner made no objection and Bobby was too surprised to protest. He stood between the two massive troopers, facing the imposing figure of the commissioner, and to Tanner he looked such a frightened, confused and very lonely little boy.

'Do you know who I am?' the commissioner asked. Bobby nodded. 'Then you know you've got to answer me truthfully.' The boy nodded again. 'The attack on the teamster was a terrible, cowardly act and a very serious crime.' He waited, but Bobby made no comment. 'It appears that whoever attacked her was looking for your uncle's nugget.' He paused again, and again Bobby didn't speak. 'You knew your uncle gave the nugget to the teamster, didn't you?' It was a direct question this time, but the boy still didn't answer. 'Come along now son, there are some serious charges against you, including one of breaking into my office, and it will go a lot easier on you if you tell me the truth. Now, did you know of your uncle's intention to get the teamster to take his nugget to Forest Creek?' The commissioner's voice had grown louder and more demanding as his irritation grew. 'Did you tell anyone what you knew?'

Bobby still refused to speak, and after a few moments of angry silence the commissioner overcame his annoyance and tried a different approach.

'You came to me complaining that your uncle had stolen the nugget out of the mine.' Bobby lowered his eyes, realising how foolish he'd been to expect justice from the law. 'And you tore the shanty apart hoping to find it.' The commissioner leant close to the boy. 'Or at least, that's what the rumours say.' He stood upright. 'Of course, rumours can be wrong. I heard one that said Tanner's nugget was in my office. Did you hear that one?'

Bobby's shoulders sagged—there was no fight left in him, and even though he was afraid it wasn't the type of fear that made a body run or fight but the empty, hopeless fear that paralyses.

'I heard you left your uncle to die in the mine after he saved your life.'

'That was an accident.' Tanner spoke for the first time.

The commissioner pursed his lips thoughtfully. 'I was just repeating the accusation you, yourself, made as it was told to me by those who saw you almost killing the boy. You did have to be dragged away from him, didn't you?'

'I was upset, irrational. I'd just learnt that it was for my nugget that Catherine was beaten.'

'And you immediately assumed it was the boy who betrayed you because he had a motive, because he knew how the nugget was being moved and when.' The commissioner returned his attention to Bobby. 'Now son, tell me the truth, did you —'

'Boy couldn't have done it.' Joey's voice was deep and troubled and his body was tense with anxiety.

'And why not?' Joey's eyes switched from the commissioner to Tanner, his face etched with desperate appeal.

'Joey pointed out to me, after I'd attacked the boy, that we'd talked over there by the dray, boy was in the shanty, even if he'd been awake he couldn't have heard us.' The boy's head jerked back and he glared at Tanner, his utter hatred of the man almost making him denounce his uncle as a liar. 'As for your office, he couldn't have done that either.'

'Why not? He was seen running and hiding in the gully not long after it happened.'

'Running and hiding he was. I spent most of the night chasing him to give him the thrashing he deserved for what he did to the shanty, and I'd've caught him too if it hadn't've been for this damned ankle.' Tanner touched his injured foot. 'Believe me, he didn't have time to break into your office.' The commissioner frowned pensively. He didn't like the answers he was getting, but he had little choice except to believe them. He indicated to his men that they could release the boy.

'Who else knew about your arrangement with the teamster?'

'Amy and Joey, but they also knew I'd changed my mind and neither of them knew when the gold was being moved.' It was another lie and Tanner wondered what the punishment was for deliberately misleading the commissioner.

'Well,' the commissioner sighed heavily, 'have you any other theories?' Tanner and Joey held each other's gaze for a moment, then Tanner smiled thinly.

'He could have been following me, watching me from a distance. He could have seen me take the nugget and put it in the dray. Catherine did carry it from here to the place where she was attacked. He could have been getting ready for the robbery, covering his face, when I collected the nugget.' There was such sadness in Tanner's voice that the commissioner was reluctant to doubt him. He made a few more routine remarks before leading his troops away.

Catherine and Loretta had appeared from the shanty, but no one had noticed them. All eyes were fixed initially on the commissioner and then on Bobby.

'You lied for the boy.' Joey's statement halted the women's advance.

'Boy didn't betray us,' Tanner said. He was still studying Bobby, who was too confused to react. Tanner switched his gaze to Joey. 'You did, you or Amy.' The remark stunned everyone and, although Tanner allowed them plenty of time, no one spoke. 'One of you told Davis about Catherine's plan, I know because he mentioned it the day I sold the nugget and he knew I had to get it to Forest Creek within two days. All he had to do was to keep watch until he saw Catherine drive off.' Tanner waited for Joey to speak, to confirm or deny. 'Tell me he was in the tent asleep the night Catherine was attacked, tell me he couldn't have done it,' Tanner challenged. Joey shook his head futilely, a part of him still wanting to defend Davis.

'He didn't always sleep in the tent. He said sometimes it was impossible to sleep being so close to Amy and not being able to touch her.'

'Ha,' Tanner laughed. 'I bet that started when I found the nugget and stopped when he thought he'd be helping to transport it.' Joey lowered his head in affirmation.

'Now Tanner, that's no proof.' It was Zeke who intervened, for he could see the potential for disaster that this line of thinking could cause. 'If you suspect him tell the commissioner.'

'I'll not send the commissioner up there, not while Davis still has Amy with him.' Tanner had raised his voice for the first time, and there was a passion in him that even Zeke found overpowering. 'And there is proof, isn't there Joey, just like there's proof that he burned the *Lady Ann*?' Tanner was yelling and Joey was loathe to answer the question. 'Answer me!' Tanner demanded.

'He could have burned the *Lady Ann*,' Joey murmured. 'It's true he lied about how he got off the ship and where he was when the fire was lit, but there's no real proof he did the burning.'

'But there is real proof that he attacked Catherine, isn't there

Joey?' Tanner's face was contorted with anger and his hands were raised as if he intended to shake the truth out of Joey. 'Something Catherine said to the commissioner was proof enough for you. I could see it in your face, I could hear it when you asked me about truth.' The intensity of Tanner's stare was as irresistible as his words.

'I didn't want to believe it,' Joey said at last, 'even after what I saw. I didn't want to be the one to put him in. I didn't want Amy to think that . . .' He stopped, unable to explain to them that he loved Amy and that to win her this way seemed underhanded.

'Get her here.' Tanner's voice was deep and gravelly, hoarse from the effort of controlling himself. 'You get Amy here.' His voice, his whole body shook and Joey was awed by him. 'Don't confront Davis, just make up a story to get Amy here.'

'Davis has a right to answer the charges.'

'No!' Tanner bellowed, then consciously lowered the volume of his voice. 'Tell Amy I'm hurt, she'll come without question then and when she gets here you tell her the truth.'

'But —'

'For God's sake, Joey,' Tanner yelled, then once again he regained control, his voice becoming one of appeal. 'She'll never accept a man who could do what Davis has done, and what do you think he'll do to her if she refuses him?'

'He'd not hurt Amy.' Joey was genuinely astonished by the suggestion.

'Don't make me go up there, Joey.' Tanner's voice was a cry and he drew breath to steady himself. 'Because if I ever see him again I'll kill him, and if anything happens to Amy I'll hunt him down to do it.' Tanner's body was suddenly still and there was a frightening calm in his voice, and not one among them doubted that he meant what he said. Joey looked from one face to another, but none would oppose Tanner. For an instant his eyes rested on Catherine, her broken body testament to Davis' capabilities. There was nothing else to say, nothing else to do, and he trudged wearily from the camp. The climb to his own claim never seemed more difficult.

Catherine walked unsteadily forward. 'Tanner,' she wheezed. The hardness faded from his face as he saw her and moved to support her.

'What are you doing out here?'

'It was going to be a surprise.' She leant heavily on him, resting her head on his chest. 'I want to go to Melbourne,' she said, 'I want to go today. Paddy can have my dray and I'll trade what's left of the team for a cart.'

'I already have a cart.' Tanner felt her arms tighten around him.

'Forget it, Tanner, just walk away.' She looked up at him. 'Please.'

'What about Amy and Willie?'

'Amy will be here soon, Joey will bring her, you'll see.' There was desperation in Catherine's voice as she fought for enough air to keep on talking. 'When she comes we could just go, Joey would look after Willie, or Paddy or Zeke.' She looked to them for confirmation. 'There's nothing here worth packing. We could start for Melbourne straight away.' She paused to catch her breath, his body seemed so unyielding. 'We could be married if you still want me, I'd come with you on the sea, we could buy that ship you were wanting. I've money I could put with yours.'

'No,' Tanner moaned, kissing her on the forehead. 'I'd not take your money, not to put in a ship that could end up at the bottom of the ocean. You buy land with your money, something that'll be there no matter what happens. And you make your decision about sailing and marriage when we've not got the spectre of Davis hanging over our head.'

Tanner turned to face Bobby, who had not moved since the commissioner left. He stood motionless like a bystander, watching, hearing, but detached from the proceedings. Nothing made sense to him, not the commissioner's questions nor his uncle's lies, even the revelations about Davis had meant nothing to him. He had recognised his uncle's anger and the power of it might have frightened him, but it seemed distant and directed elsewhere.

'I intend to sell the mine,' Tanner informed him. 'I've been offered two hundred pounds. I'll put the money in trust to be turned over to you and Jilly when you're twenty-one.' Bobby heard his uncle's words but they had no effect, and it surprised him to realise that it didn't matter any more. He frowned at the thought—it had mattered so much before, the mine had been all his parents' hopes and dreams, the only thing he had left of them. He felt the burning of tears in his eyes, and for the first time since his parents' death he allowed them to fall. Tanner reached out awkwardly to comfort him. 'It'll be easier once we're back in Melbourne.'

Jilly appeared from behind Loretta's skirts. 'Are we really going to Melbourne this time?' she asked.

'As soon as Catherine can travel.' Tanner brushed his hand across the child's untidy hair. 'But for now I think she should rest.'

'No, I want to sit up for a while.' Tanner wrapped his coat around her and sat her by the fire. Bobby also moved to the fire, and one by one the others joined them.

'I still think maybe we should get the commissioner,' Zeke said.

'Maybe,' Tanner agreed, 'when Amy and Joey get back.' Zeke stared pensively at the track.

'And maybe one of us should have gone instead of Joey.'

'Maybe,' Tanner agreed again, 'but it's too late now.

CHAPTER 29

++++++++++++++

J OEY CAME upon his camp sooner than he expected, he was panting, the urgency of his mission made his body hurry but his mind was still sluggishly behind.

'What's wrong?' Davis asked, for it was obvious that something was wrong.

'Amy.' Joey called.

'What's the matter?' Davis insisted.

'I've got to get Amy, take her down to the lower camp.'

'Why, what's happened?' The two men stared at each other and Joey's guileless face couldn't hide his feelings, the sadness, the loss, the shame—they were all there for Davis to read.

'Amy,' Joey called again.

'Why such a rush?' A calculating note crept into Davis' voice.

'Tanner's hurt,' Joey said, without conviction.

'I'll get my things and come with you.'

'No,' Joey answered too quickly.

'Why not?'

'He just wants Amy.'

'Who wants me?' Amy emerged from the bushes.

'Your uncle seems to have hurt himself,' Davis said.

'What's happened?' Amy asked.

'I don't know,' Joey said hesitantly. 'They just said you were to come.'

'I'll get the horses and we'll all go.' The simple fact that he wasn't wanted made Davis determined to go.

'No.' Joey's voice halted him. 'It's not wise for you to go there.'

'Why not?' There was a keenness in Davis' face, an inflection in his voice that Joey knew well and he'd never been able to resist it. He looked helplessly at Amy, if only she would take charge and tell Davis to stay put while she came with him.

'Well?' Davis insisted.

'Commissioner's been there,' Joey said at last, 'asking a lot of questions.'

'So?' Davis prompted.

'There was only me, Amy and the boy that knew Catherine offered to take the gold.'

'And?' The soft cajolery vanished from Davis' voice.

'They were accusing the boy, I couldn't —' The look on Davis' face froze Joey mid-sentence. 'Tanner knew anyway,' Joey managed to add.

'Knew what?' Amy came forward, the concern she felt turning to fear.

'So they sent you up here to get Amy away from me before the commissioner's men move in, is that it?'

'Tanner's not told the commissioner.'

'Of course,' Davis laughed. 'He's got no proof, just more of his wild accusations.'

'There's proof,' Joey breathed heavily. 'I saw the welt on your back where Catherine tried to fight. I saw them bits of cloth you used to cover your face when you robbed her, the gloves you put on your hands to stop them being cut when you beat her.'

Amy gasped. Finally she understood, someone had to tell Catherine's attacker that she was carrying the gold. Bobby knew no one to tell and she had told Davis, hoping that his inclusion in the plan would help smooth things over between him and Tanner.

'Oh, Davis, why?' she implored.

'Surely you don't believe his stupid lies?'

'They're not lies,' Joey protested.

'Can't you see what he's trying to do?' Davis moved close to her, his voice persuasively soft. 'He's in love with you Amy, he has been for months but he hadn't the guts to tell you or to challenge me like a man.' He took her hand and began caressing her fingers. 'He just waited his time, got close to your uncle, waited his chance to come between us. He probably had it worked out that eventually Tanner would come up with something like this and he had it in his mind to be on hand to comfort you. God, I'm surprised he had the guts to come up here himself.'

'Stop it,' Amy screamed, wrenching her hand away from him. 'Stop it,' she sobbed bitterly. It was possible that Tanner would use trickery to separate them, that he'd accept any unsubstantiated accusation to discredit Davis, but not Joey, Joey wouldn't lie, even if he did love her and she believed now that he did, Joey wouldn't lie. 'Couldn't there be a mistake?' she beseeched Joey.

'Oh Amy,' he sounded near tears, 'we could pretend we didn't know about the *Lady Ann*, but not this.'

'What about the *Lady Ann*?' Amy could hear her heart pounding as all the fear and suspicions burst into her mind.

'He told us he got off when she docked, long gone before the fire started, then he admitted being with Tanner not twenty minutes before she burnt. There's no way he couldn't have known about it, the whole town knew.'

'All right, I admit I was on the ship when the fire started, but it doesn't prove anything.' Davis sounded calm, almost offhanded.

'Why lie?' Amy demanded.

'Because I knew I'd be accused by your uncle and his kind, all the high-minded bastards out to damn a man for trying.'

'Uncle John's no different to you,' Amy yelled, and she was struck by how true and untrue her statement was. 'He's no fine gentleman, looking down his nose at you.'

'Amy,' Davis began softly.

'He didn't make this up, did he? Even if you didn't burn the ship, you were the one who almost killed Catherine, weren't you?' She wouldn't let Davis take her hand. 'The truth Davis, for God's sake, tell me the truth.'

'Amy, I love you.'

'No.' Her misery extended the word into a cry. She reached for Joey and he took her arm.

'I didn't do it,' Davis yelled. 'Maybe I talked a bit freely, maybe I was the one that betrayed her, but not on purpose.'

'How do you explain the things Joey saw, the welt on your back, the bits of cloth?'

'I scratched myself on a tree and the cloth —' He searched desperately round the campsite. '— the cloth was wrapped round a carcass I bought.' It even sounded plausible, but Amy knew in her heart he was lying. She linked her arm through Joey's.

'We'll take the cart and horses, they belong to Uncle John, Nanny and the chickens too. I wouldn't trust an animal to be left with him.' She choked back the tears, trying to salvage some dignity from the humiliation of her gullibility. 'It doesn't matter about my clothes or anything else.' They turned towards the place where they tethered the horses.

Suddenly Davis felt cold, the bitter, angry cold that occasionally possessed him. There was no sense of urgency as he picked up the small log from beside the fire, no feeling of frenzy as he swept across the short distance between himself and Joey, no exhilaration or horror as he struck him. Amy heard the dull thud as the wood made contact and she heard a muted groan. She felt the spasm in Joey's hand before it became limp as he slumped to the ground. For an instant she didn't understand what had happened, then she heard the dull thud again and the grunt of exertion as Davis delivered another blow.

'Joey!' she screamed, falling on her knees beside him. He was lying so still. She found his face, and it was wet with blood. She sobbed as she searched for some sign of life. She felt Davis' hand on her arm, then he jerked her roughly to her feet. 'You've killed him.' She struck out wildly, catching Davis across the shoulder, hurting herself more than him.

'Amy, listen to me.' He held her by both arms, gripping her firmly but not causing pain. 'I did it for us, Amy, I did it so we'd have our fine house and you'd be a fine lady with everything you want.'

'No.' She tried to pull free. 'I'll never marry you, not after what you've done.'

'I've done nothing wrong,' he pleaded, and he sounded for all the world as if he believed it.

'You burnt the *Lady Ann*,' she replied in astonishment. 'Five men dead and the captain.'

'I started the fire as a diversion, I never meant it to get out of control. They left me no choice, Amy, I had to be with you, that's all I wanted.' His voice had an almost child-like appeal, but she wasn't taken in.

'Is that why you killed Joey?'

'He's not dead,' Davis said dismissively.

'How do you know?' Amy tried again to pull away.

'I never hurt anyone more than I intend to,' he said, and the strange quality in his voice frightened her.

'You meant to do that to Catherine?' She swallowed, trying to make herself sound steady.

'She asked for it.' Amy was shocked by the contempt in his

voice. 'She could've told me Tanner had taken the nugget, but she just kept screaming over and over that she didn't have it or yelling at me in Chinese, stupid bitch. She's nothing, like Joey, nothing, stupid, ugly, disfigured, ignorant, dirty, nothing!' Each word came with greater emphasis, until in the end he was shouting at her.

Amy inhaled sharply as she was gripped with panic, and all the memories of Tanner's warnings about Davis crowded in on her.

'Don't you see, Amy,' it was the gentle, winning voice again, 'I was so close before the bastards robbed me. It was so near I could see it and they robbed me, my partners, the men I'd worked with.' The appeal had become a cry. 'I'd lost it all and Tanner knocks me to the ground, kicking me while I was down. Then he goes and finds that nugget. He didn't have to grub for it or work for it, it just landed in his lap. He didn't count it up day by day, ounce by ounce, the way I did, feeling the dreams becoming a reality, one day it's just there and he hardly knows it's happened. It wasn't fair, not after all he'd done to me.' He released his tight grip and drew her to him, holding her firmly to his chest. 'I knew from the first moment I saw you that you were the one. I could see you even then standing on the front stairs of our house, great sweeping roadway leading up to it lined with poplars . . .'

Amy closed her eyes; she'd heard it all before and she knew it would go on and on. She wanted to cry, to beat him on the chest and call out for Tanner. She gulped back the tears, a vestige of anger returning to drive back the fear. It was Tanner's fault, he'd known all along that it would come to this, he should have stopped her going with Davis. Surely he could have thought of some trick to keep them apart, how could he have let this happen? Why hadn't he come himself? Why had he sent poor, hapless Joey?

Amy stifled the sob that rose in her throat. It wasn't fair to blame Tanner, who'd given her so much, a chance at a new life and the confidence and courage to make the best of it. He'd taught her things too, not just how to look after herself but all about people. The anger came again. Why didn't he teach her what to do now, if he knew it was going to happen why didn't he prepare her, he'd taught her to lie and cheat and dissemble, why . . .?

The anger and the panic died, leaving only the thought: he taught her to dissemble. She held the thought for a moment, then the sound of Davis' voice came to her: he was talking about the bedroom, a huge four-poster bed with white lace curtains. If she could let him think he'd swayed her, if she could make him believe she wanted to go with him, if she could make him trust her, maybe she could find a way to escape him. He was talking about the dining room with lead-light windows, herself at the table presiding like a lady. She tried to speak but no sound came, and she tried again.

'Those things don't matter.' Her voice was weak and she had to force the words. 'I told you a hundred times they don't matter. I love you, not the things you promised me and I do love you Davis, in spite of everything.' Amy listened to her speech and she feared it lacked sincerity. She had been so angry a moment ago, so full of condemnation, how could she expect him to believe that she had suddenly changed her mind 'What you did was so wrong—if only I could be sure it would never happen again.'

'What if I promised, would you come with me then?'

Amy caught the nuance of suspicion in his voice. 'I don't know, I want to, but how can I be sure it won't happen again, even if you promise how can I be sure?' She buried her head in his chest, mainly to prevent him from seeing her face.

'I did it for us.'

'I know, I understand that, but it was still wrong. Say you know it was wrong, say it won't happen again.' Amy felt the panic rising again, and she didn't known what to say next. Joey moaned, the low guttural noise of a man drowning in his own blood. 'Oh God,' she sobbed, 'this is all my fault.' Davis didn't contradict her; he rocked her gently in his arms.

'I did this for you,' he murmured. 'I knew it was wrong but I did it for you.'

'Then I'm as guilty as you are.' Although this statement was contrived it sounded as genuine as the previous one. A smile spread slowly across Davis' face—he would have taken her by force if he had to, of course he would prefer her to come out of love, but he would settle for guilt. He loosened his grip. It was only natural for her to blame herself, it was the type of thing a fine lady would do and if he encouraged it, if he let her share the blame, it would be an even stronger bond than love or marriage.

'I did it for you,' he repeated.

'I know, I know.' Amy stumbled over the words. 'I'm sorry.'

'We've got to get away, Amy, a long way away. They could hang me for what I've done for you.'

'Oh God,' she gasped, for the possibility really did frighten her.

'Come with me, Amy, that's all I ask, and I promise one day we'll have our fine house.' She nodded her agreement, not trusting herself to speak. Joey moaned again, a horrible, strangled sound. Amy felt a spasm run through her body and she wondered if Davis felt it too. 'We should get help for him,' she said, then added: 'We can't just go and leave him here.'

'He'll be all right. Tanner will be here soon or the commissioner's men.' He watched her for reaction, but there was none. 'We have to hurry, leave before they come.' He read the expression on her face as indecision rather than frantic thought. If he could just get her to make the first step and come with him of her own free will, from then on she'd be trapped by her blindness and bound to him by their shared guilt. 'Come on.' He began to lead her towards the horses.

'We'll need supplies,' she said. 'It won't be safe to go near the towns. You get the horses, I'll pack a few things.' He glanced at Joey—there was no chance of him waking up, no chance of him spoiling things now.

Amy listened to the sound of Davis' retreating footsteps. She held her breath, straining her ears to make sure he was gone. This was the moment she'd been waiting for, the moment she worked so hard to create and now that it had come she didn't know what to do. She might be able to find her way down the track to Tanner's camp, she'd been over it enough times, but the minute Davis found her missing he'd know that was the way she'd gone and he would easily overtake her before she could get far. She rubbed her fingers through her hair as if it might stimulate the brain. If she went at right angles to the track then down to the valley floor, she might be able to find her way out, except that Joey had said it was rocky and steep. Uphill she would run into Davis and she had no idea what lay on the far side of the ridge.

Joey moved slightly and groaned and a panic seized Amy, making her heart pound and her palms sweat. She had to get help for

Joey, she had to get away, she was wasting time and she couldn't think. Maybe some of the other miners would help, and she tried to remember the direction of the nearest camp. She listened, but the valley was full of sound echoing back from ridges and hills. The panic and the desperation grew, but she wouldn't let the fear paralyse her. She forced herself to move and found herself heading at right angles to the track, across the rocky ground towards the valley floor.

The first few paces were taken quickly and with confidence, but then she reached the perimeter of the camp. She felt her way from one tree to the next, feeling each step with her foot before taking it. Then the ground became steeper and the trees further apart. She crouched down, testing the ground with her foot and searching the air with her hand. Each step was so painfully slow and she had so little time to spare. She found a low shrub and inched her way around it. It was easier when she had something to hold on to.

She hurried forward, her agonising fear of the darkness in which she lived momentarily outweighed by her fear that Davis would find her. She found another bush and moved round it more quickly this time, her eagerness making her recklessly assume that there would be another a little further on. She groped forward, but there was nothing and suddenly her feet slipped from beneath her and she was falling, rolling and sliding down the craggy slope, the sharp edges of the rocks and the prickly bushes tearing at her skin and clothes. She clutched desperately at anything that came within her grasp, scrambling with her feet, hoping to arrest her descent. The branches of a large bush whipped across her back and tangled in her hair and she grabbed at them frantically, the tiny branches tearing at her fingers before her grip tightened around them, bringing her to a halt. She searched with her foot for a foothold, then eased herself uphill until she was able to wrap her arms around the trunk of the bush. She lay beneath its rough branches panting and sobbing, her face buried in the stones and gravel. Then it came, the soft enticing voice.

'Amy.' Then louder and more insistent. 'Amy.' Her heart began racing and she couldn't breathe for crying. 'Amy!' The anger in his voice was terrifying, and she knew he'd realised that she'd tricked him. Now he would come looking for her, maybe find her and there was so much anger in him.

She held her breath, praying that the tiny bush would obscure her if he searched in that direction, hoping against hope that he'd go the other way. She channelled all her conscious effort into listening, trying to catch the sound of him moving. There was a small bird chirping in the bush above her, and down in the valley to her left men were laughing and talking, so many sounds but no footfall, no telltale rustle in the bush above her. She strained to hear, but only the sound of the miners reached her, their language seeming alien and distorted and it was impossible to tell how far away they were. Then at last it came, the sound of horses galloping, Davis riding down the track towards Tanner's camp.

Amy released the breath she'd been holding for what felt like an eternity. He was gone but he'd not given up, she was sure of that for he'd taken both horses, one for himself and one for her to ride when he caught her. She let go of the tiny trunk and climbed cautiously backward down the gully wall. It was rather like descending a ladder and Amy reasoned that she was no more disadvantaged than a sighted person under similar circumstances. Her feet came upon an area that felt like solid ground. She rolled into a sitting position and probed her surroundings with her hands and feet. Earth with grass on it and a few large rocks, not too great a slope, so she slid forward on her backside, testing the area in front of her before edging forward again. The sound of laughter came to her, the same laughter as before but closer this time. She angled her descent slightly so that it took her in the direction of the sound. Steadily and painfully she edged her way along the ground. She was too afraid to stand up, too afraid to hurry, even though she had to reach them before Davis came back she couldn't take the risk of falling again.

Davis reined in his horse, dragging it to a halt. He was almost at Tanner's camp and all logic told him she couldn't possibly have come this far, yet he felt an urge to ride into the camp, to confront Tanner for the last time. He fingered the rifle he carried. Tanner may not be alone, Paddy and Zeke could be there and Zeke, he knew, carried a pistol. He glanced back towards his own camp. Amy had tricked him but she couldn't have gone far; perhaps he'd missed her riding so quickly down the track, or she could have wandered off to one side or even hidden when she heard him coming. He headed his horses uphill again, riding more slowly and scanning each side of the track for some sign of her.

Tanner raised his head, his brows furrowed as he listened intently.

'Horses at a gallop,' he said, more to himself than anyone else.

'Aye,' Paddy agreed, 'but Joey wouldn't be riding at that speed with Amy in tow.'

'They've stopped anyway,' Zeke added.

Tanner rose irritably to his feet. 'They've been too long,' he said. 'Even on foot they should be here by now.' He paced a few steps then paced back again.

'Perhaps they've stopped to pack a few things,' Paddy offered.

'Why would she pack?' Tanner snapped. 'She's supposed to be rushing to the aid of her poor, injured uncle, remember?'

'Maybe Joey told her the real reason you wanted her to come,' Zeke said thoughtfully.

'That's what I'm afraid of,' Tanner called over his shoulder as he entered the shanty. He returned a few minutes later with his brother's gun.

'Tanner, no.' Catherine rose unsteadily to her feet. 'Please Tanner.' She stumbled towards him.

'Please Tanner what?' He put his arm around her. 'Don't go?' he suggested. 'Even if Amy never comes back? Or wait perhaps? For how long? Until he's made good his escape, taking Amy with him.'

'Joey wouldn't let him take Amy.'

'Joey couldn't stop him.' He held her at arm's length. 'Look at yourself, Catherine, he's the man who beat you mercilessly even though he knew you didn't have what he wanted. He's the man who set fire to the *Lady Ann* rather than be separated from Amy. Do you think he'd let Joey take her from him now?'

'Then let Paddy or Zeke go, they could talk to him, you and Davis hate each other too much.' The congestion in her chest made every word she spoke an effort, and the sound it produced accentuated the force with which she pleaded.

'I have to go.'

'Not alone,' Zeke said.

'This is my fight, I'd not wish to see anyone else hurt by it.'

'Your fight is it?' Zeke laughed. 'Well, if you're relying on your skill with that weapon, you've lost already.' Tanner didn't argue. 'But if it's gun play he's after . . .' Zeke patted the sidearm he frequently carried. 'Well, I'm considered something of an expert.'

'Oh God!' Catherine cried, slumping back into her seat.

'Anyway, the more the merrier,' Zeke continued, 'eh, Paddy?'

Paddy looked a little surprised to find himself included. 'I suppose so,' he said, looking at Tanner. 'Maybe we should get a few of the men from some of the other mines.'

'And have Amy caught in the middle of a war?' Tanner snapped at him. 'Look, I just want to find him quietly and get Amy away from him, without it coming to a fight.' Zeke studied Tanner shrewdly, but Paddy spoke before he could dispute Tanner's intention to avoid confrontation.

'Well,' Paddy said, 'if I'm coming would you mind if I rode your horse?'

'I thought I'd ride the horse.' Loretta interrupted.

'You're not coming,' Tanner began.

'And why not? I'm a better marksman than you, John Tanner.' She produced a small pistol from her purse, which would probably only fired one or two shots and was the type of toy at which a man might scoff. 'He'll pay no heed to me if he's busy with the three of you and this'll be the bullet he won't expect.'

'Don't argue with her, Tanner, she's more likely to shoot him than you are and less likely to be prosecuted for it.'

'We're wasting time.' Loretta headed for the horse. Catherine got painfully to her feet and returned the coat Tanner had given her.

'Be careful,' she said.

CHAPTER 30

++++++++++++++

AMY HAD found a straight stick of reasonable strength and length, which she used to probe the ground and empty space in front of her. She moved more quickly than before, but still her hoped-for sanctuary was beyond her reach.

She stopped to listen for some sign of Davis returning, but her ears were filled with the rasp of her own heavy breathing. She held her breath: no galloping horses, no one careering noisily through the bush, just the rowdy laughter from the camp to which she was heading. She concentrated on the sound for a moment—their language wasn't English, she was sure of that, but there was something else that set the conversation apart from the usual chatter of the diggings. It was too loud for one thing and there was too much laughter. As she came closer to the men Amy detected a slur in their speech, which she suspected was not part of their habitual accent. She slowed her pace as she realised that she would soon be within their sight, they were to be her salvation but now intuition warned her to keep away. She stood still, willing herself to have the courage to go on, then the wind blew in her face and even the redolent wattle couldn't disguise the stench of alcohol.

A loud whistle filled the air, accompanied by calls of appreciation, and Amy knew that they'd seen her. One man called out to her again, and encouraged by his friends began to walk towards her. They were French, very young, very homesick and very drunk. The young man slipped and fell, rolling helplessly on the ground while his companions hooted and jeered at his attempt to reach her. He called to her appealingly, and even though she didn't understand him Amy knew his words were meant for her. More than once the drunks from the inn in London had cornered her, and although their language was different she knew their meaning and intentions were the same and there was no auntie here to ask more than she was worth, no one to say that she was just a child.

Amy edged slowly back up the hill, away from the camp, away from the direction in which she wanted to go. Then she began to hurry as the catcalls and whistles grew louder, and they seemed to follow her as she retreated into the bush. She tried to move faster, stumbling and falling, colliding with low branches, her only direction away from the mocking laughter. Eventually the sound faded and she collapsed against the trunk of a tree, sobbing and gasping for breath, her hands, her face, her legs scratched and bleeding, every part of her bruised and her side aching from the effort of hurrying.

She took time to regain her breath, then sat up and listened. By now Davis would have realised his mistake and returned to the camp. She thought fleetingly of Joey, of how badly he might be hurt and how desperately she cared what happened to him. Her mind returned to Davis. He'd search for her of course, and the way she'd come was the only viable alternative to the direct route to Tanner's camp. She wondered if Tanner was looking for her yet, if he would think to come this way. She wished that it was night so that Davis had to search for her in her own environment, but even at night the stars and moon were there to betray her. She remembered the London fog, so thick you couldn't even see your own hand in front of you, and she wished for one to descend upon them now.

Davis finished searching the perimeter of the camp. It seemed logical that she should hide there, hoping Joey would regain consciousness and rescue her. His eyes swept the area again as he tried to think, if not here or on the track then where? Uphill and she'd've run into him getting the horses, over the ridge and she'd be in the next valley, miles from anywhere. He glanced down towards the valley floor: it was an impossible climb, far too rough for one who couldn't see. Suddenly Davis felt sick, the awful sickness that comes just before fear manifests itself in thought. If she couldn't see she wouldn't know it was too rough until it was too late. She could be lying broken and bleeding at the bottom of the valley and he would never find her.

'Amy,' he bellowed, for he was certain that if she was hurt she wouldn't refuse his help. He started down the rocky slope, trying to find a path amongst the crags and bushes.

Amy didn't hear him call; his voice was absorbed into the endless echoes of the diggings. She had lost the straight stick and the confidence to use it, instead she crawled on her hands and knees, heading mainly downhill with a strong bias away from the Frenchmen's camp. Her thoughts became jumbled as the exhaustion and panic took over. She remembered her first meeting with Tanner, how she'd lacked the courage to run from him, even in the comparative safety of a London street, even though she was certain he'd blinded her. Now she was running or rather crawling from Davis in the untamed Australian bush, and she wasn't even certain that he'd hurt her. It was funny in a way. Her thoughts turned to Catherine and Joey. She wished she knew what they looked like, she had a vision of Tanner and it bore a strong resemblance to her father. She wished her father could see her now, he would be proud of her.

'Amy.' She froze. The voice was a long way off but instinct told her it was coming her way.

The Frenchmen halted their revelry and stared blankly at Davis.

'A girl,' he panted, 'have you seen a girl?' They shook their heads and mumbled among themselves.

'A girl.' He grew impatient. They shrugged, then one of them suggested.

'La fille?'

'Ah, oui,' his friend agreed, 'la fille.' They pointed in the direction Amy had taken.

Despite the injuries he'd received in his recent spate of accidents, Tanner made better time up the hill than anyone else. Loretta rode at the rear, afraid that if she rode beside Tanner it would force the pace faster. It was, therefore, Tanner who first came upon Joey's motionless form.

'Oh, dear God.' He knelt beside Joey, unable to bring himself to touch him in case he was dead. Loretta pushed past Tanner, immediately rolling Joey on his side to allow the blood to drain from his mouth and throat. He'd been choking on it and his lips were blue from a lack of oxygen. His eyes were black, his nose disfigured and streaming blood. Loretta ran her hand across the back of Joey's head and neck.

'He was struck from behind,' she said, 'then again in the face.'

'With this,' Zeke added, holding up the small log smudged with enough of Joey's blood to confirm his assumption.

'These horses have been ridden.' Paddy indicated the cart horses

281

still warm from their gallop to Tanner's camp. Tanner stood up, surveying the surrounding area.

'Where are they?' Zeke followed the direction of Tanner's gaze.

'On foot, that's for sure,' Paddy answered.

'Why?' Zeke began.

'Because Amy ran from him.' Tanner turned to face them. 'She got away from him somehow, tricked him or hid from him, and when he found her gone he rode these horses almost as far as our camp and then turned back. We heard them, remember? While he was gone, she either came back and tried to revive Joey or put as much distance between herself and Davis as she could. If she'd come back here he'd've caught her, in which case they'd be on horseback, so my guess is she ran.' He scanned the surrounding bush again and vocalised his thoughts as they came to him. 'If she'd headed down to our camp he'd've caught her or we'd've seen her, which only leaves up the hill, over the ridge or down to the valley. Three choices gentlemen and three of us. Zeke, I don't suppose you'd mind climbing the hill seeing as I'm sure Paddy would prefer to take the ridge?'

'Leaving you the valley?' Zeke queried.

'Why not?'

'It's the way she's most likely to have gone, isn't it?'

'Down there?' Paddy sneered. 'Any bloody fool can see there's no way a poor, blind girl could get down there.'

'Any bloody fool can see,' Tanner said patiently, 'but a poor, blind girl can't. She'd reason that if she got to the valley floor she could follow it until she came amongst the diggings and then ask for help.'

'Maybe we should all go that way,' Paddy said doubtfully.

'No, we spread out,' Tanner insisted. 'There's no telling what people'll do when they're scared.' Zeke handed Paddy the rifle he'd been carrying.

'Take this and one of the horses,' he said. 'Fire a shot if you need us.' Tanner headed for the rocky slope. 'You, take a horse too.' Zeke called after him.

'I can't ride a horse down there.'

'Then lead the damn thing, but if he's caught Amy and they're walking out along the valley floor, with the head start they've got you'll never catch them on foot.'

Davis moved quickly after he left the Frenchmen's camp. He was so relieved to find that Amy was apparently uninjured that he gave little thought to the direction in which he was going, and he'd travelled some distance before it occurred to him that it was the wrong way, that Amy would only have come this way to avoid the Frenchmen, that her ultimate destination lay in the other direction. Davis looked around him, wondering how far Amy would have gone out of her way before turning back. He closed his eyes and tried to think like a blind person. Sound, it all depended on sound, if she couldn't hear them she would assume she was safe from them. He backtracked until he was within earshot of the camp and then he began his descent.

Amy's knee caught on the jagged edge of a rock and sent her sprawling face down in the dirt. She lay there, too tired and scared and disheartened to get up again. Far away she could hear the Frenchmen still laughing and talking, their voices blending into the background noise of the diggings. Close by something rustled through the leaves, a bird most likely because it was too cold for snakes, and in the middle distance she could hear something big coming through the bush, a kangaroo possibly or a horse or a man, Davis. She scrambled to her feet, half running, half crawling, grasping desperately at the trees and shrubs around her. She couldn't outrun him, she knew that, she had to hide. She needed a large bush or a giant tree, something big enough to obscure her totally, something she could move round keeping it always between herself and the sound of him and the sound of him was coming nearer. She grabbed hopelessly at the skinny saplings and scrawny bushes that lined her path. She could go no faster and the sound of him was almost upon her. She tried to run and fell. She tried again.

'Amy, stop!' His voice was so full of anguish that Amy stopped dead in her tracks. 'Amy.' He breathed heavily. 'Listen to me, you mustn't move.' He swallowed to steady his voice and his breathing. 'There's been a land slide, the ground in front of you has been washed away. There's a fifteen foot drop not four feet ahead of you and it curves round you to either side.' He paused again to give her time to accept what he was saying. 'Just stay there and I'll come and get you.' There was an imperativeness in his speech, a sincerity that most people could not put there by design, but Davis wasn't like most people and to Amy it seemed incredibly convenient that she couldn't move forward or to the left or right, just backward to him.

She dropped down into a sitting position, testing the ground in front of her with her hand. It felt moist and flat like the land at the bottom of the valley and by her estimation that was where she should be. She edged forward, reaching out as far as she could, feeling the ground ahead of her. She had tricked Davis and perhaps now he was tricking her, and it would be poetic justice if he was. The ground still felt firm, so she slid forward again. She could hear Davis coming, already it was too late to try to run from him but, at least, she would know for sure if he'd lied to her. She slid forward again, four feet he'd said and then she should feel the edge and if she didn't . . .

Maybe there was a slight warning, a tremor before it happened, but if there was it didn't allow Amy enough time to save herself. The land simply fell away from beneath her and she was falling, dirt and stones all round her, the sharp edges of the embankment ripping at her as she slipped past them. Then the ground hard and sudden, knocking the air out of her lungs and sending prickling pain through every part of her body and burning agony to those parts of her that took the full force of the fall. She gasped and gulped, her need for air overshadowing all the other pain. She had heard Davis scream as she fell, and in the short time before she hit the ground it had occurred to her that he had been telling the truth.

The pain in her chest eased and her breathing became more natural. She could hear Davis calling to her as he searched for a way down the embankment. It was her last chance to escape him, if she could find somewhere to hide, if she could evade him until Tanner came looking for her. She tried to get up but one leg gave way under her weight and an agonising pain gripped her. She felt the leg—it was broken. She lay flat on her back, tears streaming down her cheeks. Davis was coming, she could hear his ragged breathing and the sound of him slipping and sliding down to the valley floor.

She was lying so still when Davis drew near that for an instant he thought she was dead, then he saw the rise and fall of her chest but his relief was tinged with regret. He came closer. There were tears on her cheeks and her face was scratched and bleeding, bruised and dirty, her skirt was pulled back to expose her leg and even to Davis' untrained eye it was unmistakably broken. He took her hand gently, which was bruised and torn like the rest of her.

'Oh, Amy, why?' He was crying and she had no answer for him, for he could never understand the differences that would forever separate them. 'I wouldn't hurt you. You must know I wouldn't hurt you.'

'Really?' she murmured. 'What makes me so different?' It was difficult to speak, but she was determined to say the words. 'What makes me so different to Joey or your mates on the *Lady Ann*?'

'I love you,' he said without hesitation. 'You're a part of me, the only one I ever wanted, the only one I ever cared about.' Even as he spoke Davis realised that those dreams were lost. Alive she may be, but so far beyond his reach that she might as well be dead. Soon they would come for him, Tanner and his kind, to catch him if they could and hang him or worse, and she couldn't run with him now even if she wanted to and run he must, but he couldn't just leave her there alone and in pain. The Frenchmen's camp was the closest, but he'd rather see her dead than in the hands of those drunken sots. He caressed her fingers as he had so many times before and she winced in pain. Davis looked about him helplessly, there was a doctor in Golden Gully and for all the gold he had maybe this doctor would come, if he was sober, if he could find the place. He laid her hand across her chest, then used the rifle to help himself to his feet. He gazed at her fragile form. If she was a horse he'd finish her and they'd say he'd done the right thing putting her out of her misery. He closed his eyes and tears ran down his cheeks. His instincts told him to leave her in the hands of a God in which he did not believe, but she was his one priceless possession and he could not just abandon her to the bush.

Davis glanced back up the gully wall. Tanner would have found Joey by now and be searching for them, but he wouldn't find Amy in time, he'd assume that she was heading down the valley to his camp and by the time he organised a search it would be dark and the next day they'd start looking in the wrong place. It would be days before they found her, days of agony and fear. He looked at Amy again and at the rifle in his hand, he felt his throat closing as if some outside force was choking him. In all his life he'd felt nothing but contempt for every other human being, but Amy was different, he wanted her so much it was frightening, he wanted her not just as a man wants a woman but as something inseparable from himself, and killing her would be like cutting off his own hand.

He swallowed the tightness in his throat. It was not his fault if she should die now, it was Tanner who had brought her to this, Tanner and his endless mistrust, Tanner and his groundless accusations, Tanner and his questions, Tanner and his damned nugget. Davis' vision blurred and he knew that he was crying, and it was not his love for Amy that brought him to tears but his hatred of Tanner. It rose within him like a bitter bile so strong that he could taste it. He could kill Tanner. Already they would hang him for what had happened on the *Lady Ann*, and they could only hang him once. He could kill Tanner and Amy too, the punishment would be the same. Amy tried to sit up then fell back, succumbing to the pain. It would be easier on her to finish it now, easier on her, easier on him and hell for Tanner. Even the sight of her now would rip Tanner apart, yet if she was dead and out of pain his grief would be even greater.

Davis' eyes focused on Amy again. She could have been his fine, fine lady. He waved the rifle in front of her sightless eyes. Amy sensed something moving and reached out to touch it, she gasped as she felt the cold metal of the rifle.

'Davis,' she murmured, but he didn't answer. She waited, but the silence continued, then suddenly the fear gripped her again and she began to drag herself away from him. He rested the barrel against her chest and she dared move no further. Tears prevented Davis seeing the terror on her face. He blinked his eyes and looked up at the tree tops—he could see it still, the poplar-lined drive and the sweeping staircase, her waiting for him by the door, and it was that vision he would carry for the rest of his life, not that of the broken body that lay before him.

CHAPTER 31

✦✦✦✦✦✦✦✦✦✦✦✦✦

TANNER BURST into the Frenchmen's camp, yelling questions about Amy and Davis. They looked at him blankly, then made some insulting remarks about the English. Tanner didn't know much French, just enough to ensure his survival, and for a man who'd smuggled goods to and from the European coast enough included such words as murderer, kidnapper and police. His grammar may not have been the best but his meaning was clear, and the Frenchmen moved with deference to show him the way.

At first Tanner moved quickly into the bush then, just as Davis had done, he stopped to consider his position. Their final objective must be the valley floor, so Tanner headed downhill, still moving as quickly as he could. He glanced back in the direction from which he'd come. He should fire a shot to warn Paddy and Zeke, but such a shot would warn Davis, too, if he didn't already know. Tanner slowed his pace, his movement through the scrub suddenly seeming very loud. The element of surprise could have been useful to him and he regretted not having taken more care. Finally he stopped and a feeling of hopelessness engulfed him—there were so many different directions they could take, and in the bush he could walk within a few yards of them and still not see them. He raised his eyes to scan the bush once more. There was movement to his left, a splash of coloured cloth—Davis!

Without thinking, Tanner took aim—now was the moment to kill. Davis was in his sights and Tanner knew he could kill him, kill him for what he'd done to Catherine, kill him for Buchanan and the *Lady Ann*, kill him for what he was doing to Amy, strike at him without warning just as he had struck Joey. Tanner's finger closed on the trigger, but for all that he hated Davis he couldn't pull it. For a moment Tanner held his breath, willing himself to finish it. He exhaled heavily.

'Stay where you are Davis,' he called. There was, perhaps, a fraction of a second's hesitation before Davis dived for cover. Tanner fired the shot, but even if Davis had remained still it would not have hit him. Tanner dropped to the ground, but there was no return of fire. He lifted his head and listened as the echo of the shot died, and it occurred to him that Paddy and Zeke wouldn't be able to get any idea of the distance or direction from the reverberating sounds. He crawled forward to the place where Davis had stood and, in the absence of any other response, began to look for a body or at least some telltale drops of blood. He had risen to his knees when he heard the movement behind him, and before he could turn something cold and hard was pressed against the back of his neck.

'You're a lousy shot,' Davis hissed. Tanner didn't argue. Davis would never believe that he had missed on purpose. 'Get up,' Davis instructed, and Tanner complied. 'Now, put down the gun.'

'And if I don't?'

'I'll shoot you.'

'And if I do?'

'I'll not shoot you anyway,' Davis laughed. 'I'll take you to Amy.'

'Really?' Tanner said, still keeping a firm hold of his gun.

'Yes, really.' Davis sighed bitterly. 'You see, some damn fool filled Amy's head with the stupid idea that I'd hurt her, so she ran from me, Tanner, and she fell.' Davis prodded him with the gun. 'And she was hurt.' He prodded him again. 'And now your friends are on their way, with the commissioner's men no doubt, so I've got to go and you wouldn't want me to leave her there all alone, would you, Tanner?' The gun barrel hit Tanner harder this time, knocking him off-balance. 'You'd rather I took you to her, wouldn't you, Tanner?'

Tanner felt the gun poised to push him again. 'All right,' he said, and he carefully put the gun down. Davis lowered his own weapon and circled round him, then with lightning speed Davis jammed the butt of his rifle into Tanner's ribs. Tanner dropped to his knees, gasping for air, retching while the world spun around him.

'I owed you that,' Davis hissed.

'I used my fist.' Tanner mouthed the words, but no sound came. Davis picked up Tanner's gun and edged his way up the hill.

'Don't go anywhere,' he said. 'I'm just going to get your horse. I'm going to need a fast one if I'm to get away alive.'

By the time Davis returned Tanner's condition had improved to the point where he was barely able to speak but not yet able to stand.

'You don't mind me taking your horse, do you?' Davis stood over him smirking.

'I warned you before of the penalty for stealing a man's horse,' Tanner wheezed. Davis laughed mirthlessly, pulling Tanner to his feet.

'And what's the penalty for sending six men to their grave and what do you think the teamsters and miners will do to me for what I did to that ugly bitch of yours?' Tanner didn't answer. 'Empty your pockets, I'll need as much money as I can get.' Tanner obeyed, but when Davis went to take the cross and ring Tanner withheld them.

'They're Amy's,' he said.

'A wedding ring?' Davis queried.

'It was my mother's.'

'And a cross,' Davis said bitterly. 'Well, I don't believe in either any more.' He took them from Tanner, smiling at him curiously. 'Not much to show for a life, is it? I'll bet it's all you've got left of your mother.' He laughed sardonically. 'It was really only Amy's second-hand, wasn't it?' He thrust them back in Tanner's hand. 'There's nothing to show for her life at all.' He grabbed Tanner and headed him downhill. 'I could have given Amy everything, a fine house and children, all the things that live on once you're dead and gone, but you had to interfere.' He pushed Tanner, shoving him so that he staggered and fell. 'You always interfere, so sure you know what's best, but it wasn't best for Buchanan was it? And I'll tell you something, it wasn't best for that ugly bitch of yours either, dragging her back to a life where she'll never be anything but the butt of every man's joke.' He stood over Tanner, looking down at him. 'Some people are better off dead.'

Davis watched dispassionately as Tanner got painfully to his feet, then pushed him again though not so hard as before, just hard enough to indicate that he should continue downhill.

'You know, it's strange we've ended up being enemies,' Davis said. 'After all, we've got so much in common. We grew up the same way, poor men's sons, educated from birth to know our place and punished if we ever thought to better ourselves, taught endurance was a virtue and ambition was a sin, rich men's lies to keep us in our place.' Tanner stumbled and this time Davis caught him. 'You ape the gentleman too well not to have dreamt of being one, but you're still just a cheat and a liar because you've learnt the hard way that it's easier to live up to their expectations than it is to try to change them.'

'Tell a man he's nothing and he'll stay nothing, tell him he's evil and he'll become evil. If that's your excuse, Davis, I'll not except it. A man can only be pushed or led so far, inhibited so much by other people's perception of him. In the end he must decide for himself.'

'Up to himself, is it?' Davis pushed Tanner forward again, prodding him with the rifle to keep him moving. 'Well, I believed I could start over here and so did Amy and Joey, but you turned them all against me.'

'I didn't turn them against you, though not for want of trying— you did it yourself with your lying and your stealing and your killing.' Tanner managed to finish the sentence before the butt of Davis' rifle slammed into his ribs again. He fell to the ground, the pain making him dizzy and sick. Davis lowered the gun, resting it on Tanner's chest so that it was aimed at his heart.

'This land was a dream for men like me and you, a chance to be what we could never be back home.' He moved the barrel of the gun up under Tanner's chin so that it forced his head back, compelling him to look at Davis. 'Don't tell me you didn't feel it, Tanner, when you held that nugget in your hands, don't tell me you didn't feel as if all your dreams had come true. Well, I felt like that, too, the moment I heard about the gold. No,' he stopped, 'no, it was the moment I saw Amy. I wanted it so much,' he said, and the poignancy in his voice triggered a fear far in the back of Tanner's mind. 'Get up.' He took the rifle away from Tanner's face. 'Get up and I'll take you to Amy.' Tanner didn't move, for the nameless fear seemed to intensify with Davis' last words. 'Get up.' Davis kicked him.

'I can't,' Tanner gasped.

'Oh, I doubt that.' Davis prodded him again. 'I rarely do more damage than I intend.'

'Rarely?' Tanner used a nearby tree to haul himself to his feet.

'The fire on the *Lady Ann* was bigger than I intended and I was out of control that day you punched me to the ground. I'd've killed those lads that took over my claim and there'd've been no purpose in it.'

'What was your purpose in beating Catherine?'

'Hurt you, didn't it,' Davis grinned. 'Hurt you more than if I'd taken that nugget.'

'My God.' Tanner lurched at Davis, but he brought up the rifle, pushing it against Tanner's chest and using it to stave him off as much as to threaten him. 'Catherine is not my possession, she's not an extension of me.' Tanner was yelling, his fear of the gun lost in the anger and the grief that had taken hold of him. 'Her life has relevance beyond my existence and in spite of the way she looks and the way she's been forced to live she still feels pain and fear and humiliation, she still has hopes and dreams as important and probably more worthy than yours.' Yelling had hurt Tanner, so his next words came with as much passion but less volume. 'If you wanted to hurt someone, why didn't you hurt me?'

'There's time enough for that yet.' He prodded Tanner with the gun to get him moving again. 'But first I want to take you to Amy.' The oft-repeated phrase suddenly had a strange sound to it. 'I wish I'd been there to see the look on your face when you found that ugly bitch of yours.' He continued to poke Tanner, picking out the ribs bruised in his previous attacks. 'It was your fault that I attacked her,' the rifle connected again, 'your fault, too, that Amy fell. She'd've never run from me if it hadn't been for you.'

Tanner felt cold, a prickling in the back of his neck, a shudder as if someone had walked over his grave and the fear that was hovering in the back of his mind began to take form.

'How badly is Amy hurt?' he asked, but Davis didn't answer. He waited, then said, 'Can she be moved?' The noise that came from Davis' throat was something between a laugh and the sound of a man choking.

'Yes,' he said, 'you can move her.' Tanner felt a pain in his chest that was not the result of Davis' assault, and he didn't have the courage to ask if Amy still lived, but the more they walked the more convinced he became that she did not. He wondered if she had died in the fall or if Davis had finished her. She might not have been badly injured at all, but Davis would rather see her dead than turn her over to him. He glanced over his shoulder and caught a glimpse of Davis' face, which was stained by tears.

Tanner felt his heart beat quicken and his body become tense, signs of a more urgent fear than the one that already possessed him, for with the belief that Amy was dead came the realisation that Davis was going to kill him, too. He had only kept him alive this long because he'd wanted to see the look on his face when he saw her. Davis jabbed the rifle into his ribs again and Tanner promised himself that the next time it happened he would take the gun from Davis and kill him, if he could, and if he died in the attempt then he'd have lost nothing.

Tanner slowed his pace and tensed, his body ready for the anticipated blow. The jab came, hard and sharp, and Tanner dropped as if hurt, turning towards Davis as he did so. Slowly Tanner regained his feet, glancing quickly at Davis to ascertain his position. Davis was standing over him holding the rifle in both hands, the barrel pointed harmlessly into the bush. Tanner took a deep breath and closed his mind against the pain he knew would come.

He thought he heard himself yell as he rushed at Davis, and it sounded like a wild animal cry. He grabbed the rifle and the momentum of his attack drove Davis back, causing him to lose his footing. Both men fell and for an instant Tanner was on top, his weight pinning Davis to the ground, but Davis seemed to slide away from under him. Tanner rolled and twisted, trying to wrest the rifle from Davis' grasp. Another day he might have won easily, but every time he found a foothold in crumbling soil his weakened ankle failed to hold him against Davis' strength, and every time he braced himself and took a deep breath for that final assault it was like a knife being stuck between his ribs.

For a time each man held his own, neither one being able to pin the other down, neither one being able to break away with the gun in his hands, but Tanner could feel himself losing, and each time they rolled the pain became more acute, each time Davis forced the gun against his chest it took him longer to push it away, each time the gun was wrenched and twisted his grip grew weaker. Suddenly Davis jackknifed away, drawing his knees up under him, and as they rolled he came out on top, his knees forced into Tanner's bruised and broken ribs, the gun rammed against Tanner's throat. For a moment Tanner pushed against the overpowering weight, trying to force back the gun, but he couldn't breathe. Great waves of darkness began to drive at him, each one sapping more of his strength, then Davis shifted his weight and it felt as if his knee was going to break through Tanner's ribs, flattening his lungs against his backbone. The darkness overcame Tanner and he felt the gun being ripped from his grasp.

Tanner opened his eyes in time to see Davis take aim, and his face bore the same look it had when he attacked the young men at his mine, the same passion, the same loss of control, the same capacity for violence. Tanner lowered his eyes to the barrel, the muzzle, the tiny orifice from which death would come. He waited for the flash of light, the first rumble of the explosion, the last things he'd ever see or hear.

Tanner felt himself take a breath, then another, and after the third he raised his eyes to look at Davis again. He was like a man caught out of time, the grimace fixed on his face, his finger poised on the trigger, the breath caught in his chest. Tanner was loathe to move, to break the spell that held him, so for a moment both men remained frozen like grotesque statues.

Davis moved at last, his face losing all expression. He backed away from Tanner, leaving him room to get up.

'I don't care much for anyone on this earth,' his voice was almost a cry, 'but I loved Amy and I hate you. I could have killed you then,' a hint of a smile flashed across his face, 'you know that, don't you?' He waited for Tanner to nod in confirmation. 'But it would spoil my plan.' He laughed, a bitter, humourless laugh. 'And I couldn't let you spoil this plan like you spoiled all the rest.' Tears sprang into his eyes. 'Now get up and I'll take you to Amy.'

Tanner trudged down the hill, his body and mind numbed by the result of the fight. Suddenly Davis grabbed his arm, pulling him back from the very edge of the embankment.

'She's further down that way,' Davis tilted his head in the appropriate direction, 'but here's the only place you can get down.' He gave Tanner a shove, sending him slipping and sliding down the bank. 'Don't forget it was me that brought you here, Tanner, as long as you live I want you to remember that.'

Tanner watched as Davis mounted the horse. He dare not turn

his back on him, and even when he was out of sight Tanner was reluctant to go in the direction Davis had indicated. He walked slowly, his mind primed for the sound of Davis returning. It made no sense for Davis to have brought him this far and not to wait until he'd found her, not to savour his anguish and despair, not to kill him in the end.

Suddenly it occurred to Tanner that Amy may not be there at all, that she may be bound and gagged back where he first saw Davis, that Davis had simply caught him and led him away from her, that he hadn't killed him because Amy would hear the shot. Tanner had all but convinced himself that it was so when he saw it. No more than a hand span of material poking out from beneath a bush, but he recognised the garment as one of Amy's. Instinctively he moved towards it, then checked himself, looking back up the embankment quite expecting Davis to be there. He was not.

Unwillingly, Tanner's eyes returned to the dress, and hesitantly he moved towards it, each step a massive mental and physical effort. He sank to the ground, feeling beneath the bush that all but concealed her.

'No,' Amy sobbed, and Tanner was too stunned to speak, too shocked to move. He stared as she tried to drag herself further under the bush crying out in pain each time she moved the broken leg.

'Amy.' He forced the word and the sound of his own voice released him, he scrambled under the bush and, searching out her arms and shoulders, he drew her to him.

'Uncle John.' She clung to him. 'Davis, Davis.' She choked on the word.

'He's gone.'

'Davis . . .' She tried again to speak, but her throat seemed to close around the words and her head ached at the sound of her voice.

'It's all right now.' He patted her shoulder and pulled her head on to his chest, then his voice failed him too. For a few minutes they both just lay there, slowly recognising the pain that fear had blocked out, gradually coming to terms with the fact that they were both still alive and that they'd both almost died.

'Joey?' Amy managed to ask.

'He's all right.'

'Blood,' she stammered, 'blood all over his face. Davis . . . Davis . . .'

'I know, I know what Davis did, but Joey's all right, I promise.' Tanner held her a moment longer, putting off for as long as possible what he had to do next. 'I'm going to have to move you,' he said at last, 'and there's no way I can stop it from hurting.' He pulled her clear of the bush. 'Are you all right?'

'Yes.' Her voice was strained.

Tanner turned his attention to the injury, studying the broken leg with a mixture of concern and relief.

'It's a clean break,' he announced. 'It'll hurt when we splint it but it'll heal straight.' She tightened her grip on him as she felt him try to get up. 'I want to light a fire.' He eased himself out of her grip, but kept talking as he made the fire. 'Fire'll keep you warm and maybe lead Zeke and Paddy to us. I fired a shot before, but I doubt they could get a fix on it.' He added a few larger sticks to his collection of twigs and leaves. 'I doubt we'll get a cart this far up the valley, might be we have to carry you out on a stretcher.' Amy was shivering and the hastily constructed fire was reluctant to burn. Tanner sat beside her again, putting his coat around her and holding her to him as he had that first night in London.

'Davis.' Amy tried again to speak.

'He brought me here.' Tanner thought he owed her the truth, owed it to Davis too.

'Kill me.' Amy fought the tears, the desire to bury her head in Tanner's chest and cry until all the pain was gone. 'Thought he was going to kill me,' she sobbed, 'put a gun to my heart, sounded so strange.' She swallowed, trying to hold back the tears a little longer. 'Tried to hide from him, thought if he came back after dark, wouldn't find me.' The effort became too much for her and the broken sobs became one long cry.

Davis' horse ambled to a halt and the cessation of movement jolted Davis back to reality. He gazed about him at a land that few white men had ever seen; a grim smile crossed his lips, the commissioner would not think to search for him here, not in the vast emptiness of this land. The smile faded—the commissioner would not search, for few could survive in this place but he had a compass, two guns, ammunition and water, thanks to the recent rain. He had a better chance than most. He could head north or west, perhaps in time sneak back to Melbourne, get a ship heading home. Once the initial furore died down he'd be just another face in the crowd.

He urged the horse on again, and for the first time in his life he had no plan, no dream. He succumbed to the temptation to think of Amy, to remember how she'd tricked him and run from him, to recall how much she'd wanted to be free of him. He pushed the horse on faster, let Tanner have her, let him be judged and damned by her idea of right and wrong. The angry thought didn't help for he knew it wasn't Tanner who'd have her. He had studied human nature for too long not to recognise the bond that had grown between Joey and Amy and not to realise that it was only their loyalty to him that had held them apart.

'Joey,' he murmured disgustedly, 'what in God's name could she see in Joey?'

Tanner watched as Zeke and Paddy lifted the stretcher from the cart.

'Put her in the shanty,' he said. 'I'll be along in a minute.' He crawled to the back of the cart, then drew a deep breath in an effort to summon the strength to climb down.

'Commissioner's looking for you.' Catherine appeared at his side.

'Tell him I'm unconscious.'

'By the look of you I could tell him you're dead and he'd believe it.' Tanner put his arm around her and it was impossible to tell which one was supporting the other. They followed the stretcher into the shanty.

'Amy.' Joey tried to crawl to her as they laid the stretcher beside him.

'Don't you dare get up.'

'Amy.' Joey ignored Loretta's order. 'Oh, God, look at you, all bruised and scratched and your leg . . .' He leant close to her and she reached out to him, gasping in horror as she felt his battered face.

'Oh Joey, I'm so sorry.' She searched out his hands and held them tightly. 'It was all my fault.'

'No, no.' He moved closer to her. 'I should never have left you with him. I should never have waited so long to say my piece.' He lay down beside her and Loretta arranged the bedding accordingly.

'Come on you two,' Loretta ushered Zeke and Paddy out of the shanty. 'Let the injured get their rest.' She paused at the door and turned to survey the scene. 'Well,' she said, 'Davis has made a right mess of the lot of you.'

Tanner smiled at the vanishing figure, then led Catherine to the untidy bed they now shared. He found a position in which they could both almost be comfortable.

Amy edged closer to Joey. 'I am so stupid,' she said, 'to be taken in by promises of gold, to believe all those daydreams of his.'

'He believed them too.' Joey put his arm around her shoulder. 'And I don't think the gold really mattered all that much to you, did it?'

'No, but it did to him and people who love each other should want the same things, believe in the same things.'

'You must have loved him very much.'

'I don't know that I loved him at all. He wanted me so much it seemed wrong not to love him in return.'

Joey shook his head sadly. 'It's not enough to have someone love you, you've got to love them too.'

Amy turned towards Joey, her fingers moving gently across his misshapen features. She smiled at him.

'You're a beautiful man,' she said.